Coven Chronicles: Magickal

Lorena Bisset

Bisset House Press

COVEN CHRONICLES: MAGICKAL

ISBNs

979-8-9911069-0-0 (Hardcover)

979-8-9911069-1-7 (Paperback)

979-8-9911069-2-4 (eBook)

Copyright © 2024 by Lorena Bisset of Bisset House Press

First Edition

Cover Art and Design © 2024 by Jessica Darling

Contents

Katiyana

Monday, September 7, 2020

IMAGES SPUN PAST ME, settling into the scenery as my partner twirled me around a dance hall. The body I inhabited glanced down to check her footing and I caught a glimpse of purple lace swirling about her knees, beads sparkling between the floral patterns. She looked back up over our partner's shoulder, out across the crowd at another woman. This one had long nutmeg-colored ringlets trying to escape her updo as she was spun around, her partner grinning wide as he blew blonde hair out of his face. They both looked agonizingly familiar, right on the edge of my memory. They were in a daze of happiness, and I felt my host's wave of deep jealousy, tinged with happiness that her best friend was having such a wonderful time.

She wasn't paying any attention to her partner at all, and I think he got the hint because as soon as the song ended, he dropped her hands and walked off with a sigh. My host didn't seem to care; he was just another name on her dance card. She turned to step toward a long banquet table set up along the wall, picking at the various tiny desserts and finger foods laid out.

"Can I help you with a plate, miss?" A voice sounded from our left and my host whirled to face it, her eyes landing on a waiter. Her thoughts flitted across my mind, *Oh isn't he beautiful?* And I had to agree. The whole blonde hair and blue eyes thing was really working for him.

"Oh, thank you." She spoke with a high-pitched New York accent. One of them wasn't born in this place. His accent didn't match my host's, so he had to have been a foreigner, or maybe she was.

Then the most terrible beeping started up and didn't stop. The two continued conversing softly and politely, but I didn't hear a word as the beeping grew louder and louder, until finally my eyes flew open and I realized it was my alarm.

"Cripes," I grumbled, smacking the flashing screen of my phone to shut it up. The word had gotten stuck in my head thanks to my cousin and her constant repetition of it. I buried my face back in my pillow and sighed, wishing I could stay for just ten more minutes. A luxury not afforded to me on the first day back to school.

I compromised with myself and stayed in bed for just a few more moments. Two minutes later, I was bumbling to the bathroom for a shower and twisting my hair up into a clip. There was no way I was gonna wash it today with no time to dry it.

"Katiyana? Finally up?" My brother called from the kitchen, the banging of the cupboards signaling his attempt at breakfast.

"Mmyeah," was all I managed, and I snapped the bathroom door shut before Nick could delay my getting ready any further by asking me more questions or divulging the plot of the latest anime episode he'd watched.

I showered, dressed, quickly pulled my curly chestnut locks into a braid that hit the small of my back and decided not to care if it's lopsided. *Who's gonna notice?* My glasses were still a little foggy from the steam of the bathroom as I headed into the hall, but it faded pretty quickly.

"I made you breakfast." Nicolae beamed as I wandered into the kitchen with all my new school supplies.

One look at the plate told me he'd definitely *tried* to make breakfast, but had instead ended up with a single serving of scrambled eggs that were somehow burnt on one side and raw on the other. Yeesh.

"My stomach is in knots with nerves. I don't think I can eat." No way I was touching that. White lie would have to do.

"Fine, it's not like I slaved over this stove for thirty minutes or anything just to serve my dearest little love, my baby sister, breakfast on her first day back." He punctuated his lament by loudly scraping the food into the trash and tossing the plate into the sink in such a way it made me wonder how it didn't break. I successfully hid my cringe and avoided his dark glare, tucking my chin and pretending to dig for something out of my bag. His eyes were always dark--*almost* black--but when he glared, they became black holes. Especially contrasted against his pale skin, which was nearly printer-paper white due to hardly ever leaving his bedroom.

Change the subject. "I had a weird dream this morning before I woke up." I didn't need his pity-party right now.

"Oh? Do tell." He turned toward me with full interest, elbows on the counter, chin in his hands, eyebrow hiked up in curiosity. It took a lot of self-control not to make a face at his expression. I could actually feel the condescension waiting to roll off his tongue.

"It was probably the 1920s, at some big fancy party. I was dancing with someone but I wasn't interested and he gave up. Then I went to get a snack and ended up talking to the waiter." The finer details were already escaping me, but I could remember the basic premise. A quick glance at Nick told me to ready myself for his attempt at dream analysis.

"Hmmmm, hmm, hmm," was a shockingly short analysis.

"Maybe it was a past life," I joked, smirking half-heartedly. It might have been, who knew? Nick's loud scoff and push off the counter was the all the response I needed, but he didn't stop there.

"You always jump to the most romantic and dumbest possible conclusions." His voice took on a mocking tone. "Oh it's the twenties, it must be a past life." I didn't see him roll his eyes, I could *feel* it. I sighed as quietly as I could and gathered my school things again. "Yeesh Katiyana, we just watched Gatsby like three days ago, of course you're dreaming about parties in the twenties."

It had actually been six months ago that we'd watched the newest Gatsby. I had pinpointed the date because Nick had decided it was the most pretentious and unimportant remake of a film he'd ever seen in his life—despite not ever watching the one from the seventies, or from the forties, and never reading the book—and had literally tossed the DVD in the trash. I'd had to fish it out because it was a borrowed copy. But sure, three days ago. Another huff as I hiked my bag back onto my shoulder.

"Your dad's flight to Germany just landed. He made it safe." I glanced to the hallway to see Mom coming out of her bedroom, pulling her bag onto her shoulder in a similar manner to me. "Wonder how much it cost Robin to send that text..." As much as I wanted to hear about Dad, Mom's attention was immediately stolen. She looked to Nick and then to me, eyebrow raised with an unspoken question.

That expression was the only thing that made Nick look like her son. Otherwise, he matched Dad almost perfectly. Mom and I were also practically twins––the same dark brown hair and silver eyes, the same face shape, everything. We'd even picked out similar glasses last time we'd needed new ones, just for fun. Nick and Dad both had dark brown eyes, with Nick's just so much darker, and sharper faces than Mom and me. Unfortunately, we were of Scottish blood, and therefore pale enough to sunburn in ten minutes, but somehow Dad got off easy; he actually tanned.

"Okay, I need to get to the train station. I'll see you after school." I had already started walking out of the apartment when Nick called behind me. Mom still hadn't said a word, but joined me in the doorway after waving to her son. He probably didn't even notice.

"I have to tell you about Boruto—" The door closed with the most satisfying click before he could.

"What was that all about?" Mom asked, her hand on my shoulder as we walked together to the elevator. I rolled my eyes with the most exaggeration I could muster, sighing just as dramatically.

"I had a weird dream last night, told Nick about it to keep him from forcing 'breakfast' on me, and he told me

I was stupid for thinking it could have been a past life just because it had twenties fashion in it."

"Ah, hence the Gatsby comment." Mom sighed, much more softly than I had, and shook her head. We'd reached the elevator, and she took care of the button pressing while I gripped my things to my chest.

I took a moment in the elevator to close my eyes and ground myself, leveling my breathing and imaging tree roots growing down from my feet and spine, deep into the earth. I let all of the nervous and annoyed energy filter down through the roots and into the core of the earth, letting it change and develop into something more beneficial. Mom stayed quiet beside me. She'd taught me this process and likely knew what I was doing.

By the time I heard the third ding, the one for the lobby, I felt lighter than I had on the fourth floor and shook my head to clear the rest of the annoyance. *That's just typical Nick, Yana, you know he does that every time. You know it's normal for him to think of stuff that doesn't make any sense because he never pays attention to details.* Nick's conclusions were always wildly wrong and out of left field. The one time I'd had a spirit show themselves to me, I'd run to Nick since he was the only person home, and he said the spirit was an ancestor that was angry with me because I hadn't done my homework yet, even though I could see the spirit shaking its head furiously. I explained it to Mom later that day, and she'd suppressed a laugh and explained it was the guardian spirit of the building we lived in, probably just popping in to check on our unit. I'd confirmed that story later with the building owner.

"You know Nick is just being Nick, right? Just because he says it with confidence doesn't mean he's right." Mom's words echoed my thoughts, and we strode through the lobby together.

"Yeah, I know. Doesn't make it any less annoying though."

I smiled at the doorman as he held the door open for us, sidestepping the neighbor's tiny Pomeranian. The train station was only a couple blocks away, ten minute walk. No problem, plenty of time to catch the train. With Mom making the trip with me this morning, it would be far more pleasant than normal. Yet I couldn't shake the urge to run just to get away from the apartment faster. I made myself walk at Mom's pace, arriving at a normal time, and sitting in my normal seat. Mom sat next to me while we waited for her train to arrive.

"If you think it might be a past life dream, you need to start writing them down and keeping track. You have been waiting since April, after all. Usually they come much quicker after a sixteenth birthday. Your Aunt Pearl's were basically down to the minute, but she's always been much more in tune with her intuition and foresight." Mom's voice was nearly inside her bag as she dug into it, finding her phone and checking the local transit app. Both our trains were on time. Then she lifted her eyes to meet mine, silver gazes mirroring each other. "So no matter what Nick says, go ahead and follow your gut." She smiled and nudged my arm with her elbow. I smirked back, nodding.

"I know. I remember all the rules." I chuckled, letting my shoulders drop as the last of the Nick-induced tension faded away. The coven had taught me well, so I knew what to do if the setting and people from my dreams appeared again.

Mom and I sat in silence together for a few more minutes before her train showed up. She left me with a kiss on my head, another smile, and some final words of wisdom before disappearing into the train car: "Legally we're Randas, but we're still of the MacAskill line. You know what to do." I slumped back into my seat. Our ancestor, Angus, had come over from Scotland centuries ago and founded the island. The family line had (mostly) kept his name and position as leaders of Faodail. We'd also inherited his magic.

I was alone at that moment, but Alena would be there soon, then Jamari and Fleur, and then the train. School, lunch, school, then home again. An easy enough pattern. I ran my fingertips along the corners of the pages of a book, spacing out to the noise it made.

"Hello, earth to Katiyana." My attention was snapped back, and the first thing I saw was a rolled up piece of

French toast with ham and egg in the middle. Alena's stepmom's cooking. I could have drooled.

"Is that for me?" I asked, looking up. Alena's soft almond-shaped hazel eyes and impatient expression warred with each other, pinching her round face ever so gently. Her fawn skin tone still held the slight pink of a healing sunburn from our last trip to the lake before school started.

"Why else would I be waving it in front of you? Katherine knew you would need it. Don't ask me how." Alena sat down next to me so gracefully, her silky elbow-length black hair barely moved.

"She was right. Nick attempted eggs again this morning." Alena made the most appropriate *yuck* face and pushed the treat at me harder. "You and your stepmom are my lifesavers." I gratefully enclosed greedy fingers around the little toasted wrap, briefly losing myself to the pleasure of a well-cooked and still surprisingly warm breakfast. "I was going to ask you for one of your emergency granola bars, but this is way better."

"Hah, you bet it is. There they are." I followed Alena's gaze to the end of the platform, watching two figures move toward us, one shorter with long sunshine blonde hair and one taller with a barely tamed Afro. If it had been colder, Jamari would absolutely have her dark brown, purple-tinged curls hidden under a beanie. The two siblings were aesthetic opposites, Fleur's cool-toned light skin and hair contrasted by her sister's warm, reddish-brown skin and dark hair. The opposition was even in their eyes, with Fleur's clear gray paralleling Jamari's rich umber. The four of us matched in our school uniforms: white short-sleeve button-up shirts, gray plaid knee-length skirts, and dark dress shoes. Jamari wore slacks instead of a skirt. All the schools on the island used the same uniform, so it made going between Cridhe, Inntinn, and Corp easy for those who did.

"Bets on how long it takes Jamari to yawn?" Alena grinned.

"Ten seconds."

"Five."

Alena and I waited in anticipation of our bet as our sister-friends moved closer, then started counting as they sat next to us. Jamari collapsed like a tumble of clothes dumped from a hamper while Fleur settled like an anchor sinking into sand. It was hard not to make ship puns at Fleur after she'd decided last year to switch from they/them to she/her pronouns, calling herself "a machine of her own making, feminine in the way a ship is." Jamari's hand went up to her purple-tipped curls and, eleven seconds after sitting down, her face was just about swallowed with a yawn.

"Damn," Alena whispered.

Fleur looked over, smirking. "Eleven seconds."

"Are you guys still betting on my damn yawns?" Jamari crossed her arms and rested her head against the back of the seat.

"Mhm," I managed around a bite of my heavenly breakfast.

"It's our favorite waiting-for-the-train pastime." Alena smiled haughtily at Jamari, who groaned and closed her eyes, sinking her head against Alena's shoulder.

"'This is the way,'" Fleur quoted as she brushed her golden locks away from her high cheekbone, behind an ear, and secured it with a blocky black barrette, somehow making it look perfect without a mirror. "Also, they wouldn't do it so often if you didn't stay up all hours of the night hacking into government databases," Fleur continued before opening her ever-present planner to study it. We didn't even have our schedules yet, but she was already blocking out times for extracurriculars and homework. *Filling out her manifest*, we teased her.

Jamari didn't get a chance to snap back at her sister as the train pulled up, putting a halt to all conversation, brakes squeaking, doors opening, and the din of people conversing on the morning commute breaking into the previous near-silence of the station. Alena and I managed a grin at each other before all four of us pushed into the crowd, Fleur and I dragging Jamari behind us as she tried to shuffle instead of hustle.

Vincent

Monday, September 7, 2020

IN COMPARISON TO THE starched and dark plain uniform I wore, the rest of the room was gilded. Shimmering and glittering dresses, cufflinks, and jewelry twinkling in every square inch of the ballroom. I stood with my hands behind my back, suffering under the oppressive tightness of my collar, waiting for someone to need help. I could feel jealousy—the softest touch of it—rising from my chest, trying to fight out the relief of just having a paid gig. A woman with a close-cropped wavy haircut and purple lace swishing about her knees wandered over as the latest song ended, poking at a plate of desserts and moving toward the other finger foods, seemingly unsatisfied with the selection. *Aha, this explains the uniform.*

"Can I help you with a plate, miss?" I asked, stepping to her side. I barely had time to place the accent that wasn't my own tinging my dream voice when my breath caught as I locked gazes with the brightest, sharpest silver eyes I had ever seen in my life.

"Oh, thank you," she said sweetly, her New York accent ringing in my ears and sending a delightful chill down my spine. The next thought to cross my headspace wasn't mine: *I will never tire of listening to New York women speak.*

"The cream cheese and pimento sandwiches are light enough to keep you dancing without feeling like you're carrying around a ten-ton weight, if that's what you're after." I gestured at the platter holding the little rolled-thin slices of bread with the aforementioned concoction squished between them. She chuckled softly––politely––and nodded.

"Sure, that sounds wonderful."

I spun to pick up a plate for her when the dance hall...boomed? As if someone huge were slamming their fists repeatedly against the ceiling. No one else seemed to hear it. My body kept moving on its own, filling the woman's plate with little tongs produced seemingly out of thin air, but all I could hear was the pounding.

Then it clicked. *Oh no.*

"Vincent if you don't open this goddamn door right this minute I will BREAK IT DOWN!" Her voice was shrill and cracked from behind the plywood, which was definitely also going to crack if she kept pounding on it. I scrambled out of bed and flung it open, jumping back a few steps and holding up my hands. I still had to duck to miss her next "knock."

"Sorry! I'm sorry! My alarm didn't wake me up!" I kept my head down, but my hands up. There was silence for a moment, then the sharp huff of a sigh. I dared to glance up. Mom glared down over her glasses, the black hair I'd inherited swept back with a pastel pink headband. The shade complimented her light tawny skin, but probably would have looked odd against my darker version of the same tone. But I was no artist, what did I know?

"Fine. Get your ass moving then. I'm not driving you to the station." She turned on her heel and stomped down the hallway. I stood there in shock for a moment. She never drove me to the station normally, so why bring it up now? *Add it to the list of mysteries that will never be solved, I guess.*

I scrubbed my hands through my hair and sighed. *Alright, no time for a shower or even breakfast. Get dressed, get running.* I closed my eyes just for a brief moment, sucking in a large breath and holding it for the count of four before letting it out slowly through my mouth, imagining all the tension and annoyance leaving my body with it. I gave myself one more round of that before I slapped on some deodorant, tossed the tube in my bag for later, and pulled on some clothes. If I changed at school, I wouldn't be a sweaty mess all day, and my uniform would stay...well, not pristine, but it wouldn't get any worse than it already was.

I took off toward the station, somehow managing to untangle my earbuds and slip them in while running, thankful my phone had saved my last played song even on the home screen. Lacey Sturm exploded into my ears and I kept the song's beat with footfalls, managing to make it to the station right as the train pulled in. I caught sight of a blonde head adorned with sunglasses slipping through the doors and dove in after it, collapsing next to Dan as the train departed. With my earbuds in, the sound of my heart pounding in my ears was louder than normal, and I begrudgingly took them out so as to not give myself a headache.

"Ah, the birthday boy returns to the land of the living." Dan snickered and nudged his still-summer-tanned shoulder against mine. I turned my head––rested against the back of the train seat as it was––and glared at him, still trying to get my breathing under control. His blue eyes absolutely sparkled with mischief, which on a normal day I would have returned, but my own brown eyes were far too dull to match him today.

"My birthday was two days ago." I closed my eyes and let out another big breath, ignoring his further shoulder nudging.

"Well, I didn't get to see you, so it's today for me. Why did you get here so late?" Even without looking at him I could feel his brow knitting in concern, definitely noticing the bedhead I didn't have time to tame and the pillow line still on my cheek.

"I woke up right before I had to leave."

"And you didn't have time for breakfast?"

"I did not."

"Mom is psychic, then." I opened my eyes to see Dan pulling a small container out of his bag. "She said to bring this to you."

I melted into the seat. I wouldn't have to go until lunch without eating. It was just scrambled eggs with bits of ham mixed in, but it was a godsend. "Tell her thank you!"

Dan's response was drowned out by the sound of the train stopping and the doors opening. I quickly sat up properly and pulled my legs in to allow a group of girls to pass, one of them basically dragged by the others. And I thought *I* was tired. After a moment, I recognized them as some classmates, ones Dan knew better than I did. The blonde one parting the crowd was named Fleur, and the one being dragged was her sister Jamari. The scene made sense once I'd realized who it was. I barely managed to catch sight of Katiyana and Alena as they passed.

"This never happens, man, what's up with you? It's the first day back and you're already trying to wreck your perfect attendance?" It was followed by a snort and a smothered laugh, and I turned to glare at Dan again.

"You're such an asshole." I sighed, slumping back against the seat again. Lacey's voice was just barely audible--small and tinny--from my headphones. *Ah, hell.* I popped my earbuds out of the jack, pausing the music until I needed it again.

"Aaaww, I knew you loved me. When are you going to propose?" Dan leaned his head on my shoulder and I dropped my head onto his, regretting the action and pulling back immediately as his sunglasses stabbed into my cheekbone.

"As soon as you stop wearing those stupid pointy things on your head. You almost took my eye out." I jostled Dan off my shoulder and rubbed my cheek, making a spectacle of it.

"Oh, psh." He pulled them off and hooked them on the collar of his shirt instead. "There, now we can get married." He grinned and I smirked, shaking my head.

"If I had to pick a dude."

"Wow, all this love I've harbored for you for the past sixteen years—"

"You've known me for seven, stop." We'd met in fifth grade.

"SIXTEEN YEARS—"

I snorted and ducked my head to smother my own laugh, pretending to ignore his theatrics, which immediately ground to a halt when he looked out the window at one of the train stops, putting his sunglasses back on just to peer over them dramatically.

"Ohhh mama, oh wow. Look at *her*."

I twisted my neck so I could look out the window without having to get up, and sure enough, a busty, beachy boho-type was perched on one of the station seats, all perfectly tanned skin and dark blonde hair with an overabundance of braided jewelry on both wrists.

"She's old enough to be your mother, Dan."

"Well she can mother me aallllll she likes, woof." He basically had his face pressed up against the glass, and to my amusement and his chagrin, she looked up to see it with wide eyes. The confused and slightly repulsed look she gave him through the glass was enough to deflate Dan, and he sank back into the seat, leaning heavily against my side. I wrapped my arm around his shoulders and patted his arm roughly.

"One day you'll stop being so disgusting toward everyone you find attractive, and then maybe they'll like you back."

"Oh, you hate me." He whined against my shoulder, clinging to my shirt.

"No, no, I just enjoy watching you get rejected when your first offer is always of a sexual nature. You do realize you're sixteen, right? No older woman in her right mind is going to give you a second look, not to mention any older dude. Actually, if you start off that way with everyone, no one is going to."

"Stop giving advice that makes you sound like you're forty." Dan pulled himself up and ran his fingers through his hair, getting it to stay in the perfect spikes he aimed for. He looked like he stepped out of a boy band music video from the 2000s, but that was probably his goal. He'd even loosened his tie and left the top button of his shirt unbuttoned. I made an internal bet with myself about how long it would take a teacher to tell him to fix it.

"Someday you'll be begging me for it." I shrugged as he pouted and turned his attention to Instagram, flipping through a slew of selfies likely taken in the bathroom this morning. I heard his mocking grumble and just laughed to myself. *Classic Dan*. He would feel better after his new selfie post got a few likes.

After a minute or two more of silence, the train screeched to a stop once again and we stood up together, waiting our turn to step onto the platform.

"Let me do your hair when we get to school." Dan was already picking at it, fussing with the cowlick on the back of my head I usually ignored. I waved his hand away.

"Sure, just don't spike it."

The station was right at the school gates, so it was nothing for Dan and I to slip into the bathroom and get me presentable before the first bell rang. We'd done this so many times before that it was down to a science— change clothes, Dan does my hair while I brush my teeth, then I rinse my face off while Dan stashes my other clothes away. Done and done in five minutes flat. Dan may have been overbearingly dramatic at times, and his obsession with dating and fooling around was way out of my comfort zone, but he took genuine care of me. I couldn't remember a time when he didn't help me spruce myself up for school or bring extra food just so I could have something to eat. He may have been a horndog, but he was a true friend, and I was grateful.

We settled in the auditorium for the traditional First Day of School speeches with two minutes to spare. I popped my earbuds back in and slumped in the seat. The auditorium was dark enough that none of the teachers could tell, and Dan always smacked at my elbow if something important was going on. As my eyes closed, I immediately saw those brilliant silver eyes from my dream and swallowed a gasp, keeping my eyes shut so I could burn them into my memory. Dream girl, indeed. I'd never seen such beauty.

Katiyana

Monday, September 7, 2020

THANKFUL FOR THE DIM lights in the auditorium, I held my notebook on my lap and doodled. The lace pattern from my dream felt so...distinct. Like I needed to remember it. If I was having past life dreams––and I hoped I was––maybe the lace was a specific manufacturer's pattern or something. So here I was, attempting to sketch it out as the principal read out a list of school rules to the new students. I'd heard them before, so I didn't feel the need to pay attention. Then I heard a familiar voice, a tap on the microphone, and the same familiar voice. I looked up and grinned, seeing my cousin Sinéad on stage. She was Faodail's current leader, the Bruadarach. Her nutmeg-colored hair was swept back into a half ponytail and she tapped the side of the podium with what I knew to be perfectly-manicured fingernails, her silver eyes scanning my classmates. The iris color was a family trait, passed down through the MacAskill line. Most of my cousins and aunts had it too.

"Hello, yes, hello everyone. And so begins the best time of the year: school." She smirked at the boos and groans she was expecting and held up a hand for silence. "Yeah, I know. But hey! At least you get to pick what you study here, right?" That got a few hollers and cheers, and Sinéad smiled again. "So, what I'm really here to announce is that everyone's favorite fireman is here to tell you about the new syste—"

She didn't even get through the entire word before the cheers shut her down, and she just set her chin in her hand and motioned toward the wing of the stage. Leon Regulus stepped out from behind the curtain, waving and offering up a grin which only made the cheers louder. Sinéad stepped away from the podium and surrendered the mic, but Leon had to hold up both hands to get the crowd to calm down first. Then it hit me. The blonde man I'd seen across the dance floor looked like Leon! My cousin's partner, the other Bruadarach. The woman he had been twirling around bore a striking resemblance to Sinéad, as well. My surprised expression must have been blatant because Jamari and Alena both gave me questioning looks, and I tapped at the lace design on my notebook, then pointed at Leon with the pencil. I'd told them about my dream on the train, and they both looked up at the man on stage then back at me, still questioning, but now for a different reason.

"Alright, yes, alright, thank you, thank you." Leon was speaking again, shaking his head at the uproar he'd caused. He was something of a celebrity around the island, having been the fire chief for decades along with being the guitar teacher at Cridhe before Mr. Cromwell took over. It didn't hurt that he was "devastatingly handsome," as most people put it. For as long as I'd known him, he'd always looked about twenty-five. Good genes, I guess. "As your Bruadarach was saying, I'm here to tell you about the new fire suppression system we installed over the summer."

The rest of the assembly wasn't nearly as eventful—it was hard to be on stage after Chief Regulus had appeared. None of the other speakers managed to grab the students' full attention, and I returned to working on the lace design in my notebook. Within moments it was over, or at least that's what it felt like. We all shuffled off to our various homerooms to gather our new schedules and regroup before class and the glorious freedom that was lunch.

The truth is, the boos and groans during Sinéad's speech were mostly for show. This school wasn't bad, but none of us would be caught dead saying it was good. We were teenagers, after all, so we had generational reputations to uphold. The classes weren't overly long thanks to having about eight in a day, the homework was light, and the teachers were all fairly compensated and didn't have to purchase supplies out of their own pockets. Just another benefit of being your own sovereign nation. I never wanted to leave Faodail.

Vincent

Monday, September 7, 2020

THE CHEERING HAD JOSTLED me awake from my doze; I had almost fallen completely asleep. I opened my eyes and blinked around, realizing the fire chief was on stage and everyone was cheering for him. *Ah, that makes sense. He's so popular.*

"As your Bruadarach was saying, I'm here to tell you about the new fire suppression system we installed over the summer." That was the only part of his speech I heard before I tuned back out.

The next speaker, Mx. Shore, the drama teacher, mentioned auditions opening up next month for the winter musical, and I perked up. I loved musicals, and had always wanted to be involved with the drama department somehow, but hadn't worked up the courage. Maybe this year I could take my chance. Dan showed he was mimicking my thought with a playful tap on my shoulder and a grin, and I nodded with a smile of my own as the rest of the auditorium finished their hooting and hollering.

After the other faculty members wrapped up the assembly, Dan and I let ourselves be tugged downstream with all the other students heading to their homerooms. We'd been in the same one since Freshman year and weren't worried about different ones anytime soon. Somehow, things had a way of working out how Dan wanted them. At least in school. As I had witnessed on the train that morning, his love life was an exception.

"I wonder how long they're taking course corrections this year?" Dan mumbled to himself as we slid into our desks, his nose buried in his schedule. I shrugged and made sure my phone was silenced, grimacing at a missed call from my mother. She knew I was in school. I'd deal with the fallout from not answering her later. It was easier to deal with than getting in trouble for having my phone out.

"I just really don't want to take home ec, Vinny, I really don't." Dan sighed, fanning himself with the schedule as our teacher settled behind her desk.

"But you'd get to bake pies for all the girls in the class." I grinned at him, tugging my own schedule from the binder where I'd stashed it. If the school was still accepting course corrections, I could maybe hop into the actual drama class Mx. Shore taught.

"Oh, gracious me." Dan rolled his eyes exaggeratedly, dropping his hand onto his desk. "Like I know how to cook, Vincent."

I chuckled softly, as he rarely used my full name. "That's kind of the point of the class there, Dannyboy."

"Alright, enough chatter." Our homeroom teacher tapped her pencil against the edge of her desk, and the class silenced. "The school day has begun."

Katiyana

Monday, September 7, 2020

JAMARI HELD HER HANDS to the sky in the biggest stretch her already lanky frame could reach, closing her eyes and sighing in the warm afternoon sunlight, mumbling something about taking the longest nap as soon as she got home.

"Not if our moms have anything to say about it. Plus, Isabelle will need a walk once we get back." Fleur had her attention mostly focused on her school planner, the little spiral bound thing resting on top of the stack of books in her arms. She was jotting down her class schedule on each day, matching lines to class periods. Without the Captain, this ship of friends wouldn't be half as organized as it was. Jamari groaned as she dropped her arms, tucking her hands in the pockets of her pants.

I chuckled softly. Jamari and Fleur's mothers were both teachers and took their children's homework—and pet care—very seriously. As juniors, Alena and I only had a little bit, and Fleur had probably picked up all the extra credit work a sophomore was allowed. But Jamari was a senior who'd almost flunked junior year, which meant she would absolutely not be getting any sort of nap until her homework was complete. My musings were broken by Alena's voice.

"Do you want to stop somewhere before we head to the station?"

"Hm? Where's that?" I personally would take almost any excuse to get home late, but I had suffered through a few chess club meetings for that precise reason and had since raised my standards.

"Ladine's. Katherine's birthday is in two weeks, so I figured it would be the best place to shop for her." Alena shrugged nonchalantly, but if you knew her like we did, you knew she was giddy with excitement about finding the perfect gift for her stepmom. Katherine was the furthest thing from an evil stepmother that could possibly exist.

With a noise of agreement, Fleur nodded once to seal her bond to this new mission, and flipped up the flap of her messenger bag to stash everything she was holding into it.

"Aw, you guys want me to go in on my day off? Why you do hate me..." Jamari sighed, but the quick smirk after it betrayed her true feelings on returning to her workplace.

Ladine's Gem was the local café-slash-metaphysical shop-slash-ritual space, and one of the oldest buildings on the entire island. I'd basically grown up there, since my mother and aunts were part of the coven that based its operations out of the little shop. Jamari had worked there part time for about a year.

"Awesome. If we keep our browsing under twenty minutes, we should be able to catch the train after the one we normally take." It was clear Alena had been planning this out all day. I smiled fondly at the thought, and we set off together. Luckily we didn't have to physically drag Jamari this time.

My phone buzzed as we walked and I tapped open the Faodail messaging system, following Alena out of the edge of my vision. Basically everyone on the island used Comms since it was more reliable than texting. It was Sinéad.

Bruadarach

What were you drawing during assembly? Also I wanted to come say hi but had to run back to the office.

I giggled, and my friends turned to look. "Sinéad JUST left Ladine's."

"Aw, missed a chance to see our leader in action," Jamari teased, pulling out her own phone to snap a photo of the sign and send it to the group chat we had with Sinéad. She read out her message as she typed: "Why did you leave without us? Sad face, puppy dog eyes, crying face."

Alena followed suit and grinned while pulling out her phone, swiftly changing expressions to send a sad selfie, also reading aloud as she typed: "Why didn't you wait for us?"

I hadn't stopped giggling throughout all of this, and Fleur's big huff of resignation made the giggles worse. "Fine, fine, I'll join in." She held her hand to her cheek to take a wistful selfie, telling us her caption before typing it: "My face when Sinéad abandons us."

Everyone burst out laughing at that one, and I had to lean against a nearby wall to catch my breath. All four of our phones pinged as Sinéad responded.

Bruadarach

> **THAT'S IT I'M MAKING LEO TURN AROUND**

We all typed back at the same time, giggling.

LilTriquetra

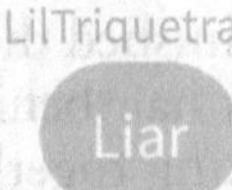

QueenofGambits

> **Prove it.**

BlondeBrainiac

> **I don't believe you.**

GameznStuff

> **Yeah right!**

Immediately Sinéad started typing, and we all hurriedly shoved our phones into pockets and bags, snickering. We bustled into the shop as a unit, moving aside when we almost ran into an elderly woman, giggling our apologies as she just smirked softly and slipped out the door. After a moment more of looking at her, I recognized her as Smilté, one of the coven members and the Head of the Faodail Education Department. Her white braid was longer than mine and tied with a ribbon instead of an elastic. She caught me looking and we locked eyes for a second. I gave her an extra big grin. Smilté returned it, the expression lighting her gray eyes. She then bowed her head calmly, turned, and left. She'd always been a serene and grounding presence at every event I'd been to, and she left traces of that energy behind as she departed.

"Welcome! Hello again," Alexis, the shop owner and coven mother, called from behind the counter, finishing ringing up the last customer's purchases and wrapping up a large quartz sphere. The customer waiting for it ignored us, not bothered by a bunch of loud teenagers wandering into the shop. Alena responded first.

"Hello! I'm looking for a gift for my stepmom, Katherine. I think you know her?"

"Ah yes, I do. Quite well, in fact." Alexis chuckled as she finished the transaction, and brushed her short, wavy black hair behind an ear, the rings on each of her fingers clinking together softly with the action. They sparkled against her fingers, a bright contrast against the terra-cotta shade of her hand. "Let's see..." her eyes scanned the shelves and pegboards, squinting toward the corner. "She came in here the other day looking at these pendulums." She moved from behind the counter over toward the corner she'd been squinting at, running her fingers along a stock of hanging pendants along the way. The tinkling noise and sparkle caught my attention, and I followed Alena over to look at them while she and the shopkeeper looked at pendulums.

"Here, this one." I heard Alexis say before my attention was wrapped up in a crystal pendant, a raw amethyst point wrapped in silver wire and hung on a matching chain with a little triquetra pendant. I reached up to check the price, immediately attached to it, and was pleasantly surprised to see only eight dollars on the tag. Fleur was wandering, letting whatever current that existed in the shop carry her, even though little there suited her religious tastes. She paused at some angel statues in the corner, looking each one over in detail. Jamari appeared at my shoulder, resting her chin on it as she looked over the pendants too.

"I hung all these up during my shift last weekend. They made me think of you. Did you find one you like?" Jamari asked, lifting her head and reaching to look through them herself. I lifted the little point in my hand to show her, and she nodded her approval.

Alena moved to the register with Alexis and I followed, leaving Jamari to eye an onyx point pendant similar to the one in my hand.

"Alright. That's eight dollars, then," Alexis was telling Alena. Fleur appeared before us, looking questioningly between Alexis and the price tag on the small angel statue she was holding. Alexis caught her expression and grinned. "That one is slightly busted. On the wing there, see the chip? The Cottage over in Richmond sent it here since it sat on their shelf for half a year, and Siroun said she felt it would get more love over here. Looks like she was right."

Alexis was multitasking, bagging up the pendulum and even counting out Alena's change as she spoke. Alena stepped out of my way and I presented the necklace to Alexis, who smiled at me in recognition. She took the pendant and began ringing in my purchase, still talking. "You know we have a teen witch class here every Monday, right? You should all come join us, instead of just Jamari and Katiyana."

"Oh, I'm not Pagan—" Fleur interjected, shaking her head softly.

Alexis interrupted gently, "We welcome all those who are open-minded and kind. Also, witchcraft and Paganism aren't actually the same thing. You can practice witchcraft while still loving and worshiping your God."

Fleur seemed to be mulling it over, running her thumb along the chip in the angel's wing. I grinned at her, knowing she would end up coming with us now that a formal invitation had been extended instead of just her friends begging. As Alexis held out my change, her tone switched to one of familiarity rather than sales.

"How's your mother doing, Katiyana?" She asked, and I brightened with a smile.

"Great actually. She and the aunts are heading to Richmond here in a couple days."

"Ah yes, helping Siroun with prophecies." Alexis chuckled. "I'm sure I'll be getting a call from her soon, begging me to call them back."

I chuckled along, nodding. "I think they use it as an excuse to go on vacation every year."

"Exactly right."

Alena suddenly gasped and patted my shoulder. "The train, we need to leave soon."

"Oh, let me purchase this real quick then." Fleur nudged her way between me and the counter, setting the angel down gently. Jamari's hand shot out from her other side and slapped the onyx pendant down, as well.

"I'll pay you back, this is just for speed." Fleur glared but paid for it anyway.

"As if you don't have a shift within the next two days," Alexis teased, and Jamari grinned sheepishly.

Within moments the transaction was complete——Jamari's new pendant around her neck, the angel tucked safely in Fleur's bag——and we were on our way. We made it back with time to spare, settled into our seats on the train, and separated at our individual stops. I was the last left on the train and took my few minutes of solace to ready myself to face Nick, knowing he would complain about me not being back right after school.

Sure enough, when I got home he said, "Well you sure took your time," before I even had the strap of my bag over my head. I stifled a sigh.

"We ran an errand with Alena." *Of course, the day I run a spontaneous errand is the day mom works late.*

"Oh? Who's we?"

Another stifled sigh, and I turned to head down the hall to my room. "Alena, me, Jamari, and Fleur. The normal crew, Nick. Why does it matter to you?" Oh, why did I say that? The slap of the remote on the coffee table made me wince, and I shut my eyes against his shouting.

"Oh, *excuse me* for wondering if my little sister is hanging with the wrong crowd, and making sure she's safe while walking around Ceangal on her own. Pardon me for taking charge like our parents asked me to." He was behind me in the hallway and I could feel the red hot irritation oozing out of his aura. I put my hands up and turned to face him. Mom and Dad had never once asked him to look out for me or "take charge."

"Sorry. It's fine. Everything is fine. I'm going to go do my homework," I said meekly, keeping my hands up while he glared, black holes threatening to swallow me whole. After a moment his face softened, and he reached out to ruffle my hair. My shoulders dropped, thankful he didn't shout again.

"Alright. Off you go, go study. Then you can make dinner."

I rolled my eyes at that one. *No kidding Nick, of course I'm going to make dinner. You can't cook and you don't dare to learn, despite being twenty-two.* I stalked off to my room and forced myself not to slam my door, shutting it firmly instead and locking it. Nick had a habit of walking in on me while I was changing and didn't seem to care that it bothered me. Mom and Dad had tried to talk to him about it, but he didn't listen, so they'd just gotten me a knob with a lock.

I changed out of my uniform and into normal clothes, plopping down at my desk to work through the sheet of algebra problems we'd been assigned. I took twice as long doing it out of spite. Nick could wait longer to eat.

Vincent

Monday, September 7, 2020

DAN HAD HIS ARMS draped over my shoulders as we waited for the train, telling me all about some guy he'd matched with on Connect. I had him partially tuned out, scrolling through my Recent Calls list. Mom had called me no less than ten times during the school day, and texted me double that. A whole stream of "where are you" and "why aren't you answering me," with worried——I couldn't tell if it was real or for show——messages peppered in-between. It was as if she had completely forgotten today was the first day back at school, despite being the one to make sure I got up on time this morning.

"Vinny," Dan said, shaking me lightly.

"Mm, what? Sorry, Mom texted me like twenty times today so I was skimming."

"Wow Mila, rude. I asked if it was dumb of me to go on another date with this guy who said that pink is an ugly color." Dan sounded ridiculous but was completely serious, raising his eyebrows at me over his sunglasses. I held back a snort of laughter.

"People are entitled to their own opinions, Dan, you can't just not go out with someone because they don't like a color." I grinned at him, tucking my phone back in my pocket. I'd talk to mom as best I could in person. Dan exhaled loudly and looked off into the distance.

"Ugh, Fleur said the same thing. I guess you're both right. That *was* the only red flag I noticed. But he also didn't even try to hold my hand or kiss me or anything!"

"Remember what we talked about this morning?" That brought a groan that got drowned out as the train pulled up.

He dramatically flopped into the seat beside me and spent the rest of the ride home sighing and showing me pictures of other people he'd matched with, asking my opinions on them. I did the best I could just going off of a photo or two, and knowing what he wanted to hear. I had a couple years of practice doing this with him.

"Okay last one—I know your stop is next. Katiyana has been on the edge of my radar for years." Dan turned his phone and showed me a girl with long brown hair. The same girl that had been dragging Jamari onto the train. The same girl I'd had on the edge of *my* radar for years. But that wasn't what caught me: it was her eyes. Bright silver, not as strong as the ones from my dream, but similar enough that my breath caught. I knew she had them, but I hadn't made the connection before now.

"Right?" Dan chuckled. "Her profile says her friends dared her to make the account, and she's not really looking for anything right now. But isn't she just so pretty?"

"Yeah, she really is." I'd thought so from the first time I'd met her. But, of the two of us, Dan was braver, so if he made his move and it landed...Well, he had a much better chance than I did, that was for sure. Dan swiped back and forth between her two photos, one with the school uniform and the other one with her wearing a triquetra shirt. *Ah, she must be Pagan. Interesting.*

The train screeched to a halt and I looked up. "If you message her, be polite. Don't say anything sexual." Keeping the sigh of resignation that was threatening to show itself from *actually* showing itself was a feat of Herculean proportions. I hefted my bag strap over my head, standing up and giving Dan a little salute for a goodbye. He blew me a kiss and I rolled my eyes with a smirk, hopping off the train and onto the platform. My good mood from getting out of the house and being around Dan was starting to fade with the prospect of going back home. If Mom was there, she would immediately go after me for not answering her despite being at school, and then I'd have to remind her about school, which she would probably pin on me for "not telling her," etc., on and on, big sigh. Well, no other choice. Five blocks to contemplate how to handle this and all the possible ways it could go. I untangled my headphones, popping them into my ears and turning Flyleaf back on. It may have been an older band, but it held up.

I meandered home, purposely taking the long way. Maybe I shouldn't have, because it only made Mom's wrath worse that she'd had to wait to dole it out.

"Where the ever-loving hell have you been all day?" She was standing right inside the doorway with her arms crossed, watching me head up the sidewalk.

Inadvertently, I tucked my head down toward my shoulders and looked down at the ground instead of her. I hadn't done anything wrong, I'd just gone to school, but it was instinct at this point.

"It was the first day of school, Mom," I said quietly as I got to the porch. She had me trapped. There was no way I was going in without physically moving her, and I wouldn't dare.

"How the hell am I supposed to remember every detail of your life, boy! Why didn't you say anything this morning?!" She was glaring at me, tapping her foot in impatience.

"I woke up late, I'm sorry." It would be best to leave the fact she blatantly refused to take me to the station out of the equation.

"You lazy ass kid, I thought I raised you better."

"I'm sorry." My response must have been too quiet for her liking.

"You what? Speak up, you idiot." She reached out and slapped me across the face, hard enough to make me stumble and have to catch myself against the door jamb. I felt my cheek immediately swell up, and I held my hand to it, trying to breathe normally and failing. *Well, we made it a week and a half this time...*

"Oh knock it off, I didn't hit you that hard. You little baby, get your ass up and get inside." She slammed the door open hard enough that I heard it hit the wall inside the living room, and then she stalked off down the hall. I took a moment to gather myself again and pick up my phone, as I'd dropped it with the hit.

She was, thankfully, nowhere to be seen as I made my way into the house, and I hoped that meant she was in her bedroom so I could head into the bathroom and assess the damage to my face. My prayers were answered as I heard our only television set in her room blaring, and I let my shoulders sag in relief.

The bathroom light flickered a couple times as I switched it on. I'd have to remember to replace the bulb before it went out completely and she yelled at me for using too much electricity. If it hadn't happened once before, it wouldn't have even been a thought in my mind.

A quick inspection of my cheek, inner and outer, led me to discover what would likely be a bruise in the morning and a small cut on the inside where my teeth had caught the skin. I wasn't bleeding too badly, just a little. It would stop within the hour. After quickly rinsing my mouth out, I slipped into my room as silently as possible and shut the door without so much as a squeak. Instead of the overhead light, I flicked on the desk lamp, hoping to give the impression I was asleep. It was more likely she would leave me alone that way.

After hanging up my uniform, I managed to drag myself through my homework, having to reset my brain back to Latin verbs instead of running the argument through my head over and over. Sometimes these days legitimately made me want to run away, to just hop on the train and take it all the way to Dubhan. Honestly, slipping into the waves just off of the little fishing town and letting them rock me to sleep sounded even more tempting. But I had to finish this Latin homework. Mr. Rossi would be disappointed if I stopped turning in work, considering that for the past two years I'd been on time with full marks for every assignment. I snorted at myself, regretting it as the bruise on my cheek twinged. I rested my hand on it but still smirked, amused with myself that a perfect streak of Latin homework was keeping me in my chair.

The last time I'd told Dan about my temptation to give myself over to the sea, he'd tried to drag me to the school counselor. I'd managed to convince him it was just a joke, and after a while he'd let it go. But the look of worry and near pity he'd given me was enough to make me never tell him one of my "jokes" again.

I flopped onto my bed as soon as I finished my homework. I sighed, sinking back into my pillow. Maybe tomorrow morning I could get up on time.

◆━◇━◆

The next thing I saw was a different gilded room than the one from my dream the night before. I felt a smile on my face before I realized I was the one causing it. *Oh, is this a lucid dream? That's unusual.* I quickly reverted to the pose from the last dream. It felt right. I stood there quietly, watching the guests of the party mill about the room. There didn't seem to be any dancing tonight—maybe it was a different sort of gathering? There wasn't even any music, which struck me as odd. I turned to glance out the window, noting it was bright daylight instead of night like last time. I tried listening in on the conversations, but there were just too many going on at once to really pick them apart. I answered the guests' questions about the food as best I could. The knowledge seemed to just simply be in my brain, so I ran with it.

After a while, I heard the unmistakable sound of someone tapping a knife against a champagne glass, and the room silenced. I followed everyone's gaze to the little platform in the corner of the room and saw a man and a woman standing together. He looked elated, sweeping his black hair out of his eyes. He held his champagne glass to the room, giving everyone a big grin. The woman smiled, but even across the room I could see how strained it was. She was gripping her glass so hard her knuckles were nearly glowing white. With a bit of squinting I recognized her as another woman from the previous party, one who'd been dancing across the room.

"Hello everyone!" The man called out to the room, his grin never dropping. "I have an amazing announcement to make!" He took the woman's hand and lifted it, bringing attention to a large diamond ring sparkling on her finger. "Clara has finally agreed to become my wife!" The woman smiled, still tightly, and it didn't reach her eyes. She hid it with a sip of her drink as everyone else in the room cheered and clapped.

In spite of the jubilation surrounding her, Clara looked miserable. The man with black hair was still holding her other hand, and now it was his knuckles that were shining white. Yikes. Even from a distance and with only a tiny glimpse into the relationship, it was clear that this was forced. My musings were interrupted by a meek, polite voice.

"Excuse me? Are you the same waiter that was at the dance hall?" I turned and was greeted by those gorgeous silver eyes and a shy smile attached to the woman from last time. She was no longer in a purple lace dress, but a black one made of thicker material. I grinned, forgetting I was supposed to be a waiter right now, and nodded.

"Oh, yes, I am. Hello again." I was purposely avoiding any greetings that sounded too much like they were from the future, and then scolded myself for it. This was a dream, what did it matter? I focused hard on the accent coming from my own mouth again, and finally placed it as Russian. But all thoughts faded as she giggled softly, and I went completely blank. I probably looked like a fool. I could feel the lopsided smirk on my face and everything. Thank god it was just a dream.

"Hello again..." Her voice trailed off as she looked at me curiously, and I realized why.

"Jackson, miss."

"Jackson." She chuckled, turning to look at the spread. It was definitely smaller than last time, and seemed less luxurious, but judging by the way everyone was scooping it up, it didn't seem to matter. "What's your suggestion this time?" The woman glanced over at me, then back to the food, tapping her fingers softly on the edge of the table. A thought quickly flitted through my mind: *Oh, how I would love to hold her hand and silence that nervous jitter.* But of course that's not proper in any decade. I ignored the whim and looked across the spread, my gaze landing on a small platter of cookies.

"Well, these are infused with lavender. They remind me of your dress from the dance hall." *Oh, damnit, was that too forward? Wait, this is a dream. Who cares?* I smiled at her, allowing myself to be a bit more daring, a bit more like Dan. It was safe here. Her soft blush and small giggle were all it took to send my heart thumping and put the lopsided smirk back on my face.

"Oh, goodness." She stepped to the side just a bit, toward the platter, when the woman who had been on stage, Clara, appeared and wrapped both hands around her friend's upper arm.

"Marie, Marie. We have to disappear, please," Clara pleaded, her eyes wide. Marie—boy, was I glad to learn her name—dropped the smaller plate she'd been holding and turned to hold Clara's arm, smoothing an escaped ringlet back into place. The black haired man from the stage was across the room, preoccupied by other partygoers seemingly congratulating him on the engagement. Clara was twisting the ring around her finger, obviously trying very hard not to pull it off in front of everyone.

"Let's slip into the parlor, the one that Reginald never goes into," she said, rubbing Clara's arms soothingly. Clara nodded with a sigh, then Marie looked up at me.

"Please don't tell anyone where we went, even if you get asked." I was ready to answer when Clara chimed in.

"Please, swear you won't tell Reggie." Clara's voice held the most desperate but quietest plea I'd ever heard, and I just nodded. My brow furrowed in concern, and I clasped my hands behind my back to avoid reaching toward her to offer more comfort.

"You have my word, miss," I managed right before the women took off. The rest of the dream was fairly uneventful. I noticed Reginald looking around in bewilderment for his betrothed, but he apparently didn't think to come over and ask about her. Maybe he was used to this kind of behavior from her? What an interesting supporting cast for my new recurring dreams.

Katiyana

Tuesday, September 8, 2020

M y e y e s f e l t l i k e they'd been glued shut when my alarm went off. Since I'd taken so long to make him dinner, Nick had decided to tell me exactly what he thought of my "dedication" to housework and my share of the chores. By the time he was done, I was so angry that I slammed my bedroom door shut, locked it, and shoved my desk chair underneath the knob. Normally on nights like that I'd text my friends, but I didn't trust Nick to not try to read over my shoulder later. So instead I ended up angry-cry-writing into a notebook, then tearing out the pages and mixing them in with my school notes to hide in my locker. The lengths I had to go to for any sort of privacy from my brother…I would have talked to Mom, but I'd passed out before she'd gotten home.

My alarm was still blaring through my thoughts and I rolled over to smack my phone, groaning and nestling my face in the crook of my elbow. You always hear about people sleeping better after they've had a good cry, but it was the opposite for me. I always felt like I'd been dipped in cement and left out to dry. I could only vaguely recall my latest dream at that point, but I trusted it to come back to me later. I forced myself up anyway, slipping my glasses on and looking around my room for a minute. My chair was still shoved under the knob—probably a fire hazard, but eh, oh well. I left it there as long as I could, gathering my school supplies together and picking out uniform pieces from my little stash. When I finally opened my door, I was face-to-face with Nick, who looked like he'd been crying himself. *He'd have blood-on-the-moon eyes if he'd gotten the*

MacAskill eye color. I tried to push past him, but he caught my arm. I closed my eyes so I didn't whirl around on him and just snap.

"What."

He pouted at me, but released my arm and took a performatively meek step back. It was the same song and dance I'd seen every other time he'd made me storm off and lock myself in my room for the rest of the night, even forgoing dinner sometimes. Next up would be a non-apology that still blamed me.

"I was mean to you last night, but you just left me hanging on dinner. I'm sorry that being so hungry made me testy and rude," he said, literally tapping his index fingers together like some sort of damn anime character. I seethed internally but swallowed my comments, instead just shaking my head and going down the hall. "Katiyana?"

"Save it, Nick. I need to get ready for school." I shut the bathroom door behind me, locking that one, too. I definitely wouldn't put it past him to try to come in while I was showering just to "make sure his apology was accepted." I mockingly whispered the words to myself under the cover of running water, and jumped when Nick started banging on the door.

"God damn you, I just want to apologize for how I acted last night and here you are shutting me out! What's wrong with you? Ungrateful little wench." One more good bang that rattled the shelf near the door and he stomped off down the hall. *Oh by the gods.* I was suddenly very glad there was a locked door between us for the next thirty minutes as I did as much of my morning routine as I could in the bathroom. I even texted Alena and asked if there was any possibility of me getting breakfast again, and told her I'd explain why on the train. She immediately said yes, so I breathed a sigh of relief. I sat in the bathroom and listened for a minute, trying to determine where Nick was in the apartment. I hadn't heard Mom this morning, either. It was rare that she left before I woke up, but it happened sometimes. I caught the faint tune of an anime opening, so he was either in the living room or his room. His room was more doable; living room I'd have to basically sneak out. Alright, well, no way around it. I needed to get to school.

I made it down the hallway and back into my bedroom with no issue, switched my pajamas for my school bag, and darted down the rest of the hallway to the front door. I had just turned the handle when I heard Nick get up from the recliner in the living room. Damnit. I tried my best to slip through the door before he got to me, but he grabbed it and followed me out.

"I have to get to the station. I don't want to be late for school." I stabbed the elevator button and willed it to come sooner. *Please be faster, little machine.*

"You can run to the station then, just stand the hell still and let me apologize to you, damnit!" I stepped back into the elevator as soon as it dinged open, shaking my head at him.

"I don't want to be late for school, Nicolae!"

He reached through the elevator doors as they were about to shut, and they slid back open. Nick planted a firm hand on either side to keep it from shutting and loomed menacingly into the elevator. "Katiyana, your big brother is trying to be nice to you," he growled, and I planted my feet where I was, refusing to cower like he wanted me to.

"Nick, just let me go to school." I was trying so hard to keep my voice from shaking, to keep it nonchalant, and the deepening furrow of his brow told me it was working.

"You stand here and let me apologize to you." He slapped both hands on either side of the elevator door, literally trapping me inside. I heard a door shut down the hall and peeked over his shoulder, praying it was a neighbor I knew so Nick would have to calm down and not cause a scene. It was Valerie, with Mom standing next to her as they chatted quietly. *Thank goodness.* Valerie looked up as she was locking her door and paused, key still in the knob. Mom peered over Val's shoulder with a narrow gaze, and I felt her sigh of exasperation. I stared at them wide-eyed as Nick realized someone else was in the hall and dropped one of his hands, changing his tone.

"Now Katiyana, you be careful on the way to school, alright? I don't want you getting hurt before you've even started your day!" My stomach turned at how swiftly his voice went from terrifying to saccharine. Valerie had made it to the elevator and tapped Nick on the shoulder, Mom a couple steps behind. He spun with a wide grin. "Miss Valerie, how nice to see you this morning! I was just seeing my darling little sister off to the station. Hi Mom!" The disgustingly sweet tone in his greeting caused mom to raise a single eyebrow and step past him to hold the elevator door open.

"Hello, Nick," she said, her tone causing his smile to falter.

Val's face remained stony as she stepped past him and into the elevator, situating herself between us. I allowed myself to look away, to stare down at the book in my arms instead of up at Nick's fraudulent grin.

"Well you've seen her off, and now you know she's with us, so you don't have to worry about her safety." Valerie grinned, and Nick took a step back. I'd always thought Valerie's canine teeth were a bit too long. They were very good for giving someone who hadn't seen them before a scare, and Valerie never smiled much around Nick. Couldn't blame her.

"Yes, I suppose you're right. Thank you. See you when you get back, Mom." Nick turned tail and scurried back to our apartment, and as soon as the elevator doors slid shut I slumped toward Mom with my forehead pressed to my book. I felt Valerie's hand on my shoulder, Mom's on my back.

"Is he being unbearable? You know you can come stay with me until Etta's trip is over." I almost cried at her words. Valerie had been my neighbor for as long as I could remember, and Mom's friend for longer. I looked up at her, grateful.

"I'll be okay. I think it's just because you're about to leave. He gets all high and mighty when he thinks he's in charge." I gestured with my head toward Mom, who rubbed my back, attempting to comfort me. "He's been trying to read texts over my shoulder and demanded that I tell him where I went after school yesterday, as if he needed to know. I basically barricaded my door last night just to get away from him." My head dropped back to my book and Valerie stood straight, sighing.

"Well, the moment you feel unsafe, you pack your shit and come to my door." Val patted my head. "Told you that you and Robin both leaving at the same time was a bad idea," she grumbled toward Mom, who was about to respond when someone else joined us in the elevator. It was a neighbor I recognized but didn't know, and he gave me a concerned look. Valerie gave him a reassuring smile and laid a hand on my head. The other neighbor got off in the lobby, and we were right behind him, Mom taking my hand.

"I wish you'd come to me with this sooner. How long has he been doing this? Why didn't you tell me last night when I got home?"

I ducked my head into my shoulders a little. "I don't know, I thought it was just a one-off thing I guess. It's just been the past couple of days really, not long. Since school started."

Mom exhaled deeply and squeezed my hand. "I should have waited to talk to Valerie and stayed in the apartment this morning, I'm sorry. I'll call him before I get on the ferry. And please, go stay with Val the second he makes you feel worse––I don't want you to feel unsafe in your own home. But I will remind him of boundaries and letting you keep your privacy. I'll tell your father what's happened, as well. He'll probably call Nick later."

"Okay." I picked at the strap of my bag, mentally kicking myself for not bringing it up to Mom the first time Nick had "accidentally" read over my shoulder.

"We'll walk with you to the train station. I am so sorry we have to leave you alone with him. The aunts and I tried to move the trip."

"I know, and I know Dad tried to move his, too."

Valerie shook her head. "I just don't trust him. I know he's still young and has his own issues, but he's always been...weird. Around you." She gave me a sideways glance, and I knew she was dancing the line between appropriate non-family-member talk and her own thoughts.

"Thank you for your input, Valerie." Mom's tone had a bite of finality to it, warning her friend she was toeing that tenuous line. She focused her attention back on me after Valerie closed her mouth. "I'm so sorry, honey. I'll talk to him."

"At least give him time to calm down; he's so angry right now. We got into a fight last ni— well he...he just yelled at me, really, but I stormed off and it made it all worse. I made him mad."

"Sweetheart, that's not your fault, you know he has issues." She sounded tired of the reason, and I didn't blame her. I was tired of it too. "I'll also talk to him about going to therapy again. Can you hold out until we get back?"

"Yeah, and school starting helps. Plus I'm sure he'll chill out after a day or two." We were almost to the station. I saw Alena waiting for me, a little Tupperware-looking container in her hand. Mom spotted her, too, and waved with a smile.

"You have very lovely friends to turn to, as well." We three walked across the street to the station, joining Alena near the bench seats. As her train pulled up, Mom wrapped me in a tight hug. "I won't be too busy for you, Yana. Call me when you need me. Lean on Valerie and, hell, call Sinéad if you need to. You know she'll drop anything for you." Mom's voice was really soft, and I heard her heave a gentle sigh. "I wish I could fix this."

"I'm not mad at you. We'll figure it out when you get back. I love you."

"I love you, too, Yana."

We said our goodbyes and Mom climbed on the train, carrying a suitcase I'd been too wrapped up in my own nerves to notice. I leaned my forehead on Valerie's shoulder, tapping my books against her arm. "Thank you. I'm really glad you were getting in the elevator at the same time I was." I gave her a half-hearted smirk and she patted my head in return.

"I had a sense I should leave a little earlier today." She smiled and tucked her phone in her pocket, then immediately pulled it back out as it buzzed. "Ah hell, I forgot Alexsander wanted to do breakfast." I chuckled softly, grateful for the change in subject, but also just her presence in general.

"When are you going to marry him?" I teased. Alex had been her boyfriend for as long as I'd been alive, probably longer.

"When he stops acting like a vampire and staying up all night." Valerie was punching a text into her phone and I laughed. As soon as Valerie's attention shifted, I got swept up by Alena's hug, blinking in surprise at her as she held my shoulders and studied my face.

"Are you hurt? In danger?"

"Nick and I got into a fight last night. I tried to sneak out this morning without talking to him, and it didn't go well." I shrugged, trying to downplay it, but the fact Valerie and Mom had walked me to the station made that impossible and I knew it. Alena mercifully took the explanation anyway and pushed the little container at me.

"Okay. Here's breakfast! Katherine also wants you to come over while your mom's gone so she can make sure you're not getting malnourished at home." Alena grinned, and Valerie laughed.

"I love that woman," Valerie said, then looked up as the train pulled in. "Alright, you two head to school. Call me if you need me, Katiyana." I nodded and looked around, confused for a moment.

"Where are Jamari and Fleur?"

"Oh, they got a ride this morning from Renée. I guess she had a meeting in Meadhan and took them to get breakfast?" Alena shrugged, and I returned one of my own. It was probably in the group text message I'd ignored earlier.

We got on the train with the other passengers, and settled into our seats. Alena had brought me oatmeal with brown sugar and fruit on top. "I made this myself, just for you!" She was so proud of it too.

Alena didn't ask any more questions while we were on the train, or even during the little amount of time we had while waiting for classes to start. I was as grateful for that as I was for breakfast. I had come to her crying more than once, and she let me talk in my own time. She only ever wanted to know if I was hurt or in danger, and that was the only answer she ever forced out of me. Everything else could come later.

Vincent

Tuesday, September 8, 2020

I managed to wake up with more than enough time to not only eat breakfast, but shower, get to the train station, and actually wait there for a little while. Miracles upon miracles, and I wasn't about to look a gift horse in the mouth. A lot of it had to do with the fact that Mom had a shift that started at midnight or something ridiculous like that, and wouldn't be home until after I'd already left the house.

I was hunched over my phone, typing up the details of the past couple dreams in the Notes app. It was getting a little hard to remember the first one, but I did the best I could. I remembered everyone's names, and the small glimpses I had seen into their relationships. Reggie definitely seemed like the villain of the story, if his grip on Clara's hand was any indication.

I'd been staring at my phone screen long enough it went dark, and I blinked at my own reflection. The bruise on my cheek was small, thankfully, but I had been keeping my hood up as much as possible and carefully leaning on my hand to cover the bruise when I couldn't wear it. Then another face poked into the reflection next to mine, and I smiled. Dan had found me.

"Vinny, are you staring into the void?" He asked, draping his arm over my shoulders and planting a kiss on my temple. I ducked down from him and batted at his chest, shaking my head.

I scrubbed my temple with my hoodie sleeve and he laughed, taking his arm back. "You gotta stop doin' that, man."

"Aw, I thought you loved me," Dan pouted, a tube of lip balm halfway to his mouth. I rolled my eyes.

"I do, but the kissing's just weird. I don't mind if you hug me or have your arm around me, though."

"Oh, fine, whatever you wish, my darling." Dan returned to his lip balm, using his own phone screen as a mirror. I shook my head again.

We sat in silence for a few minutes, Dan flipping through Instagram and his other socials, me trying to pull more details about my dreams from my subconscious. The train came and we bustled onto it, the ride to school much the same as the wait at the station. It was such an oddly calm and nice day, despite only just beginning, and I was starting to wonder if something terrible was going to happen. There had to be a catch, right? There had to be. Nothing ever went well for this long.

I checked my phone again, certain Mom was going to call and demand why I'd left the house without telling her two days in a row. At some point, I had started bouncing my knee, and Dan set his hand on it with a concerned glance.

"Okay, I know that's an anxiety thing and not a conscious thing, but you good?" He had lowered his voice, which I appreciated. He'd also not mentioned the bruise, which I appreciated even more. I shrugged.

"Mom called and texted me like forty times yesterday, remember? I'm certain she's gonna do something like that again. I can feel it. Today started off way too smoothly." I had inadvertently begun talking faster with each sentence, and Dan's hand moved up to my shoulder.

"Easy babe, easy. You gotta breathe." He lifted his other hand—still holding his phone—and guided me through a couple breaths, lowering and raising his hand with the inhales and exhales. I felt better by the time the train stopped at the school station but zipped my hoodie up for some extra mental security. I had to reassure Dan that he didn't need to hold my hand and I was alright, but he hovered nearby anyway. It was comforting even if I tried to say it was annoying. He would have never believed me anyway.

Upon settling in homeroom, those of us who had requested and been approved for class changes were presented with new schedules. I looked up eagerly upon seeing the teacher make her way toward me, but she passed me by and handed a paper to the person behind me instead. My shoulders sank. *Okay, there it is. There's the thing I've been waiting for. No drama class for me this year.* Despite their best efforts, the administration wasn't always able to get everyone into the classes they'd asked for. Classrooms only had room for so many people, after all. I stifled a sigh. It was no use fighting them on it. I couldn't shake the disappointment, but it wasn't worth it. It just wasn't worth it. *Get over it, Vincent.*

The next few class periods passed in a sort of blur, as I was too busy being at war with myself to focus on anything else. *I needed to get over this, it's just that I had been waiting for so long. But it's not like any particular deity was out to get me, there just wasn't enough room. Just stop thinking about it, Vincent.*

By the time lunch came around, Dan had visibly had enough of my silence and finally just bapped me on the back of the head with his textbook. "Okay, enough. What is it? Why are you so upset? Is it still Mila or something else?" He was exasperated and I sighed, pulling my hood up.

"It's nothing, it's dumb. Don't worry about it," I mumbled, shrugging.

"Alright, fine, whatever you say. But next time you're sitting in every class staring at your paper instead of writing notes, I'm not sharing mine with you." I nodded; that was fair. He didn't have to take notes for me in the first place. I was glad he did, though. As we joined classmates in the lunch line in silence, he huffed, never being one to stand the quiet. "Do you want to go somewhere after school?"

"Sure. Where? I don't have any money right now."

He waved his hand dismissively at me. "Dad refilled my card. I have money burning a hole in my pocket right now and no dates blowing up my phone, so I'm going to spend it on you." He had given up his crossed arms and stern countenance, diving right back into his Instagram spam. I smirked.

"Alright, then. You still haven't told me where."

"Oh, the little café down the street. You know, the one that's been there since the dawn of time?"

"You mean the witch shop?" I laughed softly, loosening with it.

"Is that what it is? I knew they sold stuff but I never paid attention." Dan was texting while talking, someone he'd met on the dating app judging by the emojis next to the name. I'd unfortunately learned the organization system he used for his contacts.

"Yeah dude. You want to cast some spells, do ya?" I teased, nudging his arm with my elbow. If I was honest with myself—and I rarely was—it would, in fact, be nice to see if Dan would buy me a couple things I'd been thinking of getting. I didn't want to use up all his money, but the idea of a new book was incredibly tempting. I'd read about a series online that guides readers through each step of the initiation process for this church/temple/coven up in New Hampshire.

"Can we cast a spell to get me laid? Because I am dying right now. This dry spell is *killing* me." Dan said this completely nonchalantly, not even looking up from his phone. I groaned.

"Daniel, I do not need to know the fine details of your love life." I cringed, shoulders nearly meeting my ears as I saw the person ahead of us look over their shoulder at Dan with wide eyes. "And no, I will not cast you a spell like that, because you are a minor, dumbass. I don't need that on my conscience."

"If the other person is a minor, it won't matter!" Dan protested, giving me a pout that I peeked at between my fingers.

"Not doing it, dude. No chance." He finally just grunted and turned back to his phone, and then it was our turn to load up our trays. We gathered our food and headed to a corner table, taking up as much of the lunch period as we could just chilling and Dan showing me more people on his app. This must have been one helluva dry spell, with him going on Connect binges two days in a row.

Classes resumed, and this time I was focused enough to take notes and pay attention. I had a string of impeccable grades to keep up, and I didn't want to let it slip.

◆

The end of school came quicker than I thought it would, and I found myself following Dan around the corner and down the street instead of getting on the train. Neither of us had gone to Ladine's before and while it aligned with my interests, it definitely had nothing to do with Dan's. Knowing him, this trip had something to do with a potential suitor.

"Vinny, did you get lost in your own thoughts again?" Dan tapped my forehead, and I realized I had, but I snapped back to attention quickly.

"Yeah, wondering why you want to hit this place up." I tapped his forehead in return and he swatted at my hand, waving his phone around as he did so.

"I'm just curious is all!" He said, far too defensively for it to be true. I grinned as he frowned and turned around with a huff, picking up his pace to walk briskly down the block. I followed him with a laugh.

"Curious about some*thing* or some*one*, eh Danny?" I teased, jogging after him. Neither of us were paying attention and Dan had looked over his shoulder to shout at me but ended up slamming right into an older guy and nearly falling over. I dodged out of the way just in time, watching the dude brush his shoulder off and glare at us both. His eyes were so like black holes I feared they would swallow us whole. His uniform betrayed his workplace as one of the local fast food joints.

"Why don't you watch where you're going, brats," he spat at us, switching his shopping bag to the other hand as if we were going to take it from him. He glared for a second longer then stomped off, grumbling something I didn't quite catch beyond "ingrates" and "kids these days." Pretty sure I heard a curse word or two in there, as well. I tried not to laugh, because he couldn't have been much older than we were, but here he was acting like an old man.

I helped Dan pick himself up off the sidewalk and we walked the last half block to the café. The bells tied to the door let out a small, pleasant tinkling noise as we pushed it open, and the scent of incense hit me immediately. I took a big, deep breath as we stepped in, closing my eyes to just bask in the immediate wave of comfort and peace that washed over me. I got so wrapped up, it took me a moment to realize that Dan had moved on without me. When I opened my eyes, he was making a beeline to the counter where a blonde woman was sitting and organizing crystals. I blinked, realizing it was the beachy-boho lady from the train station yesterday. Faodail was small, sure, but how the hell had he found her? Dan had probably stayed up half the night browsing all the companies in the city just to see if her photo was posted anywhere. What a damn creep. I shook my head and left him to his flirting, if you could call pretending to care about crystals flirting.

I moved over to the book section to see if the ones I'd been looking at online were on the shelves. I passed a rack of sparkling necklaces, all raw crystals and wrapped wire. They caught my eye, and upon further investigation, I noticed an amethyst with a tiny triquetra attached and I reached up to hold it gently. It was gorgeous, and it looked like someone agreed with me, as there was one missing from the frontmost hook. I smirked softly and let it go, continuing my journey to the shelves.

I had found the book I'd researched, the first one of the series, and was four pages into it when Dan knelt down beside me with a sigh. I hadn't even noticed myself sinking to the floor, but there I was, cross-legged and absorbed. I looked up, blinking back to reality.

"Miss Valerie has very politely turned me away and spoken very blatantly about her long-term boyfriend, and our age gap, to the point of mentioning she wishes she had a little brother like me, so my efforts have all been for naught." Dan slumped dramatically, leaning back lightly against the bookshelf. I laughed.

"Why are you surprised? You tracked her down from one look at the train station without even knowing her name, and showed up at her work unannounced. You probably started the conversation off with something sexual, too, didn't you?" His groan was all the answer I needed, and I reached over to slug him on the arm softly. "You'll learn your lesson one day, and I sincerely hope it's not with a slap to the face." I flipped the book closed, standing up to put it back on the shelf, and Dan took it from me, reading the back.

"Do you want this?" He asked, his plight forced away and forgotten. "I did say I wanted to spend money on you."

"Oh, you don't have to. It's not a big deal." He was already standing up and heading back to the counter.

"Did you see anything else you wanted?" He called over his shoulder, and I relented, running my list through my head. The only other thing that came to mind was the necklace I'd held for two seconds. I must have glanced toward it in an obvious fashion, because Dan took off down that aisle without me saying anything. "Something over here?" I took a deep breath and followed him. There was no dissuading him now.

"Which one?" He had reached the display rack and was tapping some of them lightly, and I stepped forward, lifting the amethyst one gently. Dan pulled it off its hook, setting it on top of the book before heading up to the cashier. "Miss Valerie, I'd like to purchase these for my friend, please," he said sweetly, definitely leaning into the little brother angle. She grinned back at him, sliding the book and necklace to herself to tap the prices into her register.

"You're such a sweetheart, buying things for friends. Is it a birthday gift?" She asked, the question directed at me. I shrugged, and Dan stepped back up to the plate.

"A late one, but it's also a back-to-school present. He's gotten straight As every year that I've known him, so this is to give him good luck in our last two years of high school."

Dan's grin was bright enough to power a small car, if cars ran on solar power. Valerie matched it with a much calmer smile.

"That's so kind of you!" Everything was rung up swiftly, and Dan handed over his card before even being told the total. Within moments, Valerie had the necklace in its own special bag and both items in a larger paper bag branded with the store's logo.

Dan and I made our way back to the station, him absentmindedly swinging the bag with my new things in it and me mulling over the few pages I'd read. I must have gotten unnervingly silent again, as Dan tapped my forehead, this time without a word. Just a look, a raised eyebrow.

"Sorry."

"What are you thinking about now?"

"That book, actually." I shrugged. "It seems interesting, but a little outdated."

"Why did you want it?" The question was absent-minded, but I didn't mind. Dan had only a passing curiosity in my interests, but he always supported them.

"I've been interested in Paganism and witchcraft for a while, and after some research, the series that book's from seemed like the best place to start."

"Is that why you won't cast a spell for me? Because you don't know enough?" Dan laughed. "Is there a level system? Oh my gosh, are you a level-one witch?" I chuckled with him, softly.

"Nah. Honestly, I'm more like a level *point*-one. I know some very generic—well, basic is a better word for it—basic stuff, but I haven't been able to read any books or do deep research." I reached up to sweep my hair back. Dan had convinced me this morning to let him style it again, and it had been falling in my eyes all day.

"I didn't know there was so much homework involved. You're such a nerd. Schoolwork AND religion work? Couldn't be me." Dan held the bag out to me as we got to the train station, and I took it. He slid his arm through mine and we just hung out waiting a few minutes for the train. Our ride home was about the same as the one to school: quiet and chill. A nice bookend to the day.

Unfortunately, the peace was shattered ten seconds after I walked in the front door and accidentally kicked a partially empty beer bottle over. The noise it made was minimal, but the line of moisture that spilled from it was the issue, as my mother shouted not a mere second later.

"VINCENT! WHAT THE HELL!" She stomped towards me, throwing another bottle on the floor. That one not only left more moisture on the floor, it shattered, and I had to glance down to make sure mom was wearing shoes. Thank goodness she was—one less mess to clean up.

"I'm sorry! I'll get the mop right now, and the broom too! I'll clean it up; it'll be like it never happened." I held my hands up again, ducking my head down as she swung. Whenever she drank, her blows got wild and it was easy for her to miss. I was thankful for that, but definitely didn't look forward to these moments, as it made her temper worse.

"You fucking better! You little shit-for-brains, what did you have to go and spill shit on the floor for!" She shouted again, slamming the front door, which I'd accidentally left open. She spun around and stomped back to the couch, falling down on it amidst a bowl of what seemed to be a mixture of popcorn and Pringles. I closed my eyes briefly, moving down the hallway to put my stuff in my room, and then came back to clean up the mess I definitely didn't cause, but didn't want to deal with fighting about. It only took about five minutes, and I had the mop rinsed out and hung up in the bathroom swiftly. While in there, I took a look at my cheek and gladly noticed the bruise was turning yellow at the edges. It was healing fast, maybe because it was a partial mouth injury. Those always healed quickly. I hated that I knew that, but I would definitely be using the knowledge for as long as I was in this house.

Back in my bedroom, I dug through the bag from the café shop and pulled out the necklace. I was drawn to it, but it definitely seemed too fancy for me to wear. I looked around my room—maybe I could hang it up somewhere? I must have spun around looking for possible places at least three times, and the chain ended up around my neck anyway. I blinked at it. I seemed to be doing a lot of things absent-mindedly lately, but none of them had really turned out badly. The pendant felt nice against my chest, so I just shrugged and left it on, but tucked it under my shirt. It wasn't really a secret, but it didn't feel safe to wear visible jewelry around Mom.

Katiyana

Tuesday, September 8, 2020

My left hand was gripping my new necklace as I unlocked the door with my right. I was so glad Nick was
working tonight. I probably wouldn't see him until ten or
eleven p.m., which meant I didn't have to deal with him
confronting me about that morning. Valerie had texted me
after school, telling me that if things went wrong or I felt
unsafe to text her and she'd be right over. That helped.

It really was unfortunate that my neighbors had to make
safety plans with me just because of my brother, but I was
thankful nonetheless. I felt fine so far, nothing beyond
my typical desire to avoid him, so I wasn't scared yet. Just
anxious.

The pendant didn't leave my hand until I had successfully made it to my room and set down all my things after
taking a stealthy peek into Nick's room to be absolutely
certain he wasn't there. After changing out of my uniform,
I tucked the amethyst under my shirt and settled at my desk
to read the few pages I needed to catch up on. I'd been far
too distracted during class to read along and had ended up
doodling the lace pattern from my dream in the margin
of the book. Something about it was just sticking in my
mind, despite the rest of the fine details having escaped my
memory. I was deep in the assigned story when my phone
buzzing against my desk jolted me out of it, and my hand
flew to my chest in surprise.

It was Alena reminding me that Katherine wanted
to see me, and I smiled softly, imagining Alena's stepmom peering over Alena's shoulder, her Afro held back
with a brightly patterned bandanna and her sparkly lit-

tle stud earrings glittering beneath it. She was the type of woman you trusted immediately, a mom of the highest caliber. I quickly assured her that I would visit before the week was out, complete with heart emojis and kissy smiley faces. She must have stolen Alena's phone, because the response I got back was definitely not from my hold-loved-ones-at-arms-length friend, as she called me "baby girl" and "dear heart" multiple times. I giggled softly and set my phone down to continue reading. The next day was going to be so lonely with her and Jamari across the street taking classes at Inntinn and Fleur across the river at Corp. I'd gotten pretty used to being alone on Mondays, Wednesdays, and Fridays while they all went to their specialized courses, but it didn't make me miss them any less.

Ten pages and a sheet of grammar questions later, I fashioned a passable dinner for myself and sat down to eat it with some cartoons before retiring to my room. I shut my door but didn't lock it, as I still had plenty of time before Nick's shift was over. I would lock it while I slept, though.

I stood in the center of my room and fiddled with my necklace again, staring at the little cabinet that rested on top of my dresser. Mom had given it to me when I'd turned thirteen, and it contained supplies passed down through our family for generations. I hadn't formally started any training yet, but I knew enough to cast a spell or two by myself. This Samhain was supposed to mark the start of my official training with my mom, aunts, and the rest of the coven.

Moving in front of my dresser, I tugged one of the small drawers open and pulled out a small blue pouch. I turned it over and deposited the contents on my palm, the cool surface of the stone slowly warming against my skin. It was a carved sandstone with light, mottled colors mixing on the surface. The front was carved with a woven cross, the back an eternal flame, both symbols of Brigit. I wrapped my fingers around it and shut my eyes, reaching out my senses, breathing slowly. My aunts had given this to me with the cabinet, believing I had a connection to the Celtic goddess. I had never tried anything beyond holding this stone and sending out energy toward her, but they also assured me that deity work could and likely would come long after my formal induction into the coven.

After a few precious moments of meditation with the stone and receiving a sense of protection and comfort, I glanced at my phone for the time and decided to try and sleep.

With the door locked against Nick, Brigit's stone still in my palm, and my favorite blanket bundled around me, I allowed myself to relax and be whisked back to the gilded room of my dreams. I hadn't been able to control anything last night; I just watched Clara's engagement get announced, talked to the waiter again, and then comforted Clara in a different room. The pattern was becoming obvious. It was all the same people and the same couple locations. Maybe I'd text Sinéad later. She might be a little looser with info about how the dreams worked. The rest of the coven sure wasn't.

Oh damn, I never sent her the lace pattern like I said I would. Unfortunately, my phone was on my desk across the room and the coziness of my blanket was too good to sacrifice for a single photo. I'd do it later. I let my eyes close again, giving the Brigit stone a little squeeze, and dozed off.

———◇———

The next thing I saw wasn't the crystalline gilded room from before. But it was the same waiter. He was behind the counter of a bakery, grinning over a display of perfectly decorated pastries. I glanced down, and noted the little gloves on my hands, which were clasping a tiny matching purse. I grinned back up at the waiter, who seemed to be serving as cashier here, and silently thanked whatever deity was letting me see him again.

"Well, this is a surprise," he said, and I giggled.

"I thought you were a waiter?" I teased, shifting a little, my skirt swishing around my calves. Off-white this time, no lace. He laughed gently, leaning his arms on the top of the counter and settling his chin on them.

"Some of us downtown have to work more than one job." He smirked, and I watched his eyes roam down to the hem of my dress and back up. It was definitely an approving glance. I had to fight a blush.

"Oh, that never crossed my mind." In the back of my head, I felt a thought that wasn't mine: *Oh, it definitely has.* The girl I was currently embodying had gone out of her way to find out exactly what his other job was so she could just "happen" to run into him. I leaned closer to the counter, peering at the array of delights. "Did you make these?"

"No, no, Charles made those. I made these." I looked up as he gestured to a different cabinet, filled with dainty chocolates in all sorts of colors, with an impressive array of fillings. I stepped over to that display, gasping softly at the artistry contained within. Even the marbled colors on a few of the chocolates seemed completely intentional rather than random, and I pressed my fingers softly against the glass.

"Would you like any?" Jackson's face was on the other side of the cabinet, grinning at me over the shelf. I nodded.

"Oh yes, please, a whole pound box!" I straightened, and he did at the same time, smile never dropping.

"Which ones?"

"All your favorites!" He laughed at that, shaking his head softly.

"You're making it difficult to choose." It was a tease, and his tone made it blatant. I giggled.

"Surely there are some that are more fun to make than others?" My hands went behind my back, clasping my little purse there, and I tilted my head at him. His eyes widened just slightly and I saw a flash of pink across his cheeks, before he bowed his head to look back into the cabinet.

"Well, I suppose I can think of a few." His voice was muffled as he reached into the cabinet to start filling the empty box he'd produced from below it, and I bided my time by watching him work. In a few moments, the box was filled, wrapped, and tied with a purple ribbon suspiciously similar to the lace dress I'd had on during the party. I gave him a knowing glance, smiling ever so slightly, and the flash of pink traced his cheeks again. He cleared his throat and rubbed the back of his head, turning to the cash register with the box in his hand.

"Would you like to pay cash or should I write you an invoice?" He asked, tapping the keys on the register. They made such a satisfying clunk with every number he punched in.

"Oh, they're not a gift?" I giggled, already opening my little purse to see what kind of money this woman had. My eyes shot wide as I saw a hefty stack of cash inside. I couldn't tell what all the bills were and couldn't remember what counted as a lot of money in the twenties. So hopefully she had enough for chocolates.

I was counting out the bills—there was enough—when the little bell on the door jingled as someone opened it, and Jackson glanced up with a polite, customer-service smile before turning back to me and finishing the transaction. Then I felt a hand grip the back of my neck. Not hard, not threateningly, but definitely possessively.

"Marie, I wondered where you wandered off to." His voice was cordial, but laced underneath with the threat that if I "wandered off" again, I'd be paying for it. My body was rigid in response, and Jackson was eyeing the man over my shoulder, one hand poised under the counter. There must have been a weapon or an alarm button under there, and either way I prayed he didn't need to use it.

"Sorry, I just wanted to see inside this shop. I didn't mean to leave you behind." The girl turned, smiling up at the man whose hand fell from her neck to her shoulder. My lucidity was fading. He smiled back, but it absolutely did not hit his eyes. *Yikes.*

"Please tell me next time, instead of just walking away." The girl nodded, and the man looked over at the counter. "Did you already pay for those?" The disgust in his voice was thinly veiled, and I recoiled from it. Thankfully that reaction didn't translate to her body. She just nodded, picking up the box and the bit of change off the counter.

"I did. They're specialty chocolates absolutely worthy of your mother. They'll be a gift," she said, holding them to her chest loosely but protectively. The mention of a gift for his mom flipped some sort of small switch in the man, and Marie laid a gentle hand on his chest. "Lucas, she'll love them." He sighed but nodded, patting her hand before grabbing it and tugging her out of the shop. Marie glanced over her shoulder at Jackson with an apologetic smile, which he half-heartedly returned. Marie and Lucas left the bakery, and I felt more than saw Jackson's heart drop.

◦◦◦◦◦

My eyes opened not long after the dream ended, and I peered into my dark room. My hand had loosened around the Brigit stone and instead wrapped itself around my amethyst pendant while I slept, and I just laid there for a while holding it. Jackson's face as Marie left was stuck in my mind, the longing and almost loneliness Marie felt while she left with Lucas filling my heart to the brim. It was all I could do not to cry. I wasn't sure what was going on with these dreams, but I probably needed to try and distance myself a bit before Marie's emotions started leaking into the real world. It took me a few more minutes to compose myself, and I rolled over onto my face to block out my room until I could. The cool stone that was still on my bed pressed gently against my cheek, and I welcomed it. That little touch was like a soft reassurance from Brigit herself that I was back in my own life and not living out Marie's. With a soft sigh, I got out of bed and settled back at my desk with my blanket still wrapped around my shoulders. There was a single sheet of algebra homework to look over still, and I'd been avoiding it since I didn't like algebra. Instead, I flipped through my notebook to find the doodle of the lace, snapping a photo and sending it off to Sinéad. I stared at the math but couldn't bring myself to do it yet. It wasn't due for a couple days, anyway, so I really didn't need to do it right that second. I usually did my homework the day it was assigned, but dang this math just wasn't it right then.

In the midst of me musing more about the dream and this new character, Lucas, Nick came home. He tried to open my door but the lock stopped him, and then he called for me to open it. I heaved out a breath, pushing myself up and relenting because I knew he'd just stand there and whine and knock until I did. He pushed in immediately and flopped onto my bed, still in his work clothes. Considering he worked at a fast food joint, it wasn't exactly pleasant. But I had a nice linen spray from Ladine's I could use before getting back in bed, and hopefully it would be enough. Better than arguing with him about why I don't want my bed to smell like grease.

"Aren't you going to ask me how my day was?" He droned from the bed, seeking attention. I rolled my eyes, confident he couldn't see since my back was to him, then put on a shockingly saccharine voice.

"How was work?"

"Horrible as always. They made me mop the floor twice." He sighed over-dramatically, and I sighed inwardly.

That's what happens when you half-ass the job. He'd screwed up every other job he'd had, so why not this one, too? Things I wanted to say but would never. "I'm sorry," I offered up instead.

"Oh also, I went to Ladine's, and as I was coming out, I ran into a couple boys from your school. They slammed right into me, probably on purpose, and didn't even apologize. If you see them, make sure you tell them off for me." He was waving his hat around as he talked, and I turned to give him an incredulous look at that last sentence.

"Nick, how on earth am I supposed to just know what two kids bumped into you on the street? You know how big the school is, right?" It may have been four years since he'd last set foot in it, but gods, his memory couldn't be that bad. He exhaled loudly again, but this time irritably.

"You won't let me apologize to you, you won't help me out when two kids you probably know and probably put up to it slam into me and nearly knock me down on the sidewalk...You just don't care about your older brother at all do you?" He sat up, hat twisting between his hands as he glared. I slumped against the back of my chair, chin on my arm.

"Why would I ever put two random dudes up to that?" I knew the question wouldn't get a proper answer, he had already spun up the story in his mind.

"Like I just said, you don't care about your poor, tired, yelled-at-by-his-managers older brother at all. You'd probably prefer it if I was just gone." He moved toward my desk so that he was standing over me, and looked toward the wall above my dresser where Mom's old athame was hanging. I used it as decor rather than a tool since I hadn't gotten any training yet. I stood up, moving to block him from it.

"Nick if you're going to be like this, I'm going to call Valerie." My voice was firm even though my hands were shaking, but he stopped moving. His eyes narrowed, and he spun around to stomp out of my room, slamming the door hard enough that the frame on the wall next to it rattled. I scooped up my phone and found Valerie's messages.

LilTriquetra

Val, pls be on call, nick is home from work and freaking me out. He's not in my room, I'm gonna lock my door now.

She responded almost immediately.

LoveWitch

I heard that door slam all the way down the hall, you good?

LilTriquetra

Yeah, that was Nick leaving my room. I'm good right now.

LoveWitch

I'll be awake for a while. Call me if you need me, okay kid?

LilTriquetra

Of course, thank you val

LoveWitch

No problem sweetheart.

With Val made aware of the situation, I was able to relax a little before hitting the sheets, going to bed properly this time. It was a little hard to drown out the sounds of anime from Nick's room, but I settled for a white noise video on my phone and perched it on the pillow next to my head. It helped drown him out but was a different sort of annoying. It took a few tries to find the right volume and position for sleep and noise cancellation, but in the end it happened, and this time I didn't dream.

Vincent

Wednesday, September 9, 2020

I WOKE UP WITH my hand wrapped around the amethyst and the memory of chocolates. I was halfway through my shower when the details of the dream came back to me. A bakery, Marie, and someone new. I tapped all of the new details into my phone as I was walking down the hallway, bag slung over my shoulder and my new book tucked safely inside. I was planning on getting some reading done during lunch, or, if I could be sneaky, homeroom and lulls in class periods. I'd even gotten up a little earlier than normal to meet Dan at the train station before his train over to Corp took off so I could read while waiting for mine. It was the first day of his specialized classes over at the other school and he was nervous for some unfathomable reason.

"The shit is that around your neck?" I heard, and stopped to find my mother standing at the end of the hall, arms crossed, glaring at the pendant I'd forgotten to hide under my sweater.

"Oh, Dan got it for me as a gift. It's just a pendant. He said it was for good luck." All of this was true, and easily omitted the fact I'd gone shopping with him.

"You're dating, then?" The question had been asked before, and I cringed against what I knew came next. "You and your little faggot of a boyfriend, huh?" She glared harder.

"No, Mom, no. It's just for good luck." I tucked my phone in my pocket and shook my head. Arguing about her usage of derogatory names was something I'd learned not to do—with a bruise on my ribs and a slap to the face.

"Sure, just remember what I said would happen if I caught you being gay in my house." She was closer to me now, looming over me with only a couple inches of extra height, her eyes dark. My head tucked back, shoulders rising up to meet it, and I nodded.

"I remember." This is one of the reasons I never invited Dan over. I didn't want him to censor himself, and I didn't want him to be somewhere so clearly unsafe for him. Mom seemed to accept my two words as enough, and I gratefully stepped around her, forcing myself to not just run for the door. I did run the first block though, just enough to help shake out all the nervous energy and get myself back down to manageable levels.

When I got to the station, Dan was waiting for me, a little Tupperware tucked under his arm. Fleur stood next to him, flipping through her tiny ever-present planner. She was much more Dan's friend than mine, but I'd come to enjoy her company, as well. She was headed to Corp too, just like every other year they'd been traveling across the river together.

"Heeey boy, that pendant do look good on you though." Dan wiggled his sunglasses at me, tapping the arm behind his ear to make them jump. Fleur nodded, agreeing with his assessment quietly. I smirked half-heartedly back, finally tucking the pendant under my shirt. Dan pouted. "Did you not believe me?"

"I believe you, I just don't want the wire wrapping catching on my sweater." I showed him the little fray it had caused earlier, thankful I could use that as a reason and not my lingering unease from my mom's comments. Fleur eyed me, squinting ever so slightly, and I avoided her pointed light blue gaze. She was about a million times more perceptive than Dan was, and it wasn't nearly as easy to skirt around subjects with her. But thankfully, that perception also led to her knowing when not to pry.

"Oh, alright." He settled into a station chair and I sat next to him, accepting the offered Tupperware. Inside was a generous serving of fried rice, an unusual choice for breakfast anywhere outside of the Weber household. Dan's mom tended to make whatever she wanted while cooking, not bothering to consult society's restrictions on what was acceptable at what time. I kind of admired her for it. There was a plastic fork nestled on top, so I plucked it out of the grains and got to work emptying the container. Not long after, Dan and Fleur's train showed to carry them across the island.

"Have a good day, Vinny." Fleur patted my shoulder as she was leaving, and I looked up in shock to find her offering a soft, reassuring smile as she stepped onto the train.

Alright, my mood must be really blatant if Fleur of all people is offering physical comfort. I should work on a better poker face. I sighed, opening my book to read until the next train showed.

At lunch, I was sitting on my own when a tray plunked down across the table from mine. I looked up from my book to see Katiyana, without her normal entourage.

"Can I sit with you today? I know Fleur and Dan are both off at Corp, and Alena and Jamari couldn't make it back across the street from Inntinn—"

She was shy about it, despite the fact we'd shared a lunch table with the others together before, and last year we'd had a class together. I was staring up at her in a bit of shock and confusion before I managed to shake my thoughts—*Katiyana would rather sit with me than alone*—and actually answer her.

"Oh, of course, yes. Please feel free."

She smiled gratefully and sat down on the bench, leaning her chin in her hand as she picked at her food. I returned to paging through my book and eating with the other hand, wondering if I should try to talk to Katiyana about it or not. I'd overheard her talking about her mom's coven, but beyond that, I didn't know any of her personal beliefs or practices, or anything really. I was so busy ruminating on it that before I knew it, the bell was ringing and lunch was over.

"Thanks Vincent. See you later!" It was friendly enough, and she smiled again, but I cursed myself for not actually having a conversation with her. I managed to lift my hand in a half-wave, almost too late, but she turned in time to see it.

Next time, Vincent. Next time you'll talk to her.

The school day continued as normal. I read my book during the snippets of time that I could, and Dan invited me over to his house as we were waiting for the train back home. Mom's comments were still lingering in the back of my head, so I declined and asked if I could the next day. Dan could definitely tell something was off, but just nodded and gave me a quick hug goodbye before heading off down the street instead of getting on the train. Probably to go bother Valerie again. I smirked softly, and settled into my seat.

As I was walking into the house, Dan texted me and I opened it as I shut the door.

Beefaroni

Bro

RedSam

lol what dan

Beefaroni

I need to tell the world we're bros

RedSam

?? okay, put it on your insta or something??

Beefaroni

whispering we're bros

RedSam

Beefaroni

You're my whole world, bro

The last message was sent with a flurry of sparkling heart emojis and a couple of kissy faces. I laughed, then immediately stopped as my phone was slapped out of my hand. I hadn't even realized Mom was reading over my shoulder. She spun me by the shoulder and grabbed the collar of my shirt, dragging me to her face. Her teeth were bared in anger. I couldn't even fight back, she was already throwing me to the ground.

"I told you what would happen if I caught you being gay in my house, you little faggot!" She shouted, then she was on me. I couldn't even begin to tell which direction the next blow was going to come from, if it was a foot or a fist, or even a knee. I covered my face as best I could with my arms and curled into as tight of a ball as possible. It was too late to explain to her it was just a meme, he was just copying someone else's post on the internet. I grunted as a blow hit my stomach, taking it until she either tired out or got bored or both. She finally stopped, kicked my phone down the hall, and stomped out of the house. I shakily got to my knees, feeling new bruises forming along my sides, arms, and legs. I was just glad she hadn't kicked at my ribs this time. I followed my phone's path down the hall, scooped it up, and scuttled to my room to barricade myself in. I hadn't noticed if mom was in her work uniform or not, so I had no idea how long she was going to be out of the house. I dumped my backpack by my desk and curled up on my bed, staring at the absolutely innocent text from Dan that had set her off. I wanted to cry. He hadn't meant anything by it, he was just trying to make me smile, make me laugh, because he was a good friend. My sinuses were burning but I sniffed hard and fought the tears trying to break, swallowing a few times to force them down. If she *was* going to come home soon, she couldn't hear that.

She'd just break into my room and "give me something to actually cry about," as she always said.

I thought briefly about Dubhan. I even opened the public transit app to see train times. I thought about the cliffs, then started thinking about what it would feel like to be supported only by wind, wondering how much different it would be from being supported only by water. My phone screen had turned off as I drowned in my thoughts, staring into the void once more. Dan had just tried to make me laugh, and here I was bruised for it. I couldn't tell him. I'd have to come up with something tomorrow when he caught sight of one of the bruises or saw me cringe in pain. It had been a really long time since mom's downward mood swings had gotten this bad, since she'd been violent a few days in a row. I was praying this would be the last day, and she would be on the upward swing again. Maybe I should skip school tomorrow. What did it really matter if I had straight As, anyway? It's not like Mom cared, not like I had parental support or guidance. Even if I wanted to, I couldn't go to a college off Faodail. I had no money. We were lucky the landlord hadn't evicted us, so there was no chance of a college fund for me. I needed off this island, one way or another. And unfortunately, the cliffs were looking far too appealing.

Katiyana
Wednesday, September 9, 2020

THANKFUL FOR NO FURTHER incidents with Nick before school, my morning was easy and, honestly, a little boring. But sometimes boring was nice. I was half asleep on the train, as the rest of my night had been restless thanks to my late nap and its accompanying dream. I hadn't figured out yet what the new guy's problem was, this Lucas dude. I thought about running it by my friends, since I'd only told them about that first dream. Maybe at lunch, or after school.

My chance at lunch didn't come because literally none of my friends were able to join me. Fleur was over at Corp all the way across the island, Alena and Jamari across the street, and, as I had come to find out, Jamari had gotten lunch detention. That was a new record, Jamari getting detention on the third day of school. From what I'd been told, she'd fallen asleep in class, and it was a teacher she'd had last year so they just went straight to lunch detention.

I'd planned on just eating on my own, but thankfully spotted Dan's friend Vincent at an otherwise empty table. My shoulders slumped in relief that at least someone I vaguely knew was still at Cridhe today. I plunked my tray down and was halfway into some overly long excuse when he answered.

"Oh, of course, yes. Please feel free." He said it like he was absolutely shocked I'd even asked, and shifted his tray and book closer to him to make room. A glance at the book told me it was one sold at Ladine's, one Valerie loved but mom wrote off as "far too Wiccan for her tastes." I hadn't read it, but I'd been told the teen witch class took a lot of inspiration from its structure.

Well alright, if he's reading I'll leave him be. I ate quietly, thinking over the next art piece I'd been assigned for class. The dreams were prominent in my mind, so I wanted to do something with them, but I had to stay within the teacher's instructions.

These thoughts filled the time for me and I tapped little bullet points into a note on my phone to discuss with my teacher. Before I knew it, the bell rang and I stood up to head out.

"Thanks Vincent, see you later!" I called cheerily. I didn't know his next class, and I glanced back in time to see him giving a small wave, as if he had been too caught up in his book to realize I was leaving. *Huh, must be pretty good then.*

Afternoon classes came and went, but I jotted down my homework as it was assigned in my planner this time since Fleur had gotten on me about it the day before. It did help, I just had to make it a habit. While I waited for my friends outside the school doors, I texted Sinéad.

LilTriquetra

Did you get the picture of the lace

Bruadarach

Shit, yes, sorry, I did, it's been a madhouse

LilTriquetra

Lmao no worries

Bruadarach

It looks lovely, probably from the 1920s, that pattern was super popular back then

Aha, perfect. My suspicions were confirmed. Sinéad had a decent knowledge of historical fashion trends, so I trusted her judgment. The twenties were pretty blatant in terms of fashion, but it was still nice to have confirmation from someone who definitely knew what she was talking about.

LilTriquetra

That's what era I figured my dream was from. I've had more about the same people for a while now, too. Three so far.

Bruadarach

Three? All with the same people? Yana those could be past life dreams

LilTriquetra

Maybe??? Mom said so too, I'm trying not to jump to conclusions though

Bruadarach

Well let me know if you have any others. Leon had a life in the 20s so he might be able to match things up

LilTriquetra

There was a guy who looked like him in the first one, actually. And a girl who kinda looked like you but different?

I didn't get another message from Sinéad after that, but as she was the leader of Faodail, I was used to it. Her work pretty consistently took her away from our conversations, so I was more than content to wait for her to say something when she had time.

"Who were you talking to so intently?" Fleur was at my shoulder, tapping her books gently against my arm. I smirked and nudged her books, happy to finally see her after being without her all day.

"Sinéad. She asked to see that lace pattern and I finally sent it to her."

"Ahh gotcha." She dropped one hand from her books and interlaced her fingers with mine, and we stood like that waiting for her sister and Alena. "I hope Jamari only got lunch detention and not after-school detention." *Ah, that's why she wants to hold hands.* Fleur would never admit it, but when she got anxious, she reached out for physical comfort. She needed an anchor, as it were. I squeezed her hand gently.

"I'm sure it was just lunch. It would be pretty wild for teachers to give two detentions in one day." I grinned at her. Jamari would have had to totally mess up to get both.

Sure enough, not long after, we heard Alena's voice very obviously telling Jamari off for falling asleep and not taking school seriously enough. Fleur and I stifled our giggles. Jamari hung her head in the appropriate amount of shame, and nodded along to Alena's lecture.

"I did say I was sorry, Alena."

"Well instead of just apologizing constantly, you should maybe try actually fixing your sleep schedule, so you don't fall asleep and cause problems!" Alena even had her hands on her hips, and Fleur and I shared one of those *don't laugh* looks that hardly ever works. Sure enough, we burst out laughing. "And just what on earth is so funny?"

"Oh nothing, *Mom.*" Jamari put emphasis on the title, snickering and hiding behind her hands. Alena's eyes widened and she moved to swing her bag at Jamari, who jumped back and took off down the sidewalk. Fleur and I followed, still hand in hand, and Alena darted after us. She ended up pinning Jamari against the wall at the edge of school property, her arm against Jamari's chest. Jamari put her hands behind her head and leaned back against the wall.

"Gosh, not even going to ask me to dinner first? Just gonna pin me right up against the wall, eh?" She teased, and Alena immediately blushed hard enough she looked like a tomato. She dropped her arm and huffed.

"We have been on four dates!" Alena crossed her arms and Jamari laughed, dropping her own arms to wrap them around Alena. It took a second but Alena softened to the touch and hugged her back.

"Thank you for caring about me, Alena, I'll try and do better." Jamari's voice was soft, and Alena nodded, pushing her away gently.

"Good! Now, who wants another adventure?" We all looked at her curiously. "I want to go to Ladine's again."

No one needed any further convincing, and we all set off down the road to the little shop. With the tiny bell on the door rung and the scent of incense inhaled, I took a glance around the shop and saw another person in our uniform standing at the counter talking to Alexis and Valerie. It was Dan, and he seemed absolutely intent on making Valerie laugh. She caught my eye from across the room and smiled. *Seems he's flirting outside his normal age range.* I waved, then followed Jamari to the stack of precariously balanced crystal spheres. She was peering at one on the bottom, purple-and-black swirled. It matched the colors of her hair.

"That's pretty," I noted, tapping it ever so gently. "Why do you always like things that are out of reach?" I chuckled, nudging her with my elbow. She groaned.

"Life is so difficult for us gamers." She tapped the sphere after I did, then turned to move to the counter. Alexis was half-listening to Dan talk, but she looked up when Jamari moved closer. I glanced around to take note of where Alena and Fleur were—studying the bookshelves on separate subjects—and followed her.

"Alexis, the sphere that's calling me is on the bottom of the pile," she said as she laced her fingers together in front of her, something she did when she was trying to look as innocent as possible. She had developed the habit alongside a string of reprimands, mostly for falling asleep in class or not bothering to turn in assignments. Alexis nodded as Valerie rambled on about Alex at her side. Dan was looking a little forlorn, and I held back a chuckle.

"Oh, allow me to help you then." Alexis laid her hand on Valerie's shoulder as she passed, a gesture that was so soft and familiar, it sent a strange sort of longing through me. I had no problem being affectionate with my friends, or them with me, but something about a touch that'd been repeated over and over for a decade or more...I wanted that kind of relationship in my life. I looked at Jamari again, then glanced at Alena and Fleur. I truly hoped we'd make it that long. I idly followed Alexis and Jamari back to the aisle—I wasn't really looking for anything in particular, just taking in the vibes.

"Which one were you looking at, dear?" Alexis said, gesturing at the pyramid. Jamari pointed to the purple and black one.

"This charoite one here." Jamari tapped it softly, then tucked her hands back in her pockets. Alexis somehow, someway, managed to pull it out of the pyramid and tuck a different sphere from a lower shelf in its place without toppling the whole thing. Both Jamari's and my eyes widened at the feat.

"How did you do that?" Jamari asked as Alexis placed the sphere in her hands. I watched her fingers curl protectively over it immediately, and Alexis chuckled gently.

"You learn a lot of things when you work in this shop as long as I have. I'll teach you someday." She was making her way back to the counter, Jamari at her heels.

"Are you telekinetic? That was amazing!"

"Well, that specific answer is my secret." Alexis smirked, picking up a little ledger to check the price of the sphere. There were no price tags directly on any of the stones, and I was thankful for that. Discovering a bit of adhesive you'd forgotten to remove after you'd put the rock in your velvet-lined drawer was far too annoying. "That sphere is ninety-five dollars." I blinked at the price, and leaned back a bit. The sphere was only a little bigger than a golf ball. Alexis must have seen our expressions because she continued with a small laugh. "It's very rare, from a river in Russia. That's why the price is so high." Jamari nodded wordlessly and looked down at the sphere. Obviously she didn't want to let it go, but ninety-plus dollars for a rock was a bit of a staggering price for a high schooler working part time.

"I might have to put it back," Jamari said in a small voice, frowning at the round stone between her hands. Alexis reached across the counter and laid her hand on Jamari's.

"If you want to add a few more shifts to your roster, you could work it off. Maybe help with the planning for the Mabon festival."

"You'd give me a charoite sphere if I worked a little more for you? Is that legal?" She asked, laughing a bit.

"Well, if you consider the rock as adequate compensation, then yes, it is." Alexis was putting the ledger away and Valerie had excused herself to the back. Dan was still there, but now leaning against the counter and peering at me over his sunglasses. I gave him a side-eyed half-glare, raising my eyebrow at him questioningly. Jamari and Alexis' conversation had faded into discussions about hours available and how many Jamari would have to work to earn the sphere.

"Well hello there, LilTriquetra." Dan grinned, crossing his arms in a way that was probably meant to be alluring. His expression was way too pleased. I frowned harder. How did he know my screen name? We were only the vaguest of acquaintances—I didn't even have his phone number.

"Why are you calling me that?" I asked, crossing my own arms defensively.

"You have a profile under that name on Connect, don't you?" He pushed off the counter to step closer, the sunglasses on his head catching the light. "I recognized you from your photos on there."

Oh good lord, I'd forgotten entirely about the app all the high schoolers on the island used for dating. Anyone over the age of eighteen or below the age of sixteen was literally not allowed on it. I'd been dared into making a profile and did the bare minimum just to get the peer pressure to stop, all in one sleepover.

"Oh geez, no, I don't even have it installed on my phone anymore." I waved a hand in Jamari's direction. "They put me up to it." Dan laughed.

"I saw that in your bio. And that explains why you never messaged me back."

"Yes it does."

"So...in the interest of re-sending my message, where should I send it to?" His grin got wider. I blinked. I'd had guys flirt with me before, but not that brazenly. I laughed. "Why don't you just tell me it now?"

"Well then." He slid an arm on the counter to lean against it, his face much closer to mine now. I could smell his cologne—actual cologne, not that spray stuff most the boys my age wore—and it wasn't bad. "How about you cast a spell on me and we see what these lips can do?" His smile was genuine, but I still recoiled at his words. The look on my face must have been obvious, because he leaned back.

"Really? Dude, even if I had the app on my phone still, I would have never responded to that. In fact, I probably would have blocked you." I tugged my bag strap up higher on my shoulder, turning slightly away from him. "That's a terrible way to start a conversation with someone."

He sighed softly and frowned, turning his gaze down as his hand lifted to the back of his head. "I've never heard someone put it so blatantly before." His voice was low, sheepish, even, and I took a little bit of pity on him. Maybe he just didn't know how to flirt.

"Look, if you wanna try again, my username is the same on Instagram. Come up with a better line, and let's actually talk. Deal?" I held out my hand, offering to shake on it. He brightened a little and took my hand, shaking it a few times before releasing.

"Deal." Dan's smile was again genuine, and I offered him one back. No harm in second chances. He flipped his sunglasses down and pointed some finger guns at me, walking backward toward the door. "See you on Insta, then, Lil'Triquetra." I smirked and nodded, waving at him as he turned around and headed out of the shop. He was much more Fleur's friend than mine, and I knew he had a reputation of being a bit of a playboy, but he'd always been nice enough.

"Gosh Katiyana, did you just talk to a boy?" I heard Alena's teasing tone behind me and I slumped back, staring at the ceiling. Oh no. *Here we go.*

"Yes, I did. Alert the newspapers." I groaned, turning to face her and give her a deadpan look. She grinned back, Jamari and Fleur mimicking the expression behind her. Jamari had a little bag in her hands, so apparently she and Alexis had worked out a deal.

"You know, with your cousin being the Bruadarach, that IS actually possible," Alena giggled, patting my arm. I groaned again.

"Nooo don't, Sinéad's teasing is a million times worse than yours. Don't tell her, I beg. Besides, it's just Dan." My friends chuckled at the quick shift from unamused to pleading in my tone, and I even heard Valerie chuckle from the counter. I shot her a quick glare, which made her laugh aloud.

"Sinéad has nothing to tease about, you should have seen her as a teenager when she first met Brian *and* Leon," Valerie said, leaning her chin in her hands with a wide grin.

"Hah, that's true," Jamari said. "Imagine turning sixteen and discovering you're bound to this hot older dude."

"Smokin' hot older dude," Fleur muttered, pretending to be absorbed in her phone. We all gasped; it was rare Fleur showed any interest of the sort. I took advantage of the attention shifting to her.

"Oh? Should I text Sinéad right now to tell Leon that he has a fan? Should we ask her to bring him here?" I poked gently at the hand holding her phone and she yanked it back protectively, glaring at me. Her cheeks and the tips of her ears were turning red.

"No! Oh my goodness, it was just an observation!" Fleur pocketed her phone and tried to turn and hide in the next aisle, but I could hear even Valerie and Alexis chuckling behind the counter. With a wide grin, Jamari hurried to follow her sister.

"Fleur, do you have a crush on Leon?" She called, Fleur was busy trying to leave the shop. We followed her and I called a quick goodbye to Alexis and Valerie, who waved back. Valerie was pulling out her phone, definitely preparing to share the story with Alex or someone else.

Fleur was running full sail down the sidewalk, hurrying to get away from us and our teasing. We laughed as we followed her, all the way to the train that was waiting at the station. She couldn't escape us on the train, but we did lighten up and eventually stop when she slapped her hands over her ears. She'd love us again in the morning.

Once I got home, Nick was off at work again. I took advantage by playing music loudly—but not loudly enough to annoy the neighbors—while I did my homework and ate. The other neighbors weren't as tolerant about noise as Valerie. After locking the bathroom door, I also indulged in a bath, using it as a cleansing meditation. I felt soft and at peace by the time I went to bed, but for some reason I dreamt of the cliffs along the side of the island and the ocean waves below. And not just being there, but diving off those cliffs, underneath those waves.

Vincent

Thursday, September 10, 2020

Somehow, I had fallen asleep despite the pain and the aches. Unfortunately, that also meant I hadn't plugged in my phone, and now had to deal with bruises and a dying battery. I sighed, plugging it in to juice it up as much as possible before I headed out. I counted myself lucky that it hadn't died completely, leaving me without an alarm. Before leaving my room, I stood still and listened. The house was silent, so Mom was either asleep or at work. I had no idea if she had come home while I slept or not, or when she'd be back, so I took advantage of the quiet and swiftly—*swiftly*—got ready for school.

I tugged the hood of my hoodie up as I rounded the corner closest to the station. The bruise on my cheek was fading but still there, and I'd gained a new one closer to my jaw on the same side. Luckily, that one was easy to hide with my hand, too. I hated how good I was at this.

"Vinny! Vinny, why didn't you text me back last night? I know you read my messages." Dan's voice got me to lift my head, and he slid into the seat next to mine. He took one look, noticed the bruise on my jaw, and his eyes widened. "Vincent, what happened? Please don't lie to me." He reached out, probably just to comfort me, but I cringed back.

"Please, don't, I really don't want to talk about it." I knew my voice was smaller and softer than intended, and I tucked further back into my hood.

"You can't hide from me in sweater town." Dan leaned around to look me in the eye, and I dropped my gaze. I felt his frustrated huff deep in my soul. I knew he just wanted to help, but I couldn't let him get involved. "Do you have any others? Are you okay? Do we need to go to the hospital?" He'd lowered his voice, which I appreciated, but the way he was leaning would still draw attention.

"No, no, don't worry about it." I shook my head and nudged his foot with mine. "Just sit down, okay? I don't want other people seeing."

"You and I are talking about this later, but I'll leave you alone for now." The tone in his voice was one I'd never heard before, something determined and almost commanding. But he relented and leaned back in his own seat, crossing his arms and actually leaving his phone in his pocket. Yeesh, that made me feel even worse.

"...can I still come over after school?" I asked, peeking at him around my hood. He brightened a little, softened his rigid, protective stance, and nodded.

"Of course, Vinny darling, you know you can grace my bed with your presence anytime." He winked, nudging me gently with his shoulder. I laughed slightly. It hurt a bit to laugh due to the bruise spread across my right side, but it was worth it to see Dan smile instead of pout.

Fleur caught sight of us at the school gate, her concerned expression obvious even from across the sidewalk.

"Vincent, are you alright?" She asked quietly, tugging me to the side and out of the main walkway. The other girls were hovering nearby, talking about some video or other they'd watched. I saw Jamari glance over, frown softly, then leave her sister to tend to me and Dan.

"I'm fine, please don't worry." I tried offering a little smile to reassure her, but winced as it pulled on the bruise. Fleur's expression hardened.

"Come with me." She took hold of my sleeve and led me and Dan into the school, abandoning her friends for the moment. We followed silently to the little alcove the restrooms were tucked into, and Fleur pulled out a little sponge and a jar of something from her bag.

"Why do you have foundation in Vinny's skin tone?" Dan asked, taking the little jar from her and opening it. She took it back, dipping the sponge in and then carefully nudging my face toward her.

"When this happened last year, I stole Jamari and Alena's foundations when they weren't looking, but the mix didn't match as perfectly as I wanted it to. So I judged the difference in shade at the store later and, well, I've just had this ready to go ever since." She shrugged as if it was no big deal, as if carrying around foundation in your friend's skin tone to hide his bruising was normal. I stared at the bag strap on her shoulder as she worked, trying to process this situation. "It's still not an exact match, but it's close enough."

"Fleur! That's so nice! Why are you being so nice?" Dan was cooing, strategically blocking my face from passersby with his body. Fleur just shrugged again.

"Vincent deserves some niceness." She patted the sponge gently on and around the bruise, and Dan vocally admired her skill with the makeup. When she was done, my shoulders dropped and I smiled gratefully at her.

"You're an absolute lifesaver." I would have reached out to hug her, I was that grateful, but she was already tucking everything into her bag and getting ready to head to her homeroom. She grinned though, and nodded.

"I try. Don't touch your face too much. I don't have any setting spray to help it hold." She mimicked spraying a bottle near my face, then turned to leave. "Keep an eye on him, Dan!"

"I will!" He sounded overly joyful at being given that order, and linked his arm through mine so we could head off, as well, and I was glad for the touch. Fleur just immediately leaping to my rescue like that had left me in a daze.

Thanks to her command, Dan was even more stuck to my side during school than normal, walking me to classes that we didn't even have together and convincing a couple other students to switch seats for the day in the two classes we weren't already next to each other in. I didn't mind; his overprotective care of me had kept me going through similar spells. I just had to hold out until mom calmed down again. Everything would be fine as soon as she did.

Lunch was harder. There were too many people too close, especially when you're trying to secretly protect bruised areas. I was grumbling by the time we made it to the front of the line, and even more as we tried to find a table. It didn't help that I'd had to push my sleeves up to keep the cuffs from getting into whatever soupy mess was currently on my tray. The school lunch that day was just a miss. But not everything about Faodail could be perfect, I guess.

After school, Dan literally grabbed my arm and made me sit with him on the train as my stop passed, restraining me from running away from our deal to talk at his house. I couldn't help but chuckle at him, even if it meant opening up to him about what happened the night before. His persistence was admirable.

"Okay. You're in a sacred and safe space now." I was sitting on his bed, Dan on his chair in the corner, his phone face down on his nightstand. I perched on the side of the mattress, rubbing one of the bruises previously hidden by my hoodie. Dan had literally shut his door and stripped me from the waist up, and I knew I wouldn't be able to fight him on it. He'd inspected me and then let me put my shirt back on, but bundled my hoodie to his lap.

"I don't really know how to explain this." I laid back on his bed, resting the top of my head lightly against the wall.

"You don't have to babe, I think I know what happened," Dan said, crossing his arms. I rolled my head to look at him, frowning and wishing it hadn't come to this. My gaze went back to the ceiling as I tried to forget we'd gone through something similar last year.

"I wish you didn't."

"Kinda figured."

"Mm." I heaved out a dejected breath, closing my eyes. Dan's frustration with my avoidance was palpable. I could feel it pressing into every corner of the room, and I put my arm over my face. It was easier if I didn't look at him.

He stayed quiet instead of questioning me further, which was a shock. I peeked under my arm at him, just barely enough to see. He was sitting with his arms crossed, looking down at my hoodie in his lap. He didn't speak for a few minutes, and I stayed silent with him.

"It was Mila again, wasn't it? Do you want to tell the security force? I know last year you didn't because you were afraid and stuff but..." His voice trailed off, his eyes still down. I lowered my arm to stare at the ceiling. I really didn't want to think about last year. Dan had been convinced we needed to call the security force but I'd begged him not to because I was afraid they'd believe her and not me, afraid she was going to pull the "he's just an angsty teenager, look at the marks on his arms" card. I didn't have marks on my arms anymore, though.

"I...don't know," I admitted, still not looking at Dan.

"You know my mom and dad would let you stay here if you needed to."

"I know, and I'm grateful, but...it feels like I'd just be a burden."

"Why?" Dan was looking at me now. I felt the curious and frustrated stare. I met his gaze only for a moment, then closed my eyes with a sigh.

"I don't know—I'm not their son, I'm not able to contribute anything, I'd be another mouth to feed..." I sighed hard and dropped my arm, lacing my fingers together over my stomach. Dan started laughing.

"Vinny, you're a teenager. Who told you that you had to contribute?" He leaned forward, planting one hand by my head and using the other to tap at my forehead. "Your only job is to go to school, crush on girls and gays and theys, and then graduate. Parents are supposed to take care of the rest."

I kept my eyes shut but nodded.

Dan was quiet for a moment but stayed where he was, sighing softly. "I know this is why you never invite me over to your place. You don't have to hide this from me, of all people."

"Dan I...I know. I guess I just never wanted to make you worry?"

"Vinny, baby, as if I could worry about you more than I already do." He rolled his eyes and came over to lay next to me on the bed. "Why does she do it? Do you know?"

"I have a theory."

What followed that admission was a repeat of the long tale about how mom had gotten pregnant fairly young and broke up with the guy before she even knew about it, and she'd never been able to find him again. With Faodail being as small as it was, it was likely he'd been a tourist. I told him my theory about how she took that resentment out on me, and how she'd become an alcoholic due to feeling like her life was ruined by unintentionally becoming a mother. I was also pretty sure she was severely bipolar and unregulated, but I wasn't a psychiatrist so I couldn't really make that claim. What I'd seen from light research seemed to line up, though. Especially the cycle of manic and depressive episodes.

"You'd think she would have just given you up for adoption or something," Dan muttered, chin resting on his knee. As I'd talked, he'd moved back to his chair, I'd sat up against the wall instead of hiding, and was currently staring up at the ceiling getting the rest of my mental notes in order. I rolled my head to look at him, cheek pressed to my shoulder.

"Y'know, sometimes I wish she had. But I would have probably ended up off the island." I grinned at him, reaching over to knock his hand off his shin. "And then I wouldn't have met you." Dan groaned and swatted at my hand.

"Oh good lord, don't excuse your abuse because you have a friend. Even if that friend is me!" He pulled the pillow from behind me and whapped it in my direction. I laughed and shielded myself with my arms.

"Okay, fair point."

"You still haven't told me what you want to do about it." Dan pulled his pillow back and settled it on his knees, arms and chin resting upon it. I shook my head and looked down at my hands, picking at a hangnail on my thumb.

With a heavy sigh, I shrugged. "I'm just hoping she'll calm down in a few days, she has before. So I'm going to give it a few more days."

"You should move in with me instead."

"You'd have to move the treadmill out of your room." The state of the art machine was perched in the corner, taking up a good fourth of Dan's bedroom. He looked over at it and tilted his head toward the door.

"There's room for it in the living room."

"Tell me about something else, I don't want to think about this anymore. Please." I closed my eyes and stole Dan's pillow to hide under. I heard him sigh, but his phone hit the bed and he gave in to my request.

"Fine. You know that girl I showed you on Connect?"

I peeked from under the pillow. "Katiyana?"

"Mhmmm. I saw her at Ladine's yesterday." He smirked, crossing his arms smugly. I sat up and his expression turned smug, as well.

"Well? Is that all?"

"Aw, Vinny has a crush!" He knew I did, and was absolutely using it to rile me up, and damnit, it was working.

"Dan just tell me! You tease!" I smacked him with his pillow as he laughed, raising his arms to shield his face.

"Hahaha, make me, crush boy!"

It took a decent amount of pillow beating to actually get the story out of him, and he told it breathlessly due to laughing so hard, but by the time he was finished I was more curious about Katiyana than ever. Maybe *I* needed to sign up for Connect...

Katiyana

Thursday, September 10, 2020

WAKING UP FROM THE cliff-jumping dreams to my alarm was bad enough, but Nick had to add onto it by rattling my doorknob. I put my pillow over my face for a fraction of a second, letting myself imagine how great it would feel to just scream into it, but I didn't. Instead, I slapped my phone to silence it, glaring at it as I moved to unlock and open my door.

"Can't you let me just wake up?" I pleaded, and he crossed his arms.

"I just wanted to know why you didn't come straight home yesterday." He was glaring down at me when I realized what else he might have done. He'd done it before.

"You didn't."

"What?"

I turned and pulled my phone off my nightstand, flipping through the settings and location sharing. Nick had turned on my tracker and set my phone to send the location to him through parental controls. I held it up and shoved the screen in his direction. "Why are you tracking me? What's your problem?" I was struggling not to shout, and I immediately tried turning off the tracker but was blocked by a passcode. "Nick, tell me the passcode right now! You can't do this!"

"Well it seems I already have, Katiyana." Nick was leaning in my doorway, arms still crossed. His eyes narrowed at me as I stood up straighter to hold my ground.

"I'm going to call Dad. You can't do things like this! We live in Ceangal, not Detroit! I'm in no danger on this island!" I threw my phone on the bed and regretted it as the device bounced and landed on the floor. Nick chuckled as I ducked to retrieve it. "Just tell me the passcode."

"I won't. As your older brother, it's my duty to keep an eye on you and protect you." I couldn't see him from behind the bed but I could hear the satisfied smirk on his face.

"Nick, we are literally cousins of the Bruadarach. If we're in trouble the entire island is going to protect us!" I sighed, finally pulling my phone from under the night-stand where it had landed.

"Why did you go to Ladine's twice this week?" He changed the subject and I sighed, turning to get clean clothes from my dresser.

"Why do you care?"

"I want to know if my little sister is getting mixed up in the black magic our mom's friends teach. I want to know if my darling baby sister is going to go down the wrong path," he said, taking a step into my room. I whirled, heat rising up my back with my anger.

"Mom's coven does NOT teach black magic! First of all, that term is outdated and racist as hell, second of all, mom's coven is literally a branch of the MacAskill magic! It's not like I'm learning anything from a Mortmore!" I was fully shouting now, not caring who might hear. With luck, Valerie would. Nick scowled, his eyes boring into me. Though they were always dark, they were tainted now, filled with rage. *Oh, damnit.* I picked up my phone again. "You take one step toward me and I'm calling Valerie." I turned my phone to show him her contact info already pulled up on the screen, my thumb hovering over the call button. Nick paused, still glowering, but relented. He stood straight, his almost-predatory hunch disappearing. I gripped my phone tighter to disguise the tremble in my hand.

"If I see you go to that shop again, I'll come find you myself."

Remembering the shopping bag in the trash that I hadn't brought home, I shouted after him, "Then why do you shop there yourself?" I moved to my bedroom door as he walked down the hall.

"It was a cover so I didn't look like I was casing the joint." Nick slammed his door with the last word, and I was glad for the conversation to be over, but still furious he was not only being a hypocrite, but dishonoring our ancestral line. I gathered my things and slammed the bathroom door, then noticed a text from Val.

LoveWitch

You know slamming doors wakes neighbors, right?

LilTriquetra

Nick turned on the traker on my phone so he can see m y location an d won 't giv me the passcode

LoveWitch

Well that's disturbing. Did I also hear you shout something about black magic?

LilTriquetra

He said the covem was teachin it an i shouldn't go to ladines

LoveWitch

Rich coming from someone who came in two days ago… Do you want me to text your mom?

LilTriquetra

Yes

LoveWitch

Get to school, do you have somewhere else you can go afterwards?

I thought about it then realized yes, I did.

LilTriquetra

I can go to alena's

LoveWitch

Good idea, let Katherine feed and take care of you. Then let me know when you're headed home. Etta says I should come in with you. I can bring Alex?

LilTriquetra

Okay, tell him to look extra scary

LoveWitch

LOL you have a deal.

I smirked at that, feeling calmer than I had since the night before. Alexsander, Val's boyfriend, had such blatant vampire vibes he made me wonder if they were actually real. I didn't think I'd ever seen him in the daytime, he wore all this silver jewelry, and sometimes talked as if he were from centuries ago. But he was also head of the local theater so...it was likely just an act.

With a quick prayer of thanks to whatever deity was listening, I made it to the station just barely before the train pulled in, my friends already there. They waited until I was done huffing and puffing to ask what'd happened, and I cringed as I relayed the morning's unfortunate events. They all had expressions that ranged between horrified and disgusted, and that alone reassured me I wasn't overreacting to the situation.

"Valerie says I should go to your house after school, is that alright?" I asked Alena, who nodded immediately.

"Oh yeah of course, mama Katherine wants to feed you and hasn't stopped hassling me about it since the first day of school." Alena was texting her stepmom, confirming it was alright to have friends over on short notice. She looked up at the train as the doors opened.

"Can I come over, too?" Jamari said, and Fleur glared at her.

"It's rude to invite yourself to people's houses," she said, elbowing her sister in the side. Jamari faked being hurt, clutching her side.

"I was asking, not inviting myself."

"Yes, everyone can come over. I think Katherine would be offended if you didn't, especially if she's cooking." Alena laughed.

The ride to school was blissfully normal, an excellent transition from the annoying and, quite frankly, disturbing events from the morning. Alena and I watched Tik-Toks, Fleur wrote down notes in her planner, and Jamari had somehow snuck her Switch out of the house and was playing Animal Crossing. She was halfway into getting her fossils assessed when the doors opened again.

We bustled off the train, Fleur holding onto Jamari's sleeve so she could keep her eyes on Blathers instead of the platform and sidewalk. Once out of the way of the crowd, Fleur caught sight of Dan and Vincent not too far away and headed over to talk to them. Vincent had his hood up. Jamari somehow managed to expertly save her game and stow the device away before the teacher standing at the door saw her, and I shook my head.

"One day you'll be a few moments too slow."

Jamari laughed. "They can't catch me, I'm a Power Ranger!" She threw up her hands and did a little fake karate motion, and I rolled my eyes.

"You took one year of Toso Kune Do, that doesn't make you a Power Ranger."

"Yeah, that just makes you a teenager with attitude," Alena quipped, reaching up to stretch a curl away from Jamari's Afro, letting it spring back as she darted away giggling.

Jamari's jaw dropped as she stared after Alena. She turned to me briefly, and I gave her a questioning look.

"Remind me to pin Alena against the wall next time," she huffed, hurrying inside as I blinked and blushed a little, wondering if I caught the implication correctly. I didn't have much time to think it over, as the warning bell rang and we all dashed to our respective homerooms.

At lunch, we were gathered around one of our favored lunch tables, having already eaten and just taking the rest of the period to slack off, be on our phones, and in my case, text both Valerie and my mom back.

I turned my attention to the group chat my mom had started long enough to see that she'd be calling Nick to tell him to remove the tracker from my phone, and as soon as she and Dad were home, they were going to have a serious talk with him about moving out. The idea probably shouldn't have made me smile as much as it did, but there we were. I tucked my phone away as the bell rang, becoming trapped as Alena and Fleur both slid their arms through mine, Jamari doing the same on Alena's other side. It was a silly thing we did sometimes, linking into a chain and trying to make it through a crowd without having to unlink. We all parted ways in the hallway, heading back off to classes.

After school, heading to Alena's place instead of mine felt like a blessing. I had caught sight of Dan a few more times throughout the day and each time he grinned at me, I was reminded I hadn't responded to his message yet. I promised myself I would do it on the train to Alena's. I fiddled with my pendant in one hand while my phone was in the other, finally reading his message.

Beefaroni

this is me sending you a better message than before, I would like you to know that your eyes are strikingly gorgeous and I think you should post more photos of your art on here

I smiled softly. It was a far better message than his first try, and it sounded like he actually thought about what to send rather than flirting. "Good job, Dan," I whispered to myself.

LilTriquetra

I like this message much better, thank you. And thank you for the compliment. As far as my art goes, I'll have to dig some up, haven't painted in a while. =)

"Aww, that's cute. He tried so hard." Jamari was reading over my shoulder and I startled at the sound of her voice, whapping my phone against her arm with a glare. She laughed, setting her bag down to dig her Switch out of it.

I shrugged it off and within moments, she was absorbed back onto her island, chopping down trees. It didn't take much longer for Alena and Fleur to find us. Alena was on the phone with Katherine, assuring her that she didn't need to cook a four course meal just because some friends were coming over. I chuckled a bit. I wouldn't have minded eating that much of Katherine's cooking. After a few "alright, yes, okay, alright, see you soon"s, Alena got off the phone as we made it to the station. She sighed and slumped into a seat.

"She is adamant that you need to be fed the biggest dinner you've had since Christmas."

"I don't think any of us mind." Fleur giggled softly, settling next to Alena.

"That's because you don't have to help wash all the dishes afterward," Alena grumbled, a hand over her face.

"We wouldn't mind doing that either," I chimed in happily.

"Go ahead and try telling her that—I dare you."

Alena's house was the biggest one out of our little groups'. Mine was obviously the smallest, being an apartment, with Fleur and Jamari's in the middle. Alena's dad was an extremely successful software engineer, and he'd built a few systems that not only the entire island ran on, but also a few places off-island. As a result, he'd bought one of the antique manors on the island. He had filled it with his favorite things, mostly video game paraphernalia and chess sets. He'd definitely lucked out when those ended up being his children's favorite things, as well. As the resident Chess Club President and reigning champion, Alena took after him in looks *and* skill.

"Katherine?" Alena called as we stepped into the door, hanging her backpack on the hooks near the entryway. We followed suit, kicking off shoes and shedding jackets to burden the coat rack with.

"In here sweetie!" Katherine called back from the kitchen. Jamari took off toward her first, and the rest of us followed. We were greeted with the scent of baking chicken, roasting potatoes and green beans, and the promise of a cheesecake being whipped up in the stand mixer. It smelled like some divine facet of heaven. Alena's little black cat appeared from a different doorway, and she scooped her up immediately.

"Mama Katherine, it smells so good in here!" Jamari said, walking over to peer into the stand mixer. Katherine laughed and patted Jamari on the head. Jamari actually looked more like she could be Katherine's daughter than Alena did. Alena's parents had split when she was eight, and Katherine had stepped up to the stepmom plate a couple years after. They'd gotten a lot closer when Alena's mom had passed a couple years ago. Katherine's sparkly stud earrings—little diamonds that had been a gift from Mr. Chen when they'd gotten married—caught the light as she laughed. She wore them at all times, no matter what kind of outfit she was wearing. That was true love, and she wanted to show it off to the world.

"Well thank you sweetness. How're all my kids doing?" She draped a cloth over the stand mixer and left it to run on its own, turning to face all of us. It was amazing how quickly Katherine could make anyone feel at home. It didn't matter who you were, she made you feel listened to and respected and wanted. She was only biological mom to Alena's little sibling, Mori, but she loved and cared for each and every one of us as if she'd given birth to us herself, and we absolutely adored her for it.

Over dinner, Jamari chatted about her new responsibilities at Ladine's. Though she hadn't worked a single extra shift so far, she was due to start on Saturday. She got the life teased out of her for that, enough that she ended up deflecting the conversation to Dan's sudden interest in me.

"Yana had a boy message her on Instagram," Jamari broke in, silencing my laughter and turning my face red. Katherine was a mom incarnate, and that also meant she wanted to know everything about our budding love lives. Almost on cue, she turned to me with a curious, excited glance. Mori groaned from the other end of the table.

"Uuuugh do we HAVE to talk about boyfriends? It's sooo annoyinnnng." They dropped their head low enough that their short dreads nearly dipped into their roasted potatoes, and Katherine laughed.

"Mori, baby, you'll learn when you get older." Katherine reached over to pat her child's hair softly, and Fleur shook her head.

"Yeah, you'll learn that alloromantics love to talk about nothing else," she teased, putting her hand over her mouth to hide her grin. Katherine turned and gave her a fake scathing look, then chuckled.

"Alright sweetheart, you got me. Not everyone loves romance," Katherine conceded, then turned back to me with her chin in her hand. "Now who's the boy?" I flushed.

"It's just one of the kids at school, Fleur's friend Dan. He tried messaging me on that dating app I deleted the moment that sleepover was over, and then he caught up to us at Ladine's day before last." I poked at my food, trying to look completely uninterested in the story. "I'm not really interested. He seems like he's too high energy for me."

"Well being around people who are different from you is a good thing. Broadening your horizons rarely turns sour."

Katherine was back to eating, and I took it as a sign she'd leave me alone about it. Thankfully, I was right.

We all did our homework together after dinner on the same table, as it was hard to pass up a chance to spread everything out as far as you could. It also helped to have Alena and Fleur within earshot. Fleur may have been a year below us, but she understood our math problems better than we did. The little cat took advantage of the foodless table by laying in its center, a luxury only allowed to her when Alena's dad was at work.

I watched the time tick away on the grandfather clock in the corner, knowing I'd have to catch the train home soon and dreading it. I sat there pretending to read a passage for history, wishing I could stay, but wasn't sure how to ask. I was thinking about how much of an imposition it would be when a message pinged on my phone.

LoveWitch

Are you still at Alena's?

LilTriquetra

Yeah, doing homework over here

LoveWitch

What train are you planning on catching? Alex and I went out to dinner, I want to make sure we're at the apartment with you.

My heart lightened, and I let out a slow breath through my nose. That's right, Valerie would be there. She'd promised this morning. I could still see the message at the top of my screen. I could go home and be safe.

Valerie was waiting for me at the door to the apartment building by the time I got there. Alex stood next to her, leaning against the building and glaring toward the setting sun. I fought back a laugh that almost broke through my nerves. I really didn't want to go in the apartment, but I also didn't have much of a choice. It was my home

"Hey kiddo," Valerie said brightly, reaching out for me. I nearly ran into her arms, leaning my head on her shoulder and letting her embrace me.

"Hi Val."

"You ready to go in, kid?" Alex asked, reaching over to pat my head gently.

"No. I actually don't want to go in at all. But I want the tracker off my phone and I don't want to be scared of my own apartment." I pulled back from Valerie just enough to show her the determined face I had mustered up, and she grinned back at me.

"Alright. Let's go put some well-deserved terror into your brother, then. It's only fair."

As I unlocked the door, Valerie tied her hair back and Alex adjusted the leather cuffs on his wrists. It almost looked like they were gearing up for a fight, and I prayed it wouldn't come to that.

"Katiyana? Is that you?" Nick called from down the hall, and I heard him running. "I've been so worried, you were supposed to be home hours ago, where were—" His string of questions stopped as he caught sight of Alex and Val—especially Alex—and he crossed his arms defensively. "What are *you* doing here?"

Valerie answered, stepping into the apartment ahead of me. "I'm here to ensure you listen to your mother." Alex joined her in the apartment, with me behind them. I shut the door.

"I haven't done anything," Nick lied, and if Val and Alex hadn't already known, the lie was made obvious by Nick dropping his gaze and shuffling his weight from one foot to the other.

"What's the passcode to turn off the tracker, Nicolae?" Alex asked, and this time his voice did sound a little more threatening. Nick looked up as if to retort, but his comeback was cut short by Alex's glare.

"Forty-six fifty-seven," he muttered, dropping his arms and turning to head into his room. Alex followed him, and Val turned to me so we could make sure he'd given us the right code. No wonder I hadn't been able to guess it. He'd picked a random set of numbers instead of using one that meant something to him. I tapped it into the Settings prompt and immediately turned off the tracker when it accepted the code. That simple act was such an enormous relief, enough to make me let out a huge sigh. Then the relief was broken by a shout.

"You're not my father or my boss! You have no right to tell me what to do!" Nick was yelling back at Alex, who I assume had been calmly explaining to him that his overprotectiveness and possessiveness of me was unacceptable, as he'd promised on the way up. Nick continued shouting similar things, and I heard a crash that was probably him knocking his computer chair over. I shuddered and moved closer to Val, who wrapped an arm around me protectively.

After a few minutes, Alex strode down the hallway, adjusting his leather jacket and looking unbothered. Valerie squinted at him, but he just shrugged, then turned to me.

"Nicolae has exhausted himself by shouting at me. I think he is likely to sleep for the rest of the night. Do you feel safe staying here on your own?" He asked, and I gave him a confused look. Nick falling asleep before two a.m. was a rarity that usually only happened when he was sick. But if Alex said he was out, I was inclined to believe him.

"We can stay a bit longer if you want us to," Valerie added, squeezing me gently to her side. I smiled at her.

"I think I'll be fine if I lock my door. He has an opening shift tomorrow, so I shouldn't see him before school." I still didn't want to be near Nick, but with both of our doors shut—mine locked—and Valerie on-call right down the hall, I'd be alright.

"As long as you're sure. And you know you can call me and I'll be right here." Val smiled at me, wrapping me up into another hug. I squeezed her back, once more grateful beyond belief to have her in my life. "Alex is staying at my place tonight, as added security." She winked at me as we pulled back, and I chuckled.

"I've actually threatened to call you twice now and it's worked. That's one of the main reasons I still feel safe. I don't want to be pushed out of my own home." Valerie nodded along and I hugged her one last time, turning to hug Alex as well before they left. He seemed startled at the touch but accepted it, squishing me lightly against his leather jacket. "Thank you both so much."

"It's no problem at all, kiddo." Alex smirked tenderly and I suddenly saw exactly why Valerie had fallen in love with him. He was all bristly and poky on the outside, but there was a heart of gold underneath all those spikes.

They took their leave after making me promise again to call if anything more happened, and I settled into my room with the door locked, more content than I'd been all week. I texted mom quickly to let her know the results of her calculated assault with the neighbors, and she sent back a pleased response with a GIF of Anna of Arendelle clapping. On a whim, I tucked the Brigit stone under my pillow again. She made me feel safe, guarded. And I could definitely use more of that feeling.

Vincent

Friday, September 11, 2020

My uniform was the same, but this room wasn't quite as fancy as the other two. Still elegant, still high class, but it was the woodwork that shone instead of gold and brass plating. The chandelier was smaller, older, and the room itself was smaller, as well. Honestly, I liked it more than the others. It felt more welcoming and less...show-off-y. Like when rich people buy things just to prove they could. This room had the mark of old money, generations deep.

"Jackson." Someone called my—his—name from behind me, and I turned, greeted by Marie's smile and sparkling eyes. A grin was on my face before I noticed it spreading

"Hello, Marie." That wasn't me; Jackson had spoken with the softest tone I'd heard from him in the short time we'd been hanging out.

"Hello." Her smile broadened as she laced her hands behind her back. She was an absolute vision this time, dressed in the palest purple lace and satin, in what was probably a daring choice for the time period. That was based on the surprise I'd felt from Jackson, and the way he was trying to keep his eyes off the neck and hemlines of her dress. I could tell he felt absolutely inadequate next to her. "I asked my father to book your company specifically for tonight." She swayed a little, like girls do when they're shy. Our hearts melted.

"Is it because you wanted to see me?" Jackson asked, tilting his head inquisitively. Marie giggled, turning her head into her shoulder. A thought—barely words, more of a feeling—flit across Jackson's mind. He wanted to reach out and embrace her, kiss her, and cursed the social setting they were in that was keeping him from doing so. "What's the party for this time?" He asked, keeping his tone as casual as he could, despite wanting so desperately to flirt.

"Oh, they didn't say?" Marie teased, tilting her head to match Jackson's.

"Unfortunately not, miss."

Marie leaned in a little, looking around before lifting a hand in a conspiratorial whisper, "It's my birthday." She laughed lightly, then turned to chase after Clara, who caught her by the arm, and they took off dancing.

If I didn't know better, I'd say she was six, Jackson chuckled to himself, and I agreed with him. There was something oddly innocent about heiresses; maybe being sheltered and pampered all their lives did this to them. And yet, here Jackson and I were, absolutely enamored by it.

There was one of those little shifts that dreams do, that little glitch that drives you forward like scrubbing through the timeline of a video, and suddenly it was later in the evening. The guests were dancing less and migrating to the sides of the room, talking amongst themselves. There was the occasional peal of laughter, both masculine and feminine, both echoing across the room to where Jackson stood, his feet aching and temple throbbing with the promise of a migraine. Was he the only one working this party? I hadn't seen Charles or any of the other waiters from the first dream. This one must not have been the same scale of importance. He snuck a look at the clock, and I followed his gaze—not that I had much choice on that matter—to notice it was nearing ten p.m. Five hours? Standing? Yeesh. I couldn't imagine.

"Jackson!" He turned before she'd even finished saying his name, his grin from earlier replaced with an exhausted smile.

"Ah, the birthday girl returns." Jackson bowed his head, bending slightly at the waist as if he were addressing royalty. "You darted away before I got a chance to wish you the happiest of birthdays, miss." He straightened, and she dipped her head briefly in acknowledgement.

"Why thank you." She laid her hands on the table between them, leaning forward. "You were right before, I did want to see you again." Her grin was infectious, lighting up the corner of the room, and Jackson was hooked, already bound to this woman he'd spoken to a total of three times.

"I'm honored," Jackson said quietly, his tone from the last dream returning. Then he smirked softly, leaning forward to share her conspiratorial tone. "Although next time, try to get your father to spring for Charles, as well." He winked at her, then leaned back as she laughed. A full laugh, not a giggle hidden behind a hand or hat. Her head went back with it, hand to her chest, and she had to clasp both hands over her mouth to stifle herself. Jackson's grin was unmatched.

"You, sir, are very naughty to suggest what your employer should do." Marie was still laughing, and she batted at him with the fan that was dangling from her wrist. Jackson chuckled.

"Ah forgive me, my manners must be muddled. Your bright grin has shot my mind right to the moon."

Marie's jaw dropped ever so slightly and she flushed, laughing again, hiding behind her fan. "Sir! You are far too forward." Another chuckle was Jackson's only response before a shadow fell over the table and he turned, paling at what he saw.

"Marie, your father is looking for you." Lucas' voice was the opposite of Marie's laughter, low, rough tones tinged with anger and annoyance. "I was, as well. Why are you lingering in the corner at your own birthday party?" He glared at her, and all the light she'd projected into the room shrank back inside her. It was the worst thing I'd ever seen in any of these dreams.

"Sorry, Lucas." Marie's voice became small and her gaze dropped to her hands, the floor, her shoes, anywhere but up at Lucas. Jackson stepped back and pretended to check the stock of the dessert table. A wise choice if the glare Lucas was focusing on him was any indication of what would happen if he chose otherwise. Had I my own body at that moment, I would have shuddered.

Lucas took hold of Marie's upper arm and led her away without a word. Her head was still drooped, and when Lucas called out to someone, his attention briefly off her, she turned and smiled weakly over her shoulder at Jackson. He lifted a hand in return, smiling back.

He was silent and had easily slipped back into the mind-set of being a waiter instead of being a flirt, but I could tell he was warring with himself, trying to decide if breaking societal boundaries—and possibly a few of his own bones—was worth her grin.

The little voice deep in his heart whispered, *Yes, yes it is.*

That calm determination stayed with me as I woke up, and it was so strong I had to stare at my own brown eyes in the mirror to convince myself they weren't blue and I wasn't Jackson. A text from Dan helped, bringing me back to reality far more effectively than the chilly shower I'd been forced to take. Mom had a habit of draining all the hot water right before I needed it.

Beefaroni: are you a lvl3 witch yet? what level do you need to be for love spells??

I laughed softly, dropping my phone to finish getting ready for school. I'd talk to him on the train home since he had Corp today. As I walked, my mind drifted to Ladine's, thinking about the warm and familiar energy there. It felt so safe. Maybe over the summer I'd see if they were hiring, then I could save some money to start stashing away for college. Hm. It wouldn't be enough for full tuition; but if I could get a scholarship...

School was easy enough. I sat on my own at lunch and half expected Katiyana to join me again, and this time I was determined to talk to her. But a glance up at a sudden chorus of showtunes made me realize she'd sat with Alena and Jamari instead. I sighed, and returned to my book.

After school, I was sitting at the train station and wondering why I hadn't just gotten up and joined the girls, why I hadn't just moved my tray to go and sit with them, when I heard a call over my music.

"Vinny baby!!" I broke out of my musings and pulled my headphones out of my ears right before Dan wrapped both arms around my shoulders and tugged me close. "Vinny, darling, you'll never guess what I did. You'll be so proud of me."

I grinned, shaking my head. "What? I'm already proud of you." Somehow Jackson's soft sincerity had found its way into my voice, and I gleefully watched as Dan flushed and froze for a moment, just like Marie had.

"Oh no. No no no, I'm rubbing off on you!" Dan dropped his arms from my shoulders and held up his fingers in an X shape, shaking his head fiercely. "You can't just turn around and flirt with me after denying me for five years! That's cruel! Don't get my hopes up when you've already thoroughly dashed them!"

I tried to stifle my laughter but it escaped, and before I knew it I was bent over my knees, gasping for air between chuckles. A glance up showed me Dan was having none of my laughter and instead waiting impatiently for me to finish, arms crossed.

"I'm done, I'm sorry, I wasn't trying to flirt with you." I patted his shoulder in the most "bro" manner possible to solidify it, and he huffed his acceptance with a roll of his eyes.

"Fine, I believe you, but if you do it again I'm deleting Connect AND Instagram and you're stuck dating me forever." Dan pulled out his phone, flipping to his Instagram messages. "Anyways look, I took your advice." He showed me a conversation between himself and a girl and I laughed incredulously.

"You did it, you had a normal conversation with someone. I am so proud of you!" I draped my arm around his shoulders and patted his arm, grinning at him.

"Uh-huh I did, and I'm going to continue. To think it's the same girl that told me off in Ladine's!" He wiggled his shoulders a little and I let go as the realization sunk in.

"Wait, it's Katiyana?" My arm dropped to my side and he looked up, only a little sheepish.

"Well, you've never gone after any other girl you've looked at, so I figured she was fair game." Dan shrugged, looking back at his phone so he wouldn't have to meet my gaze.

He wasn't wrong, and that's what felt so bad about it. I really hadn't gone after anyone, ever. There had been a few girls we'd gone to school with that I thought were pretty or I liked the way they spoke up in class, but I hadn't done anything. He wasn't wrong about this girl, either.

The most I'd done was admire her from afar and think about her. I hadn't even ever told Dan my full thoughts on the matter. I kicked my foot against a crack in the platform concrete, swaying with the rush of air as the train sped in. The train ride was awkward and silent, me mulling over Dan's words and my own thoughts, Dan not knowing what to say and not wanting to upset me further. I wasn't even actually upset, but I didn't know how to tell him that. It was more like I was...disappointed. Mostly in myself, that I'd become so predictable and passive that Dan barely thought to talk to me about a girl I'd mildly shown interest in before pursuing her.

We barely spoke at his house either, until Dan finally sighed and broke the silence.

"Okay Vinny look, I'm sorry. I will stop talking to her if you want me to," he said, staring at me until I responded. It took me longer than it probably should have, but that was partially due to the food that I was still chewing.

"I've been thinking about it this whole time and honestly Dan, it's fine. You have your go, and if it works out, awesome. If it doesn't, maybe I'll finally shoot my shot." I shrugged, twirling the pasta his mom had made on my fork. "It would be a first, wouldn't it?"

Dan groaned quietly. "Vinny I didn't mean to make you feel bad."

"I know. I'm not upset with you."

"You're upset about something. It's all over your face."

Oof, he had me there. I exhaled deeply, setting my fork down and trading it to cradle my chin in my hand instead. "I'm upset that I've become so...passive, I guess."

"Aw, Vin—"

"It's not on you, Dan. It's on me. Acceptance is the first step to recovery, right?" I offered him a smirk, but I knew it was unconvincing. I loved him for accepting it anyway.

"It is! And no matter what, I'm here for ya buddy." He pointed and wiggled his fork at me, and just like that, the friendship was mended. Not that it had ever been broken, but Dan had a tendency to jump to the worst possible conclusions without consulting anyone. He'd thought our friendship was over at least ten times now, but each time it had only lasted about a day at the longest. I shook my head, returning to my pasta. I really was lucky to have him on my side, even if he did need to learn to ask before leaping. But I also needed to learn to speak up before he even reached the edge.

Katiyana

Friday, September 11, 2020

It seemed as if Valerie and Alex's intervention had stemmed Nick's need to "protect" me, for now at least. He didn't say a word to me after I got home from school, just turned up the living room television a little louder. I shrugged and grabbed some leftovers from the kitchen before holing up in my bedroom, closing the door but not locking it as a test. I truly did not mind if Nick decided to completely ignore me from now on.

Homework was basically non-existent, one reading to do and a few thumbnail sketches for my first painting project of the year. I sat at my desk and scratched out scenes from the parties, smudging a little bit of graphite here and there in the vague shape of partygoers. I wanted to paint them all.

But unfortunately, none of them felt right for this assignment. It was supposed to be an architecture study, and we were allowed to pick indoors or outdoors. There weren't supposed to be people in it but...maybe if I stretched the meaning a little? Meh.

I pushed away from my desk, deciding to figure it out later. Instead I pulled my notebook out from under my mattress, navigating to the pages I'd been keeping short dream notes on. It wasn't anything elaborate, just somewhere to record what felt like key details. I was storing much more info on my phone. Writing was just easier than typing first thing when I woke up.

New York City, 1920s. Marie: some sort of heiress/rich girl. Jackson: waiter boy, bakery boy. Clara: heiress, richer than Marie. Reggie: asshat but also a love interest for Clara, maybe? They were engaged but Clara seemed to hate him. Lucas: thinks he owns Marie, not sure if related or love interest.

I hoped Lucas wasn't a love interest; he was such a dick. I mused over the little bit I'd learned of him, chewing on my lip while doing so. Marie definitely didn't want to be near him, but seemed forced into it. Maybe it was an arranged marriage of sorts? It would make sense given their social status and the time period...

I awoke to a buzzing against my leg, unaware until then that I'd dozed off. I grabbed my phone to see Alena had messaged our group chat.

QueenofGambits

> **Lunch tomorrow?**

BlondeBrainiac

> **Can't get enough of us during school & after, she needs the weekends too**

QueenofGambits

> **Fleur one day you'll admit you love me**

BlondeBrainiac

> **Lmao, yeah I'm down for lunch. Jamari will be half asleep, and also working**

QueenofGambits

> **As per usual, nothing strange there**

GameznStuff

Why am I the butt of the joke again?

QueenofGambits

You make it too easy, babe, sorry.

I chuckled. The easy relationship we'd all developed was so dear to me.

LilTriquetra

I'm down too, where tho?

QueenofGambits

Ladine's

BlondeBrainiac

You're addicted to the incense smell in there now, aren't you?

QueenofGambits

Yeah what of it

LilTriquetra

I always figured it would be me dragging us into witch stuff, but shocker, it's alena.

GameznStuff

Well, I'll already be there, so, count me in

LilTriquetra

Me too, maybe I'm addicted to the incense as well

QueenofGambits

You know what maybe I'll just go by myself

BlondeBrainiac

Lmao, how does 11:30 sound

QueenofGambits

Read my mind

GameznStuff

I hate all of you for making me get out of bed before 1pm on a Saturday

LilTriquetra

No, you love us for making you eat good food and walk in sunshine

GameznStuff

… yeah I guess

BlondeBrainiac

It's alexis doing that to you not us

GameznStuff

Yeah but I can't blame her so it has to be piled onto you dorks

A slew of laughing stickers/GIFs popped into the chat, a few from myself, but mostly Alena and Fleur. Jamari tried to counter with some of a very cute sleepy panda but got buried under the others. I was chuckling, scrolling back and forth through them when another notification popped up, this one from Instagram.

Beefaroni: Why don't you paint more?

Another actual question rather than the nonsense he'd started with. *Good streak. Keep it up.*

LilTriquetra: Got distracted over the summer, and now school work comes first.

Beefaroni: That makes sense. you're painting in school though right? I hope so.

LilTriquetra: Hah yeah, we just got our first assignment today.

Beefaroni: Show me?

I rolled off my bed, meandering to my desk to flip my sketchbook back open and snap a photo of the thumbnail sketches. It's not like he'd recognize anything. *I* barely did in those messy little squares.

Beefaroni: A party? Your assignment is painting a party?

LilTriquetra: LOL no, it's supposed to be an architecture study, I just thought the room needed some people in it

Beefaroni: Rooms always need people in them, shit's too quiet otherwise

LilTriquetra: Normally I'd agree with you but sometimes quiet is nice

Beefaroni: Oh no, not an introvert! I already adopted one of those! he's actually asleep on my bed right now

He sent a GIF of a vampire hissing away from sunlight and I snorted softly.

LilTriquetra: You adopted two if you count fleur. And hey now, life can't be all parties and ragers

Beefaroni: Says you. i for one plan to spend every single night after graduation at a party of some sort

LilTriquetra: You have fun with that lmao, couldn't be me

Beefaroni: I'm taking that as a challenge.

LilTriquetra: Good luck!!

I set my phone on my desk with another chuckle and turned back to my thumbnails. Before I really registered it, I was sketching up one more. The room was the same—the lighting, the decor, everything. But instead of the whole party, it was just Marie and Jackson talking quietly at the edge of the room, over the snack table.

That was it, that's the one I wanted. It would show off enough of the room to make Mx. Darling happy, and it was a direct scene from a dream to make me happy. It was too bad all the canvases and paints were at the school or I could have started the painting right then and there. I settled for making a larger version of the thumbnail, as detailed as I could get away with. Getting the finer points down before even getting paint on your palette was never a bad idea.

Vincent

Sunday, September 13, 2020

I'D SQUEEZED OUT AS many new details about this latest dream as I could. My phone was dropped to my chest in defeat as I stared up at the ceiling, arms spread out across the bed on either side of me. I would have killed for some sort of calendar to be in the room during Marie's birthday. I could have done much better research from there. It wouldn't be hard to find a wealthy daughter listed on some census or another, could it?

Wait a minute, what was I thinking? This was a dream. These were *dreams*. My phone dropped to my lap as I sat up and I left it there, gaze moving to the window and the street beyond. There's no way I could really be dreaming about a real person from the 1920s. My eyes dropped to the new book Dan had bought me, and I squinted at it for a moment before finally picking it up and flipping through the table of contents. It was a level one book, the first in a series of eight, what kind of info—*Oh.* My eyes widened in shock and I blinked a few times, making sure what I was seeing was correct. "Past Life Regression" was literally listed as one of the exercises. Alright then, I completely misunderstood what "Level One" meant in terms of Paganism. It would be skipping ahead by...ten or so lessons...but I went and looked at the exercise anyway.

It was a meditation. The book had come with a CD set with all the included meditations, and thanks to Dan and his laptop, said meditations were now on my phone. I paused, listening to the sounds of the house. I'd heard the front door slam and Mom's car speed off hours ago, but I had no idea if it was for work or something else, and therefore no idea how long she would be gone. My phone told me the meditation was about forty-five minutes long.

It was worth a try. I grabbed my earbuds and got comfortable, settling on my bed. The dude's voice was really chill—he definitely knew what he was doing. It didn't take long before I was swept up into the meditation, following along as best I could since I'd skipped all the lessons that were supposed to come before it. But soon enough, I was back in the gilded room, watching the dancers swirling about. It was an exact play-by-play of the first dream I'd had, stopping right when Marie was about to speak up.

The guided meditation led me back to the land of the waking moments before I heard the door slam back open. *Oh, that was close. But worth it.* This was something I could go off of, despite getting no new info. I had remembered details that I hadn't written down, and I added them to my note document the moment I felt awake enough to do so. A skeptical voice in the back of my head was ranting away, saying that of course it was the first thing I would cling to after having so many dreams in this fashion. I could probably silence it with another meditation when Mom was at work next.

She must have gone grocery shopping, because I could hear her bustling around in the kitchen. I cringed and prayed she hadn't only bought freezer meals and junk food. Even as a teenager who craved those things regularly, I'd been taught to eat my fruits and vegetables by Dan's parents.

Finishing up my notes, I stashed the book back into a drawer of my dresser under the clothes. I wasn't about to have my mom find it. I was lucky she hadn't seen it last time she'd banged into my room, shouting at me to take out the trash or sweep or something else that I'd already done while she was gone.

Maybe looking into a census was a good idea after all. I was still wavering between believing my dreams could be a past life and not, but I couldn't get the idea out of my head. A few Google searches couldn't hurt. The Wi-Fi at my house was definitely too slow for any database I had access to, and researching things on a phone was a pain anyway. The library it was, then, if I could just slip past Mom. I lifted my backpack to my shoulder and made my attempt.

"Where are you going?" She asked as I hit the hallway, leaning around the corner that led to the kitchen. My shoulders reached for my ears and I dropped my gaze immediately. Her tone was softer than I'd expected it to be.

"I have an assignment to finish, but I have to type it up, so I need to go to the library," I explained as calmly as possible. It wasn't a lie, I did have things to type up for school, I would just be doing my own extra studies on the side.

"Oh. Maybe we should look into getting you your own laptop so you don't have to go to the library all the time," she said idly, setting a bag of carrots and what looked like onions, but smaller, on the counter. I stared at it, absolutely bewildered.

"That might be nice," I mumbled, testing the edge of what was sure to be the deep end. "I'm totally okay going to the library though, so don't worry!" There was no way to know what sentence could be the wrong one.

"Alright. Did you come out to join me for dinner?" She shook the bag, and I hid my cringe at the sudden motion as best I could.

"No thank you, I just wanted to tell you where I was going," I said cautiously, hiking my backpack further up, trying to prove my schoolwork point with the gesture. She just nodded and returned to putting the groceries away, and I took it as my sign to leave as quietly as possible. I was so glad for an easy encounter, but after the past few days I wasn't ready to push my luck.

The Faodail Learning Center wasn't really far. I could walk there in twenty minutes if the trains weren't running, but I preferred the trains. The employees recognized me, since I did a lot of my schoolwork there. They'd even let me stay after closing to finish up assignments a few times. They were wonderful people, and I was glad to know them. I waved at one, Raphael, and he pushed his long blonde hair out of his face to grin back. He was bent over an old book, likely trying to restore it or translate it, so

I let him be. He and the others would be there if I had questions. The study rooms were on the third floor and I settled into the one I normally sat in, logging into the borrowed laptop.

Forty-five minutes later, I was ten articles deep in a few different databases and had exactly zero words of my assignments typed. I only knew the exact amount of time that had passed because the little pop-up appeared letting me know I'd have to log back into the computer in fifteen minutes to continue using it. It was annoying when I was there for the long haul, but if keeping time like this helped prove the library computers were getting used on a regular basis, I was here for it.

I'd found a lot of information about the steel industry and the people who ran it, the Carnegies and the Morgans, but not a lot about other wealthy families yet. It would have been easier to find if my current search hadn't been limited to "marie + heiress + 1920s." There had to be another way to go about it. I pulled open the note on my phone, scrolling through for ideas.

"Clara + Reginald + 1920s" I muttered as I typed it in. They'd gotten engaged, surely there would be some sort of announcement? Wealthy people showed off every chance they got, right?

Sure enough, a newspaper clipping appeared. There was no photo attached, so I couldn't be sure it was the right ones beyond the names and era, but it was the most I'd gotten thus far. I had to squint and control + scroll my way around the paywall to read it, but I managed to copy down a few lines and snap a photo of the headline.

"Coal mine heir to wed. Reginald Warburton and his longtime sweetheart are tying the knot! Clara [messed up letters] is the daughter of [unreadable]. The pair will wed next year in spring, details to follow at their engagement party next week."

A coal mine? That didn't seem like the right level of wealth, but who was I—a teenager in 2020—to speak about what made money and what didn't in the 1920s? Content with the little bit of knowledge I'd managed to dredge up from the internet, I set about typing up my assignments and printing them to turn in tomorrow.

As I was leaving the library, I waved once more to Raphael and mulled over the article. One last name to go off of was better than none, but it was also of the person most disconnected from the people I wanted to know about. I didn't notice I was frowning until I caught a glimpse of my reflection in a window. I shook my head, shaking the thoughts away for now. I had a good starting point now. I could dig from there.

And after all, it was nice to know that skeptic in the back of my mind would be squashed under that newspaper article. I would have to listen harder for Reggie's last name in the next dream.

After hopping off the train, I walked home in a rather good mood, humming softly to the music playing in my earbuds. My amethyst was bouncing gently against my chest as I walked, a pleasant reminder of my first steps into real spirituality.

Paganism felt like home immediately.

Katiyana

"IF YOU SEE ANYONE, you can drag me out, and I'll know it's a sign." My dream began with those words, and as my subconscious focused, I saw Clara frowning deeply at Marie, whose hands were on Clara's shoulders. I could feel the encouraging smile on Marie's face.

"Are you sure about this? Lucas was so angry last time. I thought he was going to punch a hole through the door." As Clara spoke, Marie just nodded encouragingly. Clara bit down on the edge of her lip, sighing. "Fine, alright. But Leon and I are going in too." Clara adjusted her glove, fitting the little lace garment around her wrist just so, and stepped to the side of the bakery door. Behind her, unmistakably this time, I recognized Leo, arms crossing his chest as a look of resigned acceptance clouded his features. Marie's smile widened.

She more or less danced through the bakery door, the little bell ring sounding as merry as she felt. Her eyes scanned behind the counter, searching out the only person she knew here and, therefore, the only person she would come here to see. Leo and Clara took up a post near a display shelf, pretending to look at the displayed wares but actually watching out the window.

"Miss Marie?" His voice floated to her across the store and she turned. He was coming out of the back room with a box of pastries in his hands. His face was streaked with flour, and he looked like he'd been at the shop all day, but it didn't stop him from grinning. "To what do I owe this pleasure?" The pastry box found its home on the counter, and Jackson pulled a cloth from his apron pocket to mop his forehead with. Marie's dancing gait didn't stop as she made her way to the other side of the counter, mirroring his grin all the way.

"I wanted to apologize for how Lucas treated you at my birthday party. He's very rude and is used to everyone just following along with what he wants." Marie's voice had softened and sobered enough by the end of her sentence that I felt bad for her. I knew this guy was a dick, but what had he done to her to make her so scared to even speak ill of him in (relative) private?

"Oh, I've been treated worse. It comes with the job unfortunately." Jackson smiled and rested his hands on the counter, taking advantage of a customer being there to take a break. "Is there anything I can get you from the displays?"

"Oh! Oh, hmm." Marie obviously hadn't even thought of buying something at all, not even to cover her trail, to give her an excuse to be there. I had never even been in this situation and knew it would have been a good idea. Jackson must have had similar thoughts, because he just chuckled and started putting together another box of chocolates for her. She blushed softly and dug in her purse.

"You can have these as a birthday gift, Miss Marie." Jackson's sincerity was so thick, so palpable, I was sure that if I reached out in this dream-space I would have been able to hold onto it. He set the box down with a gentle tap, smiling up at Marie in such a way it made even my heart do a flip. Oh, I fully understood why she wanted to sneak to the bakery. She blinked rapidly a few times to clear her thoughts, obviously distracted by that smile, and managed to give her own in return.

"Thank you. That's so, so kind of you. Are you sure it won't come out of your wages?" Marie's eyes shifted to the back room where someone else was making noise. Jackson shrugged.

"The money from your birthday party will make up for it." His smirk was teasing, and he threw in a wink. Marie laughed and rolled her eyes, copying his tone.

"Oh, I'm paying for my own birthday gift, then?"

"No, your father is."

"Oh gracious." Marie reached forward to swat at his arm again, like she'd done at the party, but Jackson caught her hand, raising it to his lips to kiss the back of it softly. "Oh...gracious." Marie whispered, her blush sending heat across her cheekbones and all the way down her back. Jackson smiled over her wrist, eyes holding hers.

"Once more, happy birthday, Miss Marie." Jackson released her hand, replacing his fingers with the chocolate box. Marie (and to a lesser degree, I) was stunned, but managed to take hold of the box. She huffed, not able to hide the blush but able to at least salvage a little bit of her dignity with a joke.

"Well, if you're done flirting with all of your customers—" Marie stuck her nose up just a little, but broke after a moment and giggled. Jackson leaned against the corner of a display, hands interlaced beneath his jaw, with a soft grin.

"Oh, I only flirt with the ones that flirt back." He chuckled, then straightened as the other person in the back came to the front. "Oh, there you are."

Charles was carrying another three boxes, all stacked on top of each other, and he glared at Jackson as he set them down. "You were supposed to be helping me." His thick Irish accent was unmistakable, without even considering the red hair and the freckles across his nose.

"We had a customer." Jackson gestured to Marie, stepping away from the counter to pat him on the shoulder. Charles looked over, amused.

"Ah, Miss Marie. From the big party," he said, then nodded to the chocolates in her hands. "Can't stay away from our sweets, can you?" It was innocent, he absolutely meant the chocolates, but another flush spread along her cheeks anyway.

"No, I can't seem to." Her eyes darted to Jackson just long enough for Charles to catch it, and he smirked, but mercifully didn't say anything.

"Best in all of New York! Come and get more anytime you like!" He waved and wandered off to the back. Jackson looked up from the pastries he was stocking, through the glass at Marie. Her blush refreshed itself. I couldn't blame her, his eyes were on her like she was the only woman in the universe. Most women would kill to have someone look at them like that and mean it. And, boy oh boy, he meant it.

"I, uh, I had better get going. I promised to meet a friend," she stammered out, hugging the chocolates to her chest. Jackson stood up, draping his arms over the top of the display he had been working on.

"You're welcome back anytime." He smiled and inclined his head to her ever so softly. Marie managed to return the expression. Her heart was pounding like she'd run a marathon.

"Thank you! Thank you for the chocolates, as well!" She turned and scurried out of the bakery as quickly as she should, Clara catching her arm as they hit the street. Leo was only two steps behind, looking around as the girls talked.

"Why were you flirting so much?" Clara asked as they made their way to the train station. Marie's cheeks were still tinged pink, and she shook her head fiercely.

"He was too," she breathed, hugging the box to her chest. Her thoughts were already three blocks away and counting, back in the bakery, back with Jackson. She was so wrapped up in it, she didn't register the look of concern cross Clara's face, but I did. *Oh, dear.*

—◇—

I woke up feeling confused and groggy, with Clara's expression still in the back of my mind and Marie's breathless infatuation in my heart. I needed to document this one immediately. Rolling over, I pulled the notebook out from under my mattress and sat up to click my pen open and scribble down all the key points I could remember. I would flesh it out later, but I needed to get the most important details down first, like the fact that it absolutely *was* Leo. How strange. I hadn't heard anything about his past lives, or Sinéad's, but it was weird that he looked exactly the same as he did now, just with shorter hair.

As I made a note of "kissed her on the hand" a blush raced up my spine, over my cheekbones, and even to the tips of my ears, reverse of how Marie had felt it. Good lord. *I* was going to fall in love with Jackson at this rate. Snapping the book closed with the last of the notes safely inside, I tucked it back under my mattress and set about my morning, gathering my homework from the weekend and stashing it away. Thankfully, Nick was still more or less ignoring my existence, and I took advantage of it by walking right through the middle of the living room, in front of the TV, just to see if he would say anything about it. He didn't, and I suppressed a giggle.

Getting to the train station and to school was just as simple. Things were looking up at the moment, it was just a shame I'd had to have Alex threaten Nick for it to happen. But I wasn't about to complain about a vampire-shaped bodyguard. Jury was out on if he was actually a vampire, though. The jury, of course, being me and my friends.

On Saturday, Alexis had reminded us again about the beginner witch class, so we'd all agreed to go after school. Another thing to look forward to and keep me out of the house for a bit.

The sun was directly on my face as we walked to the café, and I turned my head up to meet it, eyes closed and drinking it in. Once Mom and Dad were home, they'd kick Nick out, or at least force him into acceptable terms, and everything would be fine. I just hoped Nick would continue to basically ignore me until they got back.

Witch class was super basic, as it seemed to be the first of a new round of them. We learned about energy manipulation—making little balls of swirling energy between our palms and seeing how dense we could make them. By the time class was over, we'd all managed to make at least one decent energy ball and we were feeling good about ourselves.

After the mess that'd been last Thursday, it was really great to have a day where I actually felt normal for once. Well, as normal as a MacAskill descendant on Faodail could be, of course. The magic of the island's ley lines was singing in tune with me as I walked home from the station, and my phone pinged.

Bruadarach

> why are you in such a good mood that I can feel it over the line?

I laughed; I'd forgotten how in tune Sinéad was with the lines as Bruadarach.

LilTriquetra

> we went to alexis' magic class for dummies, it was a good time.

Bruadarach

> tell me she didn't name it that

LilTriquetra

> LOL no, she didn't.

Bruadarach

> Oh thank the gods. I'm glad it was a good time though ! Going back next week?

LilTriquetra

> Yeah, absolutely!

Bruadarach

> Auntie etta will be so sad you started your training with valerie instead of her

LilTriquetra

Is this legit MacAskill line training??

Bruadarach

Hahah kinda, it's the LiteTM version. The real training is a lot more intense. You'll see

LilTriquetra

Stop making me scared of it

Bruadarach

LMAO sorry, sorry, it's not scary, just intense. You have the fortitude for it.

LilTriquetra

thank you

Bruadarach

Welcome boo.

The text conversation lasted me from the lobby, up the elevator, and to my living room, where Nick spoke the first words of the day to me.

"Did you go to that class at Ladine's?" He asked, side-eyeing me from the recliner in the living room where he'd been that morning. Had he moved at all?

"Yeah, I did. Sinéad even encouraged me to go." I crossed my arms, keeping my spine straight.

"Hmph. Just because she's Bruadarach doesn't mean she knows everything," he grumbled, turning back to the television.

"She knows good magic when she feels it." I left it at that, heading down the hall quickly enough that I couldn't hear his reply, but not so fast that it seemed like I was intentionally escaping from him.

On a bit of a whim but also the running magic high of the class, I propped up the little Brigit stone against my bedside lamp and laid a plate of grapes and a little cup of apple juice next to it, whispering that it was for her.

Settling into bed later that night, I tapped the stone with my fingertips as I laid my glasses down, thanking her for whatever blessings she was bestowing upon me. It was the most restful sleep I'd had all month.

Vincent

Wednesday, September 16th, 2020

SHOCKINGLY, I HADN'T HAD a dream since Sunday night—well, Monday morning, really, since it had happened right before I woke up. Something about Jackson gifting Marie chocolates as a belated birthday gift. It was really sweet. The blonde man from the very first dream had appeared again, and he still looked so familiar. I needed to pin that down.

Waking up Wednesday morning without one in my head was a little strange, but it wasn't like they'd been every single night thus far. My count was up to four dreams in nine days, all with the same people and settings. There wasn't any pattern to it, either. It had started with two dreams in a row, nothing for two nights, then one, nothing for two nights again, then Sunday/Monday's dream. The math was simply not mathing, as my peers would say. I huffed out a discontented breath. I was supposed to be paying attention to Mr. Rossi, not trying to figure out if my dreams were mathematically logical. I glanced up at the board and jotted down the Latin that was on it. I had missed the explanation for it but I could probably figure it out with context clues. Benefits of taking the language for two years. If all else failed, I'd just ask Mr. Rossi.

Mercifully, class ended not long after and I gathered my stuff to head to the cafeteria. After sitting down, I was surprised by a hand on my shoulder and a tray clinking onto the table next to mine.

"My darling baby boy, how are you today?" Dan asked as soon as he sat down, and I laughed.

"Aren't you supposed to be across the island?"

"Supposed to be, but I have a dentist appointment in the middle of the school day and Mom didn't want to drive across the river to get me, so she called Corp." He grinned, ruffling my hair and then immediately re-styling it with his fingers. "You look so, so cute today." Dan held my face, a hand on each cheek, and squished it softly.

"Thanks. Now release me."

"I get to be here with you! Isn't that great?" He asked, leaning heavily against my arm, expression shining with the brightness of ten thousand suns.

With a roll of my eyes I just accepted it, using his phone pinging for his attention as an advantage to get lost in my thoughts once more.

Everyone in the dream seemed to be at least twenty-ish, so if I wanted to find birth certificates or any sort of announcement in the newspapers, I'd have to look around...1900? Would that work? It would be easier to narrow down the years if I knew the precise age of at least one pers—

"Vinny?" Dan's voice shocked me out of my thoughts, and I jumped a little, blinking over at him.

"S-sorry, what?"

"I hadn't said anything but you were definitely on another planet over there, babe." He shook my arm lightly by the sleeve. "You good?"

"Yeah, sorry. Latin is just getting difficult this year so I got super distracted thinking about it." I gave him a preoccupied smile that faded quickly and he rolled his eyes at me.

"Uh-huh, sure booboo." He patted my shoulder, nodding in fake belief. "That's not a Latin homework furrow in your brow. What's going on?"

I tried to think of an answer that wouldn't sound insane. *I think I'm dreaming of my past life. I'm dreaming about this girl from the twenties and I might be falling in love with her. She's literally a dream girl.*

"Vinnyyyy." He nudged me with his elbow.

"I...hm." I sighed, still trying to figure out how to explain. "You might think it's weird."

"Vincent D'Avaranches, we literally live on Faodail, of all islands, where the local coven is half the Cabinet. Where we attend a Samhain festival every year."

"Okay fair point, very fair point." I half-laughed, running my hand through my hair and pushing it away from my eyes. "Well, I've been having these dreams. It's been happening since the night of the sixth." I tapped my fork against my tray, glancing up at Dan who was chewing and waiting patiently for me to continue. "It's about this girl—"

I didn't get any further before Dan started giggling. "Oh! Oh a girl!" He dropped his fork and settled his chin in his hands. "Please, do go on."

"Pff. Yeah. So it seems to take place in the 1920s. Her name is Marie and she's just..." I trailed off and sighed absent-mindedly. I didn't even realize how dreamy my expression had gotten. That is, until Dan snickered. I shot him a glare and continued. "Yeah. She's beautiful and intriguing and I think she's a sheltered rich kid but she's got this...innocence about her." I lifted my hand, holding my pendant through my shirt. "She's so amazing Dan, she snuck out to this bakery just to talk to the guy whose eyes I've been watching through."

"So it's not you in the dreams?" Dan asked, all teasing dropping as he went back to his food.

"No. I'm watching through this guy named Jackson who works at that bakery and is also a waiter for some sort of catering company." I poked at my own food, waiting for a response.

"Sounds a bit like Romeo and Juliet without the murder."

"Kind of. Although there is this other dude, Lucas, and I'm pretty sure he'd kill Jackson if he could get away with it. Seems really possessive of Marie. I can't tell if they're related or engaged or what." I frowned, shrugging.

"Ew, what a douchebag."

"Yeah. But, the reason you might think it's weird, well..." I chewed on the thought and my food tapping my fork against my tray again. "I think they might be past life dreams. I did a meditation from that book you got me and all the visions and info it gave me were through Jackson's eyes still. And I found this." I dug my phone out of my pocket. I'd taken a photo of the article along with copying down the parts I could read, so I showed both to Dan.

"Vinny, I know you can read, but this says Clara and Reginald, not Marie and Jackson." He slid my phone back across the table, furrowing his brows at me. I laughed.

"I know, Clara and Reginald were also in my dreams. They got engaged, but Clara definitely didn't seem happy about it." I tapped the photo to make it bigger, looking it over again.

"Wow. All this in ten days?"

"Uh-huh. Wild, right?"

"It really is. Maybe that book of yours has more answers." He shrugged, and for some reason I briefly saw Charles overlaid on him. I tilted my head, then shook it. I was letting the dreams get to me. Not everything from them connected to real life, even if it was a past life.

"Yeah, I'll figure it out."

"You will babe, you're smart." Dan smiled at me, and that was enough reassurance to carry me through at least three years. I grinned back in thanks.

School was easier to focus on with my secret shared and Dan on my side. The rest of my classes flew by, and soon I was settled on the train with Dan dozing lightly on my shoulder. It was a little overcast, and days without sun always drained his energy. I patted his knee to wake him as his stop came up, nudging him off my shoulder as gently as possible.

"Come over." Dan pouted at me, and I gave him another grin.

"I can't, I'm sorry. Mom will start getting suspicious if I'm at your place constantly." His arms were on my shoulders and I lifted them off. He made a disgusted face.

"Oh good lord, is she still accusing us of dating?"

"Yeah." I sighed, nodding. "She'll never believe me, she doesn't think friends should be as close as we are. It's weird to text people before and after school, I guess."

"Yuck." He huffed, but gave in. "Fine, fine. To keep you safe I'll keep my distance, darling." He waved his hand, blowing me a kiss before he headed off. I laughed, taking my own path home with my earbuds in my ears.

I entered the house quietly, turning my key slowly in the lock. I didn't hear the TV or radio, or any erratic talking, so I went in with a sigh of relief. It would be nice to have mom's schedule so I would know when she would be home, but I would take what I could get if she was out for the night. The house was free of the normal tension it usually held, but I still holed up in my room for the night after grabbing food from the kitchen. I had homework, but it was the kind that would take ten minutes, so I didn't bother.

This was the perfect chance to dig into my book a bit more, since I'd only managed to get through the first chapter. It looked like the lessons were supposed to be done once a month, so I'd really skipped over a lot by doing the meditation for past life regression.

Worth it, I thought to myself, smirking as I conjured up an image of Marie again. Dan had been teasing me at lunch, but I didn't blame him. Her laughter, that grin...I caught myself smiling at the thought and laid my book over my face, laughing softly at myself.

"I gotta find out who you are, Marie," I whispered into the pages, feeling like a cartoon character with little hearts floating above my head. It was silly—ridiculous, even. But I'd really only ever crushed on Katiyana, so even if it was over a dream, this was brand new to me. It was a good thing I'd only slipped into a dreamy expression around Dan once, because if it kept happening I would never, *ever* hear the end of it.

I managed to drag myself out of her bright silver eyes, and back into my book. Only the buzzing of my phone's low battery warning reminded me to plug it in. I was swept back into the book quickly. It was so hard to put down.

My eyes were closing, but just a few more pages...

Oh it was cold, and dark. I looked up, and saw a pre-dawn sky dotted with stars. Jackson's breath formed a soft cloud in the air, obscuring the stars for just a moment.

"Get in here, the door's letting out all the heat. You're gonna ruin the bread!" A voice called. I knew it was Charles, without Jackson even turning his head. He was busy searching the stars for a specific pattern, then grinned upon finding it. The little cluster was Andromeda, chained to her rock while her mother Cassiopeia watched from above.

"Jackson!!" Charles was more insistent this time, and Jackson relented and carried his crate of flour inside. The little bags were lined up in neat rows, packaged perfectly. Little bricks of powder to mold into so many different delicacies. I wondered how many bags the bakery went through in a month.

"I'm here, I'm here," Jackson called as he kicked the door shut, the warm air of the bakery enveloping him. He closed his eyes to take a soft breath of it, letting it warm his lungs and chest to ward off the cough that always comes with cold air.

Charles and Jackson fell into their work, easy habits that came from days of repeated motions. This was their normal, kneading dough and brushing melted chocolate into molds. Jackson definitely seemed to be the one handling most of the candy-like offerings, while Charles dealt with anything that used dough or batter. This was going to be so hard to copy into my note file when I woke up.

Their peace and soft conversations were broken by a sharp rapping on the front door. They turned to look at each other, confused, then Charles went to go look. Jackson heard the soft jingle of the overhead bell as Charles opened the door, then his faint laughter.

Charles peeked around the door a moment later, a broad grin painted across it.

"Oh Jackson, you have a visitor."

Jackson's confused expression deepened, and he set down the chocolate mold he'd been working on, wiped his hands on his apron, and made his way to the shop side of the business.

His face lit up immediately. "Marie." The name was a breath, a single note, and he flipped up the hinged counter to stand next to her by the door. She was shivering, but grinning as well.

"This coat is-isn't doing much in...the way of w-warmth," she laughed, hugging her arms around her ribs. "I'm glad Charles let me in. I was afraid I would be standing out there for hours until you opened."

Jackson gave her a soft, concerned-but-thankful look, then raised a finger, disappearing into the back to grab his own woolen coat. He returned and settled it around her shoulders with his gentle, sincere smile, rubbing her upper arms briskly. Her eyes didn't leave his face, her lips parted softly. Jackson resisted the urge to see what they felt like against his own.

"Well let's get you warmed up then. Would you like some hot chocolate?" He raised the hinged counter and motioned for her to follow, which she did after a pause.

"Are you sure it's alright for me to be in the back? You won't get in trouble?" She asked as she walked past him timidly, the borrowed coat clenched tightly in her hands.

"I'm sure. Charles won't mind, and the owner lives in Chicago. We're mostly on our own here." He beckoned her forward again.

By the time they'd reached the kitchen—workshop, whatever it was officially called—Marie had calmed and was smiling instead of looking around apprehensively.

"What brings you here before business hours?" Jackson asked, after he had secured a stool for Marie across from the chocolate mold he'd picked back up. She was watching him paint it with melted chocolate, covering every bit of it in a thin layer. I knew he was going to fill it with cream, then pour another layer of chocolate over the top to seal it. I hoped he'd get far enough in his work to let me see it.

"I wanted to see you, but not get in the way of your work." Marie still had his coat wrapped around her shoulders, but had loosened her grip. She was pushing a stray crumb of chocolate across the work table, tapping at it with her fingernail. Jackson laughed gently.

"That doesn't mean you need to wake up early, Miss Marie," he teased, and she flicked the crumb at him.

"Well, I just didn't want to monopolize your time."

"Did you want to talk about something?" He paused in his chocolate painting, lowering the mold. Marie stayed quiet for a moment, keeping her eyes down. Charles had slowed his kneading but kept his back turned, and Jackson cast a scathing side-eye at him for it.

"I think I would rather you talk, and I listen," Marie said quietly. Jackson had to let it process in his mind for a moment to make sure he understood what she said. Then he smirked.

"Do you want me to tell you stories? Or my thoughts on the state of the world?" His tone remained light, on the border of teasing. Marie rolled her eyes with a smirk.

"Anything. I would..." She paused, biting her lip softly then looking at him, "love to hear all of your thoughts. I'd really like to get to know you better, Jackson."

This caught him a bit off guard. Sure, he was interested in her, and he wanted nothing more than to take her hand, wander off somewhere private, talk to her for hours, and learn her every like and dislike. If other things were involved, so much the better. All of these thoughts hit me like a truck as they crossed Jackson's mind, poised with his paintbrush over the mold as he watched her expression shift from hopeful to concerned.

"I'm sorry, I... didn't mean to overstep," she whispered, making to pull his coat off her shoulders. Jackson finally sprang to action, laying down the brush and swinging around the table to tuck the lapels of his coat more firmly around her, leaning closer so he could whisper.

"I would love to tell you every single one of my stories, Marie."

Katiyana

Thursday, September 17th, 2020

MARIE'S EYES WERE WIDE and her breath caught in her throat as she processed what Jackson had just whispered to her. It took him leaning back just enough and a gentle, encouraging smile for the knot in her throat to unlock and allow her to breathe again. I could feel her blush all the way to her ears again, and she settled a hand on her heart.

"Hah, I...oh," she stammered, dropping her gaze with a soft laugh. Jackson's hands were on her shoulders still, and she looked up at him, eyes glancing briefly over his lips.

Oh, Lucas would burn this place to the ground if he knew I was here...

The thought slapped me like a gale force wind. So were they engaged? Or was he just overprotective? She didn't have a ring on in any of my dreams, but arranged marriages were usually decided before anything was bought, right? If I had access to my face I would have frowned.

Jackson's laugh snapped me back into the dream. "I don't mean to come on too strong. My apologies." He dropped his hands and Marie quickly took one, defying her flush and timid demeanor. I was so proud.

"It's fine." Her voice was soft but firm, and Charles made a show of dropping a sack of flour onto the table as loud as he could to remind them he was still in the room. Or at least, that's what it felt like. Jackson shot him a glare that Charles pretended not to see, humming as he resumed his work. With a gentle squeeze, Jackson dropped Marie's hand and made his way back to the other side of the table. Marie swiveled on the stool, chin tucked softly into the lapel of his coat. It smelled like the bakery—flour and vanilla with a little bit of burnt sugar and chocolate. Not what most men she was around smelled like. It was nice. Lucas smelled like cigars and gasoline, car exhaust and sweat. I didn't enjoy any of those smells and it seemed neither did Marie.

"Well, Marie, have you ever heard of the myth of Andromeda and Perseus?" Jackson picked up his chocolate mold again, stirring the melted chocolate in the jar next to him with his paintbrush. Marie shook her head, eyeing the thermometer in the water basin that held his chocolate jars. He'd told her the water helped get everything the right temperature when it was on the stovetop.

"I don't know any of the Greek myths, but I've heard those names before." She leaned on the table with her elbows, settling her chin in her palms. *Clara would probably know this story,* she thought, watching Jackson's paintbrush move deftly over a different part of the mold.

"Well, it all began when Andromeda's mother, Cassiopeia, claimed herself to be more beautiful than the Nereids." The story began, and faded out as I heard the steady beeping of my alarm getting louder and louder. Dammit, even I wanted to hear that story.

<hr>

I rolled over and smacked my alarm silent, laying there with my arm dangling over the edge of my bed for a moment as my eyes tried to focus on the carving of Brigit's woven cross without my glasses. Maybe there was a book about the myth in the school library. If not, I was sure the internet would lead me to it.

As soon as I had a chance, which happened to be after I scarfed down my food at lunch, I made my way to the library, right up to the desk. The librarian was sitting behind it, taping up the ripped spine on a paperback.

"Excuse me, ma'am?" I asked, resting my fingers on the edge of the counter. She looked up at me with a raised eyebrow, but an inquisitive one rather than a condescending one. "Where would I find books on Greek myths?"

"That'll be over in the reference section, the 290s." She pointed toward the shelves to her left, and I followed her gaze. The shelves, mercifully, had numbers and arrows directing me where to go. I thanked her, heading over there.

"Why did you run to the library?" A hand landed on my shoulder and I jumped, my hand flying up to my heart as I spun. I hadn't realized anyone had followed me. Alena was staring, eyebrow raised in the exact opposite way from the librarian's.

"Gracious, I didn't know you followed me. Sorry." I took a step to be in line with her, still heading for the Greek section.

"You took off without a word. I wanted to make sure you weren't sick or hurt or something." Alena shrugged. I was touched, and also sheepish because I really hadn't said anything before I took off.

"I'm sorry. I wanted to get here while I had a chance."

"Why do you need books on Greek mythology?" Alena bent down to the bottom shelf. She knew how to navigate a library better than I did. "Which one are you looking for?"

"Andromeda and Perseus." I knelt down next to her, watching her fingers tap over the spines as she read the titles.

"It'll be in this one." She tugged out a decently thick and tall book from the shelf, dropping it into my outstretched hands. We stood together and I flipped to the Table of Contents, tapping Andromeda's name as I came to it. "Why do you need it though?" She furrowed her eyebrows at me again, and I hugged the book to my chest.

"Bear with me—"

"Katiyana, after all we've been through together...I mean, come on, we are literally studying your family's line of magic together." She crossed her arms, still watching me and waiting for an explanation. I sighed.

"Alright, well, since the first day of school, I've been having these dreams..." I divulged all of the info I carried in my head, handing her my phone to show her my notes.

Alena listened with no judgment, just processing the information, scrolling through the notes and asking a clarifying question or two.

"So you want to read about Andromeda because a boy started telling you the story in a dream?" The question was sincere, not judgy or sarcastic at all. I breathed a sigh of relief at her lack of...well, lack of being weirded out at the prospect.

"Yeah."

"Well let's get your book checked out, then." Alena nodded toward the desk, and I followed her silently. I suddenly desperately wanted to know her opinions on the matter and if she had any other leads she could think of. Maybe she was waiting until after school, when we could find a more secluded location and maybe take Jamari and Fleur with us to discuss it as a group.

With the book safely in my temporary possession, we headed back to class. It was hard to focus, and I kept sneaking glances at Alena who seemed perfectly focused on school, jotting down notes and working through problems with outward ease.

My suspicions were confirmed when she held me hostage by the school gate, waiting for the other half of our quartet. As soon as the sisters appeared, she nudged me forward.

"Alright, tell them what you told me."

I flushed, scratching at the back of my head for a moment before muttering, "you don't have to make it sound like I did something bad..." but launching into another explanation right after. Jamari and Fleur stayed quiet like Alena did, Jamari smirking every so often like she wanted to crack a joke but was holding herself back. Fleur's brow got more and more furrowed as I went on, her frown intensifying by the second.

"And that's the last dream as of this morning." I looked to Fleur, feeling like I needed to duck or lean back for safety. "What's wrong?"

"I'm concerned that if this does end up being past life dreams, you'll start trying to copy it and live out a made-up destiny for yourself, trying to find that guy's reincarnation and ignoring all the plans you have now." It was absolutely reasonable and fair, and sent a wave of relief through me that she wasn't going to say anything like I was going crazy or I needed my head checked. But I had to remind myself that we'd all literally witnessed Jamari have past life dreams last year.

I paused on my previous worry about Fleur's reaction and corrected myself. Fleur's response to Jamari's dreams had been very similar. She wasn't the kind of person to tell us it was bad or to ignore it, and it was wrong of me to project that fear onto her. I needed to sit down with myself later to figure out where that was coming from.

"Yeah, you already have stuff lined up for art school, and we wouldn't want you to throw that away for some guy you knew a hundred years ago," Jamari chimed in, then glanced at her watch. We moved toward the train station together without needing to say anything about it. "I mean, when my dreams started, I had no idea what was going on, remember?" Jamari shrugged. Part of her working at Ladine's now was because she'd gone to Alexis for help with deciphering her own dreams. "I had to go and ask the coven. Lucky for me, they *did* know what was going on."

"Alexis and Valerie might be better at helping, then." Alena spoke for the first time since we'd gathered at the school gate, and we all glanced at her and then each other. The train had just pulled in and people were shuffling off of it, so it was too late to duck into Ladine's. "We could go again later this week." We joined the group of students getting on the train, our conversation momentarily paused.

"That's a really good idea," Fleur said, and as we sat down on the train, she laid a soft hand on my knee. "Also, I'm not trying to come across as harsh, I just want you to live your life instead of Marie's."

I smiled at her, truly grateful for her perception and care. "You're not harsh, it's a really good thing to remember. Marie's life doesn't seem fully happy, anyway, and I would rather be happy with all of you instead of possibly miserable with one random guy."

Fleur got a giggle out of that, and we decided to discuss our Ladine's trip at lunch tomorrow, falling into normal patterns of video games and short videos on the way to our stops.

Once I got home, Nick made a loud show of going to his bedroom without speaking to me and slamming his door shut, hard enough Valerie texted me to make sure everything was fine. *Why isn't he at work? I thought he had a shift tonight.* Oh well, if he wanted to brush off work and lose his own pocket money, no skin off my back. It would be annoying if he'd randomly quit his job for no reason, though. He'd done it before, a few times, and never told anyone why beyond, "I hated it."

I shut my own door and went about filling in my notes more thoroughly in my cloud file, trying to write down everything I could from the dream the previous night. I wrote down a little section for the myth of Andromeda—what little I'd been able to read between classwork—as I was trying to figure out a connection between her and Marie. There had to have been some reason Jackson wanted to tell her that particular one, right?

Deciding not to puzzle over things I didn't know, I pulled the book from my bag and flipped to the right page, learning the story Jackson apparently knew by heart.

Vincent

Friday, September 18, 2020

A waiter again. Right back into the brilliantly gilded room from the second dream. This time it was decked out, streamers and fresh flowers everywhere. It seemed like even the chandeliers had gotten polished in an effort to make them shine brighter.

Jackson was looking idly around, trying not to appear too desperate to spot a specific someone in the crowd. According to the laugh from Charles at his side, he was failing.

"Would you calm down? You know she'll appear out of nowhere soon enough. She's been coming to the bakery nearly every morning just to talk to you and hear your stories. Of course she's going to find you here."

"You're right." Jackson sighed, reaching up to sweep his hair away from his face. He turned as an older lady with a little dog tucked under her arm came up to the table, asking for anything that wouldn't upset her precious poochie's stomach. Jackson had to stifle a laugh but managed to put together a plate for the little creature, elbowing Charles in the ribs for laughing when the bug-eyed dog started noisily chomping and licking at the plate, snorting all the way.

Right as I was wondering how long I would have to wait to see my dream girl again, the dream time-shifted forward and I was looking through Jackson's eyes at Marie. The grin on his face was wide, and he somehow managed to keep his hands behind his back instead of reaching out to embrace her. I'd missed a few "chapters," as it were. There were now memories of previously embracing her at the bakery coming to his mind. Lucky man.

"Jackson!" Marie said brightly, clasping her hands in front of her, probably also refraining from the embrace they both wanted.

"Hello Miss Marie." Jackson's voice and smile were absolutely betraying his proper waiter stance, and he quickly corrected himself, shifting to a more professional and less friendly tone. "I hope you're enjoying your evening." Marie made a noise like a quickly-swallowed chuckle, hiding her mouth behind her hand.

"As much fun as Clara and Reggie's engagement party could possibly be." Her voice was dripping with sarcasm, and she rolled her eyes. "No one wants to watch their best friend be forced to marry a man she hates." She had lowered her voice to a whisper, looking toward the stage area where Reggie seemed to be waiting impatiently and Clara was taking her sweet time climbing up to him, pausing to talk to people on the way. Jackson smirked at her small act of defiance.

"Why is she going along with it?" Jackson asked. Everyone's focus was on the engaged couple, and most had moved to the other side of the room to be closer to them.

"Their fathers are business partners. The marriage is supposed to strengthen the union, be good for publicity—all that nonsense." She shook her head, crossing her arms as she watched Reggie tug Clara to him just a bit too roughly, barely enough for anyone out of the loop to notice. A flare of protective and righteous fury ignited in Jackson. He only knew Clara in passing, but no one should treat their betrothed like that.

"If he causes her any pain, Leo will be on him like a cat on a rat." Before Jackson could ask who Leo was—*I* was starting to realize, though—Reggie made another announcement about the engagement, likely for the attendees who hadn't been at the last gathering. Clara dutifully waved her ring around long enough to placate him. Once he seemed satisfied, she leaned over to whisper in his ear and he nodded, releasing Clara to the crowd. She immediately spotted Marie and made a beeline for her, only stopping to thank various partygoers for their congratulations.

Jackson stayed silent as the women spoke, listening to them recount the engagement gifts Reggie had gotten Clara, figuring out what to do with all the unwanted jewelry and clothes. It seemed she wanted absolutely no reminder of him on her body, besides the ring to keep the peace. It had taken Jackson until now to notice she had never worn any other jewelry, but there had been other things on his mind. I didn't blame him; I hadn't noticed either.

"Leo's going to be so upset." Clara's voice was very soft, barely audible above the din of the crowd, and she twisted her ring faster around her finger. Marie took her hands and squeezed them to get her to stop.

"He can't do anything." Marie's voice matched Clara's. Both women stared at each other, just for a moment, and Clara let her true emotions show. Devastation and even fear were there. Even Jackson, who'd only spoken to her briefly, could see it. He glanced at Marie, who was wearing a pained expression as well, and suddenly Jackson completely understood why no one besides Reggie was pleased about the engagement.

Took you a minute, but you got there, didn't you buddy? I was shocked out of my own thoughts by the sudden onset of music, and it didn't seem to be coming from the band. It took a moment before I realized it was my alarm, and I jolted awake.

———◆———

My heart was still pounding from the sudden scare of my alarm, so I laid in bed for a moment, staring at the ceiling before shutting it off. I closed my eyes and held a hand to my forehead, letting my breathing get back under control. Chief Regulus had been in my dreams, it had to have been him. The blonde man in the dance hall, and then in the bakery, and now Clara and Marie were calling him by the same name? I got up, got ready, and headed out all while wrapped up in my thoughts and updating the file on my phone. I'd forgotten to grab breakfast and didn't realize until my stomach growled at the train station. There was nothing I could do now, so I ignored it and pulled up the fire department's website on my phone. His contact info was probably listed.

Sure enough, there was his email. I tapped it and started writing.

> *Chief Regulus,*
> *I'm a student at Cridhe but I have some not-school-related questions. I'd like to talk to you about them in person if possible. When are you free?*
> *Thank you,*
> *Vincent D.*

The note felt entirely inadequate and I immediately thought of a better way to phrase things as soon as I hit send. With a soft sigh, I resigned myself to being cryptic as hell, and leaned my head back against the top of my chair as I waited for the train. Sadly, Dan being at Corp meant I had no one to entertain me. I was alone in the torment of simply waiting.

Katiyana

Friday, September 18, 2020

THE SHOWER WAS GROWING cold as I stood there, replaying the conversation with Leo from my dream, processing the shock that it was actually him, my cousin's partner, in my dream. I needed to text Sinéad ASAP, so I snapped out of my fog and shut the water off, grabbing my phone off the counter before I was even fully dry.

LilTriquetra

Sinéad it was absolutely leon in my dream. He was with a lady named clara, can you ask him about her for me?? I think we're right about the past life dreams. They were in a bakery together and at a dance hall too.

I knew she wouldn't answer right away—she rarely did—so I went about my routine and finished getting ready for school. Nick was banging around in the kitchen, so instead of preparing a more nutritious meal, I settled for some toaster waffles and ate them by hand just so I didn't have to be in the kitchen with him for long. He still hadn't spoken to me beyond what was necessary, things like, "I need the bathroom, get out" or "I ordered dinner, don't make anything," etcetera, etcetera. Him ordering dinner the other night was actually a bit of a shock, but a pleasant one. He'd even ordered things I liked, rather than just *his* preferences. He got a couple points back in my book for that one. Alex must have scared him just enough to make him behave, or at least his version of behaving, which was basically ignoring me. Either way, fine by me.

Sinéad didn't get back to me until right before lunch, and her response was not what I'd expected at all.

Bruadarach

Go to ladine's and ask alexis for the spell I texted her about.

LilTriquetra

That's cryptic dude, you can't give me any more info?

Bruadarach

Sorry kiddo, just get the spell.

LilTriquetra

SIGH, okay, I'll tell you what happens I guess.

Bruadarach

[thumbs up gif]

LilTriquetra

[rolling eyes gif]

Bruadarach

[cat pleading and saying sorry gif]

I left it at that, since I obviously wasn't going to get anything more out of her, but it definitely made me suspicious. Sinéad usually gave me all the info she could, and if she was suddenly holding back, that probably meant I was on the right track with past life dreams. Things were starting to make too much sense, and I clung to Jamari's arm as soon as I found her between class and lunch.

"Aw Yana, what is it?" She asked, wiggling her arm free to sling it around me.

"I have to tell everyone at once because I feel like if I have to explain it more than that I'm going to explode." I squeezed my eyes shut, my hands trembling with the thought of not only discovering my past life, but it being tied to Leon of all people, and therefore directly to Sinéad. Her silence was absolutely damning, and also cryptic enough that it was starting to make me wonder if she and Clara were one and the same. It would make so much sense.

After gathering in the cafeteria, I managed to stumble through the latest dream and Sinéad's unhelpful-yet-helpful messages, handing my phone over to Alena when my hand started shaking too hard to hold it steady.

"Good thing we're planning on going into Ladine's anyway."

Fleur's voice sounded from Alena's phone. We'd secretly placed an against-the-rules phone call to clue her in while she was at Corp. "Are you alright? Your voice sounds like you're shivering."

"I...I guess it's just...so much to take in at once? The existence of past lives to begin with, even though Jamari knows about hers and I've lived with the coven, it's still weird to have it shoved in my face. And the discovery of what I'm pretty sure is my own past life, the fact Leon is there...and I don't know how this one I'm dreaming about ended so I'm scared to find out. What if it's horrible? What if Marie and Jackson get in trouble and get killed for it? Will I have to relive that in my nightmares!? How much am I going to dream about?" I had started speaking quickly, sure that none of my friends could understand me, but somehow they did.

"Hey, it'll be okay. We'll talk to Alexis tomorrow and see if she can help you just like she did me." Jamari lifted a hand to lay it on my head, stroking my hair softly. Alena nodded across the table and Fleur made a noise of agreement. "Do you want to come in during my shift?"

"I think that's for the best. Then we can all be there together." I could tell Alena was mentally checking everyone's schedules. "If we head in around noon or so, the store should be empty enough for us to talk in private, but also late enough we shouldn't interrupt any opening duties Jamari has to do."

"That's so considerate," Jamari teased, and I laughed lightly. I'd stopped trembling as my friends listened to me and helped me figure out a solution. They were right, as was Sinéad. Going to Alexis was the best course of action.

Vincent

Friday, September 18, 2020

LEON DIDN'T ANSWER MY email until after lunch. I felt my phone buzz during the next class and cursed myself silently for not putting it completely on silent. Luckily the teacher hadn't noticed, so I just continued working until the period was over. The minute I got into the hall, though, I swept my phone from my pocket and hurriedly tapped open the email app.

> *Vincent D.,*
> *I'm actually not free until after school gets out, if that's alright. Your email is shockingly vague, I hope it's nothing inappropriate.*
> *Leon*

He'd added a laughing emoji to the end of his sentence, and it made me smirk in disbelief. He was supposed to be a public official, but obviously didn't care for formality. Regardless, I now had an in. I could talk to him in the period between getting out of class and catching the train. Honestly, I didn't even care if I missed the train. If this is how I got answers, fantastic.

I screenshotted the two emails and sent them to Dan, hoping that would be enough of an explanation for why I wasn't going to be at the train station right away, or at all. My knee was bouncing in anticipation all through the rest of the day, and as soon as the last bell rang, I took off down the school steps, ran around the corner and down two blocks to the fire station. Peering through a little window on the door, I spotted blonde hair and heard a guitar playing softly behind the door. Leon seemed to be singing to himself, and it felt wrong to interrupt him, but I really needed to talk to him. So I knocked. His head lifted and he smiled kindly, coming over to open the door. It hadn't been locked, but since I wasn't one of the firemen, I didn't want to just barge in.

"Vincent D., I'm guessing?" He grinned, and I was slapped with the mental image of him giving the same grin to Clara as they danced. I nodded and followed him to a desk, where he took the office chair and I sat on a stool across from it. "What vague questions do you have for me, Vincent D.?" He was teasing, everything about him light and jovial.

"I uh..." I paused, realizing I hadn't figured out how to talk about this without flat out assaulting him with knowledge and assumptions. He looked at me patiently as I ran things over in my mind, finally deciding to just pull out my phone and the note about the second dream in the bakery. "Does any of this mean anything to you?"

He looked puzzled but took the phone as I handed it over, and his eyes widened immediately. "How...how do you know any of this?" He was scrolling near frantically, and two sides of me warred. I was glad that I seemed to be right in my assumption, but he was visibly distressed and I felt bad about that. I prepared myself to be thrown out of the station.

"I've been dreaming about it. Each dream is separated by the arrow lines, and the date is when I had the dream. Or at least woke up from it," I explained, and Leon nodded, leaning forward to rest his elbows on the desk, one hand still holding the phone, the other going to his hair. He was silent for a moment as he read through the rest of the document, gasping quietly as he got to the final bit, Clara's engagement party. I thought I saw tears well up in his eyes, but he ducked his face behind his hand quickly.

"Dreaming it, you said?" He asked, his voice cracking a little. I nodded, not knowing what else to add. He sighed and handed me back my phone, pulling his own out of his coat pocket from the back of his chair. "Hold on just a moment, alright?" He stood, tapping his phone a few times and holding it to his ear, slipping into the next room. I couldn't hear more than his muffled words, and I definitely couldn't make any of them out or even deduce who he was talking to. There was a pause, and then he sounded like he was greeting someone else, and that conversation ended quickly. He was back in the room, collapsing into his chair with another heavy sigh.

"I never imagined I'd be the one doing this..." he muttered, and I furrowed my brows in confusion.

"Sorry, Chief Regulus, what do you mean?"

Leon looked up almost like he'd forgotten I was there, and gave an apologetic smile. "Sorry, nothing. Now listen, as I'm sure you've figured out by now, that is me. It is. I remember every instance of this clearly, except the parts I obviously wasn't around for." He tapped his fingers on his desk, mulling the next thought over. "And...I'm sorry, but I can't explain any more than that." He looked up at me, the sincere apology clear as the blue in his eyes. I frowned.

"Can I ask why not?" I forced the bite in my voice back. I'd come here for answers and was probably going to leave with more questions.

"This is something that's best done by the people involved, letting them find the answers as they come to them. If I tell you the entire story, it could warp things for you, change them to my perspective instead of Jackson's. I don't want to do that to you. However, there is someone you can go to for help."

"Who is it?" I asked, probably a little too eagerly. I understood his reasoning, as mind-boggling as it was. What did he mean by changing perspective? Would I start living Leo's life in my dreams instead of Jackson's? I had a feeling he wasn't about to explain that, either.

"Alexis Easty. She runs Ladine's Gem, that café that's a few blocks away. Do you know it?" He asked, picking his phone back up, probably ready to pull up the address if need be.

"I've been there once, but I know the way." Keeping the irritation out of my voice was still an effort, but I managed. It wasn't Leon's fault. Whatever mystical rules there were to this, it was probably best to follow them.

Leon nodded, setting his phone back down. "Alright, I've already spoken to her, and she knows exactly what you need. All you have to do is tell her your name."

I sighed, both in relief and frustration. I felt like I was being led on a wild goose chase. Go here, now go here, then go over there. Leon must have felt my frustration because he stood up, came around the desk, and laid a hand on my shoulder. "I really am sorry, Vincent. After you talk to Alexis and do what she says, come back to me and we can talk more, alright?" He didn't sound like he was just placating a child, he really meant it. I respected him immensely for that.

"Okay. Thank you so much. I hope I didn't take up too much of your time." I stood, adjusting my backpack on my shoulders. I was hoping I didn't sound like too much of a snotty teenager.

"I wish I could do more right now, believe me. But I'm on strict orders not to." He gave his little smile again. "Sinéad would murder me if I didn't do this properly. Or at least try to."

Ah okay, that must have been who he was on the phone wit—Something clicked. Clara had looked familiar, too. I'd seen her ringlets and jawline on the stage at school, and in the newspapers, and at official events.

"Bruadarach Sinéad is Clara, isn't she?" I blurted out, before I even meant to, and even though Leon didn't respond, the quick glaze-over of his eyes and hard swallow were enough to confirm. He recovered, shaking his head to clear whatever fog her name had settled on his brain.

"Sorry. Go to Alexis. She'll teach you the next step." He set a hand on my shoulder and steered me toward the door, patting the same shoulder before releasing it. "We don't want you missing your train, Vincent D." He offered me another friendly smile as I gave in and left the station, again trying to ignore my exasperation.

I caught up with Dan at the train station, and he only had to give me a questioning look before I relayed the entire story. His jaw literally dropped, and I had to tug him onto the train as it pulled up.

"So it's literally him, then! Oh my gosh. That's so exciting, that's incredible. Imagine proving past lives are real!" He was waving a hand around in excitement, and I grabbed his arm in an attempt to prevent him from drawing attention to us. He leaned in closer to me, grinning. "Vinny, this means you could actually find out who Marie is!"

The thought had occurred to me, of course, and I huffed a breath at the prospect. "Yeah...I could. I just hope she's not too far from the island."

"Vinny, this is Faodail. Everything that happens here has been happening for the past forty million years." He laughed, leaning back in his seat and popping open Instagram. He wasn't wrong—the island was full of repeating cycles. I just didn't think I'd ever be part of one.

Alexis

Saturday, September 19th, 2020

Sinéad and Leon had texted me the day before, giving me the kids' names and saying they'd be coming by soon. It was just a matter of time before things got rolling. In the meantime, I had a shop to maintain. I got opening duties done before Jamari even made it in; she was half an hour late and somehow still yawning.

"I realize this isn't a full time job, but I still expect you to be here when I ask you to be." I raised my eyebrow at the young girl, my arms crossed as I watched her from behind the counter. She ducked her head in apology, slipping through the half-door that separated the storefront from the employees-only area.

"I'm sorry. I'll do better next time." Jamari looked genuinely contrite, so I left it at that for now. She hadn't been late for a long time, so a warning would do.

"I'll hold you to it, Jamari," I said simply, picking up an apron and holding it out to her. "You're going to do more of the café side of things today."

Jamari dutifully put on her apron and followed me to the small kitchen where I set her up rolling out dough for pastries and using our stand mixer to make icing. "Set a timer on your phone for ten minutes—don't let it mix longer than that—then switch out the bowl and set up the next batch. There's only two bowls, so you'll have to rinse them out between batches." Jamari nodded, tapping on her phone then holding up the timer screen for approval.

"What do I need to do with the dough once it's rolled out?" She asked, gesturing to the pre-made lumps of dough Valerie and I had worked on earlier in the week.

"Use the pizza cutter and cut it into inch-thick strips, then come find me and I'll show you how we braid it for the bread." I nodded at her and left her to work. I wouldn't be far if she needed another explanation or something went wrong. The tasks were simple enough to trust a teenager with.

For the first couple hours of the day, I went between tidying, checking the protective wards on the shop, and freshening up sigils as needed. A few customers came and went, toting their purchases happily out the door. Despite the impatience brewing in my stomach, it was a normal day of metaphysical retail. Jamari figured out the bread braiding quickly, and finished up both batches of dough on her own.

Eleven chimed on the grandfather clock that kept guard and time by the door, and I sighed through my nose. These children needed to show up already. Even though it would have complicated matters, I would have even been fine if they both showed up at the same time. I shook my head and took that thought back. It would be best if they came in at different times. It was cutting matters close enough that they went to the same school. Leon and Sinéad had called last night and said they didn't think the kids were friends, but they did seem to know each other.

"Just hold out until Mabon, please, universe," I muttered under my breath, staring at the circled date on the calendar. It wasn't exactly the most perfect date for a past life revealing spell, but the energies would be potent enough to help. "Samhain would be better," I grumbled, crossing my arms and leaning back against the counter, still staring at the date. No matter how hard I worked to follow its patterns, fate would have me tripping on my own feet and scrambling to catch up with it for the rest of time.

With a sigh, I sank down into the seat behind our register and tugged my binder over, looking over the plans and invoices for the Mabon festival we'd be having the next weekend, despite it taking place four days after the actual Sabbat. Being in business for a couple decades had taught me that festivals and celebrations never did well on weekdays. It managed to distract me enough that I didn't hear the bell on the door chime, and instead my attention was caught by a tap on the counter. I looked up into the eyes of Etta's daughter surrounded by her friends minus Jamari, who was now cleaning the kitchen.

"Hi Alexis! My cousin told me to come here and talk to you about a spell..." Katiyana trailed off, pulling her phone closer to her face, likely looking for a text message or something similar for proof. I stood up, nodding.

"I know, she called me last night to explain."

Katiyana looked relieved that she didn't have to explain further, and Fleur gently took her hand with a soft, reassuring smile. I reached for my purse hooked on the wall and pulled out a small bundle I'd wrapped with a lavender ribbon. All three girls eyed it as I set it on the counter, nudging it toward Katiyana.

"Inside you'll find some mugwort, a candle holder, and a small taper candle." I laid my hand over it as Katiyana reached up, leaning forward and looking her in the eye. "I need you to listen—this is important. Do not leave this candle burning as you sleep. I want you to stay awake with it as it burns out. It should only take about three hours, so plan accordingly." She nodded, and I lifted my hand.

"Okay. Do I need to know anything else or are there instructions?" She tucked the bundle in her bag, carefully, as if the candle was going to break with the slightest of pressure.

"There are instructions. If you can't read them, you can call or text me. My phone number is on this." I swept a business card from the stack on the counter and presented it.

"Is that all? Just light a candle, then go to sleep?" Alena asked. I grinned softly at her.

"No, she'll sprinkle the mugwort into her pillowcase, and there's an incantation to speak as the candle is burning."

"Oh, that's still so simple. I was expecting cauldrons, magic circles, more rocks...like on TV."

"Well, TV is definitely not an accurate representation." I laughed lightly. "These three items and some words will be more than enough." I nodded toward Katiyana's bag, and the girls nodded back.

"Could we see Jamari?" Fleur asked, glancing toward the back.

"Sure, let me go grab her for her break. Are you here for lunch?" The three girls nodded again. "I'll grab you some lunch then too—on Jamari." I winked, and Fleur snickered quietly.

A bit later, the girls were set up at one of the café tables, chattering and munching away. I left them to it, going back to my binder. Sinéad had texted me a few times while I'd been preparing their food, so I answered her.

Bruadarach

Did she come in yet??

Alexis???

I am thisclose to asking Connar to look her up on the grid!!

AEasty

She came in. She's having lunch with her friends.

Bruadarach

Did the boy come in?

AEasty

No, I'm hoping she leaves before he does.

Bruadarach

> **Kick her out**

AEasty

> Haha no, she's eating. I gave Jamari her lunch break to eat with them.

Bruadarach

> **Curse your great boss ways**

AEasty

> I know, how horrible of me to treat my employees like real people.

I may have let Jamari's lunch break go on for ten minutes longer than it should have, but she still had three hours left on her shift.

"Alright ladies, I have to take Jamari back," I said, settling a hand on the back of her chair. The girls didn't suppress their groans of disappointment, and I chuckled. "She'll be off in three hours." This seemed to placate them, and they tidied the table up as much as they could without flat out washing the dishes, piling them all in a neat stack. Jamari picked up the dishes, took them to the kitchen, then raced back out to hug her friends before they left.

"Thank you for letting us share her lunch break, Alexis," Fleur said politely, and the rest were quick to agree.

"You're welcome. As long as you don't distract her too much, I don't mind you coming in while she's working." I smiled at them, and they returned the gesture. One more round of goodbyes and they were out the door. Jamari looked up at me as she put her apron back on.

"What else do I need to do?" She asked, already cleaning up the crumbs and straw wrappers from her friends.

"Finish cleaning up the table, then I'll have you come to the counter and learn the new POS system." She nodded and set about her work, and I headed back to the register to be prepared to check out the customer who was currently browsing the bookshelves.

An hour later, Jamari had learned the basics of our new system and had even checked out a few customers herself while I watched nearby and finished tallying the invoices for the festival.

The bell on the door rang again, and I didn't think anything of it until I heard a familiar tone in this customer's voice.

"Excuse me? I'm looking for Alexis..." I looked up to see a young boy's face, his brown eyes full of nerves and questions.

"That's me. How can I help you?" I knew the answer to the question, as this had to be the boy Leon had told me about.

"Chief Regulus told me to come ask you about something." He glanced at Jamari, who had been watching him quietly, and a look of familiarity passed between them.

"Jamari, could you go check on the bread we put in the oven?" I asked, laying a hand on her shoulder. She took the hint and nodded, scrambling out of her chair to head for the kitchen. The boy visibly relaxed. "Are you Vincent?" I asked, lowering my voice for his sake. He nodded.

"Yeah. I'm supposed to ask you about a spell for the dreams I've been having. They've been happening since the beginning of school, and I think they're past life dreams." He was about to go on a full explanation, but I held up a hand to stop him.

"I know. Leon told me."

Vincent's brow furrowed for a split second before he smoothed it and sighed. "I feel like everyone knows the answers to what's going on but won't tell me." His voice was laced with anger, and my heart dropped for him a little.

"I'm sorry. If it were safe to just tell you everything flat out, we all would."

"What does that mean, 'if it were safe?'" He asked, clearly fighting to keep the irritation out of his voice. I came around the counter to place a reassuring hand on his shoulder, then pulled away as I noticed him flinch at my touch.

"It means we're doing our best to protect you. You're uncovering a large truth about yourself, and it's best for you to do it on your own so that you can see your memories unclouded by others' perspectives. You need to learn what *you* felt, not what anyone else felt. So until you run your gamut, we have to stay silent. And I know that's probably the last thing you need or want to hear right now."

He stared at me like he wanted to shout or rage but was keeping himself in check. "Chief Regulus said something similar yesterday," he finally muttered, and I nodded.

"Leon's been through this a few times." I smirked, remembering how he'd helped when I'd gone through my own past life dreams. I'd felt like Vincent likely did right now, wanting to scream and punch everything. "Once you do the spell, come to the café again and we can talk more. I'm here for you; Leon is here for you. I know you just met us, but we are willing to guide you through this."

"So you've gone through it, too?" He asked, a spark of youthful hope in his eyes.

"Yes. Myself, Sinéad, the majority of the coven. You've noticed the cycles on the island, right?" He nodded. "We're all part of them. We live with this island's power, connected to it, repeating things as she needs them repeated. Once you get past this hurdle, I'll teach you whatever you want to know."

My explanation would definitely leave him with more questions than answers, but I hoped my promise would soothe him a bit. It seemed to as his shoulders dropped, and he let out a big breath.

"Okay. What's the spell I need to do?" He asked, and I swung around the counter once more to pull a bundle out of my bag, this time preemptively grabbing a business card and laying it on top.

"It's all in here. If you need help, my number is on that card." I smiled, then remembered my advice to Katiyana. "There's a candle in there that will burn for about three hours. I need you to plan ahead and burn it before your normal bedtime, so you don't fall asleep with it lit. Can you remember that?"

"Yeah, I can do that." He swung his backpack off one shoulder to tuck the package into it, then looked up at me with a bemused expression. "Do people really sleep with candles burning? Seems unsafe."

"Oh, you'd be shocked." I sighed, looking into the middle distance. "There was one time a customer threatened to sue because she had left the candle burning, and it singed her curtains. She really thought I should be held accountable for selling her a flammable candle." Vincent let out a small laugh, and it seemed his anger and frustration were breaking down. I smiled. He seemed like a good kid who was used to figuring out things on his own, but this one was too big and he didn't seem to have anywhere to turn. Hopefully he would trust us in time.

I waved him off, calling out about the Mabon festival next weekend if he wanted to come. He nodded, called his thanks then headed out, and I went back into the kitchen. Jamari was perched in the doorway and it was clear she had been eavesdropping. I gave her a fake stern look and crossed my arms. She seemed immune to it as she stepped away from the doorway to let me into the kitchen.

"Did you give him the same spell you gave Yana?" She asked, pure curiosity and no regard for privacy. There was no use lying—teenager gossip took wild forms, so it was better to tell the truth and swear her to secrecy.

"I did. But you can, *under no circumstances*, let Katiyana or anyone else know."

"Why not?" She asked, tilting her head.

"They have to go through everything just like you did and figure it all out themselves. I know you all go to school together, as well, so please don't tell him either. The spell I gave them isn't meant to be performed until Tuesday."

Jamari made a disappointed face, but sighed and nodded. "You have my word: I will not breathe a single word of the brown-eyed cute nerdy boy to Yana." She put a hand on her heart, holding the other up in an oath, and I laughed.

"Thank you, now let's finish up the cinnamon rolls."

Vincent

Sunday, September 20, 2020

ALEXIS'S NOTE HAD SAID that I needed to wait until Mabon to perform the spell. The note also said that Mabon wasn't until Tuesday. Why did it matter so much? I huffed in frustration and hid the little package—opened and closed four times now—back in my drawer. That meant I had to keep it out of sight for a few more days, and then hope and pray mom had a late shift that night. Locking my door was not an option, because she would literally break it down.

I hadn't had a dream last night and I found myself disappointed over it. After getting a bunch of non-answers from both Leon and Alexis when all I wanted was straight facts, it felt like another blow to my patience. I had been pacing my room for the past ten minutes after a shower, not even fully dressed and having no idea what to do to occupy myself. I needed something—anything—to get my mind off the candle and mugwort stashed away in between socks and pajama pants.

My phone buzzed as I pulled a sweater over my head, and I leaned over to grab it.

Beefaroni

> struggling with homework. can you meet me at the FLC? i'm suffering.

The message was peppered with sad puppy-dog-eye emojis, and I smirked.

RedSam

yeah, i'll leave my house in about 15 min

Beefaroni

I'll buy you lunch if you write this paper for me

RedSam

not happening but you can still buy lunch

Beefaroni

fiiiiiine, get moving

The Faodail Learning Center was roughly halfway between our houses. We'd timed it once and had shown up there a few minutes apart from each other. Sure enough, he was leaning against a pillar by the door and scrolling through his phone when I showed up.

"Heyyyy!" He called, wiggling his fingers at me. I waved back and we went inside together, going to the desk to ask for a study room for a few hours.

"Of course, here's the key Vincent." Dorell handed it directly to me and Dan blinked in barely masked offense that he wasn't considered responsible enough to be in charge of it. The head librarian laughed. "Young man, the last time you borrowed a study room you left it in shambles. The only reason you're getting one today is because Vincent is here to keep an eye on you." I grinned, Dan huffed, and Dorell laughed. His laugh was one of those deep ones that came straight from the stomach. Had he grown a white beard, he would have been some sort of Santa Claus. His hair was silver, however, playing against the warm browns of his skin and the dark of his eyes, making him look more like a mystical wizard than a jolly old elf.

We holed up in the study room, Dan pulling out and plugging in his laptop so I could talk him through the paper he needed to write. At one point, I got up to borrow one of the FLC's laptops as well, needing to print out my own assignments and type up one more page of the same paper.

"Why are you so good at this?" Dan whined, tapping the backspace key rather roughly as he sighed in obvious irritation.

"It's just a history report, Dan. All you have to do is explain what happened."

"Yeah, but copying things word-for-word from websites or the textbook is *frowned upon.*" He mocked our teacher's voice for the last two words.

"You'll get the hang of it. Pretend you're explaining it to me, then I'll help you put it in a more formal voice when you're done. You can manage two double-spaced pages."

My advice seemed to solve his issues, because soon he was tapping away steadily. While he worked, I looked up Mabon and tried to figure out why it was so important to wait to do the spell then. It was a harvest holiday, the second of three. There was something about the veil between worlds beginning to thin, being at its thinnest around Samhain. I'd been to the Samhain festivals with Dan many times, but there was an entire set of Pagan holidays that I hadn't even known existed. I printed out a circular table of them. It was called the Wheel of the Year according to every website I looked at, and I stashed it in my binder so I could refer to it later.

Dan finished his paper, I reviewed it and removed all the slang, and we headed out for lunch. There was a diner not too far from the library that the Vercher family owned, Lara's, and we frequented it in the summer. They had really good burgers.

Dan ended up talking me into going over to his place for the rest of the afternoon and we played video games and bickered and I told him what Alexis had given me at Ladine's.

"What? No instant 'Here's Your Past Life' card or book or anything? Boo," he pouted, stripping off his shirt and turning on his treadmill.

"Nah, just a little bundle and some instructions." I flopped back onto his bed and just rested, closing my eyes to the steady thump-thump-thump of Dan's warm up.

"Well you have to tell me the results of the spell as soon as you know," he demanded, and I lifted a lazy hand in agreement. It didn't take long for me to drift off, and Dan's running was steady enough that it didn't wake me. What did wake me was my phone buzzing urgently in my pocket. I groggily pulled it out, instantly shooting awake as I saw who was calling.

"Hi Mom," I said, ready to tug the ear away from my phone if she started shouting.

"Where are you?" She demanded, thankfully at a reasonable volume.

"I went to the library with Dan to finish up schoolwork, then his parents offered to let me come over for dinner, so I'm at his house." It was a lie; his parents hadn't offered dinner at all. Dan stopped his treadmill and left the room, probably to get his parents in on the story.

"You didn't think to tell me? I came home and you were gone, no sign of anything, your backpack gone, your phone charger gone." She'd gone in my room, then. Hopefully just a glance instead of going through my drawers.

"I'm sorry, I didn't want to bother you at work. Your boss got really upset last time your phone went off, so I just didn't want to get you in trouble." My hand lifted and wrapped around the amethyst pendant under my shirt, pressing it to my heart as it started to pound. Even blocks away, she made me so anxious.

"Text me next time! So I don't come home and wonder if my son has run away and left me here on my own!" She hung up before I could say anything else, so I just lowered my phone.

"Sure, you rely on me so much, Mom," I muttered, shaking my head and flopping back on Dan's bed. Well, now that she knew I was staying for dinner, at least I didn't have to go home anytime soon. She'd been really calm for a few days now, but the thought of running away to the cliffs or the marina was sneaking back into my head.

Katiyana

Sunday, September 20, 2020

Nick had been passive-aggressively watching anime at top volume for most of the day, so I ended up at Valerie's to finish up my homework in peace. She was actually at work, but she'd stopped me on my way home from Ladine's to give me her spare key.

"Just in case," she'd said. I hoped this was what she meant, but I'd texted her anyway. It felt weird being in someone else's home without them, but I could take weirdness over louder-than-everything-else Japanese.

I laid on my stomach on Valerie's couch, angrily typing my latest book report into my phone through the cloud service I used. It absolutely sucked to write on such a small screen, and it was impossible to format, but I had stupidly left my laptop in my room and wasn't about to go back for it when I could still hear very faint music and battle noises from the apartment. I would format it at two a.m., I didn't care. Well, no, I cared a little.

LoveWitch

How's my apartment treating you?

LilTriquetra

Great, so much quieter!!

LoveWitch

I grinned at my phone, tucking my chin into the pillow I was using to prop myself up. Valerie was such a godsend, especially since Mom and Dad were still gone. I'd gotten a text from Dad this morning, asking if everything was alright, so I knew Mom had told him what was going on. I assured him I was okay and that Valerie was keeping an eye on me, and he seemed relieved. He apologized for being away for so long, but the current project was experiencing delays he'd never seen before. It devolved into his job-specific lingo that I didn't understand, then he got called away for whatever reason, so I just told him I loved him and that he was smart enough to figure it out. He sent me back a GIF of Bill Green from his favorite cartoon looking touched, and I giggled. I was lucky to have good relationships with my parents.

My homework didn't take much longer, but I didn't feel like going back to the apartment just yet, so I channel surfed on Val's TV and ended up nodding off. I'm not sure how long I was out, but a loud commercial jolted me awake. As I calmed from the scare, I noticed that I'd ended up holding my amethyst again, subconsciously in my sleep. That had been happening almost every morning now...Wait, no, it had been happening every morning that I woke up from a dream about Marie and Jackson. I made a mental note to write that down in my book when I got back to my room, tapping a basic note into my cloud file.

Listening carefully, I couldn't hear any more anime noises and decided it was safe to go back to the apartment. I locked Val's door and slid the key back in my pocket. I'd been meaning to add it to my keyring but hadn't gotten around to it. Unfortunately for me, this meant I was met with a locked door when I made it to the other end of the hall. Damnit. Nick must have left for dinner or work or whatever else he did, and locked the door without thinking. I closed my eyes for a moment, leaning my forehead against the door and imagining my roots stretching all the way down to the earth again. What could I do? I texted Valerie.

LilTriquetra

I don't think he did it on purpose but nick locked me out of the apartment

LoveWitch

Oh hell kid, damn. Okay can you hold out for 20 minutes? You can wait at my place if you want.

LilTriquetra

Ok, thank you. I'll be on your couch!!

LoveWitch

Hahah aight kiddo, be there soon.

I wandered back the way I came, unlocking her door once again. I wasn't sure how she was going to rescue me. Maybe Mom had made her a copy of the key? That would make sense. Mom was always about backup after backup.

About twenty minutes later, Val came through her door to find me lounging on her couch once more, this time scrolling through whatever endless social media app I hadn't grown bored of yet.

"Oh hi honey, I'm home," she called in a sing-song voice, laughing and bapping her purse on the top of my head. I shook my head and looked at her upside down.

"Isn't it 'Lucy I'm home'?"

"Well sure, if you lived in the fifties." Val swung around her kitchen counter and started digging through a drawer, producing a key a moment later, confirming my suspicion. "You ready to go home?"

I paused for a moment, tapping my thumb on the side of my phone. "Could you go with me? Just in case Nick's still home and just quiet?" I looked up at her, peering over the back of her couch. She gave me a soft smile.

"Course I can, kid."

We went down the hall together, Val unlocked the door with her spare key, and we listened right inside the door for a few moments. There was no noise, no anime sounds, and no snoring, so I let out a relieved sigh.

"Looks like you're safe. If he comes home and gets weird again, you can come back to my place." Val pocketed the spare and looked around the living room, making a face at what she could see of the kitchen. I followed her gaze and then immediately copied her expression.

"Well I guess we know he's getting something to eat now." Nick had tried cooking again, so every single frying pan we owned was on the counter and crusted in some sort of burnt food. How he managed to do this without the smoke alarm going off every time, I did not know.

"Yeesh. Don't do those dishes. Make him squirm." Val gave me an evil grin that made me giggle.

"Yeah, he can clean up his own mess."

"That's my girl." She punched my shoulder lightly and then took her leave with a little salute, and I locked the door behind her. A little part of me hoped Nick had forgotten to take his key, but then I remembered that's not how locks work.

Nick must have gone clear across the island for whatever reason, because he didn't make it home for what felt like ages. The island wasn't big—the trains would get you from Ceangal to Dubhan in about fifteen minutes, and then Ceangal to Meadhan in about thirty. I heard him hanging up his coat and kicking his shoes off against the wall, then he paused at my door while coming down the hall. I stayed quiet, just reading one of my assignments for school, and after a few minutes he went to his room. I shuddered. Somehow, him just standing there was worse than if he had banged on my door.

Luckily he left me alone for the rest of the night, and I tucked myself into bed. Actually, I fell asleep watching TikToks with my face nearly touching my phone since I wasn't wearing my glasses. But I fell into what was probably the most lovely dream I'd had since they began.

———⋄———

"How many more myths do you know?" Marie asked, rolling up her sleeves a little further so she didn't cover them in flour.

"All of them," Charles said with a laugh from the other side of the table, rolling out dough into a flat circle. They were teaching Marie how to make a proper pie crust.

"Not all of them. Just the ones I like." Jackson laughed gently, taking Marie's hand to put a measuring cup in it. "Here, this is the size you need."

"You like all of them, then," Charles teased, looking like he was on the edge of sticking out his tongue. For a grown man, he had the personality of a playful teenager. Jackson laughed. I never really understood what people meant when they wrote "their laugh was like the peal of a bell" until Jackson laughed just then. It was loud, clear, and happy. I wanted to hear it over and over again and I knew Marie did, too. She stared at him with softly parted lips, watching him tilt his head back at his friend's dumb comment that probably didn't even deserve that much laughter.

"Well Charles, you're not entirely wrong." His voice still held a chuckle, and he glanced over at Marie, eyes full of glittering mirth. Her heart felt like it skipped a beat, and she giggled in return. "Have I told you the myth of Eros and Psyche yet?"

"I don't think so?" Marie replied softly, knowing somewhere in the back of her head that Eros stood for a specific sort of love. *Was he implying something? Oh dear, I shouldn't think that way.* She did, however, think that way, and I laughed internally at her blush. Thank goodness she couldn't hear me.

"Well, Eros was the son of Aphrodite and Ares, the goddess of love and the god of war. Eros is also called Cupid in the Roman version of the myth, and that's where we get our little Valentine's cherub from." Jackson's eyes returned to the pastries he was working on instead of staring into Marie's eyes. Marie, however, kept watching him.

"Enough with the thesis statement, get to the actual story," Charles called from the other side of the room, hucking a bag of flour on top of a stack.

"Yes, yes. Psyche was a princess, the youngest of three. She was considered the loveliest of all, the most beautiful. Her beauty even challenged Aphrodite's, as her admirers said."

"And Aphrodite doesn't like it when mere mortals are said to be prettier than her." Charles appeared at the other side of the table, grinning away. Jackson glanced up at him with a glare for interrupting the story, but nodded. Marie's hands had stopped rolling dough in favor of just listening.

"So, hearing these claims from the mortals, Aphrodite sent Eros to shoot Psyche with one of his arrows and make her fall in love with the most vile creature on earth. Then she would never look at one of her admirers ever again, and they would all leave her alone, never to speak of her again." Jackson nudged Marie gently out of the way to take over the pie crust creation. "Unbeknownst to Aphrodite, all of the men who wanted to see Psyche didn't show any interest in marrying her. Two of them went on to marry her sisters. So her father, upset over the situation, went to the Oracles of Delphi to ask them what he should do."

Jackson's story continued, speaking of how Psyche was destined by the gods to marry a horrible serpent monster, Eros rescuing her and hiding her away, the rule that Psyche must never look upon Eros so that the secret could stay safe. He described Psyche breaking the rule, having to prove her love to Eros by performing a set of three tasks as given by Aphrodite. The story ended happily, with Psyche turning immortal so that they could be together forever and Aphrodite getting her way when the mortal men returned to worshipping her. Marie was rapt the entire time, and I couldn't help but notice she was drawing some similarities between herself and Psyche. Perhaps Jackson had done this on purpose after all.

Vincent

Monday, September 21, 2020

"THEY LIVED IN EROS' palace together after that. Psyche was immortal and therefore would never have to leave him. They were happy, Aphrodite was happy, and Psyche had proven herself." Jackson ended his story with a smile, looking over at Marie with a grin. She returned it, and even raised her hands to clap a few times.

"That was lovely!" She giggled softly, readjusting her position on her stool. "You would do great on the radio." The compliment was sincere, but Jackson laughed at it gently.

"Oh I'd love to, but it's unfortunately an exclusive club, and I don't know anyone there." Jackson said nonchalantly, not even thinking about how his words could come off until Marie blushed and he caught it out of the corner of his eye. He dropped his rolling pin and lifted his head to meet her now-embarrassed gaze. "I'm sorry, it's genuinely a lovely idea, and I would jump on it in a heartbeat, given the chance. I've actually tried at a couple stations, but was turned away each time, so I've given up on it for now. But not forever." He grinned, hoping his lingering resentment hadn't made her feel too bad. He hadn't meant to shoot her down immediately. Jackson was still working out exactly how sheltered Marie was to the world, and her having been denied very little all her life was definitely a mindset he'd been getting used to.

"Well, *I* would love to listen to your show," Marie said, and smiled. Jackson's heart lifted, grateful he hadn't been the cause of a wall between them.

"I'd be on it, as well, and I'd have to continually remind him that it's supposed to be for storytelling, not picking apart every single bit of symbolism that could possibly be there," Charles spoke up, not looking at them as he laid a pie crust in a baking dish, tapping the edges down.

"So you're signing yourself up to be the comedic relief?" Jackson asked, picking up a little ball of hardened dough and flicking it at him. Charles dodged it as Marie laughed.

"Sure, your monotone droning voice will put anyone to sleep." Charles shrugged.

"It could be 'Jackson's Bedtime Story Hour,'" Marie said through giggles, covering her mouth to hide her grin. Jackson whirled around, jaw dropped in feigned shock and offense.

"He's gotten to you! I have to ban you from the bakery so that you're never in his company!" He said, picking Marie up and making to carry her outside. He managed to get to the next table before Marie's laughter and squirming made him stop, setting her on the edge of it.

"Sir! You have no—" a pause for a breathless giggle, "no say in whom I spend my time with!" She was trying desperately to look furious, but it fell apart into more laughter. Jackson grinned. Her smile had such a hold on his heart, and I found myself looking over her face and joyous expression with him, taking it all in. I didn't think I'd ever seen a more beautiful person in my entire life. Well, except for maybe Katiyana.

—◇—

My "ogling," as Dan would have put it, was interrupted by my alarm going off, and I dragged myself out of the delightful dream with a long groan. I lay there, staring at the ceiling, burning the image of Marie laughing into my brain as deeply as I could. No wonder Jackson was already head over heels for her—she was pure light. Every time she stepped into the room it brightened, the air lightened and infused with the scent of her perfume. I closed my eyes and tried to imagine it, tried to smell that mix of floral scents while waking. It didn't work, but that was to be expected. The memory of it from the dream would have to be enough.

I took a quick moment to type out the bullet points of the dream into my notes, then rolled out of bed to get ready for school. Maybe next time I was at the library I'd research perfumes from that era, see if I could find out which one it was. Surely there were a few that had survived a hundred years? I'd seen antique perfume bottles on social media and in the windows of some of the shops in town. There had to be something that was the same.

I ended up not waiting for the library and instead researched on my phone during lunch, texting Dan to see if he knew anything at all about perfume. I ended up in a group chat with him and Fleur, whom he had roped into helping. Why they had to be at Corp instead of Cridhe today, of all days, was beyond me.

Beefaroni: Did you say it smelled warm?

RedSam: yeah, warm but floral? Does that make sense?

BlondeBrainiac: Yes, that's normal for women's perfumes. Here, look at the ones on this article, it might help.

I opened the link. I hadn't even thought of looking up stuff from fashion magazines. It was a list called "20 Perfumes Made in the 20s" that some fashion website had put up for the new decade. There were a lot of fancy bottles and what looked like French names, and scent notes I could barely begin to comprehend.

Beefaroni

That Shalimar one looks like it might be right

RedSam

i dunno, i can't smell it through the phone

Beefaroni

Read the scent notes you dummy

RedSam

dan i have to tell you i have no idea what tonka beans are.

Beefaroni

Oh, you're hopeless.

BlondeBrainiac

I think that one is a good place to start, and then Lanvin Arpège next

Beefaroni

At least Fleur knows what's up

RedSam

i am thankful to you both! Where does one go for old perfumes?

BlondeBrainiac

There's a fragrance store in the mall, and a counter at the department store

Beefaroni

YOU ARE HOPELESS

thank you fleur at least you're nice to me

Do you want me to smack dan when I see him?

yes!

Oh i'm hiding for the rest of the day. Vinny I'll take you shopping after school

Why are you hunting for perfume, anyway?

Before I had a chance to respond, the bell rang and I had to drag myself away from researching Marie's perfume and focus on school instead. I couldn't even really answer Fleur's question. I hadn't told anyone but Dan and Leon about the dreams, and I had no idea how Fleur would react. But the truth was, I didn't actually know. It just felt important to have, and it seemed like I had to give it back to Marie somehow. What a long shot that was going to be.

Dan didn't give me a chance to back out or even catch my breath after school, he just grabbed hold of my arm at the train station and kept hold of me until we got off the mall stop.

"I really wasn't planning on ditching you," I laughed, brushing off my sleeve once he finally let go.

"You tried last time we were here."

"You were trying to buy me a new wardrobe with your birthday money." I rolled my eyes, hiking my backpack farther onto my shoulders and following him through sliding glass doors.

"Well maybe you should have let me." He did an obvious "look" at my outfit and I gave him a bewildered one back. We were both still in our uniforms. I opened my mouth to retort but he started laughing and led me down the mall hallway to the first of two department stores.

We went through every perfume department and even hit up a specialty perfume store, but came out empty handed. We were sitting near the fountain in the center of the mall, Dan looking over the directory to see what other stores could possibly carry fragrance.

"Maybe it's not made anymore?" I mused, slumping down on the bench and laying my head on the top of the backrest.

"No, it is, the article explicitly said so and it's on their website." Dan frowned, squinting harder at the directory. "Let's try two more shops, then I'll resign to just ordering it online." I sighed and closed my eyes. This was way too much effort just for a perfume neither of us had ever even heard of before today. He was dead-set on it but I was ready to just let it go, despite my urgency from the morning. He tugged me off the bench as I groaned softly and shuffled behind him. This was ridiculous—it was just a perfume. I didn't even really have that much interest in finding it.

I stopped briefly. That was a lie. I'd just lied to myself. If I found it, I would know what Marie's chosen scent was, and that felt important. I shook my head of the lie and followed Dan with new vigor. Maybe it would unlock something else that the spell Alexis had given me couldn't.

The first shop we went to was another strike out; it was one of those stores you only find in malls that's filled with display swords, fountains, and incense burners. I'm not sure why Dan had wanted to check there in the first place. But we had better luck at the next shop. It was tucked between two chain stores with rivaling aesthetics, one dark and edgy, the other pink and bubbly. This one was run by an older man who had glasses on a chain around his neck, a thick book in his hand, and a name tag that said "James." The store could have been categorized as an antiques shop if it had furniture in it, but it seemed to mostly have dusty books, snow globes, and other random decorative items. Oddly enough, there was a tray full of mismatched spoons as well.

"Hello sir. We're looking for something specific," Dan said, not even giving the man a chance to answer, but he lowered his book and nodded, patiently letting Dan give his speech. "It's a perfume that has been around since the 1920s, clear bottle with a blue lid. Shalimar?"

"Ah, yes, I know what you're looking for. One moment." He set his book on the counter, then went into the back room. We couldn't see what he was doing, exactly, but heard him rustling about. Dan looked at me smugly, definitely feeling like he'd already won whatever secret bet he'd made between us and never let me in on.

A few moments later, the man returned with a small blue box with gold letters on the front that were a little worn. One corner of the box was dented.

"This is it," the man said, lifting the lid of the box to reveal the very same bottle we'd been looking at online. My eyebrows raised, and Dan gasped softly, dramatically.

"Could we smell it?" He asked, glancing up at the man and setting his hand near the box, obviously wanting to just grab it.

"Sure, but it's been around for a while so the scent may have turned." The man lifted the bottle and popped the top off, pumping the spritzer a few times before it managed a weak mist. Dan held out his arm and the man sprayed a little on his skin. After waving his arm around a little bit, Dan held it to his nose and inhaled. He fell against the counter theatrically, sighing.

"Oh, it smells like a dream," he breathed, standing up straight again. "Here." He held his arm out to me and I leaned forward to take a whiff.

Oh. He wasn't joking. My heart skipped a beat, my breath caught in my throat, and my eyes widened. "That's it," I whispered, blinking away images of Marie's smile and laughter, her holding this bottle out to Jackson to let him inspect it. That hadn't been in any of the dreams. Could this actually be her perfume bottle? The likeliness made me stagger.

"Brilliant. How much for it, sir?" I heard Dan ask, but missed the answer as I held my hand to my forehead, trying to root myself back into reality. I took a deep breath and closed my eyes, sending imaginary roots all the way down to the center of the earth from my spine. Fleur had taught me this trick last school year when she'd witnessed one of my anxiety attacks, and I'd used it since. By the time I was done being lightheaded, Dan had a bag slung over his arm and was shaking my shoulder.

"You good bro?" He asked, and I nodded, not trusting my voice to be my own. Surely it would come out as Jackson's right now. He turned and thanked the man once more, slid his arm through mine, and we walked out of the mall together. I didn't say a word the whole time. He didn't speak again until we were at the train station.

"Did you have an allergic reaction to it or something, honey?"

"No, no it just... rocketed me back to my dream this morning, I guess. That's gotta be the exact one. It smells a little... different? Maybe the plants changed over the years or something but, that's it," I said, leaning my head back and taking another deep breath. "All I could see was Marie for a good bit. It was weird."

"Well they do say that scent is the strongest memory trigger." He shrugged, digging the box out of the bag and popping it open to look at the little bottle. "Amazing that the weird knick-knack shop had it, and none of the other places. This looks like a really old bottle, too." Dan was inspecting it and I turned my head to watch him squint at it, holding it up to the light so he could see how much was left in it. "Want to take it home with you to see if you trigger anything else?" He re-packaged the little bottle, setting it securely in the small indent the box had.

"I thought you were going to give it to one of your dates?" I asked. Then it hit me, and I narrowed my eyes at him. "Unless you tricked me again and you always meant to buy it for me." He averted his gaze, then did a terrible job of hiding a grin. "Oh my god, Dan. You can't keep doing this."

"I can, and I most absolutely will." He beamed at me, dropping the bag in my lap. "Have fun spraying that on your pillow to bring about more dreams of your lovely lady." He laughed, and I grabbed the bag before it fell, considering the idea.

"I hate it when you have good ideas," I grumbled, and Dan laughed again. He knew I was just complaining to complain. In truth, I really appreciated it. It was going to be hard to hide from mom, especially since it was way more of a feminine scent than a masculine one, but it would be worth it to have Marie's scent around. I smirked and tugged my backpack off so I could stash it in there. "Thanks, Dan."

"You are SO very much welcome, my darling boy." He reached over to ruffle my hair with a chuckle.

Dan spent the remainder of the time waiting for the train quizzing me about my latest dream, and due to that I remembered I hadn't written it down beyond bullet points yet, so I told him everything as I typed.

"How long have they known each other at this point?" He asked, peering around me as the train started pulling in. I shook my head, unsure.

"At least a few weeks? I don't know if the dreams are chronological or if they're skipping around. Based on how close they're getting, it must have been long enough to feel comfortable teasing each other. Maybe a month or two?"

"If only more calendars were visible in your dreams." Dan sighed wistfully, and I laughed with a nod.

"Oh if only." Mabon was the next day, so maybe the spell would give me more answers. I voiced the thought to Dan as we sat down on the train.

"I hope so! This not knowing is killing me. I can't imagine how frustrated it makes you." He leaned back and opened Instagram, immediately tapping on the messages section. I looked away out of habit. I had read over his shoulder exactly once and decided to never do it again.

"Yeah, it's pretty bad. Guess we'll see."

"We shall indeed."

Katiyana

Tuesday, September 22, 2020

WAKING UP WITHOUT A dream in my memory banks had become one of the worst ways to start my day. I didn't get the satisfaction of learning just a tad bit more about Marie and Jackson, didn't get to see them bickering with Charles. I made a note of the non-existent dream in my book before I stumbled out of bed, pushing my glasses on and heading for my wardrobe. I'd showered before I went to bed, so I had more time to goof around this morning. Maybe I'd do my hair in a more complicated style than a braid. Maybe I'd make a fancy breakfast for myself. The world—well, the morning, at least—was my oyster. I glanced at the calendar in my room and then hurriedly glanced again as I noticed what day it was.

"Ah," I vocalized, letting my shoulders slump. It was the day I was supposed to cast the spell from Alexis. Mabon had snuck up on me, as I was hanging out with my friends and staying on top of homework. I picked idly at a stubborn bit of paint on my arm that I hadn't managed to scrub off, and frowned. I would have to talk to Nick today to see if he was going anywhere tonight. I had to do it in a way that didn't seem suspicious, either. If he were going to be in our apartment, I would do the spell at Valerie's. She'd already given me permission without me even needing to ask. Alexis must have told her something. I had gotten used to being a subject of coven gossip over the years, *lucky me.*

I stopped my brooding and changed into my uniform, pulling a sweater over my head, thankful our uniforms changed with the seasons. Cold was starting to set in on the island and our short sleeved polo shirts weren't going to cut it much longer.

Nick was nowhere to be seen when I came out of my room. His bedroom door was even cracked open enough for a peek and there was no brother in there. *Maybe he's at work.* It was plausible, it's not like he had ever once shared his schedule with me. Even Mom and Dad had only a vague idea of when he'd be gone. Oh well for now, I'd have to talk to him if he was here after school.

During lunch, Jamari was super curious about the spell and asked if I was open to spectators. I laughed through a mouthful of chow mein noodles, covering my mouth with my hand as she stared at me completely seriously. After I managed to swallow, I giggled and finally answered.

"Spectators? I have to do this right before I go to sleep. There's no way your moms are going to approve of a sleep-over in the middle of the school week."

"Damn, I guess that's true," she said, frowning and stabbing at what was probably supposed to be a meatloaf.

"Sorry Jami. Why do you want to see it so badly, any-way?" I asked, twirling myself another forkful of noodles. Fleur and Alena looked at her, as well, waiting for the answer. Jamari shrugged.

"I just want to see if it's any different than mine." She pushed a forkful of loaf-shaped meat into her mouth and ducked down, sure her sister was going to come after her with some teasing. To everyone's surprise, it didn't hap-pen. Fleur's response was calm and nonchalant, no trace of teasing in her tone at all.

"Alexis mentioned something about a group ritual dur-ing the Harvest Festival. You're sure to see another spell then."

"Oh, that's right. Are you working the Festival?" Alena chimed in, nudging Jamari's arm with her elbow. Jamari shook her head.

"I think Alexis wants it to run as smoothly as possible, and that means no newbies hanging around potentially asking too many questions. I'm only allowed to help set up beforehand."

"Can't say I blame her," Fleur laughed, her teasing tone back. Jamari was in agreement so the teasing jab was lost to the ether.

After school, home was quiet once more, and I set my bag down slowly in my room as if making a single noise other than a footstep would summon Nick from the shadows. After checking his room and even Mom and Dad's room and finding him either invisible or gone once more, I finally caved and texted him.

LilTriquetra

I haven't seen you all day so I'm just texting to see if you're dead or not.

It wasn't the kindest message I could have sent, but it would be the least suspicious. Scrolling back in our chat log, I'd sent three other similar messages in the last few months. This is what happened when you never told your family your schedule. It took him well over an hour to respond, and I'd already changed out of my uniform and was busy tidying my room to make space for a circle should I need it.

KunoichisOnly

I'm fine, don't wait up for me.

LilTriquetra

Does that mean you're not coming home tonight?

KunoichisOnly

It means I'm busy and I'm probably not going to be home until morning.

LilTriquetra

Got it.

He'd probably been trying to not answer my question, but he had. So that meant I was free to do my spell in the peace and quiet of an empty apartment, in the comfort of my own bedroom. Alexis said the candle would burn for about three hours, so I'd have to start the spell at eight p.m. I had a while until then.

The hours between Nick's message and eight o'clock felt horribly tense and anxious. I was ready to start the spell right that second, but I knew I shouldn't. I ate dinner in slow, careful bites, chewing each one far more thoroughly than necessary. I couldn't keep my eyes off the clock above the stove, the one on the microwave, and I even checked my phone lock screen probably two dozen times. Finally, I had to give up and go take a cleansing meditation bath just to calm myself down and force forty-five minutes to pass without me counting every half-second of it. Even that only worked so much, as I was still tapping my fingers on my desk impatiently while I forced myself through another few thumbnail sketches for my art assignments.

I glanced at my phone. One more hour.

I drew two thumbnails, messily shaded them in, and labeled them. Then glanced at my phone. Forty more minutes.

"Okay, how did a single thumbnail only take ten minutes?" I groaned, pushing away from my desk and standing up to pace. Why did the timing have to be so precise?! What was I supposed to do for the three hours the candle was burning, anyway? Stare at it and watch the wax drip? Those instructions had not been included on Alexis's handwritten little card. I scrubbed my fingers against my scalp, holding onto my hair out of frustration. But I'd been raised by the coven—I knew better. Surely as long as I kept an eye on the candle for safety reasons, I was free to do whatever I pleased. Sometimes spells were literally just set it and forget it. Alexis had literally said I could contact her, but I didn't know her well besides being the coven mother, so it felt weird somehow. But ultimately, I trusted her and her instructions.

I gave up and went into the living room, planning to absorb myself into the television for however long until the alarm I set on my phone went off. It was a last-ditch effort to get myself to stop thinking about the spell until it was time, and I was overjoyed to find it had worked.

A commercial break ended, my phone started playing loud video game music, and I grinned. *Finally*, I thought, *finally*. It was going to be weird doing a spell without Mom or one of my aunts hovering over my shoulder.

Alexis hadn't said anything about needing a circle for this spell, but I was used to it and felt better with one, so I set about tracing as wide of a circle as I could around the boundary of my room. I didn't have a wand just yet—Mom said that would come as part of my training—so I just pointed and imagined a beam of light flowing from my finger, almost like a sparkler. I traced it three times over and then pulled everything from my desk to the middle of my floor, near the footboard of my bed. I had a little lap desk I was using as an altar. It wasn't fancy, but it would get the job done.

I had four little sandstone animal carvings that I'd collected from various family trips and gotten as gifts over the years, and I placed them in each cardinal direction on my lap desk. A little mouse in the north for earth, a butterfly to the east for air, a lion in the south for fire, and an octopus in the west for water. Sinéad had given the lion to my mom when I was born, and Mom had kept it safe for me until I was old enough to be considered responsible with potentially breakable objects. Each one had their own little matching call, and as I whispered them to the little animals, I felt each one's presence settle around my room, patient guardians to watch over me and my spellwork. My fingertips were beginning to tingle, a familiar sensation whenever I worked magic.

The next step had always been done by Mom or an aunt, so I paused and had to think for a moment before deciding on who to call in as protective deities. Brigit was easy, and as I grabbed her carved stone from my nightstand, I felt her energy before I even said anything aloud. I laughed gently, glad she was here with me.

Calling in a god was a different matter, and I sat there for a few minutes ruminating over it, until I felt a gentle nudge and a whisper: *"Morpheus."* I blinked but nodded, asking him to join me in my dreamworking, since it would be his realm I dipped into. His presence wasn't clear, wasn't as loud as Brigit, but the heavier, darker energy to the right of my makeshift altar was enough of a response for me. It didn't matter that they were from different pantheons; the Faodail coven I'd grown up in had always worked with both.

The spell itself was about ten times simpler than casting the circle had been. I settled the candle in its holder, sprinkling a little bit of the mugwort around the base. Alexis's notes said the mugwort was to go in my pillowcase, but a little pinch around the candle wouldn't hurt anything. I'd seen Mom do this a bunch of times. I had to scramble to my desk to get my lighter. I'd really have to prepare better for my next spell.

Once the candle was lit, I took a deep breath and settled in front of the altar, looking it over and resting my hands on my knees. The pouch of mugwort was waiting on my bed where I'd tossed it, ready to be tucked into my pillowcase. I couldn't bear the thought of feeling the little flakes on my bedsheets, so I was absolutely adapting that portion of the spell. All that was left was the incantation. I lifted the paper from under my lap desk and read it over a couple times. Then I spoke, my voice gentle at first, then rising to a powerful timbre I didn't even know I had.

"By herb and flame and sincerity, bring these memories back to me.

Souls across the ages, free them from self-imposed cages.

My history belongs to me, come to my dreams, let me see."

I repeated this three times over as instructed, laying the paper back in my lap when finished. I was winded, suddenly drained, and I leaned back against my footboard to catch my breath. With my eyes closed and head tilted back, I whispered:

"So mote it be."

Vincent

Tuesday, September 22, 2020

I'D GOTTEN SO, SO very lucky. Mom was working an overnight shift, and had left around eight p.m. She wouldn't be home until four a.m. at the earliest. I suppressed the urge to dance, to shout in joy about the situation. I couldn't remember a single time where luck had been so entirely on my side. I wasted the last hour or so before my chosen start time by sprucing up the notes in my file, trying to get as clear of a picture as possible in my head before I set about the spell. I knew there was something called a magic circle, but I didn't know the first thing about making one, and I was too anxious to go and look it up. It probably required things I didn't have right then anyway.

My desk made a fine makeshift altar. I set the candle in its holder right in the center of it, pushing books and my lamp aside. I pulled the bottle of perfume that I was becoming increasingly certain was actually Marie's from its box and set it down next to the candle, but then changed my mind and set it on the nightstand instead once I remembered that perfume is flammable. It was probably overly cautious, but it seemed to be the only bottle of the stuff on all of Faodail, so I didn't want to take any chances.

After a moment of staring at the bottle, I picked it back up and spritzed some onto my shirt. Apparently Mom being gone had given me a new surge of courage. If I managed to hide the candle holder once the candle burned out, she'd never know, and surely the smell of the perfume would fade by the time she got back. Marie's chosen scent washed over me, and I shivered. Maybe the boost of scent memory would help the spell be stronger. If not, at least I was enveloped in this beautifully-scented cloud as I worked.

I scrounged up a lighter from mom's room, taking precise note of where she'd had it and bringing it back as soon as I had the candle lit. I was taking a lot of chances already, so I didn't need to add "thievery" to my list. Settling back at my desk, I tucked my nose into my shirt for just a brief moment more before sitting straight in my chair and taking a deep breath, closing my eyes and calming my energy to prepare for the spell. I had never done anything like this before, but if intuition was serving, a clear mind and a focused heart were going to be key.

The candle flame snapped once, flicking toward me as if saying, "get on with it already," and I lifted the sheet of paper Alexis had given me. The incantation was three lines long, and I was meant to repeat it three times before letting the candle burn out. Which would also take three hours. I made a mental note to look into the magical properties behind the number three.

"Alright then," I whispered to myself, squaring my shoulders and holding the paper with both hands in front of the candle. I had planned to whisper all three times, but before I knew it, I was speaking as if I were at school presenting a project in front of the class. My voice was clear and I felt the support from my diaphragm as I projected each syllable out into the universe, my eyes slipping closed on the last round, Marie's perfume rising to meet my breath.

"By herb and flame and sincerity, bring these memories back to me.

Souls across the ages, free them from self-imposed cages.

My history belongs to me, come to my dreams, let me see."

My voice felt as if it had trailed off into space, and I lifted my head to see if I could witness the energy rising through the roof and out toward the cosmos, out to any deity that was listening. Another phrase crossed my lips before I even knew what I was saying:

"So mote it be."

The Dreamers

Tuesday, September 22, 2020

THEY BOTH OPENED THEIR eyes to the familiar back room at the bakery, Charles happily humming away to whatever song was currently stuck in his head as he kneaded dough and slowly inched closer and closer to the ovens for warmth.

The girl was the first to speak, looking over at the baker with a soft grin. "He's so charming," she said, and blinked in realization as she noticed her control over the dream. She lifted her hand with a smile, wiggling her fingers to test it. She hadn't had a lucid dream in ages.

Her counterpart sat across from her at the table and looked up as she spoke. He'd already noticed his lucidity, judged solely by the way his knee was bouncing in anxious thought. He watched her move, looking over the satin and lace skirt folded around her knees.

"Marie?" He asked, unsurely, probingly. She turned and nodded.

"Y-yeah, Jackson?" Her voice sounded unsure, as well, not like it had before.

"You don't...sound like yourself." He stood, leaning a little closer to peer into her eyes. She leaned back, holding onto the edge of the table as pink flushed her cheeks and she looked away.

"Neither do you, now that you mention it," she mumbled, pushing a curl behind her ear. He sat back, noting the discomfort that had never been there before. They sat in silence for a few moments. He folded his arms over his chest and she drummed her fingers on the table, watching them move. His eyes never left her.

"Why do you sound like a teenager?" He finally asked, placing the casual accent. She laughed.

"Why do you?" She grinned at him, and despite it being Marie's face, it wasn't the same grin. This one was teasing, a little nervous. Not the same joyous one he'd grown used to.

"Well, that might be because I am one," he responded. She looked at him, bewildered.

"That doesn't make any sense, the spell said I was supposed to see my memories more clearly, something must have gotten mixed up—" The girl was stammering now, and she stood up to pace away, looking over at Charles to see if he noticed. The baker continued kneading bread.

The boy got up to follow her, gently taking a hold of her elbow and dropping it just as quickly when she startled.

"Sorry, did you say a spell? Did you cast a spell before you went to sleep?" He asked, urgency clear and fierce in his voice. She stared at him for a moment then nodded.

"I did, why do you want to know?" She crossed her arms, taking a step back and bumping into the other table. She was nervous, but still wanted information.

"I did too," he breathed, reaching back to find the table they'd been sitting at, holding onto it as his heart picked up speed. "Alexis told me to burn the candle—"

"For three hours before bedtime. Put the mugwort under your pillow," she finished, and he looked up at her, alarmed and overjoyed.

"You're on Faodail?"

"Born and raised, yeah." She shrugged, her heart suddenly racing to match his. They stared at each other, both processing what this meant, until she finally broke the silence.

"Meadhan or Ceangal?" She smirked, trying to lighten the oppressive tension, the heavier-than-air anticipation. He smirked back.

"Ceangal."

"Me too," she whispered.

He finally reached out a hand through the thick air, and her fingers slid gently into his. Marie and Jackson had held hands before, it was nothing new to either dreamer. And yet...

"So how do we find each other?" He asked, looking down at their hands. Hers pulled back. He looked up, confused and a little hurt, if he was going to be honest with himself.

"Wait, no, we need to talk a little. I know for a fact now that I'm dreaming of my past life, and if you're dreaming of Jackson, that must mean you're his...future life? This is a little confusing." She leaned back more heavily against the table, and he dropped his hand. "Okay more than a little, this is a lot confusing. How can we just both happen to be on Faodail at the same time, and Alexis, of all people, gives us the same spell, but doesn't tell us anything?" She looked up at him, her eyes darting back and forth between his as if she could read the answers there. He looked just as unsure.

"Alexis and Leon both told me that I had to figure things out in my own time, through my own eyes and thoughts. They said they didn't want to cloud any of my memories."

"You talked to Leon." It wasn't a question. "Sinéad won't even let me talk to Leon. Oh I'm going to march right to his office tomorrow and give him a piece of my mind! Oh, I hate these coven rules...I'm going to complain to the coven mother." She was growling her words, her hands lifting into claws. He suppressed a laugh.

"I don't think they're doing it to make our lives hard. Although, yeah, it is really annoying." He sighed again, pushing hair back from his face that wasn't his. "Well, why don't we just talk to them both tomorrow? We can kick Chief Regulus's door down and then go to Ladine's after school." He looked up to find she was nodding, obviously running other plans through her mind.

"That...that sounds fine, yeah. Except now I'm going to be staring at anyone who looks remotely like Jackson and hoping it's you just so we can interrogate people together." She laughed listlessly. She was still thrown off by the fact Jackson's modern-day counterpart had been practically right around the corner all along. She was also ready to march to her cousin's office and tell her off for forty minutes straight.

"That's one of the issues—I look nothing like Jackson," he said, lifting his hand to look at the skin that was many shades lighter than his own. "We're almost polar opposites." He had a realization and laughed softly, his voice lowering. "Honestly, Dan looks more like Jackson than I do."

"Dan. I know a Dan. Have we been a single person away this whole time, and Alexis and Sinéad and Leon and Valerie didn't even tell us?" Her words were quickly strung together and got higher-pitched as she spoke, as she ran out of breath.

"I guess so, if it's the same Dan." He shifted his weight to hop up on the table, leaning his elbows on his knees.

"Spiky hair, sunglasses, texts back in point-four seconds because he's always on his phone? That Dan?" She asked, copying him to sit on the other table. His eyes widened.

"Uh, yeah. Wow. That Dan." He laughed, then stopped as his breath caught. "Wait, is... is your name Katiyana?"

"How do you know that?"

"I...we...we go to the same school. Oh my god." He put a hand to his forehead, laughing in disbelief, mostly at himself. "I've literally already seen your face, and I even thought your eyes were the same. Wow, I am so stupid." He was still laughing, and she finally dropped her shoulders as realization dawned on her face.

"You're Vincent, aren't you?" Her words were accompanied by a small, slightly nervous giggle. He really *had* been around the corner.

"Yeah." He chuckled, much less nervously, much more relieved. He wanted to run to her as soon as she got to the train station the next morning.

"I guess I can message Dan and tell him to march you straight to me?" She ventured, peeking at him over her arm. He nodded.

"That works. I'll tell him the full story on my end. He already knows everything else. I've told him every dream so far."

"I've told my friends everything too."

"Group meeting, then, it sounds like," he mused playfully, lacing his fingers together.

"Sounds like," she parroted, leaning back on her hands. The moment stretched longer than it felt like it should, and she looked up to sneak a peek at him. She'd grown used to his blonde hair and blue eyes, and she was pretty sure Vincent had black and brown, respectively. It would be a bit of a trip, talking to the same person that looked so very different. He glanced up to find her looking and she looked away, pink rising to her cheekbones once more. He grinned. She might not be Marie, but it seemed she was exactly his type after all.

He doubled over, holding his side. He hissed softly in pain, struggling to breathe through gritted teeth.

"Holy shit, are you okay?" She asked, jumping off the table to hurry to him, hands trying to move his away from his side to see. He looked up, trying to memorize the slightly different shade of silver in her worried eyes.

"Meet me at school," he whispered, before jolting out of the dream and into a nightmare.

Vincent

Wednesday, September 23, 2020

"—THINK YOU'RE DOING UNDER my roof, having a fucking candle burning while you're asleep, what is wrong with you!" I heard her words through the sound of her fists striking whatever part of me she could reach, and I threw my arms up to protect my face—

But her knuckles caught me under the eyebrow and I sucked in a hard, sharp breath as pain exploded around my eye and out to my ear. I tucked my arms around my head, one palm pressed to the eye she'd struck, and curled up into a ball as she continued her pounding.

I caught snippets of her shouting, cursing me for nearly burning the house down, for wasting money on candles and fancy shit I didn't need. I hadn't even fallen asleep with the candle burning...I heard a thunk and my heart stopped; the perfume bottle. I'd left everything out and fallen asleep. She had seen it all—the remnants of the spell, the perfume—I was dead. I was going to be lucky if they could even identify my body by the time she was done with me.

She shouted, not a word but a wild animalistic noise, and I peered through my fingers as she stopped hitting me. She was holding her wrist, slowly bending and unbending her fingers as she stared at them. I hid my eye with my fingers as she looked back down.

"Now look at what you've gone and made me do. I've probably broken my goddamn finger just because I had to punish you." She kicked at my bed, then turned. I heard the perfume bottle roll across the floor and prayed it hadn't broken. I lay still, making note of all the places that hurt. I couldn't think much further past the ache in my head, and I pressed my palm against my temple probingly. I regretted the action instantly as the pain bloomed anew under the touch. I bit my lip to keep from crying out, tears leaking to my pillow. A hundred miles away, the front door slammed and mom's car started. Normally that would have brought a sigh of relief, but I just broke. It had been so good for so long, it had been such a good streak.

I sobbed. I hadn't cried in a while, and so the dam just broke. I nearly choked on my tears a couple of times. I buried myself under my blankets and pressed my face to my pillow to muffle my wailing. I didn't need the neighbors to hear me and find me like this.

I don't know how long I cried, I didn't know what time it was, all I knew is that I had been ripped from the most pleasant and informative dream I'd had all month and thrown into a gladiator ring I'd never signed up for. My throat was raw and dry, my face cracked from dried tears, and every little movement of my jaw brought a fresh helping of searing pain across my temple and eye.

Somehow, I managed to tug my phone closer by the charging cord and see that it was 5:40 a.m. Mom must have had to stay late. I sniffed and regretted it, pressing the edge of my sheet to my nose instead. I'd wash them later. I didn't care right now. My alarm was meant to go off at 7:00 a.m., but there was no way I was going to be able to sleep now.

I stumbled, nearly falling out of bed, my hand still pressed to my eye. I looked around in the dark for the perfume bottle and spotted it next to the door on its side. Thanking every single deity that existed, I picked up the unbroken bottle and hid it away in my backpack, where it should have been all along.

I needed to clean myself up. I could taste blood but I wasn't sure if it was on my face or not. Mom must have split open my cheek again. I probed both sides of my mouth with my tongue but didn't find anything, figuring that I must have a bloody nose. Sure enough, it was on my sheets when I flipped on my lamp to check. Not having the willpower or the strength to strip the bed, I held onto the wall as I slowly made my way to the bathroom, not even bothering to look in the mirror until I'd rinsed my face with warm water and gingerly patted it dry.

The skin around my eye was already turning black, the eye itself bloodshot, redness concentrated in the corner. I didn't want this face to be mine. I rinsed it gently twice more, then gave up, stripped, and stepped into the shower. I noticed more bruises slowly blossoming around my ribs and on my leg. The one that had woken me up was oddly small. It felt like it needed to be bigger, more significant. I poked it and winced. Maybe it was bigger under the skin.

The hot water and steam somehow managed to loosen my stiff muscles, and I stayed in there, lowering myself to just sit on the shower floor until the water turned ice cold. Even after I'd turned off the stream I sat there, holding my head in my hands and staring at the water running down the drain. This was the worst Mom had ever hurt me. She usually avoided the face, but that was twice in one month now. I'm still not sure exactly how long I sat there, but I suppose that's what happens when you dissociate.

I didn't go back to bed. I was on autopilot and started running myself through the normal get-ready routine without thinking. I winced as I combed my temple by accident, tossing the comb back into the drawer and ignoring the rest of my hair. I didn't care. Nothing mattered. Mom had pulled me out of my dream before I was able to make any solid plans with Katiyana, with Marie's counterpart. Meet at school, that's all we had. Involve Dan somehow. Who could say if he'd even want to help me once I told him his current romantic interest was quite literally the girl of my dreams? I wouldn't be shocked at all if he just told me to go to hell.

I pulled up the transit app on my phone. The trains were running. The marina was fifteen minutes away. I stared at the train number that would take me to it, burning it into my memory, then dropped my phone into my pants pocket and pulled on my coat. After a moment, I shoved my witchcraft book into my backpack and shrugged it onto my shoulders. Except for the bruise slowly darkening a fourth of my face, I looked like any normal high school kid in Ceangal. I was just two hours early for class.

The train station was silent, only a few people reading newspapers and drinking coffee for breakfast. I pulled up my hood in a sorry attempt to hide my face, keeping my head down and trying so, so hard not to look at anyone.

I got on the train heading to the other side of the island and curled up in one of the seats, leaning the injured side of my face toward the wall for better camouflage. With luck, it would just look like a weird shadow. The train pulled out of the station and I headed the opposite direction I normally did, letting the steady chug of the engine and wheels lull me into an exhausted sleep, my hand wrapped securely around the amethyst still around my neck.

Katiyana

Wednesday, September 23, 2020

I WOKE UP GROGGY and confused, staring at the corner of my nightstand until my memories flooded back. We'd talked. We had actually talked in a dream, and not as Marie and Jackson. I hadn't thought about the possibility of Jackson's counterpart having dreams at the same time as me, or at all. I'd always been taught that my past life dreams would be mine—no one except Sinéad had ever mentioned shared ones. But she and Leo were exceptions to this rule, or so I thought. My heart picked up speed and I turned on my bedside lamp, pushed my glasses on, and yanked my notebook from under the mattress. I wrote with such speed that I had to cross out a few words and restart because they were so illegible, but I managed to write down every single thing I could remember. I stared at the pages on my lap as I absorbed the information, remembering how the dream had ended. He'd been in pain. My brow furrowed, and I ran my finger along the sentence describing it. My other hand subconsciously lifted to my amethyst pendant, squeezing it hard.

An image of the train station hit me, along with a deep wave of pain, both emotional and physical. Wait, no, it wasn't the station I normally went to. It was a different one. The buildings around it were different. I grabbed my phone and tapped the transit app, flipping through the provided images of the stations until I found the matching one. It was the one that led to Dubhan. *Why would Vincent go there?* Why did I know it was Vincent suddenly?

It didn't matter, he was clearly in trouble and I was the only one who knew. I didn't have time to process my sudden knowledge that Jackson and Vincent were one and the same, and there wasn't time to question my intuition. I threw the covers off my legs and swung out of bed, getting dressed faster than I ever had. The closest thing to me was the uniform I'd shed after school the previous day. I put on my coat and yanked a beanie onto my head. I pulled on my boots by the door and made sure my keys were in my bag before running down the hallway, stabbing the elevator button repeatedly until I finally heard the engine whine and start rising toward me.

The moment I made it out the door of the building, I started running. I had hardly any time to catch the train that was heading out, managing to jump onto it moments before the doors slid shut. I collapsed into a seat and dug my pendant out from under my shirt again, squeezing it and praying for it to give me another flash of information. I could have cried in that moment, because it did, I saw the marina. He was definitely headed there. We'd already said we'd meet at school tomo—today. We said we'd meet today. I checked the route I was currently riding on the app and discovered I needed to transfer at the next stop—I was heading the wrong way.

I ran off one train and onto another as quickly as I could, securing a seat and settling into it. I had about fifteen minutes to ride now. A sense of dread was growing in my stomach and had been since the moment I'd seen the image of the marina, and I hated that I only partially knew what was causing it.

Vincent

Wednesday, September 23, 2020

I BLINKED AWAKE AS I heard the doors slide open, sitting up and peering out the window. The ocean was closer than I'd seen it in years, and I saw boats bobbing between docks. This was my stop. I hadn't been farther than the Ceangal city limits in so long. I stood, groggy and trembling, gripping the bar in front of my seat as I waited for an opening to slip off the train. I breathed in the cold, salty air, and made my way down the station steps, then off the concrete sidewalk, following a well-worn footpath up a rocky ridge. There was a flat part out at the top, overlooking the ocean. I kept my eyes on it as I made my way toward it, walking slowly to avoid stumbling and casting myself into the ocean earlier than I wanted to.

Katiyana
Wednesday, September 23, 2020

I JOLTED AWAKE A few moments before the train stopped and slid its doors open to release the passengers. I saw someone stand, their hood up, hand gripping the bar in front of them as they swayed. My heart dropped. I hadn't seen his face but I knew that hoodie, the same worn-out green one Vincent always wore over his uniform. I lost him in the crowd as people filed off the train, but as I scanned the area while standing on the station stairs, I spotted him taking the trail up to the overlook. I leapt off the stairs, running after him as fast as my legs could carry me.

Vincent

Wednesday, September 23, 2020

THE OVERLOOK WAS JUST a few steps away, and I dropped my backpack at the spot where the trail widened, tugging my hood off to let the ocean breeze that was slowly building to wind tousle my hair. At the other end of the area was a little bench, and I made my way to it, stepping over it and sitting down, resting my elbows on my knees and lacing my fingers together. The ocean was relatively calm, gently stirred by the wind and the boats coming in and out of the bay. The sun was peeking through a couple clouds in the east. It was a really beautiful day. I closed my eyes and breathed in the scent, slowly exhaling it out. Then I felt a thump on the bench, jumped, and looked over to see my backpack planted on it, the straps held by a girl who was out of breath and staring down at me with silver eyes.

"You—you're not...supposed...to..." Katiyana huffed, then sighed, releasing my backpack to step over the bench and sit down, holding her head and breathing heavily. "Littering is bad," she said, closing her eyes.

"I... I wasn't..." I started, but then closed my mouth. I couldn't stop staring at the same eyes Marie had, but younger. *Katiyana shows up out of nowhere when I'm about to resign myself to whatever fate the universe has in store the moment I step off the cliffs—*

"Don't do it, please," she whispered, finally lifting her head to look me fully in my uninjured eye. "I think I figured out what you're planning and I really, really need you to keep your ass on that bench."

I was completely admonished. My head hung. The small, tiny little spark of fight that I had left in me had gone out as I was ripped out of our dream that morning, so I nodded, agreeing to her request without a word.

We sat in silence for a few minutes as her breathing evened out. It felt like an hour.

"Are you okay?" She asked, and when I looked over she was trying not to look pointedly at my bruised face. I shook my head.

"No. And there's more than just the one on my face." My voice was small, quiet. I'd never admitted this to anyone but Dan before.

"The one on your side probably hurts most, doesn't it?" She asked, glancing toward it.

"Shockingly, it's the least of my worries." I managed a smirk, and she smiled hesitantly back, but her eyes were full of worry.

"Can I call anyone for you? Your parents?"

I cringed at the word and shook my head fiercely. "If I can help it, I'd like to never see my mother again." My voice was more sure than I realized. She went quiet, nodding.

"Dan?" She ventured after a moment. I lifted my hand, wrapping it around the pendant. She moved similarly and I looked over, seeing her staring off at the ocean while gripping her own necklace.

I pulled mine over my head and held it out silently. She lifted her chain over her head as well and dangled an identical pendant above mine.

"I guess you bought the first one." I smirked ever-so-slightly at her, wincing at the pain it brought to my temple. She nodded, looping her necklace back over her head. I kept mine in my hand and lowered it to my lap, tears gathering at the corners of my eyes. This should have been a happy moment. A new relationship to explore, a friend to talk to about magic and past lives with. And here she was, sitting with me in the early morning so I didn't dive off a cliff.

"Do you want me to text Dan?" She ventured again, and I sighed, but nodded.

"I guess."

"We can just go home if you'd rather..." She said, letting her voice trail off once she'd remembered what I said about my mom.

I swallowed back tears, sucking in a shuddering breath. It came out as a sob, and she pushed my bag off the bench between us to scoot closer and wrap an arm around my back. I leaned into her without thinking and ended up sobbing for the second time in one day, gripping the pendant in one hand, the edge of her coat in the other.

Katiyana

Wednesday, September 23, 2020

VINCENT WAS SOBBING AND there wasn't anything I could do but hold him and keep him from taking those few steps toward the ocean. I rested my chin on his shoulder, squeezing him close as he shuddered and cried, feeling tears of my own threatening to spill over. I never imagined being able to meet Jackson's counterpart. I had fancied the idea of him existing but not here, not on Faodail, not the same age as me. And here he was, sobbing in my arms and nearly laying on my lap out of weakness. I felt so helpless. I needed to text someone, call someone. We knew a good number of the same people, but he probably trusted Dan most. I lifted my arm from Vincent's back and dug awkwardly in my pocket for my phone, clumsily tapping to Dan's contact info and holding the phone to my ear as I waited for him to pick up. When he did, he sounded half asleep.

"Hello?" He asked, sniffing. I felt bad waking him up.

"Hi Dan, I uh, I need a big favor." I heard his sheets rustle as he sat up and cleared his throat.

"What is it? How can I help?"

"I'm at the marina. Vincent, he, um..." I paused as I realized I had no idea how to explain what was going on.

"Oh, god. I'm on my way. Don't let him go." Dan hung up before I said anything else, and I sat there for a moment, stunned by the fact that I wasn't stunned that he'd figured out the situation just from me telling him we were at the marina.

"Vincent?" I asked, leaning down to try and see his face. He lifted his head and nodded.

"Sorry." He sniffed, swallowing hard and wiping under his eyes with a sleeve. It was a little futile, he was still crying but had calmed from the shuddering sobs a few minutes ago.

"It's okay. I got a hold of Dan."

"I figured. Thank you." He was pulling away from me to sit up and I scooted a little closer, sliding my arm through his. Vincent looked at me curiously, and I just left my arm where it was. "He told you to keep hold of me, didn't he?" He asked softly, sighing in resignation. "I guess joking about this all those years ago was good for something."

My heart picked up speed and I gripped his sleeve tighter. He lifted his hand and laid it on mine until my grip relaxed, and I looked up to find him looking at me seriously through watery eyes.

"The urge has passed," he whispered, lowering his hand to his lap. I kept my hand where it was anyway.

We sat in silence, listening to the waves and the wind. I closed my eyes and reached out with my heart to Brigit, asking her to lend me just a little bit more strength. I felt her response on the wind, a gentle touch running over the top of my head and a soft renewal of hope in my heart.

"Who are you talking to?" Vincent asked quietly, and I looked over at him. His eyes were dry now, but red, and the black around his bruise was darker than before.

"Brigit," I said it before judging if I was about to be made fun of or not, and he simply nodded.

"What's she like?"

It was odd to have small talk in this situation, knowing what he'd been about to do and what we were to each other, even if it had only been in the past. But it happened. I told him about Brigit and how she spoke to me, the feeling of peace and safety every time I reached out to her. He listened wordlessly, nodding every so often, his fingers tracing the wire wrapping on his pendant. We passed the rest of the time waiting for Dan mostly in silence, Vincent looking over his shoulder around six thirty and turning us both around to watch the sun rise over Faodail.

Before we knew it, someone was running to us and shouting Vincent's name, and we turned to find Dan racing up the footpath to us, two adults who were probably his parents following. Dan's dad pulled me aside and asked me to tell him what happened, so I told him as much of the story as I could while leaving out the fact we'd been dreaming about each other for nearly a month. Dan was hugging Vincent fiercely and trying to hide the near-constant stream of tears flowing from his eyes as Vincent tried to assure him that the urge had passed and he was okay now. Dan tried to lecture him about following these urges and what he should do instead, when his mom stepped in and silenced him with a hand on his shoulder.

"Vincent, can we take you to the clinic? I'm worried about your eye," she said softly, her fingers lifting Vincent's chin with all the familiarity of a mother and son. Vincent seemed to think it over for a second, then nodded.

"Alright. I...I can't pay," he said, gaze dropping. Dan's mom pulled him into a gentle hug, and I saw his eyes well up with tears again.

"We'll take care of it," she said sweetly, kissing the top of his head. Vincent wrapped his arms around her, Dan hugging him from the other side. Dan's father rested a hand on my shoulder and I looked up to meet his gaze.

"Can we drop you off anywhere? Home? School? I don't mind going in to explain to the office for you," he said, and I smiled gratefully.

"If you don't mind, school would be fine. It's early but, oh well."

"And your parents?" He asked.

"They're both off-island right now. My mom is due back at the end of the month, so I'm under the care of my older brother and neighbor at the moment." He nodded at my explanation, seemingly satisfied, and led us back to the car. Dan held Vincent's hand the entire way back, and at one point Vincent reached out to tap mine lightly. Just his pinky against my pinky, and I tapped it back in solidarity. I checked my phone properly. It was devoid of notifications at that moment, but my friends would probably spam-text me when I didn't show up at the train station. I'd have time to tell them at lunch.

As we pulled into the school parking lot, I gathered my things and leaned forward to thank Dan's parents. They told me it was nothing and thanked me for being there for Vincent. I nodded and made to get out of the car when Vincent grabbed the back of my coat.

"Trade me," he said, holding out his pendant. I dropped my bag back onto the seat and pulled my chain over my head, settling it over his instead, and took the pendant from his hand. He smiled. "Thank you. For everything."

I grinned back. "You're welcome, Vinny."

Dan laughed at the nickname as I stepped out of the car and waved, ready to walk in myself when Dan's father got out. I'd forgotten he'd promised to help me explain to the office. We walked in together, and my shoulders slumped in relief as I saw Leon through the glass of the secretary's office. He looked up, saw me, and came rushing out into the hallway to wrap me in a hug. It was a little odd, he'd only ever hugged me at a few family gatherings, but the familiarity and comfort was enough to make me cling to him. I heard him talking with Dan's dad over my head, but I buried my face in his chest and stayed there until he pulled back and knelt down. I was by no means that much shorter than him, but I wasn't going to cause a scene.

"Sinéad woke up really anxious and sent me to check on you. Are you alright?" He asked, and I nodded.

"A little shaken up, probably scarred for life, but I'm good." I gave him the best smile I could manage, and Leon stared at me until I gave him the most basic explanation I could think of. I told him that I'd also woken up really anxious and followed Vincent to the marina, but didn't say why exactly he had gone. I just said he'd been in some sort of trouble and didn't trust his mom to help him.

"Alright. I wish I could have told him more when he visited me the other day, maybe he would have felt comfortable enough to contact me this morning." He looked and sounded absolutely stricken, and I reached out to lay a hand on his shoulder.

"You didn't know the situation he was in. It's okay. We'll come to your office when he's healed up and give you the roasting of your life for it." I grinned and Leon laughed softly and stood.

"That's fair, yeah," he said, sighing and raking his hands back through his hair. "What a morning, hm?"

"I'll be alright." I adjusted the strap on my bag, shrugging.

"I know. You're a MacAskill." He leaned down to kiss the top of my head and I blushed—I knew about forty girls my age that would be so jealous if they found out. "Get to class and come find me if you need anything."

"Thanks Leon." I was quiet for a second, then realized something else I'd wanted to ask him. "Sinéad is Clara, isn't she?"

His eyebrows shooting up was really all the answer I needed, but he further confirmed my suspicions by heaving out a breath and putting a hand over his face. I grinned and reached up to shake his sleeve in triumph.

"I knew it."

"I was banned from saying anything. Don't make this my fault, you did it." He shook my hand off his shirt and turned to head down the hall, and I giggled. Sinéad was going to tear him a new one if he broke any of the rules.

Class was easier to return to than expected. I had loitered in the library until the bell rang, and sat down in class just like it was any other normal day. And it was, until I was grabbed roughly by the arm as soon as I was in the hallway, nearly dropping my phone, which had buzzed during class and I was trying to check.

"Where were you?" Alena hissed, and I turned to find her warring between outrage and worry. I stopped and tugged her to the side of the hallway so we'd be out of the way, then wrapped my arms around her in the tightest hug I could manage, but also using the gesture to whisper to her.

"I found Jackson. It wasn't a happy meeting. I'm safe, he's safe, but I would really rather tell everyone the full story at once, okay?"

She had stiffened at the first sentence but nodded against my shoulder and squeezed me hard for a second, then let go.

"Okay, alright." Alena dropped her arms and sighed, shaking her head. "You never disappear like that, we were all freaked out. I ran across the street as soon as class let out to see if I could find you."

"I know, I'm sorry. It was a bit of an emergency, everything happened really quickly." I cringed a little, because I could have texted everyone while I was on the train to Dubhan, but I hadn't thought of it. I also could have texted while I was waiting in the library, but I hadn't. I'd have to take the brunt of that scolding later. Alena's war with her own expression had seemingly settled on "worry," so I reached out to squeeze her hand. "I really am sorry."

"You're forgiven," she breathed, turning to slide her arm through mine and lead me to my next class. I let her lead and lifted my phone to see who'd texted me.

Beefaroni: he's at the clinic, looks like no major damage to his eye or anything else. just a lot of bruises. they want him to talk to a counselor because he was honest about what happened and oh boy he is not looking forward to it. i asked if i could sit in with him for moral support and they said sure, for ten minutes, then they need to talk to just him. really rude of them i think.

I smirked at the last part of his message. I never thought Dan, of all people, would be a link to my past life like this, and now here he was giving me updates I'd never asked for but desperately wanted. It lifted a hundred pounds off my heart. Alena was reading over my shoulder and I turned the phone toward her. No use keeping any secrets at this point. I watched her expression change from confused to worried again.

"Good lord, does he mean Jackson? What happened to him? Where were you guys this morning?" She was rapid-firing questions at me and I just nodded.

"Jackson is... actually Vincent. He got hurt and Dan's parents took him to the clinic to see how bad." I gave a vague answer for now. It would still be easier to tell everyone together. My phone buzzed again.

i'll be at school by lunchtime, mom and dad say I still need to show up but they're not forcing me to go to corp. mom is staying with vinny though, so he won't be alone, if you're worried.

I was worried, thank you. You can sit with us if you want

YES thank you I don't think I can handle being alone today.

"Vincent?" Alena asked, guiding me to the classroom. "Dan's friend?"

"Yeah, best friends, it seems like. Dan literally came running after him."

Alena left me at my classroom door and took off back to her own classes. She'd probably be late to her next class and while I felt bad about it, I was so glad she'd checked on me. I slid into my seat and somehow was able to focus enough to actually learn during class, an impressive feat after witnessing what I had.

As promised, Dan showed up at lunchtime, and surprised me by wrapping me up in a giant hug the moment he was close enough. It would have been strange if we hadn't been bound together by tragedy a few hours ago. So I just squeezed him back, and we stood together until Alena jabbed me in the back with her fingertip. She and Jamari had come across the street to eat at Cridhe, I'm sure in large part due to my disappearance that morning.

"Care to explain everything now?" She asked, crossing her arms as I released Dan and turned around. I nodded, gesturing toward a spot out of the way of the crowd.

"Oh, hi, I'm Dan. We've barely met." He bowed his head to Alena who introduced herself in turn, then he smiled but it didn't reach his eyes like it normally did. "I'm probably going to be joining y'all for lunch and train rides a lot more often."

"That's fine," Jamari said, "the payment is an explanation as to what happened this morning."

I purposely made them wait until a couple people passed by to begin the story. Dan already knew about the dreams from Vincent so I didn't bother explaining any of that to him, starting instead with the spell from yesterday, the dream, and chasing Vincent to Dubhan.

"Good lord, was he going to jump or something?" Alena's voice reached peak volume and I waved my hand at her to quiet, flushing at the stares in our direction.

"I don't know, but I'm sure the whole school doesn't need to know about it," I hissed, sighing. I did know, but I didn't really want to make that known. She sank into her shoulders, sheepish for a moment, then straightened and looked at Dan.

"Did he ever tell you anything like that? Like he would?" Alena asked, and I readied myself for defense if she was about to blame Dan. Luckily, it wasn't needed.

"He did, actually. I reacted as expected, y'know—worried, and he played it off as if it was a joke. I've been keeping a closer eye on him since then. I drag him out to places to keep him out of the house as much as I can." Dan's gaze was down, all his normal bravado thrown to the wind from the cliffs. He didn't even have his sunglasses on his head, and his hair was far from spiked. "That's why I knew what was going on when Katiyana said they were at the marina. I've caught him looking at the transit app for that train multiple times." He set his forehead in his hand, swallowing hard. I reached out to rub between his shoulder blades softly. Fleur's voice came through the phone we had between us, another illegal call placed across the island.

"You did the right thing, Dan. You did all the right things. He's safe now because you told Katiyana what to do and moved as fast as you could to get him out of the situation. And now, because you came to us, he'll have a larger support group to keep him safe." She sounded so sure, so certain, and my heart lifted. Glancing to Alena and Jamari, I found Alena nodding in agreement, and Jamari looking suspicious for a moment before nodding, as well.

"What's that look for?" I asked her, reaching over to tap the back of her hand. She jumped, which was a dead giveaway something was on her mind.

"I...I wasn't supposed to say anything, but I guess it's fine now. I was in the shop when Vincent came in to get his spell from Alexis, so I knew it was him. Alexis caught me eavesdropping and swore me to secrecy, and now I just feel like I could have done something to prevent this if I'd told." She had been talking to her food the entire time, and shrugged defeatedly. Dan lifted his head to look at her.

"Hey, no. He's been like this for far longer than just this month, way longer than when the dreams started. I don't..." He sighed, the truth almost too hard to let past his lips. "I don't think any of us could have changed what happened short of having him in a different house last night. I don't like the idea but, I think it's just...out of our hands. We're just teenagers, after all."

His words hung over the lunch table like a heavy fog, and we all had to take a moment to literally chew the thought over. Dan kept tapping his phone to see if there were any new messages, and I found myself glancing over every time he did it. I was equally worried, he was just showing it.

Before we realized it, the bell rang. We said our normal "bye, we love you" to Fleur, hid the phone before we got caught, and headed out of the cafeteria. I found myself holding tighter to Alena's hand as we walked down the hallway, reluctant to let go. Jamari had her arm through Dan's, who shockingly didn't seem to mind. I saw Alena's jaw clenching and unclenching in thought.

"Let's go to my house after school," she said as we were about to head down separate hallways. "You too, Dan."

She looked directly at him and he nodded, confused but glad to be accepted so swiftly into our group. This one declaration from our self-appointed leader freed us all from the chains that had been holding us together the last few minutes, and we were finally able to let go and go back to being schoolkids. Jamari and Alena were probably late to class again, but once more I was thankful. They were willing to risk that mark on their records just to make sure I was safe.

Gathering at the school gate after our last classes with one more in our party somehow didn't feel as odd as it probably should have, but our plan to go to Alena's fell apart as we looked up to see Katherine and Mori leaning out of the car waving at her.

"Hi honey! Get in, we're going to pick up Grandma at the marina!" She called, causing Dan and I both to suppress a shudder. Alena looked at us in apology, then called out to Katherine.

"Okay hold on!!" She turned back to us, sincere regret tracing her features. "I'm sorry guys, I completely forgot. I'm so sorry." She threw her arms around me quickly, squeezed me, and then hugged everyone else in turn, even Dan. He was shocked but returned it.

"It's alright, just send us a silly grandma selfie." Dan grinned, and Fleur giggled at the thought. Alena smiled.

"I can do that." She waved as she walked off, climbing into the car with her family. The remainder of us looked at each other silently, Jamari kicking at a rock with the toe of her shoe.

"Rain check?" I ventured, and the others nodded. I nodded back. "No problem. It might be best if we all carry on as normally as possible." Somewhere in the back of my mind I heard Valerie's sarcastic tone saying the words before they left my mouth. "It's not like it's a wake, anyway." I cracked a faint smile and got a chorus of weak ones in return.

Jamari's phone beeped at her, and as she read the message her eyebrows lifted. "Alexis is asking if I can pick up a couple hours tonight. They got a shipment of supplies in early." She looked at me as if for approval, and I shrugged.

"Go do it, get that bag."

"Ask if I can tag along." Fleur leaned over her sister's shoulder and set her chin on it, Jamari tapping her screen dutifully. "She says only if you're willing to be put to work."

"I am, that's fine." Fleur leaned back and reached her arms out toward me, and we embraced tightly before Jamari took her turn.

"Vincent messaged me, he asked if I can come see him at the clinic. They're keeping him for observation and he's very displeased about it." Dan spoke up, returning Fleur's hug with a half-embrace as he read from his phone.

"You should go," Jamari and I spoke in unison.

"I guess so." Dan sighed softly, rubbing a hand over his face. "Alright. You nerds hug too often for me, anyway." He grinned, still a little weak but stronger than earlier, and we returned it. Despite his words, he wrapped me up in another tight squeeze before heading to the other side of campus and therefore the other train station. Jamari and Fleur waved as they headed down the street, and I waved back before spinning on my heel to head home myself.

Riding home on the train alone was an exceedingly rare occurrence, and I found myself leaning my head against the window to stare out thoughtlessly instead of reading or scrolling social media like normal. I probably should have asked Dan for Vincent's num—My phone buzzed, and I lifted it to see an unknown number texting me.

RedSam

> asked Dan for your number, is that okay?

It had to be Vincent. I readjusted in my seat to hold my phone in both hands.

That's totally okay, I was going to have him give it to you anyway

RedSam

did he update you?

LilTriquetra

As of everything he knew at 3pm, yeah

RedSam

okay, i'll spare you the story then

LilTriquetra

I'm sorry they're keeping you

RedSam

it's unfortunately what happens when you attempt something like that. they're all being way nicer than i thought they would, the fact they let me keep my phone is proof.

LilTriquetra

Lol, you gotta remember all the horror stories don't come from Faodail

RedSam

i guess that's true

can I order you dinner or anything?

dan's mom is bringing me stuff, but thank you, that's really sweet.

I stared at the conversation, struggling to think of what to say. There was too much between us for us to have a normal conversation now. My hand lifted to my—no, *his*— pendant and squeezed it, closing my eyes for a moment to recenter myself. As I did, another message came through.

i feel off-center too.

I blinked, shocked for a second, then remembered how I'd gotten the image of the marina earlier. Something about the pendants was connecting us and I didn't have it in me to question it.

They let you keep your jewelry too, then?

yeah, lol, i was surprised too. especially since your pendant has a much sharper end than mine.

I laughed, just a breath through my nose, and tilted my phone to snap a photo of the amethyst in my hand to send.

Before he answered, a similar photo came back, my pendant's chain wrapped between his fingers with the amethyst securely in his hand as it lay at his side.

I was halfway into my response when he messaged again.

Seven words and I could feel the emotion in every single one of them. I squeezed the amethyst hard, letting the wire dig into my palm, sending every bit of support and caring energy that I could to him. I felt so bad, I couldn't imagine not having a safe space to retreat to in your own home. Mine was far from perfect, but at least when I locked my door Nick stopped trying to come in. I squeezed my eyes shut as a realization flickered through my mind: I'd never properly taken down my magic circle from the night before.

My stop arrived before I had a chance to respond to Vincent, and as I got off the train I hoped that the energy I'd tried to send through the pendants was enough until I was safely on the sidewalk and away from the crowd.

LilTriquetra

Where would you rather go?

It was a hopeful question, one that would maybe pull him away from some of the gloom that seemed to still be hanging over him. It took him a block to respond, and when I read the message, it was clear why.

RedSam

a bakery in new york, tucked somewhere in manhattan, with a charming, loud man rolling out pastries and kneading dough as his partner tells stories to a silver-eyed young woman who's sneaking out every morning just to hear them. that's where i'd rather go.

I blushed, pressing a hand over my mouth. I'd had the same dreams and we both already knew that, but to have it out in the...well, not the open, but in real life? It was enough to make me have to pause for a moment and lean against the nearest building. I held my breath as I typed.

LilTriquetra

The conversation came to a pause once again, and although I kept my phone in my hand as I walked, I couldn't think of anything more to say. Everything was too heavy, everything was suddenly far too real. I was getting increasingly tempted to take my glasses off just so the world could be blurry instead of 4K sharp for a minute.

I made it to my building somehow, completely on autopilot the entire way. It was only when I stepped off the elevator and into our hallway that I got shocked back to life, sniffing and furrowing my brow. It smelled like incense, but not the kind Alexis carried or mom used. I'd never smelled it before in my life.

I followed the smell with dread in my heart to our door, and down the hall to Nick's room. His door was cracked open, remnants of smoke curling between the frame and the doorknob, his voice softly chanting something I didn't recognize.

Peering into the small crack, holding my breath, I leaned forward to try and see what he was doing. Magic wasn't unusual in this house, but it *was* unusual for Nick to be chanting in a language other than English, and this was assuredly not English. As I squinted into the darkness, my eyes adjusted and I finally saw the blurry shape of Nick kneeling in the middle of his room, thankfully facing away from me, with his arms raised and his head back, a bowl of whatever he'd been burning in front of him. He'd drawn a circle on the carpet with something dark and sure to stain, symbols around the edge of it that I'd never seen. The feeling of dread grew stronger, and I lifted a shaking hand to quickly aim my camera through the crack in the door and hit record. I managed to capture exactly forty-six seconds before Nick stopped, tilted his head back further in an unnatural way, and made eye contact. I quickly lowered my phone and raced to my room, shutting the door smoothly and locking it. I pressed myself against the wood as Nick's footsteps pounded down the hall, then his fist pounded against the door.

"You goddamn little sneak, what the hell do you think you're doing? I don't record your rituals, I don't touch your little candle spells when you leave them out all day, what makes you think it's okay to record mine?" He wasn't shouting, but his voice held the edge of a man who was about to. I pressed my phone to my chest and tried not to breathe. "I know you're in there Katiyana, and if you don't delete that video right now, I will come in there and do it myself." Nick's voice was dark, threatening, I'd never heard it like this before.

"I'll—I'll call Alex if you don't get away from my door right this instant!" I called back, my eyes squeezed shut against my bald lie. I didn't have Alex's number, but Nick didn't know that. Nick's fist slammed against my door once more, and he growled.

"Delete the fucking video, Katiyana Randa, or I will make you regret it."

That was enough to spook me. He had threatened me before, but never after I'd threatened him back. Threatening to get someone else involved always worked, but something had changed. I hurriedly sent the video to the last coven member I'd talked to, Valerie, and as soon as it sent—thankfully only a few seconds, bless the Comms Wi-Fi-based messaging system—I deleted it from my side of the conversation and also my camera roll, which I left on the screen as I opened my door and held up my phone.

"It's gone! Look, it's gone! I got rid of it!" Nick squinted suspiciously at my screen, then shook his head.

"Show me who you sent it to." He looked about ready to rip the phone from my hand so I tugged it back and opened my messages. Valerie's chat had gone back down the list after I'd deleted the video, Vincent and my friends back on top.

"See, look, no one. I didn't send it to anyone. Here's proof. It's clear." My heart was racing but I kept my voice as even as possible, gripping my phone tight enough to turn my knuckles white.

Nick stared at my phone and then my face, long enough I thought I was going to break, but he stomped off seconds before my mask collapsed. I slammed my door again and locked it, looking to see if Val had responded. Thank Brigit, she hadn't. She had been online just moments ago, so hopefully that meant she'd seen the video. I scrambled as far away from my door as I could get, sitting against the wall under my window, my hand unconsciously reaching for Vincent's pendant. I jumped as my phone buzzed in my hand, staring at it until my eyes cleared and I saw it wasn't Val.

RedSam

> are you okay?

These pendants were giving away far more than I'd ever signed up for. I let go of the one in my hand, pressing my hand to my forehead instead. I sat there with my eyes closed, counting four more buzzes from my phone.

RedSam

> that was a lot of intense emotion suddenly

> something about these pendants is causing us to feel each other's emotions

> it's a lot stronger after we traded, but now flashes of things from before are making more sense.

> it's gone now, are you alright? Yana?

Somehow, Vincent calling me by my nickname was too much on top of everything that had just happened. My vision blurred again but this time not out of panic, my eyes were filling up with tears that spilled over before I had a chance to force them back. I pressed my hand to my mouth to stifle a sob, feeling the false strength I'd been carrying all day finally run out.

I don't know how long I silently cried, but I was exhausted as my tears ran out and my heartbeat finally settled. The skin on my face pulled and tightened against dried tears, and I pulled my sweater sleeve up over my fist to scrub at it, rubbing under my eye and glasses as I retrieved my phone from the floor where I'd dropped it. I had a bunch of texts from different people.

RedSam

> i'm sorry if i'm being a bother, i'll stop texting.

Beefaroni

> I'm at the clinic with vinny now, I'm just assuming you want updates at this point? lmk if you don't, boo.

Bruadarach

> Leo caught me up, i'm sorry you had to go through everything you did, call me if you need me.

And in a brand new group chat that now included Dan, the silly grandma selfie that Alena had promised. She'd even drawn cat ears on her grandma and Mori, who was leaning over the entire car seat just to be in the frame. Alena—or Mori—had drawn a mustache and top hat on herself. I flipped to the conversation with Sinéad.

LilTriquetra

JSYK it's bullshit that yall can't tell us anything for sake of "clouding perception"

Bruadarch

I KNOW, I HATE IT. It's not my rule, I'm really sorry.

LilTriquetra

You're the bruadarach and you don't even make all the rules? Stupid.

Bruadarch

If you want to go with me to yell at the druids for it, feel free.

LilTriquetra

I will break down their fancy door myself.

Sinéad's response was a GIF of witches dancing around a bonfire, which I smirked at, then took a breath before I switched to Vincent's conversation.

LilTriquetra

I'm sorry, I wasn't alright, you haven't done anything wrong, none of it is on you

RedSam

well, that's nice to hear.

I was about to respond when the new group chat pinged. Dan had added Vincent to it, as well.

Beefaroni

We were missing someone, hope that's alright

BlondeBrainiac

Perfectly fine, he's family now whether he likes it or not.

QueenofGambits

YEAH!!

BlondeBrainiac

Jamari is still working but she just shouted yeah across the store when I read the text to her.

Beefaroni

Is fleur the mom of everyone or just me?

BlondeBrainiac

Everyone. however, if you call me mom, I'll banish you.

Beefaroni

Duly noted!

Vincent's chat pinged privately.

RedSam

I asked him not to do that.

LilTriquetra

Lol, don't worry. The ungendered girl gang is wonderful. They uh…they do kind of know what happened, though. I'm sorry, that wasn't really dan's or my story to tell. They just know your mom was involved really.

RedSam

forgiven.

LilTriquetra

On the plus side, they're now going to be fiercely protective of you

RedSam

nice, lol

are you okay?

LilTriquetra

I got in an argument with my brother and I guess it was just the cherry on top of the day, I broke down for a minute

RedSam

i'm sorry.

It's okay, I told my neighbor/family friend about it, she's keeping an eye on me

i'm glad someone is,

I felt, more than suspected, the typed and then deleted "I wish it were me," and found myself holding his pendant again. If this kept up, I was going to force him to trade back.

The texting went on for quite a while, even to the point of me having to plug in my phone to stay in the conversation. Vincent even talked in the group chat, albeit not much. My friends were delighted. Despite the cramped fingers, I was grateful for it, because it gave me a reason to not think about Nick and whatever he'd been doing in his room. Valerie didn't message me back beyond the same GIF of dancing witches that Sinéad had sent, and although I figured it was probably a secret code of some sort, I had no idea what.

My friend's chatter and lighthearted teasing was enough to calm me down, and after finishing up my homework and sneaking to the kitchen for a rather small dinner, I drifted off to sleep with my hand wrapped around Vincent's amethyst.

Vincent

They released me from the clinic once I woke up, and I don't think I've ever scrambled out of a place so swiftly. The nurses and even the psychiatrist I'd had to speak to were all perfectly lovely people, none of them had been rude or even uncomfortable, but being in the clinic meant that I was broken somehow, and I wasn't ready to admit that to myself. Even with it being shoved in my face in the most dramatic of ways.

Dan's dad came by to pick me up, and we finally broached the subject about what to do next. We sat in the car together, my school bag on my lap, my fingers still pressed against Katiyana's amethyst.

"Well, Justine and I have been talking about it all night, and we think you should come stay with us. At least for a while. You're not safe in that house. We'll talk to the security force and make sure it's all legal and Mila can't fight it." He said it without even looking at me, watching someone walk up to the door to the clinic and go in. I sat there, a little stunned, but also wondering why I felt that way. Dan had already offered this to me, and his kindness was a carbon copy of his parents'. This shouldn't be shocking.

"What do you think?" He prompted as I remained silent, processing the idea of it.

"I...well, Mr. Weber—" The idea of getting the island government involved was making me hesitate.

"You can call me Bradley, Vincent. I've told you before." His calm reassurance brought a new heaviness to my chest, and my grip tightened.

"Bradley...I...that's a really big offer." I loosed one hand from my backpack to hold onto the pendant, squeezing it. Less than a second passed before I felt a wave of concerned but calm energy flowing back. It was enough to even out my breathing. With a glance, I saw Dan's dad still waiting patiently for an answer, nodding at my statement.

"You've been friends with Dan for so long, it's basically like having another son anyway." He shrugged casually, reaching down to turn the key and start the engine. "We'd just have to move that treadmill, but we also discussed the idea of bunk beds." He glanced at me with a grin. "Although I know I wouldn't want to sleep in the same room as Dan's gym clothes." He chuckled, dad joke complete, and I let myself relax from the tight coil I'd wound myself into.

"If...if it's really okay. I would really like to." I was sure he hadn't heard me, I couldn't even hear my own thoughts over my pounding heart, but he clapped a hand on my shoulder as his smile widened, and everything calmed. I slumped back in my seat, staring ahead and just sitting in bewildered relief that I didn't have to go home.

"Wonderful." He shifted to reverse and left the parking lot, leaving me still clasping the amethyst and finding a relaxed smile on my face. "I know you don't have more than your school things with you, so do you want to go back and pack some clothes? I'll go in with you if you need me to."

Though the idea of packing up my entire room, minus the furniture, was incredibly tempting, a flash of panic shot through me at the idea of returning home. I didn't know if Mom would be there. The concerned look on my face must have given me away, because Bradley spoke again.

"We could also call an officer to meet us there."

Now that was sure to cause a scene, but it *would* be safest if Mom decided to throw one of her fits. She had been calling and texting near relentlessly, until I had finally just silenced her messages and started hanging up on her immediately. She was sure to be furious, and if I went in that house alone, I'd come out with more bruises than I'd gone in with.

Bradley had been driving in quiet patience this whole time, and we were nearing the library where Dan and I had met just a few days ago. It felt like an eternity.

"I'll need to know which way to go, Vin," he said softly, leaning forward to peer into the traffic around the corner. I gritted my teeth, then nodded.

"I at least need my clothes."

He answered with a nod and turned toward my house instead of his. The closer we got to the little dwelling that could almost be called a trailer, the faster my heart beat and the tighter I clutched Katiyana's pendant. My phone buzzed in my pocket, likely her texting me to find out what was going on like I'd done last night. I released my backpack fully to check.

LilTriquetra

Dude you better not be anywhere near a cliff right now. You're not allowed to make this a repeat performance just to get dan to hug you like he's clinging to a lifesaver

RedSam

i'm in the car with dan's dad, nowhere near a cliff, swear.

LilTriquetra

Lmao is his driving that bad?

RedSam

no, we're heading to my house to get my stuff,

I almost typed more but then deleted it. This wasn't a conversation to have over text.

LilTriquetra

If you keep leaving the commas you mean to delete I'm going to start finishing your sentences for you

RedSam

…sorry. i just don't want mom to be home is all.

LilTriquetra

make dan's dad go in first, and send me your location. If you want me to call the force, I'll do it in class, idc

RedSam

hah, thank you.

She sent a GIF of a cartoon character doing finger guns, and I puffed a laugh out through my nose. It was *incredibly* strange to have people know the full story other than Dan. But, if last night's conversation was anything to go off of, I was stuck with Katiyana and her friends for as long as they were willing to put up with me.

Not long after, Bradley parked in front of my house on the street, peering into the driveway. "Looks like the coast might be clear, Vin. No cars around," he said, unbuckling his belt and making to get out of the car, but looking back when I didn't move. "You okay there, champ?"

I shook my head, closing my eyes to take in a huge breath, hold it, then carefully let it out, counting to four with each step.

"I don't like being here," I whispered, but got out of the car and marched around it anyway, pulling my key from my pocket. Bradley followed close behind, his presence and willingness to help me my only solace. I unlocked the door quietly, opening it the same, and peeked in slowly. Mom had apparently gone for groceries, because plastic bags were strewn over the kitchen floor once again, and a new collection of beer bottles and energy drink cans decorated the counter and table. No vegetables. The good streak was definitely over. I didn't hear any noise or movement, so my shoulders automatically dropped as I stepped in and headed right for the bathroom, scooping up one of the grocery sacks on my way. I tossed all of my toiletries into the bag haphazardly, not even worrying when the shampoo bottle released all the water it had been secretly holding in its cap. I handed the bag to Bradley, who was waiting in the hall, and moved to my room. I had exactly one suitcase from a never-taken-but-much-promised family trip off-island back when I was a kid and things were slightly better. I would just have to fit as much as I could in it.

Twenty minutes later, I'd managed to fit all of my clothing in it, along with the small collection of books and notebooks I had laying around. I looked at my bedding, still stained with my blood from yesterday morning, and grimaced.

"We have lots at our place, but grab your pillow if you want it," Bradley said from the doorway, carrying a couple more grocery sacks. "You'll probably want whatever's in your hamper, too, huh?" He asked, and I blinked as I realized I'd totally forgotten the dirty clothes existed. I shoved them into the grocery sacks—having a very limited supply of clothing was absolutely working in my favor right now—and set them on the bed with the suitcase.

I looked around the room, trying to figure out if there was anything left, but it was mostly just furniture. Bradley moved to peer into the small closet, looking at the empty hangers I'd left and a pair of shoes that had grown too small years ago.

"What about this?" He asked, reaching up to pull down a small box and hold it out. I took it immediately, nodding. "Thank you, yes, I need this." I popped open the lid to confirm what was in it, and sighed as I looked at it all. My birth certificate and other documents, hidden away from Mom ages ago, and the only stuffed animal that remained from my childhood. Mom had taken all the rest the moment I'd turned ten, telling me I was too old for them now and needed to start growing up. But this little mouse I'd managed to hide.

"Is that everything then?" Bradley asked, gathering the few plastic bags we'd filled. I took another glance around my room, noting a couple of textbooks left on my desk. I opened the drawer briefly to check it, finding nothing but pens and pencils that could definitely be replaced. I pocketed the one that wrote best, pushed the textbooks in my suitcase, and zipped it shut. Just like that, my entire life was packed up and my room was as bare as it could be while leaving the furniture. Bradley picked up my suitcase, as well, and started heading out. I stripped the stained pillowcase off to take my pillow with me, tucking the box under my arm and following him.

We'd just shut the trunk on the car when I heard another one pull in and froze.

"Get in the car, Vincent," Bradley said, pushing my shoulder lightly. I obeyed without even looking up, locking the doors as I sunk down into my seat. I heard muffled voices, one calm, one raised in alarm, and dared to peek out the driver's side window. Bradley was standing at the edge of the lawn, purposely staying off the property it seemed, while mom yelled at him from the driveway. I pulled up the keypad on my phone, watching to see if she started to get aggressive, slowly dialing the emergency number for the island and hovering my thumb over the call button.

Bradley turned, unlocked the door, and slid into the car with a huge sigh. "Well, she's pissed. I told her to expect a call from the security force and that's what set her off."

"I'm...shocked she didn't go after you." I looked around him to catch a glimpse of her through the window. She was stomping into the house, and I swear I saw the windows rattle when she slammed the door. I shuddered, glad I was outside the house.

"Is that why you were getting ready to call the force?" He was trying to tease, but his voice was laced with concern and a bit of annoyance. I nodded. He let out a sharp breath. "Yeah, you're going to be staying with us for the foreseeable future."

"Thank you." I mustered up all the sincerity and seriousness I could for those two words, holding my phone to my chest and looking him full in the face, not hiding behind anything. He looked over and smiled as he started the car.

"You're welcome. Let's get you home." He pulled away from the house quickly enough I pressed back into the seat a little. "I don't want to come back here, and I'm betting you don't either."

"No sir, I do not." I shook my head and looked down to clear the keypad. Now that we were driving away, there was no need to call the authorities.

I sat back in my seat with a sigh, closing my eyes as Bradley turned on the radio. I didn't even hear the lyrics, I was so swept up in the near-tear-inducing relief. I held her pendant, hoping Katiyana would feel it and know I was safe, that I was out of that house. I was on my way to freedom.

Katiyana

Thursday, September 24, 2020

Vincent didn't show up on the train, and after one look at my concerned face, Dan immediately launched into an explanation that took up the majority of our train ride to school. What it boiled down to was, he hadn't been released from the clinic yet because some sort of paperwork was still backed up. Dan's parents had talked about moving Vincent in with them, at least for a while, until they decided what to do about his mother, and Dan's dad was going to talk to Vincent about it when he went to pick Vincent up. I sighed, relieved, and glad he was out of danger for now.

"By the way, Yana, what's the girl's name that's in your dreams again?" Dan slid his arm through mine as we got off the train together. I looked at him quizzically.

"Marie, why?"

"Oh, no, you've both infected me. I totally dreamed about Marie and Jackson last night. I think I was pretending to be Charles." He sighed dramatically and I snickered.

"Oh no, Dan, don't tell me you're discovering your past life now, too."

"If my experience is anything like Vincent's, I don't want it, thank you." He was very matter of fact about it, and left me at the school steps, bustling away to his locker. The possibility that he was Charles was definitely there, but I wasn't about to look into it seriously until he had more than just a single dream.

The previous day and night before had taken all of the energy out of me, and I found myself yawning and leaning against my friends far more often than usual. At one point

I must have dozed off a little in class because Alena threw one of her erasers at me, and I somehow managed to keep my jolting-awake-jump unnoticed by the teacher.

"Are you alright?" She asked as we left class and walked toward the cafeteria. I was focusing on just walking without falling over, and I stumbled a little as I tried to answer her.

"Yeah, yeah, I'm fine. Totally fine." I waved my hand dismissively, but even I could tell it wasn't convincing. Alena rolled her eyes and took my arm to keep me upright, planting me on a bench at our table. I was about to protest when she turned around and pointed, telling me to stay, so I did. While waiting, a wave of anxiety that wasn't mine filled my heart and I squinted, pinpointing it before texting Vincent. He responded, we had a little back and forth about Dan's dad, and his anxiety ceased.

Not long after, the rest of the crew filtered in and I immediately leaned on Jamari's shoulder. She straightened a little to give me a better resting point, and snickered.

"You finally meet the boy of your dreams and spend all night talking to him, hm?" She teased, and I leaned back and smacked her arm half-heartedly.

"I was talking to all of you." I folded my arms on the table and laid my head on them, tucking my chin to avoid squishing my glasses. Jamari just laughed again. I heard more people sit down and assumed it was Fleur and Dan, my guess confirmed by their voices.

"Is she alive?" Fleur joked, and I lifted a hand to wave weakly at her without lifting my head. "Oh, good."

"Is that normal?" Dan asked, and I sat up to glare at him. He grinned, looking like he was about to stick his tongue out, and I narrowed my eyes further. This made him giggle. "Oh Katiyana, we know you are exhausted from being a daring hero yesterday, we are only poking fun at you, babe." Then he did stick his tongue out. I was mildly annoyed, but he was just too charming, way too endearing for me to be upset with him, so I just put my head back down.

Alena brought me a tray, balancing hers and mine on either hand, and I took her hand in both of mine as soon as she set them down.

"Alena Chen, I will follow you to the ends of the earth," I said, and she just laughed at me, swatting my hands away.

"Eat your food, then we'll head there."

I obliged, once more immensely grateful to have such great friends to take care of me. At one point we all looked at Dan when he heaved a huge sigh, pressing his phone to his chest.

"Wanna share with the class, Danny?" Jamari asked, nudging him with her elbow.

"Vinny agreed to move in with me and my parents." He put his phone on the table and set his head in his hands, all his teasing and bravado placed aside to reveal his relief. I grinned, and reached across Jamari to pat his shoulder.

"That's so good, Dan. He'll be so much safer." As I said it, relief washed over me, as well, but not just my own. I pulled my hand back to grab Vincent's pendant, squeezing it gently to acknowledge the emotion.

Not long after, probably the amount of time it took Vincent and Dan's dad to get to their house, the group message buzzed with a photo of Vincent's stuff piled haphazardly on Dan's bed.

RedSam

oh no, dan, you're stuck with me.

Beefaroni

I ALREADY WAS YOU DINGUS

BlondeBrainiac

Wow what kind of teenager has THOSE sheets? Wow Dan…

Dan shot Fleur an astonished and hurt look, to which she burst into laughter. "I'm only teasing, Danny. So what if you have cartoon characters on your bed?"

RedSam

dan has all the best things, remind me to send more photos.

Beefaroni

Don't you fking dare, bro.

"Oh, I like Vincent," Alena said, snickering softly as she read the messages. The tops of Dan's ears were turning red, and Fleur turned to wrap her arm around his shoulders.

"Sorry Dannyboy, you're part of the full group now, which means you have to share all your secrets," she teased, squeezing him once then releasing. Dan shook her arm off his shoulders and started gathering his things, piling his garbage onto his tray.

"In that case, I renounce my spot in the group!" He got up and went over to the tray drop, and we all quickly followed. The bell would ring relatively soon, anyway. We caught up to him in the hallway and very nearly tackled him, two of us on each arm.

"Ahh! No! I told you! I'm done!" He tried to shake us off, but Jamari got her arms around his waist and lifted him up, which made him burst out laughing. "Put me down, Valkyrie!"

"That's a good title, I'm keeping that!" Jamari said as she lowered him to the floor. Dan swatted at her while still giggling, shaking his head.

"You four are too much, I need Vincent here to balance all of this out." He waved his hand, indicating all of us.

"He won't protect you from us, he'll encourage it." I giggled, and Dan turned to narrow his eyes in my direction.

"I hate that you're right." He shook his head and peered around the hallway before pulling his phone out and tapping the camera settings to set a timer. Placing his phone on the lip of a nearby window, he quickly shooed us all into formation and told us to smile, taking what he quickly sent to the group chat with the caption, "They've kidnapped me and now I'm forever stuck!"

RedSam

> oh no dan how awful. you have friends. =)

> put your phone away before you get caught, dweeb.

The sarcasm was strong even over text, and as the bell rang we continued to good-naturedly harass Dan and get him to admit that he enjoyed our company. Jamari and Dan headed off to their next class, discussing fitness regimes and a potential gym-buddy thing happening. Fleur, Alena, and I laughed at the thought—Jamari going to the gym?

I made my way to the art room, Alena and Fleur to their classes. Even after the tragedy and stress of yesterday, I wasn't anything more than tired. Everything finally felt like it was falling into place, especially with Vincent getting away from his mom. Once my own mom and aunts got back, my training could start, and now that I knew Vincent was into Paganism, maybe he could join me. We'd have to take him to the next teen witch course at Ladine's. This thought gave me the energy I needed to finish up my project and start on the next, much to the shock of my teacher. Maybe it could always be like this, I thought. That would be nice.

Unfortunately, it was all immediately ruined upon coming home. Nick was there, which might have been enough on its own, but he was casting another spell. I knew better than to linger this time, but the weird incense smell was back and even with my door shut and window open, it was infusing the entire house. Before heading into my bedroom, I'd seen marks on his door, as well, as if he'd smeared it while trying to paint his circle. It was a dark red, but I didn't want to automatically assume he was painting the carpet with blood. I curled up on the floor near my window where the smell was faintest, and read my assignments for school. I was determined to stay as far out of his way as I could.

"Katiyana!" He called, and I jumped. It took a second for my heart to settle down, which was apparently too long for Nick to wait. "KATIYANA!" He shouted, and as I was getting up I heard him stomping down the hall to my room. "Answer someone when they fucking talk to you!" He growled, slamming the door open and planting both hands on either side of the doorjamb. I slid back down, sitting with my back to the wall.

"I was getting up to come see what you wante—"

"You should have said so, goddamnit." He had smudges of the same red substance on his face and neck, and what I could see of his hands were covered in it. I really didn't want to think it was blood, but I wasn't sure what else it could be. "Are you in here recording me again, you little bitch?" I shrunk back against the wall a little more at the expletive. He'd never called me that before. I wanted so badly to snap at him or throw my textbook at him, but instead I just pointed to my phone that was on my nightstand charging.

"As you can see, Nicolae, I'm nowhere near my phone." I said it as calmly as I could, but the annoyance was hard to pull from my voice. "What secret, baneful magic are you doing in your bedroom, anyway?" I turned my attention back to my book, trying to be nonchalant, but recognized my mistake as Nick came into my room and ripped the book from my hands. He held it up as if he were going to throw it at me, and I ducked into my shoulders.

"That's none of your goddamn business, now is it?" He threw the book on the ground beside me, and stormed off. I laid a hand on my chest, the other on the carpet, twisting my fingers into it.

"Holy shit," I whispered, staring at my book that now had quite a few creased pages, but luckily no damage I couldn't fix. I sat there for a minute, hearing Nick pick up his chanting from yesterday, and got my breathing under control as best I could. After I didn't feel like I would fall over from standing up on shaky legs, I stood slowly and made my way to my door to shut it again and lock it firmly. I debated shoving my chair under the door, as well. Deciding against it, I moved to pick up my book and start un-creasing the pages, looking up just in time to see my phone screen light up.

LoveWitch

Okay why was he screaming this time?

LilTriquetra

Can I come over real quick?

LoveWitch

That bad huh? Yeah, come over.

Remembering to grab my key just in case, I slipped out of the apartment as quietly as I could and made my way to Valerie's. She wrinkled her nose as she opened the door for me, putting a hand over her nose and mouth.

"Dear goddess Aphrodite, why do you smell like bayberry and ginger? Not a good combo." She ushered me into her apartment, moving to open the living room window.

"Is that what that is?" I asked, lifting the collar of my shirt to smell it. "Nick's been burning incense in the apartment almost every day lately." Valerie turned and gave me a weird look, and I gave one back. "What?"

"There's a specific group of people on this island who use bayberry and ginger incense," she said, crossing her arms. "Is Nick also using beet juice to draw sigils?" Her voice was tinged with laughter, absolutely teasing, but when I didn't answer she silenced and furrowed her brow. "Oh, tell me he's not."

"I...I don't know for sure but whatever he's using is definitely red." I shrugged, lowering myself onto her couch. She exhaled loudly.

"Traitor." It was whispered just low enough that I barely caught it.

"Traitor?" I questioned, staring at her in confusion. "This is another one of those Faodail secrets I don't know about, isn't it?" Val ran her hands through her hair and sighed.

"Yeah, kiddo, it is." She came and sat down next to me on the couch and leaned forward with her elbows on her knees. "I might have to call your parents again. Maybe Sinéad."

"Why Sinéad?" She was family, but we didn't call on her to solve our problems just because she was Bruadarach. That would have been favoritism, and the MacAskill line strove to never play into it.

"Well, you see, the specific group that uses those things in their rituals is the Mortmores," Valerie said while staring off into space, her hands laced together, and heaved a sigh afterward. I stared at her in shock.

"The Mort—what—I...No. No way. Please say you're joking, I'm begging you." I took hold of her arm, shaking it gently. The Mortmores?? They were the family that had nearly run the island into the ground before Sinéad came back. They were the ones who had put some of my ancestors in jail on fraudulent charges. There was no way Nick was working with them, he'd be a traitor to his herita—"Oh no, Val, he literally said the MacAskill magic was the bad one, but I didn't think anything of it...what do we do?"

"I should call Sinéad," Val said again, shaking me off and standing up to get her phone off the counter. I heard her let out another long sigh, shakier than the last. I leaned back against the couch, replaying the conversation with my brother over in my head. He had straight up told me the MacAskill magic was black magic and I shouldn't learn it. I never connected the two—I didn't know there were even more than a few Mortmores left on the island. None of them were in power anymore, and Sinéad had jailed or exiled the ones who had tried to ruin Faodail. Who could he possibly be working with? How did he even know where to find them?

While I was lost in my distressing thoughts, Valerie had been quietly on the phone with Sinéad, telling her what I'd said and witnessed, and then forwarding her the video Valerie had saved from our messages. I caught the tail end of their conversation.

"I know we can't do anything legally, but—" A sigh on the edge of annoyance. "Listen, Bruadarach, this is coven business, you can't just leave us out of it. No, you're not allowed to handle it yourself just because you're his family. The coven needs to—No! Sinéad I will call Dorell, do not make me call Dorell." A pause. "That's better. The Cabinet and the coven can do it together. We might have to wait until the three get back—Yes they're still gone, do you not keep track of your own aunts?" Another sigh, closer to annoyance. "Sinéad, how do you keep anything straight?" A pause, and a soft laugh. "Well that works. They're due back on the third, yeah. As long as nothing bad happens within the next week we should be fine." She went quiet for longer this time, tapping her fingers on the edge of her kitchen counter. "Yeah, I was planning on it. Mhm. Yup. Okay. Yeah I'll see you tomorrow then. Bye." She tapped her screen, ending the call, then turned to see me peering at her over the top of the couch. Val smirked a little and leaned back against the counter. "Did you hear the verdict then?" I nodded.

"You're gonna wait til the sisters come home and then deal with it as a full coven?" I shifted, crossing my arms on the back of the couch and planting my chin on them. Val nodded.

"Yeah. If he's actually working with the Mortmores and not just copying them, we'll have trouble on our hands. But if he's just copying them, and they're not actually involved? We'll be fine. He'll just...have to be corrected." Val crossed her own arms, phone still in hand, clearly thinking over what that correction could possibly be. I watched her, not able to think of anything myself. Her phone rang, and she lifted it, answering Alexis's call and explaining the situation to her. I moved to sit back down on the couch properly.

This would be a lot easier to help with if I knew what was going on, I thought. I knew about the Mortmores, they'd taken over Faodail when Sinéad's and my aunt had died. I'd only been six at the time, so my own memories weren't super clear, but they'd nearly destroyed Faodail over the next five years. I remembered my mother and aunts doing their magic quietly, rarely leaving the house, and Valerie didn't come over very often either. There were talks about moving off the island if nothing could be done, and being the ignorant child I'd been, all I could think about was having to leave my friends behind. I'd only learned more of the story when Sinéad had come back five years ago and reclaimed the island.

I must have gotten lost in memories and thoughts, because I was jolted out of them by a buzz in my pocket. I dug it out, and released Vincent's pendant as I realized I was holding it.

RedSam

> dan is pretending to complain about all the love you gals have been showing him the past few days.

I laughed, sighing thankfully. I didn't want to think about Nick and the potential issues that were arising, at least for a minute.

LilTriquetra

> Oh he pretends he doesn't like it, lol

RedSam

i'm really glad you four scooped him up, he's a good guy.

LilTriquetra

Yes he is! We like him. We're going to keep him.

RedSam

awesome, awesome.

you know about the Mabon festival at ladine's?

LilTriquetra

Yeah, we were planning on going to it. Alexis and Valerie are my mom's friends and Jamari works there

RedSam

oh, cool

He was typing for quite a while, and the little bubble kept popping up and down as if he were typing and deleting repeatedly. I chuckled and took mercy on him.

LilTriquetra

Yes you can go with us

RedSam

oh thank you, I couldn't figure out how to ask

He sent a GIF of a guy collapsing to the ground in relief, and I giggled.

"Oh? Who are you smiling at over there?" Valerie asked, off the phone and sitting back down on the couch with me. She was placing two glasses of soda on the coffee table for us. I flushed.

"Vincent."

"Is that your dream guy?" She asked with a teasing grin.

"Am I never going to get to share my own stories?" I asked, pulling my knees up and dropping my forehead to them with a groan. Valerie laughed.

"I'm sorry, news spreads fast in the coven." She settled at my side. "Why don't you go ahead and tell me everything from your point of view?"

So I did. I showed her the note on my phone and told her about what had happened in Dubhan, Vincent and I trading necklaces and somehow feeling each other's emotions through them, everything I could think of. She read and listened quietly, asking a few clarification questions, but that was all.

"Well, I don't know what to make of the amethysts doing that, but we could talk to Alexis if you'd like. She made them." Valerie got up to take our empty glasses into the kitchen, and I turned to peep at her over the couch again.

"I don't mind it most of the time, but I catch myself holding it without thinking, and since he got my number he always texts to make sure I'm alright. Like it's sweet and thoughtful but I don't know him super well, y'know? It feels like skipping a few steps." I draped my arms over the back of the couch and sighed, and Val laughed.

"I getcha, kiddo. You two need to actually talk and have a conversation, then it'll feel less weird." I opened my mouth to speak, but didn't get the chance as she pointed at me and said, "And I don't mean texting, I mean face-to-face. You kids and your cell phones..." I giggled quietly at her. She sounded like an old woman sometimes.

I spent another few hours in her apartment, talking to her about school and my friends, and she told me what to expect at the Mabon Festival and about the last date she and Alex went on. By the time she walked me back to the apartment, the smell had faded and Nick was gone, but the smudges on his door were still there. There were a couple on mine as well now, so I cleaned them off before I got ready for bed. He could mark up his own space, but not mine.

Before I went to sleep, I texted Vincent. It was late and he was probably getting ready to go to sleep himself, but I needed it off my mind.

LilTriquetra

Can we talk about all the dream stuff soon? Feels weird having it happen and just… not saying anything yknow

RedSam

i would absolutely love to, katiyana. i'll be back at school tomorrow. if we don't get a chance then, we'll talk at the festival.

LilTriquetra

sounds great

RedSam

lol, goodnight then, Yana.

LilTriquetra

Night vinny !!

Vincent

MUCH TO BOTH OF our chagrins, Katiyana and I didn't get a chance to talk privately at school the next day. We didn't see each other between classes, didn't have any together, and at lunch I was officially welcomed to their table with a small spectacle of Broadway show tunes being sung quietly at the table. ("You're really singing *Cabaret* at school? Do you want to get detention?" Alena shushed them.) No one mentioned what had kept me out of school, and even my teachers just gave me the makeup homework without question. Mr. Rossi held my gaze for a moment longer than was really necessary, and I felt sympathy from him even though he hadn't said a word. I had a sneaking suspicion they knew something had happened, and I wanted to ask them all how much they knew. I decided in the end it was probably for the best that we didn't discuss it, and I allowed myself to let it go. After all, the security force was aware of everything, so I wouldn't be surprised if some of the school officials had also been made aware. Probably something to do with keeping Mom off school grounds.

After a night's sleep soundtracked by his snoring, Dan woke me up far earlier than normal for a Saturday morning, declaring that we were going shopping before the festival and he would have no arguments on the matter. Over breakfast, I discovered that it had been his mother's idea, so she'd be driving us around and also buying me some new clothes.

"We're going to stop and look at bunk beds, as well, like we talked about earlier. No more air mattress for you,

Vinnyboy." She grinned, twirling her keys around her finger. I grinned back, stunned, unable to say anything for a minute. Justine pulled me into a quick hug before going out to start the car, and Dan slung his arm around my shoulders to lead me out.

"Just so you know, I didn't influence this, you cannot blame me, and I refuse to take any credit." He was completely serious and somehow this made his statement even more amusing than it would have been if he were teasing, and I started laughing, a hand over my mouth. "Vinny!"

"I'm sorry! I'm just... shocked. You and your parents have already done so much for me, and now you want to do more, I just... I don't know what to say or how to react."

Dan rolled his eyes. "You say 'thank you, Webers, for taking good care of me.'" He shook his head at me and strode off to the car, and I followed quickly as Dan's mom waved to me from the front seat.

We traveled to the mall, and I glanced into the odds and ends shop we'd found Marie's perfume in with a smile as we passed it. Three stores later, Dan was holding two bags and I was holding one, and Dan's mom was nearly skipping with joy. She'd been excited and bubbly the entire time, encouraging me to try on the clothes at the shops and "hyping me up," as Dan had said, with every outfit. Dan had too, and I found myself standing a little straighter in my new jacket as we walked back to the car. While we waited for our turn to pull out of the parking lot, I leaned forward and tapped Justine on the arm.

"Thank you, so much. This means the absolute world to me," I said, willing that high level of sincerity that Jackson's voice carried into mine. "I've never had something as nice as this. I'm going to wear it forever." I tugged on the lapel of my jacket and Justine beamed at me, wiggling happily in her seat.

"You, my darling, are so welcome. I love shopping, Dan loves shopping, and now we have someone else to buy things for. You are doing us a favor by keeping new clothes in your closet and not in ours!" She laughed, clearly amused at her own joke, and Dan chuckled in agreement. I leaned back, still smiling, and lifted my phone to pull up the single photo Dan had snapped of me showing off one of the outfits I'd tried on.

"Should I send this to the girls?" I asked, holding out my phone to Dan.

"Oo, what girls?" Justine asked, and I flushed, ducking my head down.

"Oh, Fleur's group of friends, you remember the girl from the uh... marina?" I asked, praying it wasn't as awkward to think about for her as it was for me. She just nodded, so I continued. "It's her, and a couple others."

"Fleur's agender, dork, not a girl." Then his tone shifted as he spoke to his mom. "They've kidnapped us into friendship!" Dan said, pressing his hands to the top of the car. Being around his mom most of the day had made me realize where he got his energy and dramatics from. "We'll never be free of them." Justine laughed.

"Oh no! How awful! My boys have friends to care about them!" She giggled through her words, turning to check her blind spot before shifting lanes.

I ended up sending the photo to the group chat, with the caption "Dan said if I'm living with him I need to dress better."

Beefaroni

I DID NOT, DON'T BELIEVE HIM

BlondeBrainiac

Too late, I've accepted it as canon

LilTriquetra

HAHAHA you look good tho vinny!!

GameznStuff

You do bro! nice fit!

QueenofGambits

yeah that tracks as far as dan goes, and that's fire on u vincent, nice choice

LilTriquetra

When are you guys coming to ladines ???

RedSam

one more stop to make, then home, then we'll head there

GameznStuff

Break is over, see u soon guys

BlondeBrainiac

These boys are so rude, making us wait hours for them. Why did we adopt them? Let's take them back to the pound.

QueenofGambits

We can't, dan has the best camera on his phone

Beefaroni

Oh I see, that's all I'm good for

QueenofGambits

No, we needed a himbo to round out our party <3

I burst out into a fit of laughter as Dan gaped at his phone, his mom looked back curiously as best she could while driving. I was completely out of breath before I realized Dan had taken advantage of my laughing fit to get the attention off him, and was recording me wheezing to send to the group. I was too late to stop him, so I resigned myself to my fate.

LilTriquetra

Oh my goddess, alena, you murdered vincent

QueenofGambits

He's fine

LilTriquetra

We'll put your body in the middle of the ritual circle and necromancy you

BlondeBrainiac

You think alexis will let us?

LilTriquetra

Yeah probably

GameznStuff

I mean ladine's already has all the ingredients

BlondeBrainiac

STOP TEXTING ON THE CLOCK but you're right

QueenofGambits

We could copy the ritual from Practical Magic

LilTriquetra

NOOOOO oh my gods no absolutely not never do not

BlondeBrainiac

I'm with yana, absolutely not

QueenofGambits

>:)

LilTriquetra

I hate you

The specifics of my resurrection were now being planned out, sans whatever the Practical Magic ritual was, and I chuckled and watched the conversation unfold as Dan, Justine, and I walked around a furniture store looking for bunk beds. To anyone else a conversation about my death right after I'd tried to actually make it happen would probably be taboo, but since they were talking specifically about bringing me back to life, it felt fine. Some part of me was overjoyed to have people talking about wanting me alive, even if they had already let me die from laughter. I'd only been talking to them regularly for a few days, but now I couldn't imagine going back to the quiet life I'd had without my new friends. They were full of life and fire, they were intelligent and friendly, and Dan and I were lucky to have them, even if he complained about the affection. Dan matched their energy well, and I realized as Justine was discussing delivery of the bunk beds that this group of friends was exactly what I needed in my life. I got so caught up in that thought that Dan had to nudge me out of the store, trailing after his mom.

"What's on your mind babe?" He asked, sliding his arm through mine. I pressed it close to my side quickly, smiling at him.

"Just... thinking about how lucky I suddenly am and how I hope it keeps up. I feel," I laughed, just a little breath, "I feel like an entirely different person."

Dan chuckled gently, patting my arm and tugging it closer. "Well that's because you kind of are, you're Vinny 2.0 now." His teasing grin made me squint.

"What's that supposed to mean?"

He snickered. "Well, you didn't exactly come back from the dead, but you did come back from the edge of a cliff and you haven't made a single joke about going back to one since." His grin turned sincere. "And you have yourself very firmly on Katiyana's radar now."

"Well you're right about the first part," I agreed. "But I don't think she sees me like that." I shrugged. "Plus, you're still shooting your sh—" His hand covered my mouth.

"After seeing you two trade necklaces? No, no I am NOT shooting my shot. You are. And if you don't, I'm shooting your shot for you." All his love was suddenly showing as determination, and I cracked a grin.

"Never thought I'd live to see the day Daniel Weber would be the one to give up on a girl without getting rejected."

He punched my arm lightly, untangling us and moving away. "Never thought I would see the day your dreams would be infecting mine! I dreamed about Charles again last night. I'm going to complain if it keeps happening. Also, she did technically reject me, at least at first, anyway." He settled his hands behind his head and caught up with his mom, leaving me to grin after him.

"Sure, Dan, keep complaining." I whispered to myself, making a very large mental note to start marking down the times he did just that.

Katiyana

Saturday, September 26, 2020

We had arrived at Ladine's early to help Jamari, Alexis, and Val finish setting up the decorations for the festival. I was in the midst of trying to pin a streamer to the wall when Valerie ducked under my arm to get close enough to whisper.

"Did your brother say anything about coming today?"

I rolled my eyes, shaking my head at the same time. "No, actually. In fact, he told me he would rather die than be caught in this establishment."

"Hilarious, considering he just came in yesterday to pick up more candles." Valerie rolled her eyes as well, holding out her hand to help me hop off the stool. "Did he say anything about where he was going?"

"Mm-mm, nothing."

Val sighed. "I wonder if the remaining Mortmores on the island are doing a ritual today. They've been pretty good about keeping their information private since Sinéad came back." Val blew her bangs out of her face, tapping her fingers on her arm. "I hope they're not doing anything today."

"Are they Pagan too?"

"Of a sort. They don't practice the same kind of magic we do." Val smirked, waving her fingers at the decorated room, and toward Alexis who was preparing the altar in the center.

"If Nick is copying them, does that mean our magic is going to clash?" The thought made me nervous, especially with our rooms, and therefore our altars, down the hall from each other.

"Only if he targets you specifically, and can get past the protection spell we cast on you when you were born. He has the same one, but I'm sure he'd remove it if he could. He might have already, honestly."

"Wait, protection spell? Nobody ever told me about—"

"Heh, don't worry about it kiddo, your mom was in on it, and since the island about went to shit a few years later, it was a bit of lucky foresight on our part." She smirked at me, patting my head. I wrinkled my nose at her and patted my hair back down, following her toward Alexis.

"Do you do it for all the coven kids?" I asked, and Alexis looked up at the question curiously.

"Do what now? Valerie, are you sharing coven secrets?" Alexis had a teasing grin, but Valerie ducked her head all the same.

"I am not, she just found out about the protection spell we did when she was a baby." Val crossed her arms in defense. I giggled.

"Well in that case, yes, Katiyana, every child born on this island who is connected to the coven gets that same spell. But also any other child on this island whose family asks for it. We aren't exclusive about it." She turned back to the altar, adjusting a candle just so before nodding, seemingly declaring it perfect. Then she turned to me, laying a hand on my shoulder. "I'd like to talk to you and Vincent both if I could today, or soon. Together." I nodded.

"I know I would love that and I think he would too. I actually asked him if he and I could sit down and talk about stuff, as well. Things are just too... weird. And you did tell us you'd share more after the spell." I gave her a pointed look and she broke into a smile.

"I did indeed. If I'm not swamped after the ritual, I'll come find you both. But if I am, let's arrange a time later." Alexis patted my shoulder twice then swept off, her skirt trailing behind her in such a way it looked as if she were gliding.

"How does she do that?"

"She made a deal with Hecate to be ominous and mysterious wherever she goes." Val wiggled her fingers at me in the universal symbol of "spooky" and I laughed. It would have seemed far-fetched to anyone outside of the coven—or at the very least, outside of the island—but I believed it.

Valerie and I parted to finish decorating, and I moved over to my friends to help them organize the refreshments table. We had just finished the layout when all our phones pinged or buzzed, and we laughed as a group over all of the shenanigans we'd created.

"Boss?" Jamari asked as Alexis passed our little group, cross-legged on the floor and heads bent over our phones.

"Hm? Are you catching Pokémon at work again?" Alexis didn't even look up from the incense she was sorting through.

"No, def not!" Jamari closed Pokémon Go as soon as the Galarian Meowth she was after stayed in the ball. "Would you let us put Vincent in the ritual circle and necromance him back to life if he died?" Jamari's tone was so sincere, not a trace of joking in her voice, and Alexis turned to stare at us for a moment. The rest of us suppressed giggles, Alena having to clap a hand over her mouth.

"Gracious, I think I just heard Hecate herself sigh." Alexis muttered, and our laughter escaped. Alexis smiled, but threw a package of cone incense at us, and we all squeaked and ducked. Fleur caught it. "Absolutely not. You will have to use the circle outside. No reanimated corpses in my shop."

The Squad

Saturday, September 26th, 2020

IT WAS THE FIRST time Vincent had been into the base-ment, his third time in the building overall. The past two times, the shop had been emptier, just the two employees and maybe a few more people. But now it was packed, wall-to-wall almost. The only thing keeping the people away from the altar itself was the outline of the ritual circle, traced long ago in chalk and made permanent by a mosaic of colored stones cemented into the basement floor.

Vincent's back was currently pressed to the wall, his hand held by his ever-present loyal friend who had grabbed it the moment he had noticed the nerves tightening Vin-cent's shoulders. Dan knew his best friend was an intro-vert, and crowds would kick that personality trait into high gear. So Dan squished Vincent's fingers in his own, giving him a tether to the Earth so he didn't float away.

The coven mother was speaking, her voice carrying easi-ly to every corner of the room. Earlier, when the room was emptier, Vincent had noted that there were no speakers and Alexis wore no microphone. So was it magic, or was she just an excellent speaker? He wanted to ask, raise his hand like in class, but she'd already turned and begun a different speech.

"She's calling the quarters. She'll face each direction and ask the elements to join our workings." His spine straight-ened as breath tickled his ear, a lock of hair that wasn't his falling onto his shoulder. Katiyana was whispering to him, as low as she could so as to not disturb the ritual. As soon as Vincent realized who had snuck up on him, his shoulders lowered from his ears. Katiyana's hand patted between his shoulder blades, a silent apology, and they returned to listening to Alexis call upon the elements.

With a final turn around the circle, Alexis faced north, stretching her arms and fingertips toward the floor as if reaching for the Earth itself. "Great Mother, we call upon your energy, your power, to be with us at this Mabon rite. Assist us in our workings, we beseech thee!"

What felt like a deep rumbling pushed upward through the soles of Vincent's shoes. He looked down, expecting the cement floor to be cracking, but nothing. A glance to Dan revealed he didn't or couldn't feel it, and a glance to Katiyana revealed her conspiratorial smile. Their eyes met, and Katiyana's smile stretched into a reassuring grin, nudging her arm gently against his.

Alexis's voice was replaced by another. This one was deeper, reverberating, sonorous. And familiar! Vincent pulled his gaze away from Katiyana's captivating smile to see a face he'd seen almost every weekend for the past five years. Dorell, the head librarian, was now speaking. "We honor today our harvest, our abundance, and the deepening shadow. We step today toward the darkest part of the year, where we give thanks for all we have and all we are able to take into the cold months." It sounded nearly like a sermon the way he said it, even though instead of having his hands placed purposefully on a pulpit or held reverently together, Dorell had his raised on either side, his head bowed, eyes closed. He continued with his speech, speaking of the transitions of the seasons and the passage of time, the shortening of the light. Dark and cold were not to be feared, but welcomed. Accepted as a necessity. It was a time to reflect and prepare, to dig inside yourself and pull from your own warmth rather than outside sources.

Dorell and Alexis took turns calling in deities, some Greek, some Celtic, some Egyptian. They asked for each one's assistance in their workings just as she had asked the elements. Vincent was desperately trying to memorize everything, commit it all to memory, and found himself suddenly ungrounded. The dense, heavy energy that had folded around him was dissipating, floating away from him, and his ears began ringing.

Katiyana saw him flinch out of the corner of her eye, glanced over to see the hard set of his jaw, and reached out gently for his hand. Her fingers slid between his, pressing her fingertips between his knuckles and situating her palm flat against his.

The energy returned to Vincent nearly immediately.

They remained like that through the rest of the ritual, a linked trio with both of the edges doing their best to keep the middle present and calm. Little did they know, he was overwhelmingly aware of every single energy in the room.

Dorell was speaking of gratitude now, of thanking those on the island that took care of her citizens, the security force and emergency responders and firefighters, and anyone else with a role that meant public service of the noblest sort. He asked the gathered crowd to add their gratitude to the workings, to send it into the island below and add the thankfulness to their ley lines. It was nothing for Katiyana, who had done this every year since she was seven. Dan did the best he could, though he didn't understand what Dorell meant when he said send energy down. Vincent closed his eyes, bowed his head, and let his breath out in a slow trickle, asking his gratitude to go with it and his bitterness to remain within him. Mother Earth took both, anyway.

Alena, Fleur, and Jamari found the trio during the brief interlude where the altar was moved from the center of the room and against a wall, to make room for the dance. The two trios were reunited as a whole, even though they'd only been across the room from each other.

The dance involved holding hands, arms crossed in front of you to cling to either person at your sides. Vincent positioned himself between Dan and Katiyana on purpose, and sighed silently, gratefully, when the rest of the Squad filled in on either side. He would be well separated from others.

The footwork was tricky at first, Dan and Vincent slowly figuring out what their friends already knew and had long practiced. Suddenly it all made sense that the rest of the Squad had made sure the boys were between them.

As they caught on, everyone was able to move faster and faster, most participants allowing their delight to escape into laughter, everyone smiling adoringly. It was hard not to feel joyful when everyone was a single wrong step from a hilarious domino effect.

The crowd twisted around, three concentric circles moving clockwise and gathering all the gratitude, love, and joy they could. They'd already sent some into the ley lines, but once you looked out into the room to see your fellow citizens laughing, more was easy to find.

The music rose to a glorious crescendo. Alexis and Dorell broke away from the innermost circle to stand back-to-back in the middle, their spots quickly and easily filled by reaching hands. They snapped their arms up at the same time, and half a heartbeat later everyone had stopped and followed suit, laughter filling the space where music had been.

Basking in the moment was easy; Vincent's heartbeat was pounding in his ears and his breath was ragged, but his heart felt full in a way it never had before.

Vincent

Katiyana and I flopped back in a corner of the room where no one's stuff had been piled, both still panting from the dance. The circle had been released, the quarter guardians thanked, and the deities hailed. Alexis was still in the middle of the circle, cleansing some little trinkets and tools on the altar. I watched from afar until Katiyana nudged me with her elbow.

"Did you enjoy it?" She asked, smiling at me with her head leaned back against the wall. "It was your first Sabbat ritual, right?"

"Yeah. I honestly didn't even know Mabon existed until Alexis told me about the festival." I pushed my hair back with my hand, looking over the room filled with festival-goers, paper streamers, and balloons all in various shades of orange, yellow, brown, and red. Dan and the others were gathered around a table that held all of the food from the potluck, talking to Valerie and a tall Egyptian man with black hair whom I assumed was her boyfriend.

"I think I've been to every Sabbat festival here since I was little. This is my first one without my parents, though." Katiyana tugged her knees up and wrapped her arms around them, watching the people in the room with a relaxed grin, lifting a hand in greeting to one of them. She belonged here, with these people. I caught myself watching her expressions change, flitting between content, excited, and amused. She caught me doing it. "What?" She asked, squinting and wrinkling her nose at me. I chuckled softly, turning my gaze down. I could feel heat on my face and I prayed it wasn't showing.

"Just thinking that you really belong here, is all." My voice was soft, and I scolded myself internally for copying Jackson's tone again. She must have caught it, because I saw the pink flush across her cheekbones.

"Should warn me before you do that." Katiyana lifted her hands to her cheeks, patting them as if to force the pink away but only creating more. I smirked apologetically. I understood her plight but it didn't make it less cute.

"I'm sorry."

"I forgive you." She stuck her tongue out at me briefly then draped her arms over her knees, tapping her thumbs together. "What do you think about all of it?"

"The dreams?"

"Those, and past lives, and Marie and Jackson."

"Well, it's nice to know that in some life, I was so happy I would have risked my job just to talk to someone." I shrugged, looking down at my shoes. A lace was untied so I set about righting it as I spoke. "I'm not really weirded out by it. I've figured for a while that reincarnation was a possibility. It explains a lot of unexplainable things. I guess I'm more surprised that dreams are the favored form of remembrance."

"Yeah, I guess I wasn't really shocked either, until I saw Leo. Having a family friend pop into your subconscious is weird whether it's a past life or not." She laughed, pointing with her chin to where Leo and the Bruadarach stood in the opposite corner.

"How does your family know him? Beyond the Bruadarach, I mean."

"Oh, Sinéad is my cousin. You know that whole split-soul, twin-flame thing they have going on?" Katiyana said the words as if they were perfectly ordinary, but I just stared at her.

"Split...soul?"

"You know what, that does sound weird out loud. Sinéad and Leo are bound together, they're two parts of the same soul. It came as a shock to the rest of our family too. Well, except my grandma. And my mom, and the aunts..." Katiyana furrowed her brow, seemingly taking inventory of family members who would be surprised by such a blatantly metaphysical concept. I shrugged, deciding to just roll with it for now. I could look it up later.

"I'll take your word for it."

"Vin, I don't want you to take this the wrong way but—" My heart froze for a moment as she spoke, and I glanced over to see her picking at the hem of her jeans. I stayed silent to let her continue, but internally I was rocketed back to my conversation with Dan at the furniture store. "Fleur said something to me when these dreams first started that's really been sticking out in my head the past couple days, and I think you need to hear it too. It's nothing bad, but it's helped me stay grounded as all this has been going on."

"What is it?" Still ridiculously terrified, I was sure she was going to tell me we needed to stop speaking until the dreams ended. Despite knowing it was irrational, logic couldn't stop the pounding of my heart.

"She said she wanted me to make sure I was living my own life instead of trying to copy Marie's. And I want to. And since now I know you and I were...at least *interested* in each other in the past, I don't want to just dive right into a relationship with you. I'm a lot different than Marie, and I'm sure you're a lot different than Jackson. So right now, I absolutely want to be your friend, and then let's just see how things end up, yeah?" She looked up, absolute sincerity in those astonishing silver eyes, and my shoulders relaxed. A smile spread on my face and I nodded with a relieved sigh, my head falling back to rest on the wall.

"Yes, yes Katiyana, I would love to be friends with you." I laughed, an unintentional reflex releasing my anxiety.

"You're acting like I was about to reject you." She nudged me with her arm again, and I laughed for real.

"I really thought you were going to tell me to stop talking to you for a while." I grinned, shrugging loosely. "I don't know where the thought came from, but I was suddenly just so terrified you wanted to push me away."

"Aww Vinny, poor dear." She laughed through her words, looping her arm through mine. "I'm not going to abandon a puppy I found at the marina. That would be cruel."

"A puppy?" I asked, feigning offense. She giggled.

"Yeah, you're cute and you follow us around like one." With a quick squeeze of my arm, she then released it and stood, holding out her hand. "Would you like to meet the Bruadarach? I'm planning on telling her off for keeping secrets from me about our past life together."

I took her hand and stood, still a little dazed that she'd called me cute, but I snapped out of it long enough to speak.

"Oh, right, Sinéad is Clara." I'd figured that out when Leon and I had spoken, and entirely forgotten about it.

"Yeah! Let's go chew her and Leon out." She tugged me over toward their corner. "Just make sure to call him Leon, not Leo. Sinéad said he's been zoning out when people call him Leo for some reason."

"Ah, yeah, I can do that." Boy, if I thought my life was weird before, now I was one step away from the leader of Faodail herself, entwined in some repeating cycle. But, if I were to be honest with myself, I very much preferred this kind of weird.

Katiyana

Saturday, September 26, 2020

I'D INTRODUCED VINNY TO my cousin, the leader of the island, and he didn't seem overwhelmed by it at all. Or if he was, he was really good at hiding it. I caught him reaching for his pendant once, so I had a feeling it was the latter. I listened idly as Sinéad bemoaned the rules about past life information-sharing that the druids and coven had put in place, slumping back against the wall as Leo laughed.

"This is partially your fault, you know," she said, pointing at him with her soda bottle. "Because you just had to tell me everything about my life in the seventies. They came after you for that one."

"I didn't break any rules, all I did was confirm your questions." Leo's tone was calm and measured; this was absolutely an argument they'd had before. He gave her a smug, but loving smirk. Sinéad sighed, rolling her eyes. I glanced over to Vincent to find him serenely listening, fingers curled around his own bottle of soda. He didn't seem uncomfortable.

"You two act so much like each other." I grinned as Sinéad shot me a soft glare.

"She acts like me, not the other way around." Leo chuckled around another sip of what looked like beer, but since Alexis and Valerie hadn't provided any, he must have snuck it in.

"Sure, says the man who's stolen my music, food, and clothing tastes."

"Are...you two married?" Vincent asked. Leo nearly spit out his beer and slapped a hand on his mouth to catch it, and I started laughing. Vincent looked between us in alarm. "Wh...what?"

"Not to each other." Sinéad snickered, pulling her phone out to flip through photos and turn her screen to Vincent. Her actual husband was in the frame with her, under a moon just a sliver away from full and surrounded by early winter greenery. It was different seeing it in a photo rather than being there in person. Leo's phone slid onto the table next to Sinéad's, showing his own wedding photo with his husband in his arms, Leo kissing Dominick's forehead. Vincent looked between the two photos, his cheeks flushing pink.

"I'm so sorry for assuming, you two just act like it, like you've been married for ages." He ducked his head, rubbing the back of it, and I reached over to pat his back.

"Aw Vinny don't worry, most people think that about them." I giggled, wrapping my arm around his shoulders to jiggle him a bit. He looked up at me with a thankful smile.

Sinéad and Leo talked about their respective husbands and weddings for a tad bit longer, then Leo's phone pinged with a message. "Ah, Juls is waiting for us at the apartment."

"Off we go then." Sinéad kissed the top of my head before they left, leaving me and Vincent alone at the table. The silence only lasted a few seconds.

"I still feel so dumb for assuming they were married," he muttered, rolling his now empty soda bottle between his palms. I giggled again softly.

"Don't worry, I really mean it when I say people always assume that about them. Until Dom comes into the room and suddenly it's like Sinéad doesn't exist at all. And Sinéad's wedding wasn't super public either, since she wasn't actually Bruadarach yet." I grinned at Vincent, who chuckled, then sighed. "What's wrong?"

"It's just... a lot to take in, y'know?" He glanced up at me, then back down. "I kind of suspected all this kind of magic stuff might exist but, it's kinda been shoved in my face the last few days and I guess I'm still processing. I know you grew up with it, it's probably second-nature to you."

I shrugged, tapping my empty bottle against the table as quietly as I could manage. "Some of it...well, most of it. Yeah most of it. But there's still a lot I don't know. MacAskill kids don't start training until the Samhain after they turn sixteen, so I'm not even due to start that until next month."

"It's so strange to me that just because you're part of a bloodline you get this special training that isn't offered to anyone else." His brow was furrowed again and he looked into the opening of the bottle. I sat up a little straighter, a retort forming on my tongue, but then softened. He'd been raised opposite of me, far away from the coven instead of at its center.

"Actually you know that teen witch class we told you about?"

"Yeah?"

"That's MacAskill branch magic. It's the same training. It's offered to anyone who's interested. The kids in the bloodline just kinda...get it as they grow up, I guess? With family rituals and stuff at home." I hoped I was making sense. "It's just done in case they get chosen as the next Heir Apparent—"

"Heh, Katiyana, your family has been leading and caring for the island longer than we've both been alive, you don't have to justify their traditions to me." Vincent gave me a reassuring smile, and I shushed myself, he was right. "I didn't know the class was the same, and honestly I guess I was just a little jealous. I wish I had grown up in a magic family like you did." His smile faded a bit, got sadder. I chewed on my lip, keeping my eyes down for a moment.

"You should join us at Alexis's class then. We can be your family." I hadn't realized how much I meant the words until I'd spoken them, but heck, there they were out in the open. "I bet Alexis would even welcome you as a coven member when you have enough training." Copying him, I rolled my empty bottle between my palms. I was about to speak again when he spoke up.

"You know what...I think I'd really like that." Without looking over to him, all I heard was Jackson again, so I looked directly at him to be sure I hadn't suddenly started dreaming. But Vincent's dark hair was there, his dark eyes met mine, and we shared a smile.

"I would too, Vinny."

The Dreamers

JACKSON'S VOICE WAS SOFT, gentle, as he relayed another tale of a Greek hero and the lady he loved. This time it was Orpheus and Eurydice, and even Jackson, who knew the story by heart, was praying Orpheus wouldn't turn around this time. But he knew Orpheus would, and he kept adding embellishments and more details to the story to make it last longer, to keep the tragedy further away. Charles had noticed, but had chosen not to say anything or make a taunt because he didn't like this ending either.

"Why is it so important I know what every color of every flower is?" Marie interrupted, staring Jackson dead in the eye. His brush twitched and a line of chocolate painted across the mold, but not where it needed to be. One muttered curse and a swipe of a cloth later and it was remedied, and Jackson had gathered himself.

"It's not, my apologies, I'm getting lost in the details again." He sighed wistfully, looking up at her to offer a reassuring smile, promising silently that she hadn't upset him with the question or the chocolate incident, and she relaxed. He continued his story, still adding in superfluous details here and there, but hopefully not in an amount she could detect. She was starting to suspect this wasn't a happy ending, but couldn't figure out how since Orpheus and Eurydice had only recently gotten married. Charles had normally chimed in with a taunt or twelve by now, but this time he was silent. Still, she wanted to hear the tale, and even more so, wanted Jackson to keep talking.

And so he did. Eurydice got enticed to the Underworld, and Orpheus followed, on foot with lyre in hand the whole way. He begged at Hades' feet, charming Persephone's heart with a song and adding her voice to his plea. Hades relented for a price: he must not turn to see his beloved the entire time they walked out of the Underworld. Marie's face fell as Jackson described the fateful turn, the one spin on Orpheus' heel as he opened his arms to embrace his wife just a few steps too soon.

"Oh no, oh dear me, that's so sad. I can't bear it." Her heart was heavy in her chest, and she pressed her hand to it, her other fingers lifting to wipe away the few tears that had escaped her eyes. Jackson frowned. He had nearly wanted to change the ending, but deep down inside he knew it wouldn't be right to. He tugged a handkerchief from his pocket, moving around the table to offer it to her.

"I'm sorry, I don't like the ending either. Orpheus ended up isolating himself for a long time, and it's completely understandable why. To have someone you love so dearly ripped away from you like that, I can't imagine." He reached up to dab lightly at Marie's cheekbone. She laid her hand over his and his breath caught. A quick glance up revealed she was looking at him, but not his eyes. The realization made his heart speed up. If he could have heard it, he would have known her heart's pace matched his own. She leaned first, a stray tear trailing down her cheek to meet her jawline. His other hand lifted to catch it, smoothing his fingers to her cheek, a bit of Shakespeare repeating in his head: *O, that I were a glove upon that hand, that I might touch that cheek*...would another tragedy, even if not Greek, be a good story next?

"Jackson." Marie's whisper was soft enough it could have been a breath, and it felt like one as it traced over his lip. He closed his eyes, pulling her ever so gently toward him. Her hand lifted, fingers shy at first, then sliding into the hair at the nape of his neck as their lips met. The world quieted, shrunk, until it contained Marie, Jackson, and the little handkerchief still held against her cheek.

"I'll go see who it is." Charles' unusually soft voice interrupted as a knock sounded from the front of the shop, the front door withholding a customer eager to shop before opening.

The pair startled as they simultaneously remembered they weren't alone in the room. Jackson pulled away, looking up at Marie with furrowed brows. Her face mirrored his; it was exceptionally unusual for anyone to try to come in before opening.

"Sir! This is the kitchen, customers aren't—"

"I'll tell you what I can and can't do, you Irish bastard! Get out of my way." Marie froze at the voice, but only briefly, then scurried off her stool and tried to leave through the back door. Jackson only had time to register she wasn't in his arms before a man nearly bigger than the doorway barged into the room, and upon realizing who it was, Jackson's eyes widened. Oh, heavens above, had he seen?

"Marie!" Lucas shouted, and Marie shrank against the door that she was struggling to open. "You little harlot." The word was said with absolute venom, malice, any other nasty thing Lucas could thread into it without adding physical violence. "I should have known this is why you kept coming here." He slid his narrowed snake eyes to Jackson, his fists balling at his sides. His visage was contorted into a mask of rage, a vein pulsing on his temple. Jackson stumbled back against the table, catching himself with his hands.

"Sir I've already told you, you can't be in he—" Charles was silenced by a fist slammed into his jaw, a blow hard enough to send him to the floor. Jackson's heart felt like it was ready to beat right out of his chest. Charles stayed down, not a fighter even in a fair match, and slid under one of the tables. Jackson didn't fault him, as Lucas probably had sixty pounds or more on both of them.

The man made his way to Jackson, who threw his hands up and tried his damndest to appear smaller and as submissive as possible.

"Sir, please, she's not at faul—" Jackson tried to say but Lucas' hand was already around his throat, and he choked, grabbing at the arm so much larger than his own.

"So you are then? You're the one seducing the woman who's meant to marry me? You're the one tempting her to sneak away every morning to come participate in your little tryst, here in this flour covered den? How much of your lovemaking has taken place on these tables? How many bags of flour have you soiled as you ruined another man's property?" Lucas's face was red, but Jackson couldn't be sure if it was due to Lucas's anger or his own increasingly reddened vision. Jackson tried to shake his head, to respond in any way, but the reaction was lost as sparks flew behind his eyes. The floor was suddenly beneath him and the back of his head was screaming with pain.

"You're the one trying to take my future wife from me? You filthy foreigners think you can just waltz right into our country and take whatever you please, huh? Our jobs, our women?" He slammed Jackson's head down again, hand on his throat squeezing all the tighter. It wasn't even possible for Jackson to gasp for air now, nothing was making it to his lungs. Through a partially opened eye Jackson saw Lucas's other fist draw back. He readied himself for a blow that was sure to knock him unconscious, raising shaking hands to try and block it. Somewhere in the far distance, Marie's heels clicked speedily across the floor.

"Lucas, Lucas please! Please stop, I'm begging you please!" Marie's cry was high and strained as she tugged on Lucas's arm to try and stop him from delivering the blow. "I'll go home with you right now if you stop hurting him! I'll tell Daddy I accept you! Please! Just stop hurting him!"

Lucas's hand squeezed tighter around Jackson's throat for just a moment longer, then released. Jackson gasped for air, coughing as he felt his limbs slowly come back to life, watching his vision go from red-tinged to vaguely normal. He looked up at Marie through the spots in his eyes. He couldn't bear the heartbroken and devastated image.

"Get your goddamn coat. If I ever catch you here again, even just to shop, I'll kill him." Marie nodded, moving to gather her things. Lucas caught her arm and pulled her to him roughly, the same hand that had just been around Jackson's throat. She squeaked softly in pain. "Do you hear me, you slut? I. Will. Kill. Him." His eyes were wild, determined, the vein still throbbing in his forehead. It was a sight she'd only seen once before, and hoped she never had to again. Why had her father promised her to such a horrid man? Why wouldn't he break the engagement every time she begged? "You belong to me, Marie."

Oh, how she *hated* that sentence.

"I hear you, I do. Please let me go," she whimpered, tears pouring over and sliding down her cheeks. Lucas shoved her in the direction of her things, kicking Charles's leg out of the way as he went back to the front door.

With her coat securely around her, purse clutched tightly in her hands, Marie looked at both men through teary eyes. "I'm sorry," she sobbed, running out to meet Lucas who stood at the front door impatiently.

Jackson struggled to his feet, Charles joined him at the door to the shop. Marie was leaving, possibly for the last time, and there was nothing he could do about it unless he wanted to lose his life. Lucas gave him one last threatening look, and tugged Marie out of the shop.

And as they left—Lucas's hand a vice around Marie's arm, Marie hiding her tear-stained face in Jackson's hand-kerchief—Jackson watched them go, wondering if this is how Orpheus felt as Eurydice faded from his view.

Katiyana

Sunday, September 27, 2020

My phone buzzed as I wrapped my hand around it, and a fresh wave of tears joined the ones I'd woken up with as I saw who it was.

His reply took a while, so I dried my eyes and quickly made my little list of bullet points while I waited. I wanted to forget this dream and pretend it never happened, pretend Lucas hadn't hurt Jackson and Marie both. Drying my eyes had been a useless endeavor as more tears just kept flowing, not stopping as I wrote.

I called him instead of responding, pulling the blankets over my head and rubbing at my wet cheeks as he picked up.

"Hold on," he whispered, and I heard soft rustling for a minute before he spoke again. "I didn't want to wake Dan." He definitely sounded out of breath.

We sat there in silence. I snuck a peek at the time on my phone, blown away to see it was four a.m. Mom would probably ground me for life if she found out.

"I hope that's the last time we ever see Lucas in a dream," Vincent whispered, his voice clearly coming from beneath a hand.

"I do too," I whispered back, sniffing as more tears tried to break. "What a horrible man, just horrible." I failed my fight against crying, and pulled the phone away from my mouth but not my ear in an attempt to muffle it. I heard a soft sigh from Vincent's end, and a moment later felt calm reassurance wash over me. My hand scrabbled for my pendant, clenching it desperately and letting myself cling to Vincent's energy. How he was calmer than me right now, I didn't know. He must have felt that pain, felt every smack against the floor. What it felt like to lose oxygen.

"Are you alright?" Vincent asked, his voice so gentle it nearly made me break down again. "I mean, I know you're not, but, is it any better?"

"Yeah. Thank you," I managed to whisper, shifting to hold my phone properly and press my pendant to my forehead. "Thank you."

"Thank you for letting me call you," he said, and I felt the energy ease but not go away entirely.

"I called you," I joked half-heartedly, and Vin chuckled. "That you did."

"Did you feel all of that? Everything he did?" I bit my lip after the question, remembering the tight squeeze of his fingers on Marie's bicep, wondering if I had a bruise where she surely did.

"...yeah. It... isn't something I'm interested in exploring again. I woke up gasping." Vincent's voice had grown small from its gentle confidence just a moment before. "I don't know how that didn't wake Dan, but then again, me leaving the room didn't, either."

"I'm so sorry." My heart hurt for him. Everything I'd seen through Marie's eyes he'd experienced. I just couldn't fathom it. "Are you still hurting?"

"A little, it'll fade. Most of it is probably from gasping like I did." I must have stayed quiet for too long. "I'm alright, Yana. I promise."

"I believe you. I just...I'm distraught. I want to just erase this from our history." I squeezed my eyes shut, trying to imagine a world in which Jackson and Marie could live without Lucas's shadow looming over them.

"I know. I would like that too. But it was nearly a hundred years ago. There's nothing we can do." I felt a comforting energy wash over me again, almost like a hug. It helped my shoulders loosen. "But also, who says that's the end of their story? Maybe we just know the main climax of conflict now." He sounded so sure of himself, I almost couldn't believe it. He'd gone through so much worse in that dream than I had, and yet here he was still thinking...I wasn't sure what he was thinking, honestly, but I was jealous of the hope in his tone.

"Are you just trying to make me feel better?" I said it more bitterly than I meant it, and I chastised myself. "I'm sorry. That was rude."

"It's alright. I know you're upset."

"You are too."

"Yeah. But I also know a secret." I caught the small smirk in his voice and rolled my eyes, but smiled all the same. "I swear I just felt a chill pass over my body, like someone I know is rolling her eyes at me—" Vincent laughed quietly, and I imagined swatting him like I did with my friends.

"Tell me the secret so I don't smack you next time I see you." Despite my want to sound annoyed, I knew my smile was audible.

"Usually, when the hero's plight is at its darkest, the story isn't over. It's just a sign he needs a moment to lie down and rest. Then he can pick his sword back up and go after the monster with new vigor. And since Jackson likes stories as much as I do, I'm sure he sees it, as well." How did he sound so wise for a teenager? It was a little odd, but reassuring all the same.

"What about Orpheus?" I asked, and Vincent quickly smothered a laugh.

"Yana there's exceptions to every rule." He was trying to sound annoyed like I had, but failing miserably at it. Worse than I had. "Although it is a very, very unfortunate exception."

"I wish he hadn't turned around," I muttered, allowing the grip on my pendant to finally loosen. Vincent had calmed me down. I hoped I'd managed to do the same for him.

"Same. Oh, big same." Vincent sighed. It was silent again for just a moment, then he stammered. "Remi-re-mind me to show you a song tomorrow, alright?"

"Alright. What is it?"

"It's a surprise. But I think you'll like it."

"Heh, okay. I'll trust you."

"What a wondrous gift." Vincent chuckled, and I grinned. The more comfortable he got around me, the more eloquent he got, the more pleasant to listen to. "And, as a tidbit, Katiyana?"

"Yeah?"

His next words were a half step from being sung, telling me my name sounded like a melody, and I felt my lips part to respond but no sound came out for what felt like a full minute.

"O-oh...gracious," I whispered, and I heard his nervous laugh at the other end of the line.

"You should go back to sleep." His voice had hit that tender note again, and my face grew hot, but not from having my phone on it.

"You should too, Vinny." How I managed to speak, I don't know. My head was cloudy, my mouth felt dry, and my heart had started pounding.

"As you command. Goodnight, Katiyana."

"Goodnight, Vincent."

As the call disconnected, I let my phone drop to the pillow beside me, staring into the darkness of my sheets. How on Earth was I supposed to fall back asleep now?

Vincent

Monday, September 28, 2020

As promised, I tugged Katiyana aside on the train to school and gave her my headphones, navigating to the Broadway section of my library to share "Come Home With Me" from *Hadestown*. Watching her facial expressions change from mildly confused to amused and then to flat out elated was fantastic, and she gave me a little pout when I didn't let it continue to the next song.

"I know, I'm sorry. They blend together," I said, taking my headphones back. "It's called *Hadestown*. It's a retelling of Orpheus and Eurydice and I think you'd enjoy it. This cast recording just came out last year. I was waiting for it."

"If the rest of the musical is as fun as that song, I think I will," she said, shouldering her bag as we stood up to file off the train with the rest of the students.

"I'm not sure 'fun' is the right word. It is that myth after all." I gave her an apologetic look and she sighed dramatically, wrapping both her arms around one of mine as we walked. I tried desperately not to tuck my face into my jacket. I could feel it burning.

"Vinny, Vinny, why did you have to remind me? I'm just going to pretend he turned around after she was safely out of the cave and ignore the actual myth, alright?" She sighed again and dropped my arm to go grab onto Jamari. The brief chill from where her arms had been left me breathless. But my heart felt lighter than it had upon waking, and lighter still when I looked up to see Katiyana laughing.

School came and went, and Dan and I had fallen into the pleasant expectation that the Squad would find us between classes, at lunch, and after school with no exceptions, and we welcomed it. The days where it was just Katiyana and me at Cridhe were oddly silent, but still enjoyable. Dan in particular was pleased with all the attention, and they had even started fixing his hair for him when they noticed a misplaced spike, or tugging our uniforms back into place. I was still getting used to it, and thankfully they'd noticed and left Dan to his normal sprucing me up.

"Is this what having siblings is like?" Dan mused aloud as Fleur fixed his collar. We were waiting for Kaityana and Alena to join us by the gate.

"It's what having you is like." I grinned at him and was met with a glare.

"Eh, Fleur never does any of that stuff for me so I wouldn't be able to tell you." Jamari laughed, ducking as Fleur spun and swung her messenger bag in Jamari's direction.

"You are constantly a mess. I would be fixing your clothes every five minutes if I took care of you like that. Dan at least TRIES to keep himself neat and tidy." She stuck her tongue out at her sister, and I chuckled. Being an only child was so, so different than having siblings.

"Mom! The girls are fighting!" Dan called, waving to Alena as she appeared on the stairs. Fleur turned back to him with her hand on her heart, jaw dropped, pure facetious hurt plastered on her face. She started a lament about how she'd been rejected from her position, and my eyes picked out Katiyana next to Alena. She met my gaze with a smirk and shifted her phone slightly from her ear so I could see she was on it. As the two final members of our "squad," as Dan kept calling it, joined us, Katiyana stood a bit away to finish her phone call.

"Since when am I Mom? I can't be Mom. That's Fleur's job. Have you seen her planner?" Alena was gesturing toward Fleur's bag, which Fleur promptly dug into and retrieved the planner in question. Dan flipped through it, and I peered over his shoulder to see meticulous scheduling, nearly down to the minute, for every single day except Sunday. That day had a single entry on it, midmorning.

"Are you religious, Fleur?"

"We all are, in our own ways, it just so happens that I follow one of the religions that meets on Sundays." She shrugged loosely, taking her planner back. "You're welcome to go with me sometime if you'd like. The church is a really lovely group of people; some of them even go to the events over at Ladine's."

"As I would expect from Faodail Christianity." I grinned, and gained one back, framed by her golden hair. If Fleur were alive when Michelangelo was, he would have absolutely used her as a model for an angel. She belonged in the Sistine Chapel.

"Vincent?" My thoughts of angels screeched to a halt as Katiyana spoke, and I lifted my gaze to see her holding her phone and looking at me expectantly.

"What is it?" I asked as Dan snickered and whispered something to Jamari somewhere on the edge of my hearing, but I ignored it.

"Will you go to Ladine's with me like, right now? Alexis still wants to talk to us." She huffed, tucking her phone into her bag. "I have so much sketching to do..." She muttered, buckling the bag back up.

I looked over at Dan who shook his head and put his hands up.

"I'm not your keeper, just tell me when you get on the train home." His phone was already in his hands, likely gearing up for a Connect binge since I wouldn't be in the same room. How he hadn't exhausted all potential suitors on the island yet was beyond me.

"Goodbyes" and "see you later"s were exchanged. Jamari took hold of Alena and Fleur and marched them toward the train station, calling for Dan. He looked up from his phone and scurried away after them, leaving Katiyana and me on our own. I dug my headphones out of my pocket and offered one to her, pulling up the *Hadestown* album on my phone once more. She grinned and took it, sliding her arm through mine, and we set off toward the café.

It took all my willpower to not just bask in the improbability of the situation I'd found myself in. Not only had I found the girl I'd been dreaming about, she was on my arm and sharing my music. And enjoying it! Despite my willpower, I lost to myself and found a smile on my face as I glanced at my reflection in a window. Then, as the moment froze briefly in time, everything clicked. I was allowed to let myself be happy about this. As long as Katiyana was comfortable with everything and I didn't push my crush on her too hard, it was fine. We could hang out, and she was obviously comfortable holding onto my arm or leaning against me. It had only been a few days and I still wanted to ask her out, but she had bluntly stated that she wanted to be friends first. So friends we'd be, and she could hold my hand as often as she wanted. I was starting to not mind the little flip my heart did every time she grabbed it.

By the time we reached Ladine's, Persephone was just barely starting to sing about summertime and bringing wine. Katiyana exhaled in mild frustration as I paused the music and took the headphones back.

"I'm just going to have to finish it myself, I guess." She shook her head, blinking dramatically as if blinking away tears, and I laughed as I pulled the door open for her. She stepped in and I followed.

"We can listen to it in bits and pieces around school, if you'd like. I'll remember where we left off."

"That would be great, but I think our five minute train rides would make it take a week."

"How horrible, to share music with you every morning for a week," I teased her, but she just rolled her eyes with a smile before turning to call for Alexis.

Not long after, we were seated at one of the café tables in the corner, each of us holding a cup of herbal tea across from Alexis who had a rather large and old book at her elbow. Valerie was at the counter very clearly pretending to not listen.

"Thank you for coming in at such short notice," Alexis said in a businesslike tone that made me smirk and Katiyana giggle.

"Why are you being so formal about it? Aren't we just here to talk about the dreams?" Katiyana took a sip of her tea, still grinning around it. Alexis laughed, that two-note huff of breath people do when something's amusing but they're being polite.

"I suppose you're right, there's no need to be the coven mother with either of you." She reached for the book, slipping a fingernail beside a ribbon bookmark and pulling the book open. "This is one of many records of the coven's history." Alexis spun the book toward us and pushed it over. Katiyana and I leaned forward to peer at the handwritten text. It was a register of members. My eyes darted until they landed on Jackson's name, and then Marie's.

"Oh, oh goodness. There they are," Katiyana whispered, reaching to touch her fingertips gently to the edge of the page. My brow furrowed and I looked at Alexis.

"Was the coven in New York during the twenties?"

Alexis shook her head. "No, the coven has always been on Faodail. Marie and Jackson moved here, and joined afterward." Alexis leaned back in her chair. "That book won't tell you everything, and I don't recommend going further than 1930 right now. Too much information could overload and confuse you."

"Why? It's our memories coming back to us, isn't it?" Katiyana had a teaspoon of bitterness to her voice, and I recognized it from part of our conversation with Leon and Sinéad at the festival. "Why can't we just get the entire story?"

"The last time we did that, it didn't go well." Alexis closed her eyes, hands shifting to fiddle with a ring, antique by the look of it. Katiyana softened, her shoulders relaxing.

"What happened?" I asked, tilting my head and hoping she could hear the sympathy in my tone. This was clearly an unpleasant memory for her. I may have shared Katiyana's bitterness, but I didn't want Alexis to think we were upset with her.

"There was a period of time, right around when you were born, Katiyana, that your aunt Pearl's past life memories were starting to return to her. We'd been waiting on it, since your mother and Aunt Jennie's memories had already come back. We got impatient and shoved the records at her, her sisters told her the entire story from their points of view, and she stopped having her dreams within a few days of us doing so. She'd taken their points of view and the records as fact, and had subconsciously—or maybe even consciously—assumed she didn't need to know anything else. We were all wrong about it and missed a key piece of info that we'd really needed. It could have helped us when...well, when Mariana was killed." Alexis sighed again, gentle but sad, and Katiyana hung her head. I didn't know as much about Faodail as Katiyana and Alexis clearly did, and I looked between them, feeling horribly out of the loop. I knew Bruadarach Mariana had been murdered, and our current Bruadarach had basically vanished for a long time but then come back not too many years ago, but nothing about where she went, or why she came back.

"I'm sorry, I didn't realize," Katiyana whispered, tracing her finger over the handle of her teacup. "I hope there aren't any life-or-death memories that you're missing from me." She looked up at Alexis, clearly reliving the same years and memories that Alexis had been, and they shared a smile. Alexis reached over to take her hand and squeeze it.

"You've done nothing wrong. I was very impatient to get my full memories back, as well. I understand. But now I hope you understand why we have to take it slow, like the druids recommended." Alexis released Katiyana's hand and took the book back, flipping further back in the pages and—I assumed—years.

"Why do the druids decide everything?" Katiyana grumbled, setting her chin in her palm. Alexis chuckled.

"They've been here longest."

Once more I was on the outside of this circle, brow knit, hands around the teacup, looking between the two women at the table. I definitely preferred this kind of weird to the kind I'd had last week, but it didn't make me any less lost.

"I'm sorry, druids?" I ventured, hoping my expression matched my confusion.

"Oh gods, Vincent, my apologies. I keep forgetting you weren't raised in the circle." Alexis shook her head at herself, putting a hand to her forehead. "You just...fit right in, it's easy to forget."

Somehow, her comment made me forget entirely that I was confused. All that mattered was that she said I fit in. The Squad had already made the declaration that they were my family, but hearing it from Alexis made me realize that my new family was a lot bigger than I originally thought.

After a much more thorough Faodail history crash course than the school offered, I was caught up on the basics of the druids and the coven and how they worked together. These druids—I was shocked to even hear they existed—lived on the smaller island a little southwest of Faodail, close enough to see the shore from Dubhan. According to what Alexis said, they were kind of a step above the coven when it came to the magical side of the island. She mentioned something about ley lines and how the druids were the main keepers of them, but the coven maintained balance elsewhere on Faodail. Alexis pointed to a few key things in her book, got up to get two more, and pointed to some crucial details in those, as well. By the end of it I had even more questions, but I definitely felt like I was on more even ground with Katiyana than I had been before.

"Alexis, the last dream we had, it was early this morning and was...severely unpleasant." Katiyana winced as Alexis stacked her books and pushed them to the side. Valerie had given up on pretending not to listen and had taken advantage of the empty store to come and sit, so she took the books from Alexis and started flipping through them herself.

"You can tell me if you're comfortable," Alexis said, folding her hands in front of her. Despite us telling her she didn't need to be formal, Alexis remained unbearably classy. It seemed to simply be in her DNA to be the most well put together and eloquent person in the room. I admired her for it.

"Well, the guy that Marie was supposed to marry came into the bakery Jackson works at and…" Katiyana cringed, her hands clenched around her now empty teacup.

"Lucas threatened to kill Jackson if he caught them together again," I finished, and Katiyana looked at me thankfully. I nodded.

"Eesh, I'm so sorry, I expected you to find out about that part much later on," Valerie said, not looking up from the book she was glancing through.

"How do you know about it?" Katiyana asked, reaching over to swat her on the arm.

"I've been here as long as Alexis has, I've read everything—of course I know about it." Valerie closed the book and lightly bapped Katiyana's shoulder with it, then Alexis reached over to take the book back.

"Coven records aren't for bonking," she said, and Valerie gave her a brief sheepish look before opening the one beneath it to continue her perusing. "That is a horrible instance, I'm sorry." Alexis looked between us, a clear apologetic expression crossing her features. "Unfortunately the memories we receive aren't all happy. But they do all contain information we need to record so that we, as a coven, aren't doomed to repeat past mistakes. That's why we keep the records." She gestured at the books with the one in her hand, then set it down. "Dorell normally keeps them, but I borrowed these for today."

I blinked in astonishment. "Dorell? From the library? The head librarian. He's the coven record keeper?"

"He's the head priest sometimes, when he feels like it. Like at the Mabon festival. He usually only does the high ceremonial things like that," Valerie answered. Alexis nodded, and Katiyana looked at me.

"I guess you were close to a coven member the whole time, Vinny."

"Guess so."

"We're all over the city. You've likely met quite a few before. You know Mr. Cromwell, at the school?" Alexis asked, grinning suddenly.

"The guitar teacher, yeah."

"He's my husband," Alexis's grin got a little wider, and she lifted her left hand to show the band on it. I laughed, shaking my head.

"This coven runs the island, doesn't it?"

"We're advisors, of a sort, but the only one of us on the Cabinet is me. The coven helps them when they ask for help. We work in tandem." Alexis nodded to me, and Katiyana giggled.

"So Sinéad calls you once a year?" She laughed. Alexis grinned and Valerie set down the book to laugh, both hands over her mouth.

"Less, usually," Alexis's grin was conspiratorial, and there was a mischievous glint to her eye as she and Katiyana shared the joke about the Bruadarach.

For the next hour or so, Alexis and Valerie shared with me the pieces of knowledge I'd not been born into like Katiyana had, and answered all my questions with patience and clarity. Our conversation bled into Katiyana and I staying for the Monday night teen witch club, joined later by Fleur and Alena. They'd mentioned Jamari had been caught up by a video game and couldn't be dragged away, complete with many eyerolls.

By the time Dan texted to see if I was ever coming home, I had a more complete view of the coven and its everyday business, along with a nice foundation of MacAskill magic. I was feeling more and more like things were lining up and going right, and as I held out my headphone for Katiyana to share as I queued up the next part of the soundtrack, I smiled without even thinking about it.

"What?" She asked, grinning back and scooting closer so the cord didn't have to strain.

"I'm just having a really good day," I said, settling in my seat. I barely heard the music above the feeling of her arm pressed lightly against mine the whole way back to her station.

Katiyana

Monday, September 28, 2020

I MAY AS WELL have been floating on a dang cloud as I took the elevator up to the apartment, humming the last tune Vincent and I had managed to listen to together before my stop. I wasn't really into musicals, but *Hadestown* really was such a beautiful retelling of the myth. I was lost in the music as I unlocked the door, but then the smell in the apartment snapped me back to reality. It wasn't the weird incense this time.

"Katiyana?" I heard Nick call from the kitchen, and after I locked the door I followed the voice and the smell to peer timidly around the corner. Nicolae was at the stove, a slightly smoking pan in front of him, and our last good spatula sitting in the middle of the hot pan. Whatever he'd been trying to cook—it looked like a frozen hamburger patty—had clearly not gone well, and he'd given up.

"Fix this for me. You were out god knows where with god knows who for hours, and you've left me to fend for myself." He scowled at me, and I took the opportunity to duck around him and rescue the last spatula not melted into a skillet from joining its brethren in the trash. It was worth the scowl and the other mean things he was likely getting ready to say to me to save our cookware.

"Where the hell were you, anyway? You know it's a school night, right? I know you're not that much of an idiot." Nick moved to lean on the counter, arms crossed, clearly not going to help any further. I bit my tongue against the insult, pulling the skillet off the burner to dump his charcoal burger in the trash.

"I was at Ladine's. The teen witch class was tonight and it seemed silly to come home for an hour and then head out again, so I just went there early to talk to Valerie." It wasn't really a lie, but I still felt bad not telling the truth. I just really didn't want him to find out about Vincent. I could only imagine the rants about purity and abstinence. I didn't need that from my older brother when Mom and I had already had a very thorough and non-shaming talk about that subject three years ago. Nick scoffed.

"Ladine's, the pit of black magic I told you not to go to. Great." He shook his head, and I ignored him by pulling a new skillet from the cabinet and new meat from the freezer.

"It's not a pit of black magic, Nick. If it were, you wouldn't go there for supplies." I heard his single footstep but didn't think anything of it until his hand was around the back of my neck, fingers tugging on the small hairs at the base of my skull, and his face was inches from mine. I stared at him wide-eyed, holding the patty above the skillet, my body as frozen as it was.

"If they weren't holding a monopoly on supplies in this town, I wouldn't have to go there, now would I?" He hissed, whispered, growled. I shuddered. He let go of my neck and stomped off to the living room, and I dropped the patty to grip my pendant. That was the first time Nick had ever grabbed me in anger.

To prevent further action on his part, I made his dinner and my own silently, keeping my near hyperventilation under wraps. When I was done, I handed him his plate without a word and took mine to my room. My phone had gone off in my bag at least six times while I was cooking. I'd heard the muffled vibration, but had ignored it for the sake of getting Nick's dinner to him in a "reasonable" amount of time. It was going to take a minute longer for my breathing to calm down, and longer still for my fingers to stop trembling, but I forced them to work properly so I could let someone know what happened. There was no way in hell I was going to do this on my own. All the texts but two were from Vincent, as expected, but I ignored them and tapped to my mom's messages instead.

LilTriquetra

Nick just grabbed the back of my neck

EttaR

What? What do you mean?

LilTriquetra

He was trying to say Iadine's was black magic again and I pointed out that he still went there for supplies and he just grabbed me and like basically growled at me that it's a monopoly and he has no choice

EttaR

Did he hurt you?

LilTriquetra

No but it freaked me out. I finished making dinner and locked myself in my room (sorry I'm eating in my room)

EttaR

It's fine.

Do you want me to come home?

I chewed on my lip, staring at the question, and even though I knew my immediate answer was yes, I didn't know how quickly she could make it back. At least not until tomorrow.

EttaR

Katiyana?

LilTriquetra

Would you even be able to?

EttaR

It might be hard, but I can look at everything and talk to your aunts.

LilTriquetra

Please? He's been really weird lately

EttaR

Have you been telling Valerie everything?

LilTriquetra

Yeah except for just now

EttaR

Okay, I'll see what we can do about getting back. We didn't keep the rental car, so I'll see if we can get another.

We got some storm warnings as well, so hopefully they don't ground any flights.

This might be tricky but I promise I'll do my best. Even if I have to drive the whole ten hours to the ferry.

LilTriquetra

Okay, thanks mom

My hopes were getting a little dashed with the mention of the weather, but knowing Mom was trying made it better.

EttaR

If you get really freaked out, please go to Val's. I'm so sorry dad and I are both gone right now, I really wish we didn't have to be.

LilTriquetra

It's ok I know you tried

EttaR

I'll let you know as soon as I know, I promise. I love you.

LilTriquetra

I love you too

Mom stopped responding, so I figured she was talking to her sisters. I flipped to Vincent's messages.

RedSam

> I'm probably sounding like a broken record but that was an intense wave of emotion

> you okay?

> answer me when you can, please?

> i'm sorry i keep doing this, i just worry when i feel panic from your end.

He wasn't wrong, he did sound a bit like a broken record. But it was a concerned and caring one at least. I let myself take a breath and grip my pendant briefly, letting him feel the calmer beat of my heart.

LilTriquetra

> Sorry, it's become a habit to just grab your amethyst when i'm freaked out. I don't mean to scare you.

While I waited for his answer I dug into my now cooled homemade burger, the first bite making me remember I hadn't eaten since school lunch. A few messages came rapid-fire as I ate, and since I could still see Vinny typing between them, I just waited for him to finish his thoughts.

RedSam

> i'd rather you grabbed it than didn't.

sorry, what I mean is, if you were really truly in trouble, and that was the only thing you could do, at least someone would know you needed help.

is that weird? i'm not trying to say i'm your lifeline or anything, i'm sorry,

and now i'm rambling.

LilTriquetra

You left a comma again

RedSam

I finished my thought!

LilTriquetra

Lol

I appreciate your thought process. Thank you for having my back like that

RedSam

don't want my dream girl to get hurt!!

I blinked at the message, which had an unusual amount of sparkly emojis to it, and exclamation points. I'd only really known Vincent for five days, but that was enough to know it wasn't him typing.

LilTriquetra

Dan give vinny his phone back

RedSam

you RUIN my fun katiyana

LilTriquetra

Lol you have my number you doofus

RedSam

YEAH BUT VINNY WON'T TELL YOU WHAT I TELL HIM TO!

LilTriquetra

Let him say what he wants!! Dan!! I'll tell fleur on you!

RedSam

damnit, understood, i'll LEAVE HIM ALONE!

I laughed, the last message was followed up by a GIF of a soldier saluting in front of a waving flag, complete with fireworks.

RedSam

remind me to change the passcode on my phone

I didn't get a chance to tell on Dan to Fleur because he ran to the group chat and exposed himself. I sent a screenshot to confirm, including Vinny's message about knowing him so well. He got a beautiful telling off about not invading people's privacy and letting conversations happen naturally instead of butting in. I mostly lurked, watching it unfold and sending relevant GIFs where appropriate, but mainly just basking in the happy new normalcy we'd created as a group.

It was enough to make me feel better about the current situation with Nick, and more willing to wait for mom. If I had my friends—my squad—on my side, I'd be okay. They had my back, and because of that I had places to run to if need be. It would be alright. Then when Mom and Dad got back maybe they'd finally force Nick out of the apartment rather than just trying to convince him and be the understanding parents they were. I was grateful for how patient they were, but there had to be a line somewhere, right? I just hoped Nick would reach it *after* they got back, instead of while I was on my own.

The Dreamers

Tuesday, September 29, 2020

THEY WERE SEPARATED, DESPITE not wanting to be. One holed up in a cliché gilded cage, the other elbow deep in flour and eggs. Marie was perched perfectly on the edge of a settee, her back straight, looking down at the letter in her hand with just her eyes. She didn't dare even lower her chin to cough right now. Every eye in the household was on her. Lucas had told her father, of course, as was expected if he'd ever found out. His droning rant in the background about immigrants "muddying the waters of America" were lost to his emotionally-absent betrothed, the last bit of joy torn from her as she read her friend's words.

Marie my dearest,

I know this likely won't come as a shock to you, but Leo and I are running away to the Catskills. I need to be away from Reggie and everything else right now. I can't take it. Please burn this letter after you read it. I hid it under your pillow on purpose. Please don't tell anyone where we went, I don't know how long we'll be gone. I honestly don't know if I'll come back. I might take this as my escape. I'm so unhappy, I can't stay there. Forgive me, I love you.

Love,

Clara

So she was gone. For now, for years, forever. Who knew. It wasn't hard to toss the page into the fireplace, to let the flame devour the words Marie desperately wished she hadn't read. Clara had been the only person Marie could have turned to with this; they'd ended up in the same situation after all. Marie closed her eyes, folding her hands in her lap as she sat back down. She couldn't even write to Clara, to beg her to send a car or come back and fetch her so they could all run away together. Why hadn't Clara asked her to come along? Marie would have, in a heartbeat.

"They're going to rise up against us if we don't stop them now, those blasted immigrants, they're already taking all our jobs—" Lucas was in the background of her thoughts, ranting on and on about some racist train of thought or another. Marie huffed the softest, one-note laugh as she remembered a phrase from a novel she and Clara had read together— "Tom's getting very profound, he reads deep books with long words in them..." Daisy was right, Lucas sounded so *profound* with his thoughts. Or were they Tom's? She'd have to ask him if he'd read the novel, as well.

———◆———

Jackson's thoughts were focused so deeply on the bread dough he was kneading. Or at least, he wanted them to be. He'd measured each cup of flour, each pinch of salt, so meticulously that Charles had sighed at him and left to go tidy the front of the shop rather than sit and wait for his turn to knead. No matter how fiercely Jackson forced himself to count the amount of times he pushed the dough against the table, Marie's eyes filled his thoughts. The guilt and anxiety in her eyes, tears overflowing, as Lucas dragged her away. The outline of Lucas's hand, bruised and reddened on Jackson's throat, pulsed gently, and he pressed his chin to his shoulder to avoid coughing into the dough.

"Please don't plague the bread, Jackson." Charles had popped in the back to get another loaf for a customer, looking at his friend and coworker with what tried to be a teasing expression, but fell short of it and became a pitying, sorrowful look instead.

"Trying not to," Jackson rasped, eyes back on the dough after glancing at his friend.

"You should stay in the back today."

"I know."

"It's...really bad, Jackson."

"I know."

"I'm not saying you're ugly or anything, just that you'd probably scare an old lady or three—"

"Charles, I know. I was planning on staying here anyway." Jackson's radio-worthy voice had become monotone, raspy, each word struggled for harder and harder the more he spoke. Charles decided, mercifully, to drop the subject, laying a hand on his friend's shoulder for a moment before moving back to the front, the bell on the door signaling an arrival.

He'd over-kneaded the bread at this point. Tossing it into a bowl to rise, he sighed and decided it would just go on the day-old cart tomorrow. No use wasting it. The next batch was no better. It couldn't keep his mind off Marie or his last glimpse of her, either.

Katiyana

Tuesday, September 29, 2020

"I just feel bad for them, you know? Thanks to Alexis and her books I know they move here eventually, but I wish they didn't have to go through all this to get here." My phone was on speaker, connected distantly to Alena's as I stared at my hands braiding my hair in the mirror.

"Yeah, that sounds really rough. I'm amazed Lucas didn't just kill him, honestly. He sounds like Kingpin." Her words were muffled; she was probably brushing her teeth. The thought was confirmed as I heard her faucet turn on.

"Haha, they are the same physically, but honestly I think Kingpin is nicer." I finished off the braid and twisted a tie onto the end, scowling at the bit of hair I'd missed by my neck.

"Well, you'd know, I still haven't finished it."

"I'll tie you to the couch over winter break." I heard her laugh from the other end.

"Deal. Now I'm hanging up, I have a train to catch." She tapped her screen in warning, and I laughed.

"Okay, see you soon."

"Byyyyyeee." The line went dead. I looked down at the screen to see some missed texts from Vincent and the group chat, glancing at them before moving back to my room to grab my stuff. I also had a train to catch, but not as urgently as Alena's.

As I stepped in my room I caught a whiff of that weird incense again, and just faintly shook my head. Nick had his door closed more often than not lately, so he was absolutely keeping me from whatever he was doing. Unfortunately, the little gap between the door and the floor didn't keep the scent of bayberry and ginger in his room. I decided to just text Valerie later, and gathered my school things before heading out early. If I was lucky I'd have just enough time to grab a tea from the kiosk at the station before the train showed up.

I was, in fact, lucky, and I sat with my tea flipping through the texts I'd missed earlier. Once the "Squad," as Dan had titled our new group chat, arrived, Vincent and I talked a little about the latest dream instead of continuing our music listening, and I realized that he and I had paid attention to vastly different pieces of the dreams this whole time. While he was looking for numbers, dates and addresses, actual info that he could have used to prove what we were seeing did in fact happen, I'd been paying attention to Marie's emotions and thought patterns and how the other people involved had affected them. Together we had a much more complete picture, and as we walked to the front door of the school, he showed me the newspaper clipping of Clara and Reggie's engagement announcement.

"Oh, wow! I wonder how long between that and when she ran off to the mountains?" I mused aloud, leaning my head on Vincent's shoulder to peer at his screen.

"I...I uh, have no clue." He paused for a moment, swallowing, and I lifted my head off his shoulder just in case it was making him nervous. I'd forgotten again that he didn't like touching as much as the rest of the group did. "I'd have to go find the webpage again. I just snapped this photo of the screen so I had proof I found it." Vincent tucked his phone in his pocket and looked over at me. "I could go back to the library after school this week and look."

"I'll go with you. We can research together."

"I'd love that." My heart did a little flip as he hit that pure, sincere tone again, and I felt a light flush briefly hit my cheeks. He chuckled. "Sorry, I forgot I'm supposed to warn you."

I wrinkled my nose at him but smiled, and not long after, we parted ways for class.

We discussed the timing of everything a bit more over lunch, and with the help of a website full of historical fashion trends that Fleur had dug up, we narrowed down the timeline to the mid-1920s as a group. Even Jamari had chimed in with the original publication date of *The Great Gatsby* after pulling it up on Wikipedia.

"That narrows it down easily to post-1925," Vincent said, tapping notes into his document.

"Why can't you just ask Alexis? I thought she had all those books?" Dan was only halfway paying attention, scrolling through Instagram.

"The books didn't make any mention of Marie and Jackson until they moved to the island and joined the Faodail coven, and she wouldn't let us read very much of it. So they didn't help at all for their life in New York," Vincent responded without looking up from his notes, and I nodded to confirm.

"Yeah, the coven books are only helpful for people in the coven, and at this point, they weren't in the coven." I set my chin in my hands, watching Vincent type, scroll a bit, and type again, adding to his notes.

"You guys should share a folder in the cloud or something, have all your notes in one place," Alena suggested, Fleur nodding in agreement.

"Huh that's a good idea. Vincent?"

"Oh, yeah, if you make one I'll add to it." Single thought spoken, he went back to his revisions, and I picked my phone up off the table, making the folder and sharing the access to it in the group chat.

"If you guys find anything relevant historically, add it please?" I requested as the bell rang, and my friends nodded or murmured their agreements as we cleaned up our trays and made to leave.

"If it's okay with you, I can make a document that holds all the relevant links, like that fashion website I found." Fleur's arm slid through mine and I squeezed it tight to my side, grinning.

"That'd be fantastic, thank you."

As the next class went on, I found myself distracted once again by thinking about how lucky I was to have this group of friends that wanted to help and lend their skills to Vincent's and my research. I made notes of other things in the back of my planner: books I remembered being mentioned in passing conversations, celebrities, anything I could think of to help narrow our search. Between classes, I checked the folder and found that Fleur had dumped in a few PDF files of old fashion magazines along with the promised link document, and Vincent had copied over his notes. I did the same, moving the file I already had into the folder as I waited for my next class to begin.

We looked things over again as a group while we waited for the train after school, heads bent together around Alena's phone since it had the biggest screen.

"What exactly are we aiming to accomplish with this research?" She asked, swiping through the pages of one of the magazines.

"Well, if we can find any legitimate mentions of Marie and Jackson, like I did with Clara's engagement announcement, it can help me find records of their existence, and we could be on our way to flat-out proving that past lives exist. To people outside of the coven, I mean." Vincent was talking without looking up from the library book he was holding, a history of coal mines in the United States. "Other than that, it's just reassurance that Yana and I aren't losing our minds at the same time." With that, he looked up at me and grinned. I laughed, joined by a few others and a light chuckle from a distracted Dan.

We set a date to head to the library together after school on Wednesday—all of us—to further our investigation. Vincent let me rest my head on his shoulder as we listened to our precious little bit of showtunes together until I had to hop off the train. Even if our research didn't prove anything beyond the fact Marie and Jackson had actually lived in New York, and Alexis wasn't just showing us two names in the coven ledger that matched, it would be a great way to spend time together as a group. We were invested, we had a goal, and it was bonding us together. I smirked at the thought of accidentally discovering Dan, Fleur, and Alena's past lives while we were at it. I couldn't suppress the thought of Charles and Dan being the same soul, especially since he'd started complaining about Vinny and me "infecting" his dreams. Now that he'd had a third dream, Fleur had made him his own note file and forced him to start recording notes in it, as well.

I was musing over the one he'd told us about during lunch, one Vinny and I had already had, when I stepped into the apartment and was slapped in the face by an even stronger blow of bayberry and ginger. I looked into the living room to see a dish of incense on the coffee table, one on the kitchen counter, and another on the table in the hallway.

"Good lord," I whispered to myself, locking the door behind me and hanging up my coat before heading toward my bedroom.

I slowed as my door came into view and with it, the red smudges on the doorframe. New ones—I was certain I'd cleaned off the ones from last time. I stopped just next to it, holding my breath and listening after I heard a rustle. It came again, and after twice more I recognized it as pages turning. With a slow, deep, steadying breath, I closed my eyes and prepared to face the reality that Nick was likely reading the diary I hadn't written in for a year, or the dream journal I'd thought was stashed securely under my mattress. I wasn't sure which I dreaded more.

"I can hear you breathing, Marie." His voice sounded ominous, and I held my breath, a hand going over my mouth as I realized what he'd called me. He had found the dream journal. "You may as well come in here and give me an explanation as to why you've been hiding this from me."

I closed my eyes, squeezing them shut as tight as I could. Maybe I'd fallen asleep on the train. This could be a bad dream, and I would get shaken awake by Alena any moment now.

"Get in here, Katiyana Randa, before I come out there and drag you back with me."

Gods I wanted to run, I wanted to just drop everything and sprint out of the apartment and find Valerie, or run all the way to Dubhan and take a boat to the mainland and find Mom. Anything but set foot in my own bedroom.

Unfortunately, my decision was made for me as Nick stomped out and grabbed my arm, yanking me into my bedroom, all but throwing me onto my bed. I landed on my journal, pages creasing under my elbow and the spine popping under my weight. Red lines from the strange substance he'd been using marked my skin, and I felt the wet smudge as he took a hold of my face, forcing me to look at him. My journal was probably stained as well. My heart sank.

"Why have you been hiding your dreams from me, Marie? Did you think I would repeat the past and beat the ass of your little lover-boy all over again?" His voice was a hiss, and his grip loosened, dropping his hand to yank the journal out from under my arm. *What?*

"Ni-Nick what...what are you talking about?" I sat up and scooted away from him, rubbing the arm he'd grabbed and trying to judge if it was going to bruise or not. I subtly flexed my hip to make sure my phone was still in my pocket. It was.

Nick didn't answer, just flipped madly through the pages, nearly tearing a few as he did, until he came to the entry with the first mention of Lucas. "September eighth. You could have come and told me that you'd met him in your dreams, we could have spoken, and we wouldn't be having a single issue right now. But instead you hid everything from me, you kept things from me, all because you were dreaming about Jackson. You wanted him all to yourself, you hid him from me again." His voice had been steadily getting louder, and now he was full on shouting. I pressed myself back into my headboard, eyes growing wide. Oh, Brigit protect me, Nicolae is Lucas.

Nicolae was Lucas. My heart was hammering, and all I could do was stare as Nick threw the book down again, banging it against the wall and likely crumpling one of the corners on the cover.

"You hid him from me again, after I've done everything I possibly can to keep you away from him, away from that coven. But you just had to listen to Etta, to Alexis and Valerie, all those other horrible, horrible women with their dark magic and demon pacts. You let them brainwash you into forgetting who you belong to. Who you were supposed to marry." Nick's hand slapped against the wall over my head, and he leaned in closer, eyes burning with anger and hatred. The gentle touch to my chin was a direct opposite to the hard look of fury on his face. "All this time I thought you were just ignoring me because I was being moody, but no, you've completely forgotten who you're supposed to be with."

His face was getting closer to mine, his hand sliding to cup my cheek, and I realized what was happening. Before I thought about it, I lifted my foot and kicked. Hard. I don't know if I hit his groin or stomach or even his hip, but it was enough for me to be able to slide out from underneath him and run down the hallway, scooping my bag up from where I'd tossed it and grabbing my coat from the hook near the door. The door didn't shut as I slammed it, bouncing off the latch and swinging back and forth. I didn't even wait for the elevator, I banged open the door to the staircase and took off.

As I ran I only had one thought repeating over and over in my mind, and the more I thought it, the more I hated it, the more I wanted to beg every god in existence to make it untrue.

Nicolae is Lucas.

I'd only realized I was running to Ladine's when I got there, and as I pushed open the door and let the first wave of gentle incense hit me, I broke. I collapsed in the doorway, the door swinging to bump lightly against my side as I buried my face in my hands and tried to muffle my struggling breath.

"Yana?" I felt a touch to my shoulders and then someone slip their hands under my arms to try and lift me up, but my legs were shaking dead weight from my run across nearly the entire city. "Yana, help me here. Stand. Just long enough to get to a chair."

I obeyed the voice I was slowly recognizing as Jamari's, and let her lead me to one of the tables and set me down. I slumped against the table, crossing my arms to hide my face once more. After a bit—the exact nature of time was lost to me just then—three sets of footsteps returned and

Jamari's hands found my shoulders again, then one lifted to smooth over my hair.

"Yana, honey? Yana?" She asked, her voice so gentle and soothing that a fresh wave of tears broke from my eyes as I lifted my head and reached out to her. She dropped to her knees next to my chair to wrap me in her arms, and I buried my face in her shoulder to finally just cry. Jamari squeezed me tight and tucked her head against mine, and somewhere in the background I heard Alexis and Valerie discussing something. I didn't care to know what the conversation was. I clung to Jamari until my shuddering sobs calmed, sniffling with my hands fisted into her shirt. She stayed as steady as a fencepost, supporting her weight and mine. I felt another soft touch to my head.

"Katiyana, are you hurt?" It was Alexis, and she tenderly smoothed her hands over my head, manipulating my hair clip out of the wind-whipped tangle I'd worked up while running. I shook my head, and finally pulled back from Jamari, but reached to take her hand. She shifted into the chair next to me, leaning forward to dry my cheeks with a napkin. She rubbed at my chin as well, and I was suddenly reminded of the red smudges Nick had left on my face.

"What happened, kid?" Valerie was across the table in another chair, and I looked up at her, sniffing hard.

"Nicolae is Lucas."

"Your brother...your brother is the dude who beat up Jackson?" Jamari was shocked, rightly so. I had been too. I just nodded, pulling another napkin from the holder to hold to my nose instead of letting it run. Jamari released my hand so she could hold her head, and I looked up at Valerie. She was staring at me as if trying to put a puzzle together, trying to connect dots.

"Did he come on to you?" She asked, and I nodded, wincing at the memory. Valerie's puzzled face quickly turned into a snarl of rage as my own expression became perplexed by how quickly she figured it out. She moved to stand up but Alexis quietly put a hand on her shoulder, and Val sat back down.

"We should call the security force or the Bruadarach or...someone, something?" Jamari looked up at Alexis, horrified. "We can't let him near her." Alexis nodded, still silent. Her eyes dropped to the table and she slipped a hand in her pocket.

"I'll call Sinéad, and Gautier, see if we can at least get a restraining order or something for the time being. It's difficult, legally, since Katiyana's parents are off-island right now." She sighed, tapping on her screen.

"Do I not count as a guardian?" Valerie asked. "Because she sure as hell has my backing, and she'll have Sinéad's, too, as soon as you tell her."

"We'd have to call Etta and get her agreement to let you act as guardian, but I'm sure she'd agree to it." Alexis had her phone to her ear, and I recognized the corner of my cousin's name on the screen. "Hello Brian, can I speak to Sinéad please?" She stepped away to have her phone call privately, presumably after Sinéad's husband had passed the phone to his wife.

Valerie reached across the table to take my hands, ignoring the snot-covered napkin in one of them. "You're staying with me until your parents get back. I have another bed in my apartment that gets used maybe once a year. We can have Alex come over and stand guard while you pack your things." She squeezed my hands and I nodded, my words still not quite working. "Okay. I'll call him in a bit, and have him drive us back." I nodded again, and looked over as Jamari stood up and went to the kitchen. She returned a few minutes later with a piping hot mug of herbal tea, and a cinnamon roll.

"I'll pay for these," she promised, glancing over at Val to make sure one of the managers knew. Val just waved her hand and pulled back to tap at her phone, calling Alex. Jamari settled back down next to me, nudging the mug closer to my hands. "Drink this, it's got rose and lavender and skullcap in it. It'll help calm you down."

I looked up and smiled gratefully at her, wrapping my hands around the mug and pulling it closer. She smiled back and pulled out her phone, hovering her thumb over the screen. "Do you...want me to ask everyone to come here or...?" I shook my head, swallowing a sip of tea before answering.

"No, no, they don't need to drop what they're doing just to come dry my tears." I bowed my head to let the steam from my mug wash over my face. The floral scent was steadying, and I breathed it in, letting it work its way right to my heart.

"Vincent wants to know where you are," Jamari said, and I peeked to see her looking at her phone with a raised eyebrow. *Oh, the pendants. Dear lord, he probably felt every single bit of that and texted the group chat when I didn't answer.* I dug my phone out of my pocket and sure enough, a string of messages from him simultaneously apologizing for being nosy and intrusive but also worried out of his mind.

LilTriquetra

> I'm sorry, I'm at ladines, can I tell you what happened later? I'm not up to it right now.

RedSam

> oh thank the gods. i'm just glad you're safe. is there anything i can do?

LilTriquetra

> Not right now, thank you tho

RedSam

> let me know the minute there's something.

LilTriquetra

> Promise

I set my phone down with a sigh, leaning an elbow on the table to support my head as I held it. The panic had left me, my heartbeat returned to normal, my breath no longer sharp. Even my legs no longer felt like they were about to fall off. Jamari was tapping away in the group chat, assuaging everyone's panic. I finished my tea and wiggled out of my coat, dropping it and my bag under the table. Jamari grabbed another napkin and I let her clean the marks off my arm, as well. Valerie returned first, telling us that Alex had agreed to stay at her apartment with us as a sort of bodyguard and deterrent so Nick would leave me alone until we could get further, more official protection in place. He'd also offered to drive me to and from school so I wouldn't have to be alone between the apartment complex and the train station. We sat in silence for a while, Jamari reaching over to hold my hand again, and we all looked up as Alexis came back.

"Sinéad is getting ahold of your mom. We're in agreement he's not to be allowed near you even if we can't do it legally right now. Gautier told me that he's just a phone call away if you want him to come over and stand guard or anything. But he also told me the same thing I told you, that we need your mother to give permission for Valerie to act as guardian or come back herself if we want to do anything legally." Alexis slid into the last empty chair at the table, sighing slowly. "I'm so sorry it's come to this. Beyond your mother and aunts, it's exceedingly rare for past life connections to manifest as siblings. Not to mention one like this."

"This hasn't happened before? Ever?" I was bewildered. Surely at some point Lucas had tried to get at Marie from beyond the grave before. This couldn't be the first time in a hundred years.

Alexis shrugged. "Not to my direct knowledge, no. I'm so sorry." The silence hung over us again, and Jamari piped up to break it.

"Who's Gautier?"

"The head of the Faodail Security Force," Alexis answered, looking at her phone as a text came through. Jamari laughed softly.

"Is there anyone you don't have on speed dial on this island?"

"Quite a few people, yes, actually." She smiled at Jamari then stood up as the door opened, ready to defend her "We're Closed" sign, but sat back down as Alex came in. Valerie got up to greet him, and he came over to our table. We decided that they'd go into the apartment with me to pack enough of my things for a week's stay at Valerie's. That would give Mom ample time to get back to the island, and then he'd stay at the apartment until Nick was dealt with.

I wasn't ready to go back yet, so as Valerie and Alexis resumed their shop duties, I followed Jamari back into the kitchen to not only hide, but distract myself by helping her make more pastries. It worked well enough; I stopped shaking and my breath evened out, but I couldn't get the look on Nick's face as he pinned me to my headboard out of my head.

Vincent

Tuesday, September 29, 2020

Jamari's texts weren't doing anything to assuage my panic, the growing pit of anxiety in my stomach that was making its way to my chest. Katiyana had said there was nothing I could do at the moment but...I couldn't just sit here.

"Where are you going?" Dan called after me, and I realized I'd grabbed my jacket and started walking to the door. I looked back at him, his phone in his hand, the group chat on his screen. "She's with Jamari and Alexis and Valerie, at Ladine's, that's the safest place she could possibly be. What do you think going there will even do?"

I didn't know, but I wasn't going to voice that. Instead I held the doorjamb that led into his room, gripping the wood before finally groaning. "Nothing, I guess."

Dan moved to take my elbow and pull me back to the bunk beds, setting me down on the bottom one that I'd claimed not long after helping his parents build them. "She's freaked out right now, and she may trust you, but she needs to be around people she's known for years, people she's not afraid to cry in front of. Don't go all white-knight and try to protect her from everything."

"Dan, this is different. Jamari said her brother scared the life out of her," I snapped, and immediately regretted my tone. I put my head in my hands, sinking back onto my mattress. "I'm sorry."

"I know dude, it's a bad time. I'm really worried about her too. But Jamari also said that Yana's gonna be staying with Valerie. They have her protected. Plus, her cousin is literally the Bruadarach, so if anything gets worse they'll probably take her to the Highlands."

"Still a weird name for a manor," I grumbled under my palms. She would be safe there, that was true. I just hoped it wouldn't come to that.

"Weird name, safe house. Take a breath, my dude." He reached out to pat my knee a few times. "She'll be okay. There are more people to keep her safe than just you and me."

I let out a long, deep sigh, and dropped my hands. "You're right, I know you're right. But I'm still going to text her."

At this, Dan stood up to snatch my phone. "No, you're not. Let her have a break. Your stress over this doesn't need to add to hers. You're only allowed to text her if it's something to make her smile, and it can't be related to the twenties at all. Well...the 1920s. The 2020s are fine."

"When did you get so emotionally aware? Where's Dan? Who's this alien I'm speaking to?"

"Oh har-dee-har, Vinny. Fleur ever so politely laid into me about not treating people as objects, and I'm attempting to take it to heart."

"When did that happen?"

"We have an anatomy class together and she managed to give me a full speech while we were doing a frog dissection."

"Incredible."

"Yeah. These peeps are something else. We're never going to be allowed to be frat boys at this rate."

He was definitely trying to get my mind off of Katiyana's situation, and it was working pretty well. When did he get so clever? "Why do you want to be a frat boy?"

"Why not? Parties, girls, guys—sounds fantastic!"

"No, no it doesn't."

Dan launched into a made-up tirade about how great Greek life was, and all the obviously fake things he'd learned from movies and TV shows, and before I could remind him that all the universities that had frats and sororities were off-island, my phone buzzed on his nightstand. He was—thankfully—too distracted to see it, so I grabbed it without his knowledge.

LilTriquetra

> Sorry for making you worry so much

RedSam

> wow no it's not your fault at all, it's not like you're being purposely reckless.

LilTriquetra

> I just always feel bad because it takes forever to answer your messages

Oof, oh. That hit me. Dan was right, my stress was absolutely compounding hers.

RedSam

> i should probably stop messaging you out of panic like that. it can't be good for you when you're having a bad time already. i'm sorry. i should wait until you say something so we can have an actual conversation about it.

She took a moment to answer, and even though it made me antsy, made me want to message her again and tell her that I was sorry for being so clingy and pushy and everything else after knowing her properly for about a week, I took Dan and Fleur's advice and abstained. Katiyana needed time to accept me into her emotional circle, and if I thought about it too hard I would realize that my emotional circle was so pliable simply because it was based on other people showing me a tidbit of kindness.

LilTriquetra: I would so, so much rather talk to you in person than over text. or even on the phone. also you're forgiven, i don't think you're doing anything wrong really, and i'm not mad at you for it. it's not even annoying, i just feel bad that you're worried but without context.

RedSam

i have anxiety, i'm always worried without context

LilTriquetra

LMAO okay that's fair

RedSam

lol. but, real talk, i'll try not to message you out of panic and instead wait for you to message me. totally unfair to you for me to add onto your stress.

LilTriquetra

I appreciate it, Vinny.

I must have been smiling at my phone because Dan finally noticed I had it, plucked it from my grasp, and read the screen while I swatted at him futilely.

"Aww, I bet that made you feel better, didn't it?" He teased, holding my phone still farther from my reach while using his gym-rat strength to hold me at bay with his other arm.

"Yes, ugh, give it back jerk." I reached again and he finished reading, handed me my phone back, then patted me on the head. I shook my hair out and glared at him while he grinned away.

"I'm so proud of you. Look at my Vinny openly being vulnerable with someone who isn't me."

"I hate you." I rolled back onto my bunk, tucking my phone under the pillow.

"Hehe, I know." Dan kicked at my back softly while climbing up onto the top bunk, then dangled his head down to look at me. "I am legitimately proud of you though, backing off was the right thing to do." He disappeared back onto his bed and I heard him swiping through TikToks, so the conversation was over for the moment.

I pulled my phone back out and saw Katiyana hadn't been online since her last message, so I decided to leave her alone for now. Maybe she'd want to talk at school. But if not, I couldn't let myself pry despite my desperate need to know what happened to her, to know what made her so scared and breathless. I'd felt like I'd run a marathon before Jamari said anything, and my heart didn't stop pounding until well after Dan had lectured me.

So, to distract myself, I closed the app and opened our shared cloud folder. I'd found some notes in the coal mining history book that I needed to add. There were a few things I wanted to run past Chief Regulus, if he was feeling up to it, but that would have to wait for tomorrow, at least. I wanted to talk to Katiyana about it all and tell her what I found, but Dan had forbidden any dream talk, so I'd just have to leave it somewhere for her to find when she wanted it.

Katiyana

Tuesday, September 29, 2020

"What did you tell the Squad?" My voice was smaller than I realized, and I had to repeat myself after Jamari gave me a puzzled look over the bowl of icing she was scraping the last bits out of.

"Oh, just that you'd had a problem with your brother and ran to the café, but you were safe and there wasn't any need to worry," she explained, popping the spatula in her mouth. I breathed out slowly. "I told them you were gonna stay with Val until your mom came home."

"Thank you." It was a whisper, but she nodded to it, and I pulled the bowl closer, taking ownership of the smaller spatula still sitting in it.

"Yeah, I figured that if you wanted to tell everyone exactly what happened, you'd rather do it yourself and in person."

"You know me so well," I said around a mouthful of icing, and she grinned.

"After this long, I'd hope so."

We sat in silence, cleaning out the rest of the icing and waiting for Valerie and Alexis to close up the store. I was grateful to her for immediately understanding what I'd want out of the situation. It was massively comforting to have someone like her on my side.

"Really? You two are incorrigible," Alexis exclaimed from the doorway, and Jamari and I both turned with spatulas in our mouths to see her with her arms crossed. "Put those in the dishwasher and start it, please." She shook her head as we giggled and did as she said, starting up the industrial machine after Jamari prepped it.

"You ready to head out, kiddo?" Valerie said, popping her head around the doorframe. I made a face at the idea. I didn't know if Nick would still be home, and I didn't know if it would be him or—I shuddered—Lucas who greeted me when I got there. Either way, it wouldn't be pleasant. "I figured. I would go in and pack your stuff myself, but I can't guarantee I won't miss anything or not punch your brother in the face while I'm at it."

"You're lucky that as your boss I'm pretending I didn't hear that," Alexis called from the other side of the kitchen, hanging up dry utensils. Valerie shrugged.

"I can go in and pack stuff, but if he's home I don't even want to look at him." I crossed my arms, hugging them close. "I don't want him to come near me."

"Understandable." I looked up at the new voice to see Alex in the doorway this time, leaning on the other side opposite Val. "I'll restrain him if it comes to it, but hopefully it won't."

"Thanks Alex." I sighed, patting my pocket for my phone and hoping I'd left my keys in my bag. "I guess we can head out, then."

"We'll be in the car," he said, moving smoothly away from the doorframe, Val nodding once and following him.

"Goodness me, he is good looking though," Jamari whispered, sliding her arm through mine. I snorted. Good looking enough for a lesbian to notice was definitely really good looking.

"Yeah but he's weird, I only ever see him when Val wants to use him as scary leverage. He also talks like he's in a period drama sometimes."

Jamari laughed. "He does have a face for Downton Abbey." She kissed my cheek and then pulled back, heading toward where our things hung on the wall together. "I'll walk you to their car."

She did just that, and I settled in the backseat of Alex's car that probably cost more than Jamari and Fleur's house. It was all leather and wood panels and more gadgets than I could even name. He'd said it was a Lexus something or other, but I had no brain for cars besides "fast," "shiny," and "safe." Mom's car was the "safe" variety. This definitely was the "shiny."

We made it back to the apartment in a much smaller amount of time than the train had ever taken me, and I only noticed my hands shaking as I went to unbuckle my seatbelt.

"Are you alright?" Alex asked, looking in the rearview mirror at me briefly, then Val turned in her seat to look at me, as well.

"If you don't want to go in, you can just tell me what to grab," she offered, laying a hand on my knee. I shook my head.

"No, I can do it. I just really don't want him to touch me ever again."

"He won't. I'll make sure of it." Alex turned off the car and stepped out, sweeping around to the other side to open my door and hold out a hand. If I hadn't been so nervous about the situation, I would have found it utterly romantic and thought about what a lucky lady Valerie was.

He helped me out of the car then dropped my hand, but I quickly took his back as we started toward the elevator that led up from the parking garage. The entire ride I clutched his hand, and Val laid her hand on my shoulder. It was like being between two surrogate parents, or a trusted aunt and uncle. No matter the comparison, I was glad they were there with me.

Valerie knocked on the door while I hid behind Alex, waiting to see if Nick would answer.

Much to my dismay, he did.

"What do you want, demon-fucker?" He growled, and Val snorted softly.

"Wow. Believe it or not, I've actually been called worse." She grinned dangerously at him. "We've come to get your sister's things."

"My sister can come get her own things." Nick's eyes narrowed, and his grip on the door tightened. "She doesn't need to hide behind you and your cult."

"She isn't," I said, stepping out from behind Alex even though I was shaking. Nick's eyes snapped to me and I saw his expression change in half a second. His voice grew sweet and soft as Alex stretched his arm out in front of me as a block.

"Katiyana, I'm so sorry I scared you. Please, just come inside and we can talk it over." He took a step forward, and so did Alex.

"She's here for her things. Not to talk to you," he said, straightening up to take full advantage of the inches he had over Nick.

"I'm not talking to you. Let me go to my room." I added my trembling and weak voice to the mix.

"Katiyana—"

Alex's hand moved from in front of me and landed on Nick's shoulder, steering him back inside the apartment with just that touch. "Let's talk in here, Nicolae." Alex's voice was firm, and Valerie reached over to take my hand. I followed her quickly to my room as Alex sat Nick down on the couch and stood in front of him, watching Val and I slip down the hallway.

"Your boyfriend's scary," I whispered to her, going to my closet for my duffle bag. She snickered quietly, nodding.

"When he wants to be. He'll keep Nick away from us, so grab whatever you need. What do you want from your bathroom?" She asked, and pulled the matching toiletry bag from the duffle as I laid it on the bed.

"All the normal shower things, my toothbrush, deodorant." She nodded at my list.

"Any hair stuff?"

"I keep it all in here to avoid Nick complaining I'm taking up too much space." I cringed at that thought, realizing how often I'd had to accommodate his wants while he never did the same for me. Val must have had the same thought because she made a face, but just nodded and headed down the hall. I grabbed my other school uniform pieces, my little box of hair accessories, and was in the midst of digging through my sock drawer when Val came back with the toiletries.

"There was a bottle of detangler and a leave-in conditioner on the counter so I grabbed those too." She tucked the small bag inside the bigger one, and moved to my desk to examine the papers. "What of this is homework you need?"

"Oh, thank you, I forgot about those." I looked at the desk across the room, and sighed. "Unfortunately, all of it. It's all art projects."

"Okay, I'm gonna have to let you pick through that. Knowing my luck I'll forget something important. Toss me the clothes you want and I'll fold them for you."

I did as she said, throwing various uniform bits, t-shirts and pajama pants, some jeans, socks, and underwear toward the bed before moving to my desk. I had sorted all my art project thumbnails into their sections in my file folder, then I jumped with a noise.

"You get out of my way right now! I will call the security force!" I heard Nick shout from the living room, and a soft thump, likely Alex forcing him back onto the couch.

"And tell them what? You're not letting your sister have peace to pack her things, to get away from you?" Alex's voice sounded dangerous, and I caught a soft chuckle after he spoke. "Hilarious." I saw Val tilting her head slightly, listening, and then she smirked.

"What?" I asked, and she let out a short laugh.

"I like it when he gets like that."

I made a face at the implication, turning back to finish organizing my homework. This was taking longer than I had wanted it to; I needed more stuff than I realized. Sure, the apartment was right down the hall and I could pop in while Nick was at work, but I'd rather not.

It took five more minutes, and me having to take a second and close my eyes to release some stress, but Val and I got my room packed up enough for me to leave for a week. Right as we were about to step out, I remembered my Brigit carving on my nightstand, and turned to grab it. Val nodded her approval, and we headed down the hallway together. Alex was still standing over Nick, who was sitting on the couch. Nick's elbows were on his knees and he was glaring at the carpet, fingers intertwined so tightly that they were white. Alex motioned with his chin for us to head out, and we obeyed. Val led me down the hall to her door, and as we were unlocking it, Alex followed us out and shut the door.

"He shouldn't bother us," he assured, tucking his hands into his pockets. He looked so cool, like the love interest in an eighties movie.

"Aw thanks honey," Val purred at him, and I internally cringed a little as I realized I'd have to be privy to their pet names and lovey-dovey actions the entire time I stayed with her. But it was worlds better than the alternative.

Val got me set up in her spare room, showed me the eucalyptus branch in her shower ("Don't let it get in the shower stream directly!"), then left me to my own devices and followed Alex into her bedroom. After a quick prayer to Brigit that the room was soundproof, I washed my face and settled in the guest room. My phone had been shockingly silent, despite me knowing I'd been clasping my amethyst at points on the ride home and while Nick was trying to talk to me. Vinny really was holding to his promise.

LilTriquetra

You're probably wondering what that was all about, but it's over now and I'm fine. I'll tell you everything tomorrow. Promise.

RedSam

i was definitely wondering, but i'm glad to know you're alright. i'll see you tomorrow then.

LilTriquetra

<3

I realized what my emoji could imply after I sent it, and turned red at the thought, but left it. I was appreciative and thankful, and that's how I showed it to my friends—over text anyway—and Vinny was my friend. He'd see it in the group chat and would figure it out.

After a bit of decompressing with dumb videos and social media, I made sure the homework that was due soon was in a finished or at least acceptable state. I had a reading assignment to catch up on, but it was only a chapter so I wasn't worried. I could read it on the train tomor—no, Alex was taking me to and from school. Whatever, I'd make it work.

With a sigh, I lay down and let myself rest. My Brigit carving was on the nightstand, Alex and Val were right down the hall, there were at least two locked doors between me and Nick. It would be alright.

It only took another hour for me to convince myself of that.

Vincent

Wednesday, September 30, 2020

I WAS PACING IN front of the school gate, Jamari and Alena huddled together a little ways away against the chilly fall air. I hadn't made myself separate on purpose, I just couldn't stand still until I knew she was alright.

"Vinny! Come over here! You're going to freeze!" Alena called, and I looked up to see that she'd hidden herself under half of Jamari's coat. She was holding her arm out and giving me a pleading look. Jamari looked pleased as punch at the situation. I smirked softly. It really wasn't that cold, even compared to last week. But this group's love language was touch, and they were offering it to me to soothe my nerves.

I had started over to them, just a few paces away, when my attention was snapped to the other direction.

"Vinny!" It was Katiyana, closing the door of a Lexus—a Lexus?—and securing her bag before running toward me. It took me a split second to understand what to do, but I held my arms out for her, squeezing her close and tucking my head against hers as she squeezed me back and hid her face against the lapel of my jacket. "Oh, gods, I'm so glad to see you." Her voice was muffled but sincere, and I could feel the tops of my ears and the back of my neck growing red. My cheeks were surely bright pink.

"I'm glad to see you, Yana." I felt the tension melt off my shoulders, even as I tightened my grip on her just slightly.

Our peaceful moment was broken as Alena and Jamari thumped into us, turning our embrace into a clumsy group hug that was absolutely blocking the walkway.

Katiyana lifted her head from my shoulder, laughing, and leaned her temple against Alena's, nuzzling it gently.

We stayed like that as a group for a few moments, then released as the school bell rang. Katiyana slid her arm through mine and I followed the memory of Jackson's lead to hold it properly, escorting her to the doors.

"I will tell everyone what happened, but I don't want to do it until after school when Dan and Fleur are back. It's hard to think about, let alone talk about." Yana's voice was strong but her last couple words quivered, and her eyes focused into the middle distance instead of anyone's gaze for a brief few seconds.

"That's fine. You don't have to tell us if it makes you uncomfortable." Alena squeezed Katiyana's other hand, and Yana smiled thankfully at her.

"No, it's important. I have to tell you all."

Katiyana kept to her word and didn't say anything until after school, when she'd convinced all of us to take Alena up on her raincheck from the other day and go to her house. We'd texted Fleur and Dan to make sure they understood the plan, and all met at the train station after calling parents and guardians to clear the evening with them. Then we headed to Alena's "house," which I quickly found out was, in fact, a mansion.

The conversation began on the train, with Katiyana explaining to us that she was staying with Valerie and that her mom was attempting to come home sooner than planned, and it was an issue getting the train sorted, finding a rental car, etc. She didn't tell us what actually happened until we were settled in the game room—*gods, a game room*—upstairs in the mansion.

"So he found my journal, the one I've been keeping all the dream stuff in. I came home and there he was on my bed, the whole apartment smelling like bayberry and ginger—" Katiyana was explaining before Alena interrupted.

"What? What does that have to do with anything?"

"Oh right, I'm sorry, I forget that you guys weren't raised to live in constant fear of the Mortmores. Apparently that's the incense they use, and Valerie got all wide-eyed after I told her Nick was using it too." Katiyana sighed.

Dan and I shared a look of confusion which was compounded by Alena and Fleur's. "Anyway. He found my journal and I guess read all of it, because he accused me of 'hiding' Jackson from him again." Katiyana took a deep breath, tugging her knees closer to her chest. We'd all ended up in a circle on the floor, like some sort of sleepover movie. Alena's little black cat was making her way around the circle, getting idle pets from anyone she rubbed up against.

"So...what happened then?" Dan probed, eyebrows knit together and looking just as confused as I felt.

"Well. He yelled at me, dragged me into my room and threw me on my own bed, nearly tore my journal and just..." Her face contorted into a grimace, squeezing her arms around her knees. "I think he was trying to kiss me. He said I'd forgotten who I belong to. It was like...like Lucas had completely taken him over." A shudder went through her, and Alena reached out to rub her back.

I bit back my rage, and then when that didn't work, I swallowed it. Watching it through the lens of a past life was one thing, but to have it be part of our lives now? If I'd been standing I would have begun pacing like I had the night before.

"No no no, what? I'm sorry no, that's...oh my god." Fleur had stood, running a hand through her hair. "This is why you ran across the city to Ladine's? This is why you're staying at Valerie's. Because your brother. Tried to 'claim' you. Dear lord." She walked to the window and pressed her forehead against it, closing her eyes. "Please tell me you called the security force."

"Alexis has the head on speed dial," Jamari informed us, shrugging lightly. "So, she did."

"Is there anyone she doesn't have on speed dial?"

"That's what I said."

I turned to Katiyana, whose gaze was on her fingers, rubbing one thumb against the other's nail. "Did he hurt you?" I asked softly, watching as the little cat shoved her head between Yana's hands. She looked up and shook her head, then paused and reconsidered.

"Only when he dragged me into my room, but it doesn't seem like my arm is even bruised, so not really?" Katiyana opened the grip on her knees and turned her arm to inspect her bicep, showing no marks at all besides a line from the seam of her pants. I let out a slow breath through my nose, forcing my shoulders to relax away from my ears.

"I'm glad," I said, and the words ushered forth a chorus of agreement from the rest of the group, even Fleur who was still against the window. Alena's cat, seemingly annoyed at the lack of chin scritches, went to find her owner. Katiyana tucked her knees up once more, setting her chin on one of them.

"Is that why you didn't take the train?" I questioned. She looked up just with her eyes, then nodded as best she could with her chin still on her knee.

"Yeah, that's Alex, Val's boyfriend. He offered to drive me to and from school so Nick didn't have a chance to find me alone between home and the train station."

"Well, I missed you." My voice was quiet, and I felt the back of my neck grow warm again. Katiyana just smiled, settling her cheek on her knee instead.

"Our little music routine is really nice, isn't it?"

"Katiyana, please control your guard dog!" Dan called from the other side of the room, pointing to where Alena was pacing between a virtual reality setup and a punching bag, hitting the bag every time she passed it. Katiyana snickered. The little cat took the aggression as her sign to leave the room.

"I can't. You're lucky it's not Jamari, though." Yana's shoulders relaxed and she smirked as she watched her friends, and I watched her.

"I'm just so ticked off at your brother!" Alena said, huffing and slugging the punching bag again. "How dare he, he has no right, none at all—"

"He really doesn't, but your pacing is aggressive and making me nervous," Dan said, scooting across the floor toward me. He was offering himself up as comedic relief to keep the atmosphere from getting too heavy, and I was thankful for it, for Katiyana's sake.

"I'm going to punch him the next time I see him," Alena proclaimed, coming back around to the punching bag and delivering a hit that slid off and only moved the bag a little. Katiyana smothered a laugh.

"Good luck with that one, Alena."

We somehow managed to muddle through our homework despite the news, with Katiyana forcing us at random points to pose as references for her art assignments.

"I thought you were doing architecture stuff right now?" Asked Jamari, holding Fleur's hand and using her other to hold the book she was reading for class. Fleur was unphased, scratching away at whatever paper she was writing by hand and then would transfer to her laptop later. Her method was too much work for me, but I wasn't going to say anything to the one person in this group with straight As and a flawless record.

"I am, but straight up architecture is boring so I'm adding some people. Mx. Darling hasn't minded yet." Yana glanced at their hands then went back to drawing, adjusting her lines every so often. I'd finished my assigned reading and didn't have anything else due until later in the week, so I was re-reading some Latin vocabulary I'd missed while at the clinic. Or at least, I was pretending to. I was actually watching Katiyana draw, watching her create something out of the nothing of the canvas. Well, sketchbook paper. I'd never tried drawing beyond doodles and stick figures, but Katiyana was making realism look easy.

Katiyana

Wednesday, September 30, 2020

I KNEW VINNY WAS watching me draw, so I'd tilted my sketchbook a bit to give him a better view. It felt a little odd, something as normal as doing homework with friends after what had happened, but it was also a relief. Being out of the apartment for an actual reason other than "I don't want to be around my only sibling because I think he got possessed by his past life persona" was somehow a blessing. None of us said much else about it, beyond Alena muttering curses under her breath and Dan asking her to stop being scary, and I was glad. I didn't want to think about it. I couldn't pretend it hadn't happened, but I wished I could.

We finished our homework, played a few rounds of games on the Chen's virtual reality headsets, and I finally got a text from Valerie asking if I was staying there for the night.

No problem kiddo, just wanted to know. Did you have dinner over there?

Yeah, katherine would never let us leave without eating lol

Hahah, you're right. Let me know when you want alex to come get you.

I will!! Thank you val

As it turned out, Dan's mom offered us all a ride home when she came to pick up the boys. After lifting the middle console in the front seat, there was room for everyone. I made sure Val knew, and settled myself next to Fleur and Jamari. Dan's mom, Justine, turned out to be the female, older version of Dan, just as expressive and infused with boundless joy, willingly shared with everyone around her. She was great. We hadn't spoken much when she and her husband had driven me from the marina to school, so talking to her for real was a treat.

"I am so glad these two have a gaggle of friends to take care of them, they definitely needed it." Justine grinned, winking at me as the boys shook their heads.

"Moooom..." Dan whined, which made his mother giggle.

"What? Having girls your age around means you'll be more sensitive and in tune with your emotions. That's not a bad thing." She turned the corner of the street that lead toward the apartment complex, and I found myself stiffening, shoulders pulling closer to my ears. Justine noticed, and softened from her teasing tone. "Are you alright, honey?"

"Oh, yeah, my brother is just stressful to be around, but my mom's best friend lives down the hall so I can go and stay with her whenever I like. She's really lovely." It wasn't a lie at all, but made it so I could leave out the precise reason that I didn't want to be around him right now. Justine frowned sympathetically in my direction, but just nodded and turned her full attention back to driving. I caught Vincent's glance over Dan's shoulder and gave him a small reassuring smile back.

"Do you want one of us to walk you up?" Dan asked as we pulled up to the front door, turning in his seat to look at me. I grinned at the thought of being escorted to Val's door like some sort of celebrity and huffed out a short laugh.

"No, it should be fine. I'm sure Nick's at work. Wednesday nights are pretty much guaranteed for him." I leaned forward to sling an arm around Dan's shoulders in a hug, then Vincent piped up.

"I think we should just in case." He sounded very sure, very committed, and I realized it was a losing battle. I looked at him, then just nodded. He nodded back and stepped out of the car to open my door, holding out a hand. Justine laughed softly.

"Oh my goodness, my sons have suddenly turned into princes." She giggled, giving me a teasing grin. I flushed softly, hiding my face under the guise of pushing up my glasses.

"Thank you for the ride, Justine. I really appreciate it." I flashed a grateful smile and slid out of the car, taking Vinny's outstretched hand as Dan got out behind us.

"She is so embarrassing," Dan grumbled as we walked inside, and I chuckled.

"She's really sweet. I like her."

"I do too," Vincent agreed, squeezing my hand he hadn't let go of. "And I am living with her now, so you can't use that excuse."

Dan stuck his tongue out briefly at Vincent, then turned to eye the concierge at the desk. "My, my Yana, you didn't tell me you had such lovely employees..."

"Dan, I don't own the place."

"Really? I figured your family owned most of Faodail." He looked genuinely shocked, and I laughed.

"No, oh my gosh, the MacAskills really don't. For the most part, it's just our own personal land." The amount of rumors I'd learned about my family in just the past few days was hilarious, and most of them were misconceptions from Dan.

"Huh. I really just thought Faodail WAS MacAskill land." Dan was "sneaking" looks at the concierge the entire time we were walking to the elevator, and Vincent finally sighed as he pressed the button to go up.

"Need I remind you what Fleur said about treating people as objects?" He asked, and Dan blushed for only a moment before shaking his head.

"No, there's no problem with admiring a lovely person from afar."

They bickered the entire elevator ride, and I just listened and giggled. They definitely acted like brothers. No wonder Justine called them both her sons. The doors slid open on my floor and Dan got out first, Vincent offering me his arm like he had before, and they led me down the hall. I'd told them Val's apartment number on the way up, so Dan was counting doorplates. As we neared mine, the lock clicked and the doorknob turned. I stepped closer to Vincent, grabbing his arm with both hands, and stopped moving. He stopped, too, and reached forward to grab the back of Dan's jacket, tugging him back. Dan saw the door cracking and moved to stand in front of me, and I lifted a hand to hold onto his jacket. Nick stepped into the hallway, and I simultaneously cursed myself for trusting his unpredictable work schedule and thanked the gods that I'd agreed to have Vincent and Dan walk me up.

After locking the door, Nick looked up. "What do you want?" There was a bite to his voice I only heard when he'd been denied something, and I shrunk against the boys.

"We're visiting a friend, is all. We didn't want to get in your way, so we waited." Dan shrugged, absolutely nonchalant, and tucked his hands in his pockets. Vincent stood silently behind him and when I glanced up, he was staring hard enough to bore a hole in Nick's head. Nick squinted at them both, then spotted me peering over Dan's shoulder. *Damn*. I'd gotten careless. I shouldn't have looked. Vincent took a step closer to me, tugging my arm close against his side.

Unfortunately, Nick had seen that.

"Let her go. She doesn't belong to you," he said, reaching forward to push Dan out of the way. "Marie, come here. I won't let them bother you anymore." His grin was lecherous, and thankfully Dan's hand came up and caught Nick's wrist as Vincent pulled me down the hall, back toward the elevator.

"She doesn't belong to anyone, you creep." Dan scowled at him, matching Vincent's grimace. Nick made a noise that I think was meant to be a growl, or whatever version of it a human could make, and yanked his arm out of Dan's grip. His freedom didn't last long as Dan grabbed his bicep instead, then his wrist, and twisted Nick's arm behind his back. Despite being taller, Nick wasn't a fitness buff like Dan, so he was easily subdued. That didn't stop him from struggling and shouting.

"Get your goddamn hands off me you little shit! I'll put you in your grave!" Immediately after the words left Nick's mouth, Valerie's apartment door opened and Alex was next to us in a flash, one arm around Nick's throat and the other taking over Dan's duty of twisting Nick's arm behind his back.

"You want to repeat that sentence to the head of the security force, Nicolae?" Alex asked, his voice low and menacing. He was really living up to his vampire aesthetic.

Valerie rushed out of the doorway toward me, spinning to stand between me and Nick. "Get back in your apartment and we won't call the force. Let Katiyana and her friends pass, and no one has to get hurt."

Nick struggled against Alex's grip and Dan moved to my other side, settling a hand on my shoulder. "God damn you all, let me go, you all know she belongs in this apartment with me! She doesn't want to go with you, ask her!"

Valerie actually laughed a little, and turned to me. "Well? Do you want to go with us?"

"More than I've ever wanted anything in my life," I said, clinging to Vincent's arm.

"What say you to that, Nick? Huh?" Val faced him again, smirking, taunting.

"You've obviously brainwashed her!" Nick shouted, straining against the arm Alex had around his neck, choking himself like a dog pulling on its leash. "Katiyana, please, come back home, please, we can set everything right, like it's meant to be, like it was supposed to be before he came along and ruined everything all over again—"

"Shut up, Lucas." I was shocked to hear Vincent speak, and I looked up to see him flat out glaring at Nicolae. If this had been an anime, his hair would have been floating and his eyes glowing. "She doesn't want to be anywhere near you. She wants to pass, and relax in a place where you're not. So leave. Listen to Alex. Go back into your apartment and let. Us. Pass." As he spoke, he took a single step forward, keeping my arm pinned to his side. A memory of watching Jamari play Kingdom Hearts, specifically of a toy cowboy and a kid with a key for a sword, slammed into my head. The comparison and trickle of amusement from it let me swallow back the last of my nerves and I moved forward with Vinny, staring my brother down as best I could.

"Go back in the apartment, Nick. I don't want anything to do with you!" I exclaimed, surprised to hear my voice not shaking at all. Much to my alarm, Nick still struggled, trying to force Alex's arm off his neck.

"Don't listen to whatever they're telling you, Marie. You know you're mine, you know where you belong!" He was shouting, and Alex finally just dragged him to the door and released Nick's arm long enough to open it and shove him in. The door slammed and Alex held onto the doorknob as Nick rattled and tugged on it on the other side. Alex motioned with his head for us to go into Val's apartment, and we followed the order immediately. As we hit the door, the neighbor across the hallway poked his head out curiously, and she just motioned to Alex, burdening him with the explanation.

"I wish he wouldn't be so physical about things," Val grumbled, hovering at the door to watch Alex. "It's getting exhausting."

"You're telling me." I sighed, letting Vincent lead me to the couch and sit me down. I looked up at him thankfully, and he gave me a soft smile in return. "Thank you, both, for demanding to walk me up. I don't want to think about what would have happened if you hadn't."

"You know we gotchu, honey." Dan plopped down next to me and slung his arm around my shoulders, and I just leaned into him. It had been quite an ordeal and any comfort was welcome. He pulled out his phone, texting his mom that they'd be a minute and he was sorry. Vincent stood in front of us, watching the door and whatever he could see beyond it. He only relaxed when Alex came in and shut the door behind him.

"He's apparently going to work tonight, but I'm not sure what kind of shift starts at this hour. I'd be shocked if he wasn't making it up," Alex reported, straightening his shirt then looking at Vincent, grinning. "That was very brave of you. Good job. It threw him off enough for me to get a more secure hold." Vinny smiled, tightly, and looked away. He had his hands in fists but was trying not to make it obvious.

"Thank you. I just couldn't stand the way he was talking." Vinny's voice was as tight as his smile, and I reached up to gently pry his fingers apart, pushing my own in between his. He relaxed enough to take my hand, looking down at it, then sighed.

"None of us could, kid," Valerie called from the kitchen, pulling out various snacks, then coming over to deposit them on Dan's lap. "Here, a treasure for your quest."

After a few more reassurances to Vincent that I'd be safe, and me standing up to hold onto his arm and rest my head on his shoulder, he finally relaxed enough to agree they should head out. I squeezed his hand before releasing it, and he looked up, right into my eyes.

"Just let me know if you need anything," he said, and I could see his desire to take my hand back, so I stepped forward and hugged him tight instead. His arms wrapped around my back, squeezing tight for a few moments before releasing. He looked more tormented than I felt, and his anxiety must have been worse than he let on. *Honestly Katiyana, it's probably trauma more than anxiety.* Dan wrapped me up in a hug as well once Vincent released me, and I giggled.

"Thanks guys. I'm glad I have two bodyguards now," I teased as Dan gathered up the snacks Valerie had offered, and they headed out. Alex followed them just in case Nick was still lurking. As the door shut I collapsed back onto the couch and put my head in my hands, shuddering with a deep exhale. Val came over to join me, tugging me against her side in a hug.

"I'm sorry kiddo. We should have met you at the door. Alex had been hearing him in the apartment all night, and we figured once it had gotten quiet he'd either left or fallen asleep." She rested her chin on the top of my head.

"It's okay, you can't be expected to just be at my beck and call constantly."

"No, but we're supposed to be protecting you right now, and we messed up. I'm really glad Vincent and Dan were there for you." Val sighed and hugged me a little tighter, and I leaned into her.

"Is that why you gave them snacks?" I giggled, and she laughed too.

"Yes. I didn't know what else to do."

Alex came back not long after, and we watched a little TV together before they headed off to bed. I washed my face, brushed my teeth, and settled in the guest room, tucking into the pillow with my phone close to my face to get a little scrolling in before I passed out. At least, that was my plan.

i don't think i like your brother very much, i'm sorry to say.

LilTriquetra

Lol, no one really does, don't worry

RedSam

i almost asked to stay.

LilTriquetra

I didn't know what else to say. It was sweet he had thought of that but the idea made me blush, even if he had been staying on Val's couch. I bit my lip and stared at the screen, trying to come up with a response.

RedSam

good lord, sorry, that was incredibly forward of me. i don't know what came over me.

LilTriquetra

The bravery boost hasn't worn off I see lol

Teasing was easier, so much easier.

RedSam

i guess not!

please forgive me, i did want to keep him away from you but Alex does a fine enough job on his own.

is it just me or is he a vampire?

I laughed, muffling it in the pillow, trying desperately to keep it quiet.

LilTriquetra

EVERYONE SAYS THAT hahahahah!!!

RedSam

he looks like one, he moved so quickly down the hall, he held onto nick with one arm…i'm seeing a pattern.

Then, the group chat pinged.

Beefaroni

So what the hell is alex a vampire or what?

GamezNStuff

Jury's still out but they're leaning "yes"

RedSam

i'd like to add evidence of super-speed

Beefaroni

You were recording???

GamezNStuff

YOU GOT FOOTAGE?

RedSam

gosh, no, sorry, i just meant he took like two seconds to move down ten feet of hallway.

GamezNStuff

You lied to me!

RedSam

please forgive me!!

LilTriquetra

Sorry vinny now you have to let her beat you at smash bros, that's the only way she accepts apologies

Beefaroni

You're kidding

GamezNStuff

Nope. Date and time, dreamboy.

RedSam

i'm doomed.

I giggled at his new nickname and watched them go back and forth over timing as I slipped off, glad that I'd plugged my phone in already. The soft light from my phone and the gentle buzz of the messages coming in was comforting, and once again I was grateful beyond belief to have the friends I did.

The Dreamers

Wednesday, September 30, 2020

MARIE WAS SEATED IN a church much different than the one she'd grown used to attending all her life. While they were both Catholic churches, this humble space was a cottage to the castle that was St. Patrick's where she had been earlier in the day. She and Clara had been baptized in the sprawling cathedral just a couple years apart. But this one in Brooklyn was where Leo had recently been baptized, after much convincing and converting him to the Catholic ways. Unfortunately, this wasn't nearly as happy of an occasion. For once, Lucas sat silently next to her, not bothering to make a comment. He had grown up with Clara, their families close, and although he hadn't shown it, she knew there had been sorrow in his heart and eyes at her funeral. Marie had pleaded with him to let her attend Leo's funeral, skipping the lunch Clara's family was hosting, and had agreed immediately to Lucas's strict condition that he attend, as well. It was better than not going at all.

"The righteous one, though he die early, shall be at rest. For the age that is honorable comes not with the passing of time, nor can it be measured in terms of years." The priest was speaking solemnly from the pulpit, gesturing at the casket settled in the nave. The second one she'd seen today. They had both been empty, and it only added to the heavy sorrow of the occasion. Marie's head hung, not bothering to lift a hand to catch the tears dripping onto her skirt.

The reading was for Leo. The most righteous of them all, the one who'd chosen St. Michael as his confirmation saint, joking arrogantly that he would become the

Archangel's right hand. Marie knew he'd lived up to the choice, what with saving countless lives as a Brooklyn fireman and constantly protecting Clara and Marie when they would meet up, pretending to go to a painting class their parents had paid for but was really just an excuse to leave the house without a chaperone. Marie didn't even want to think about the reading that had been picked for Clara. It had been so wrong, so ill-chosen. It should have been something to do with Jeanne d'Arc. Clara had chosen the French saint, while Marie had chosen Brigid of Kildare. She was content holding the idea of a proper reading in her heart, and not thinking about the parents and fiancé that didn't know Clara well enough trying to find one and failing. She had purposely pushed the wrong reading from her mind as soon as it had been spoken.

She was lucky to be able to attend both, Marie thought, forcing away the comparison of Clara's being elaborate and grand with a fourth of New York high society turning out for it, and this, Leo's bare-bones service near the firehouse with just his crewmates. The boy crying silently but unrelentingly in the front row didn't seem to be over fifteen; was he Leo's brother? Clara would have known.

Marie worked her anxieties out silently, twisting her gloves in her hands. It didn't suit Leo and Clara to be separated like this. They belonged together, in every fashion. But it didn't suit them to have been trapped in the fire, either.

Oh how she wished to run away to the bakery, to find Jackson and beg him to spirit her away. Clara had done it, why couldn't she? Maybe they could go somewhere and not share the same fate as her beloved friend.

Over the course of mass, and throughout the internment (both internments seemed very stupid to her since both caskets were empty. Why put an empty box in the ground? What's the point?), Marie got closer to making up her mind. If she could pack just a suitcase or valise with some money and the necessities, the things she couldn't leave behind, and then left in the very early morning, she could be at the bakery when it opened. She'd gone that early before, and it was easy to catch the subway most of the way and then walk the rest to the shop. Once the stupid, empty caskets were in the ground—in separate cemeteries entirely, of course they were, why would it be any different—she'd made up her mind. It was the only choice, and she'd convinced herself of it. Everyone would be leaving her alone right now, letting her mourn. She'd take advantage of it.

And so, as soon as Clara's wake dinner was over and they'd returned home, she slipped away into her room, feigning grief too heavy to carry and allowing tear after tear to spill from her eyes. She locked her door, tucking the chair from her vanity under the handle for more security. She'd done it when she was younger, so her parents wouldn't be suspicious of it.

Marie waited, and waited, lying still on her bed until she heard all the noise die down, and watched the sun set through the slit in her curtains. Then she got up, changed into her most plain traveling dress, and got to work. She knew where her luggage was stored, and slid out silently along the hallways and staircases to grab a bag that looked large enough to hold all she wanted, but not so large she couldn't manage it herself. Anything she absolutely couldn't bear to part with went into that bag, likely not packed as well as a maid would, but secured nonetheless.

The last book she and Clara had read together, some jewelry from her grandmother and mother, and others from Lucas that she'd hated the instant she saw them, but could be sold if needed. *At least he has expensive taste,* she thought, dropping another diamond necklace into the soft drawstring bag.

A few sets of clothes and her other pair of sensible shoes later, she snapped the bag shut and took a look around her room. She would miss it, of course. She'd been in this room since she'd grown out of the nursery, but she couldn't bear to be in it without Clara's light brightening it during her ever-so-frequent visits that encompassed everything from their shared lessons, to Clara finding excuses to stay away from Reggie. They'd grown up together, and Marie was loath to leave whatever remnants of the best friend who may as well have been a sister behind. But she couldn't stay here without her, either.

One last breath to steady her resolve and she stepped out the door, taking care to not let her boots click too loudly, thankful for the thick rugs protecting the wood of the floor. She slipped into an alcove or two to avoid servants who were still up cleaning or preparing for the next day, making her way to the side door that led into the garden. Surely there would be someone at the front door still, a hall boy waiting for late night visitors or people staying over to return from whatever frolic they'd gone on after dinner.

The gardens were unbearably peaceful, rudely beautiful after the tragedy. Clara had helped tend to these flowers, helped the gardener prune the rose bushes to the perfect, winding vines there were now. Of course she'd gotten mightily scolded for ruining her dresses and banned from visiting for a torturous three months, but her work had paid off. It was excruciating to look at them, so Marie left as swiftly as she could, making her way to the subway station.

The ride was awkward and silent, construction workers on their way to their job sites staring at her in confusion and the odd drunk trying to talk to her, sit next to her. Thankfully one of the workers took pity on her and sat down in the seat beside her, glaring away any other unwelcomed advances. She thanked him profusely and handed him a ten dollar bill without thinking about how much money she'd just given away. He acted like she'd just handed him a golden ticket, and tried to return it, but she shook her head firmly and walked onto the platform before he had a chance. It wasn't too much farther to the bakery. She was nearly free.

◦—◦—◦

In the few weeks since Lucas had dragged Marie out of the store, Jackson's bruises had faded, his throat was healing, and he was able to speak with only a slight rasp that showed promises of disappearing. He was certain he'd never see

Marie again and was trying to live with that fact. He'd managed to joke with Charles, to be friendly and even a little flirtatious to the customers, the ladies blushing and giggling as they took their wrapped pastries. It was starting to feel normal again, but everything still felt wrong without her smile or rapt attention as she listened to yet another Greek myth or Shakespearian play.

The bell on the door chimed, and as Jackson looked up, he stumbled back into the counter behind him. His heart was pounding, his head was suddenly spinning, and he pressed his hand to his chest, keeping his heart from beating right out of it.

"M...Marie?" He whispered, staring at the vision in the door they'd unlocked just three minutes ago. "What are you doing here? Lucas—"

"Lucas can dive off the Empire State Building for all I care." She dropped the bag she was carrying next to the door and it landed with a soft but heavy thud as she took purposeful strides to the counter. "I don't want to live here anymore. I can't." Tears filled her eyes and Jackson jumped over the counter to her, not bothering to lift the little bit of counter that was hinged for that exact purpose. She collapsed against him, sobbing like she'd been holding it back for days. And the truth was, she had. "Clara...she...and Leo...Jackson, they're gone, they're both gone!" She shook, gripping the straps of his apron and the sides of his vest. Jackson stood there, shocked, confused, but wrapped her in a tight hug anyway. Sure, he was pleased to have her in his arms again, but not like this, not after she'd just lost the person she cared about most in this world, and the one who cared about her most.

"What happened, Marie?" He asked gently, lifting a hand to nudge her chin up. She lifted her head, tears still streaming, eyes red, brows knit together fiercely.

"The fire, the hotel up in the Catskills, they...they were..." She pressed a hand to her mouth, choking on her words. Jackson's eyes widened, then closed.

"I saw, in the papers." He wrapped his arms around her again, tightly, looking at Charles as he stepped in, using his eyes to indicate for him to lock the door again. Charles took the silent command and nodded, slipping silently past them to do just that.

After letting Marie sob and empty her heart of as much grief as she could, Charles and Jackson bundled her into the kitchen, setting her near one of the ovens with a cup of hot chocolate and a plate of the best breakfast they could offer in their meager stock, which consisted of scrambled eggs and some scones meant for tea. She'd managed to eat a little, picking at the eggs and nibbling at the scones, only making it through half of the hot chocolate before asking, so softly, so apologetically, for tea instead. Charles got up to make it.

"What did you mean when you said you didn't want to live here anymore, Marie? Should I be worried that you're going to..." Jackson swallowed. "Follow them?"

Marie shook her head fiercely. "I can't stand the very idea of New York without them, Jackson. I can't live here. I don't care where I go, it just has to be out of this blasted, damned city." Her hands shook around the mug of hot chocolate she was still holding, swallowing back a fresh wave of tears. "I can't bear the idea of being in Leo's favorite place without him, and being in Clara's home without her. I can't do it, Jackson. I need to leave."

Charles brought the tea back, along with a bit of sugar, and sat on the other side of Marie. "I put a sign up on the door that we were opening late today, so we'll have a couple hours before people start pounding on the glass and trying to break in."

Marie smiled, just gently, up at him, and finally released her mug to pick up the fresh one instead. "Thank you, Charles."

"Quite welcome, milady." Then, after Marie cringed at the moniker, "Apologies."

"It's fine, I..." She took a breath and sighed it out, closing her eyes. "I am just so used to...both of us being called that. It's very odd to have it singular right now."

Charles reached forward to place a hand on her shoulder, squeezing it gently. "I understand."

"If you...want to leave New York, why did you come here first? You could afford any ticket on any ship, or train.

Why here?" Jackson looked up, confused but treading lightly. Marie's gaze dropped to her mug, and she bit her lip, finding her words.

"Come with me. Both of you. It wouldn't be safe to be on my own." She looked between Charles and Jackson, pleading, knowing the chance was slim. They had secure jobs and housing, and who knew if they had the funds to run away with her?

"There's a little island I've been curious about," Charles mused, crossing his arms and leaning back in his chair. "Have you two ever heard of Faodail?"

Suddenly, there was a glimmer of hope on the horizon once more.

Katiyana

Thursday, October 1, 2020

I ROLLED OVER TO my phone the moment my eyes opened, my sharp mind fighting clumsy fingers to navigate to Sinéad's Comms chat, adding Leo to it quickly.

LilTriquetra

Cousins, respectfully, what the fuck.

Bruadarach

Watch your mouth young lady, but I am So Sorry

DandyLion

What are we apologizing for?

LilTriquetra

EXCUSE ME? YOUR FUNERALS?? I HAD TO WITNESS THEM??? THE HELL????

DandyLion

Ahhh, that. Yes. I am sorry.

Bruadarach

I'M SORRY.

LilTriquetra

THAT WAS HORRIBLE

DandyLion

How many times do I have to relive this?

Bruadarach

I don't know what to say other than I'm sorry!!!

LilTriquetra

How did you know what I was cussing about???

Bruadarach

...dreamt about the fire again, assumed.

DandyLion

Damnit I knew there was a reason I dreamed about it too, damnit Sinéad.

Bruadarach

IT'S NOT MY FAULT! Blame the island

NO I BLAME YOU BOTH leo also who was that kid in the front row?

You can punch me next time you see me. Kid? Who do you mean?

He kinda looked like you but dark hair and lanky, he seemed heartbroken

Oh, Timothy.

Timothy?

Neither of them answered, so I got up grumpily, tossing the covers back in exasperation, then looked down at my phone as another message buzzed through.

well, at least we know why they left?

You write that one down I'm too mad at my cousins to do it

I sent him a screenshot of the group conversation, then left my phone on the bed to go get ready for school. Valerie came into the bathroom as I was braiding my hair and nudged me aside to do her makeup.

"What's the scowl for?"

"Sinéad and Leo's funerals," I grumbled. It took a moment of Val squinting but then she opened them wide.

"Ahhh, yes, 1926. Poor Leo has had so many of us remember it or remember him remembering it that he's probably had to relive it about twenty times now." She skillfully dabbed a beauty blender down a line of concealer on her cheek, on her way to an effortlessly perfect contour.

"He said I can punch him next time I see him." I tied off my braid, straightening my earrings in the mirror then stepping back from the counter to let her have all of it. She stepped in front of me immediately, the blending of her contour not stopping.

"Hahaha, he's offered me the same before, too, but good luck. He cheats." She laughed at the idea, and I shook my head and walked out to gather my things and find some food before finding Alex for a ride.

At lunch, I relayed the dream to my friends, showing them the conversation with Leo and Sinéad. Jamari had a bit of a laugh over it, not able to get over Sinéad's motherly "watch your language" before apologizing. She sent a GIF of Captain America saying "language" to Sinéad and got back one of Tony Stark rolling his eyes.

"You were on the train with a construction worker?" Alena asked, so quietly I almost had to tell her to repeat it.

Out of the corner of my eye, Jamari froze, but hid it from the others by keeping her phone in her hands.

"Yeah, he sat next to Marie and kept the other ones with less noble intentions away. Why?"

Alena fumbled for a moment, spinning her fork slowly in her fingers. We all looked at her, waiting to see what she was going to say.

"Alena?" Fleur ventured, nudging Alena's elbow softly with her own. Alena finally took a breath and answered.

"I had a dream about a construction worker coming home and telling me about a girl he protected on a train. I didn't think much of it, I just figured it was a scene cobbled together from all the period dramas Jamari and I have watched together, so I didn't think it was relevant at all. But now, I'm wondering if it is."

She had kept her head down throughout her whole explanation and I looked over at Jamari who also hadn't moved, but was grinning at her phone. She hadn't told us a single bit of her dreams last year when she'd been going through this, and she'd stayed quiet throughout our ordeals thus far. It had probably been at the orders of the coven, for the sake of our own perception. And I was beginning to suspect it was centered around a specific someone.

"It's entirely possible, I suppose," I broke the silence. First Dan complained about us infecting his dream-space, and now Alena's dreams seemed to be matching up with and filling out mine.

"It is. Why don't you add your notes to the file and we'll compare." Fleur was already making Alena her own document in our shared folder, setting up the date and basic premise so Alena could fill it out later. Jamari looked to them, then over to me, and I narrowed my eyes. She knew something she wasn't allowed to tell us, but I was starting to figure it out.

I didn't manage to catch Leo, despite keeping an eye out for him around the train stations. Valerie was right, he was definitely cheating. I'd have to wait until he thought I forgot and let his guard down, and then let loose.

"Well, that's too bad," Vincent said, grinning as we walked back toward the front door to rejoin our group. "I'm sure he would have held perfectly still." I shot him a glare, and he chuckled, ducking down into his jacket a little.

"We didn't go to the library like we planned yesterday," I announced to my friends as soon as they were in earshot, holding my arms above my head.

"Ah, right. I'm still up for it," Fleur replied, looking at the others. "Jamari doesn't have work today, Alena's club is canceled, and Dan doesn't seem to be getting a date for any night other than Friday, so we should be fine."

"How do you know so much about my dating life?" Dan asked, looking at her scandalized and holding his phone to his chest. Fleur rolled her eyes.

"Dan you tell me everything at Corp."

"My club being canceled though, how'd you know that?" Alena asked. We started walking to the train station, some of us texting parents or guardians the plan.

"Oh, I read the email over your shoulder."

And so off to the library we went, Vincent and I catching up a bit on our music habit as we rode the train to a part of town I didn't frequent very often. Not that I didn't love the library, it was just across Ceangal and my aunts and cousins usually gave me books that I ended up liking. Vincent seemed to know the place well, Dan only marginally less, and it turned out that this had been their main hangout spot for years. It'd seen many a paper written and revised, and presentations hastily thrown together on a Sunday afternoon after being forgotten about all weekend. We said hi to Dorell, and he stopped us as we headed toward the nonfiction section.

"Katiyana, I have something that belongs to you," he called, turning to dig in a drawer behind the desk. Vincent and I stepped over, leaning on the counter as he pulled out a cloth-wrapped package. "Now if you lose it again, I'm just going to let Lorena keep it down in the archives, understand?" He grinned as he said it, but I felt the seriousness. It was doubled when I glanced up and saw the archivist herself perched on a stool behind Dorell, looking over from where she was filling in for a circulation-desk librarian. Seeing her was always like looking at a ghost from the seventies.

"Yes sir, understood." I giggled as I took the package from the high priest's hands, grateful to have met him at events so it wasn't odd to joke around with him. I unwrapped it while still standing at the counter, setting it down quickly so as to not drop it the moment I realized what this was. "Where...how...Dorell, how did you get this?" I stared up at him, then returned my gaze to the little book, bound in blue cloth but missing the illustrated dust jacket I knew it'd had once upon a time.

"Marie brought it over when she moved. It was entrusted to the library after her death, kept in the archives until I asked Lorena to bring it up yesterday, and that's all I'm allowed to tell you as of now." His smile hadn't left his face, and he sat back in his chair, folding his hands over his stomach. I traced the embossed letters spelling out what'd become a keystone novel in American culture, still loved and hated and debated about over nearly a hundred years later. *The Great Gatsby.*

"Gosh. How is it still in such good shape?" Vincent asked as he leaned over, and I pushed the book closer to him to let him inspect it. Dorell laughed softly behind the counter.

"We're very good at our jobs, aren't we Lorena?" He grinned wider, and she made a noise of agreement without turning her head. "If something is entrusted to the library or museum, you can be assured it'll be taken care of with the utmost diligence."

"Thank you, I don't know what to say! This is such a pleasant surprise." I looked up at him, giving him the most sincere smile I could muster. "Thank you so much. I'll make sure to keep it looking as good as it is now."

"You are so welcome, my dear. Now I'm assuming you study buddies need a room?" He gestured at the rest of our group, who'd been hovering nearby, and we nodded. I was internally groaning at the use of "study buddies," but Dorell could be forgiven a few cringeworthy sayings.

"Yes please, if there's one open. Can we borrow a couple laptops, as well?" Vincent took over the logistics for our little research meeting, and I walked over to the group to hold out the book, threatening them with pain and suffering if they marred it in any way.

"This has to be a first edition! It's so old!" Fleur kept the cloth it'd been wrapped in between the book and her palm as she opened the cover, then gasped gently. "Aw, Yana, look."

I tilted my head over her shoulder to see an inscription, gentle cursive I couldn't quite read. "What does it say?"

"'To my darling, my Marie. May we always be beautiful little fools. All My Love, Clara.'" Fleur read aloud, and I put my hand over my mouth as my breath caught.

"Oh my goodness, I wonder if Sinéad remembers this." I pulled out my phone and snapped a photo over Fleur's shoulder, sending it to my cousin with no explanation. "It must have been a Christmas present or something after they read it together." Pocketing my phone, I put my chin on Fleur's shoulder, watching her flip through the pages.

"That's so sweet. We should get each other books for Christmas this year," Alena suggested, leaning over to watch Fleur's page turning, as well. Jamari groaned softly.

"Why do you all want me to read?"

"We want you to be smart," I said, looking up as Vincent came back with two laptops and their chargers, and a key to a private study room.

"I changed the info on my library card since I'm not living with my mom anymore. I put your address, I hope that's okay." He was talking to Dan, whose attention was on his phone, and Dan just nodded and waved the comment away. Vincent accepted it and turned to the rest of us. "Shall we?" He asked, holding out the key to me. I took it and we headed upstairs, settling in with our homework first, then getting down to research.

"Oh, oh! Valerie let something slip this morning when I told her about the dream! She said Clara and Leo's funerals were in 1926. So now we have a solid year to work around for a lot of stuff." I stretched my arms out across the table, my fingers pressing against the back of the laptop Vincent was typing away on. He looked over and grinned.

"Thank the gods, I was just about to pull up every year's fires between 1925 and 1930." He closed a few tabs, clicking away on the touchpad to refine his search.

Vincent and Fleur had taken the laptops, and Fleur had first scoured the library catalog for more history and reference books that could have possibly been of use, then directed those of us not at a keyboard to go find them all and bring them back to the room. Dan had ended up locked out once, and faked crying after we let him in, only stopping when Vincent begrudgingly wrapped an arm around him and let Dan rest on his shoulder. It was absolutely ridiculous, but Dan never failed to bring light into a room.

I also remembered to add the details of the funeral to the document, after learning Vincent hadn't dreamed about it at all, and had instead gotten a dream about Jackson and Charles reading the papers about the fire. We matched up our dreams and realized they'd converged as Marie walked into the bakery. I laughed at myself, just a little, for assuming Vinny would dream about a place Jackson hadn't been.

"I think I found something," Fleur said, her voice the first noise we'd had in the room for twenty minutes. "You said Marie told Jackson about a fire at a hotel in the Catskills, right?" She spun the laptop around, showing us a newspaper clipping about a fire in a place called Haines Falls, at the Twilight Inn. "Do you think this could be it?"

We all peered closer, me squinting a bit since she was on the other end of the table and the clipping was small. She flipped through a few more clippings of the same event, then back to the first tab. "I didn't find Clara or Leo named on any of the lists, but it looks like there were a lot of people that went unidentified. So maybe?"

"Let me text Sinéad. She would know better." I pulled out my phone, blinking at the time, shocked we'd been there for two hours already, then texted my cousin who hadn't responded to the photo of the book.

LilTriquetra

Haines Falls mean anything?

She saw the message immediately, but then went offline just as quickly. I stared at the screen and was rewarded a moment later with a screenshot of the same article Fleur had just shown us.

Bruadarach

Yeah.

LilTriquetra

We just found that clipping and like five others

Bruadarach

I keep them on my phone

LilTriquetra

Morbid, macabre.

Bruadarach

A reminder to not make the same mistakes.

"Sinéad sent me back the same article so it must be the right one." I showed my friends the clipping on my phone, then plopped my phone back down on my lap. "She says she keeps them on her phone to keep her from making the same mistakes, whatever that means." I set my chin in my hands, looking at Alena who had taken the laptop from Fleur and was reading the clippings more intently.

"Well you said Clara and Leo ran away, right? Maybe she's reminding herself not to run away again?" Jamari asked, not looking up from her Switch. She'd given up on helping with research early on, pushing the few books she'd grabbed to the middle of the table and devoting the time to her island instead. I snorted.

"She ran away when I was eleven, but Leo didn't go with her that time, so maybe the reminder worked."

We didn't find much more information besides the clippings about Haines Falls. We packed up and returned all the books to a cart at Vincent and Dan's insistence. They said it helped the library to know books were getting used, so we followed their instructions instead of taking them back to the shelves.

"Well, it wasn't a very fruitful research session, but at least we found something of note," Dan said, hands on his head as we waited for the train at the nearest station. Turned out, Dan's house wasn't far from the library, so the boys were going to walk back.

"Yeah, wasn't a total waste of time," Jamari added, zipping up her Switch case. Fleur pinched her arm.

"Says the one who didn't help at all," Alena scolded, shooting a glare in Jamari's direction. Jamari pouted, but Alena and Fleur just rolled their eyes. I chuckled.

The train pulled in not long after, and after hugging Dan and Vincent—Vinny admittedly just a tad bit longer—we took off. I texted Valerie and she said that they'd meet me at the door this time, just in case, and I felt myself relax at the message. Nick was easier to handle when Alex was there to stem his nonsense and aggressiveness, but I still hoped I didn't see him at all.

"You really like him, don't you?" Alena asked, sliding her arm through mine and resting her head on my shoulder. Fleur and Jamari were bickering softly in the seats across from us. I flushed.

"Well, he's a nice guy, and not like, a Nice Guy, y'know. He's sweet and listens to me, and he's a good person," I rambled, and Alena just giggled at me.

"It's okay to crush on him. Fleur's speech when this all started was just all of us not wanting you to rush into anything. You already told him you wanted to be his friend first. And so you are. We have two really good guys in the group now, and it's been great. So let's just keep it as it is and see what happens, yeah?" She looked up at me and I smirked, nodded, then rested my head on hers. She was getting sleepy, and when she was sleepy, she was at her cutest and most sappy. We teased that she'd be even worse if we ever saw her drunk.

"You got a deal, Alena."

The Dreamers

Friday, October 2, 2020

CATCHING THE TRAIN HAD been harder than Marie had thought, but Charles and Jackson hadn't been worried at all, and she trusted them. She'd never traveled anywhere by ferry before, and was looking forward to it. Jackson watched Marie's awe over all the small details of traveling third-class instead of first, like not having a private carriage, and as they'd boarded, he'd had to gently take hold of her elbow and steer her farther down the platform to the proper carriages.

"Your muscle memory is too strong, Marie." Charles laughed at her, and she blushed and playfully batted at him with her valise.

The two days leading up to the trip had been stressful, with Marie hidden away in Charles's neighbors' apartment, staying in their back room and hardly daring to peer out a window, let alone go outside. But it had worked. Lucas had indeed come to the bakery, raging and red-faced and demanding Jackson hand her over, but the men had lied so convincingly that he'd gone to interrogate Clara's still-grieving family instead, and gotten himself thrown out and banned from the estate. Marie only found out because it had been in a gossip rag that Charles had smugly brought her, and she tucked it away in her book as a prize. But now they were getting away from all of that. The owner of the bakery had been furious but had found replacements quickly enough to keep his ire and guilt-tripping at bay.

"What do you think it will be like?" Marie asked, her fingertips pressed to the window as the train chugged along, heading toward Massachusetts. The ferry would take them from that coast to the little island. Charles glanced over to her, looking up from his book, and just shrugged. Jackson shrugged as well, but answered.

"I'm hoping it will be somewhere that's open to anything." They smiled at one another, and in those smiles, they shared their hope, their wishes for the future to be better than their recent past. Their longing for a fresh start.

The roughly five-hour train ride was uneventful, making a couple stops along the way to pick up and drop off other passengers, and the trio took turns dozing off. Before they knew it, they were in Boston.

"One more train to Chatham, then we get to the ferry." Charles yawned, scrubbing a hand through his hair and looking around for the bellboy that was meant to be transferring his and Jackson's luggage. Jackson went off to procure dinner, coming back with newspaper-wrapped sandwiches and pickles. They ate in near-silent companionship as they waited for the next train.

Marie very blatantly headed to the right part of the platform this time, much to the amusement of both Jackson and Charles.

The train station in Chatham was smaller, and the next bellboy left them to deal with their own luggage instead of helping them transfer it to the dock. Jackson seemed perturbed by this, but didn't let it show besides a small frown as the boy left after getting paid.

The ferry wasn't due for another hour or so. It made near-constant trips back and forth between Chatham and Faodail, so it was either just docking on the island or in the midst of returning. And so the companions rested on a bench near the dock, idly talking, reading, taking turns to get up and pace impatiently. Marie did the most pacing, anxious to leave her old life behind.

While she was sitting down and Jackson was taking a turn pacing toward the railing of the dock, watching the ferry approach, a hand landed on her shoulder. She jumped violently and the hand fell off as she scrambled upright, reaching for Charles's arm as her worst nightmare came true in front of her eyes.

"Come home now and we won't speak of this ever again," Lucas growled, his eyes hard and angry, narrowed toward Marie. "I have searched every train station in New York for two days and finally, I catch you heading here."

"You followed us all the way?" Marie's voice was high, nervous, and Charles stood to stand between her and Lucas, holding an arm out in front of her. Jackson had heard her cry and came over as well, taking his place beside Charles, leveling Lucas with a glare.

"Get out of here," he said, reaching back to hold Marie's hand. "She doesn't want to go anywhere with you." Marie gripped his hand, holding her other to her rapidly beating heart.

"You've obviously brainwashed her." Lucas's voice shifted from menacing to some fake sweetness, looking at Marie. "Marie, just come home. You know you belong there with me."

"No she doesn't," Charles snapped, glancing around in hopes of finding a police officer. Unfortunately, there were only a few concerned fellow travelers watching warily.

"I'm not talking to you, you blasted Irish bastard." Lucas swung a fist toward Charles, but he leaned back in time to avoid it, having learned his lesson after the last time they'd been in the same room. "Stay out of this."

"Neither of us will be staying out of it. Marie wants *us* here, not you. Now leave, and don't cause a scene. Unless you want your face plastered over every gossip rag on the east coast. Or did Clara's family kicking you out already accomplish that?" Jackson asked, letting his mouth quirk into a bit of a smirk that dropped as he ducked from another wild swing from Lucas.

The ferry's horn sounded, and Charles ducked to quickly grab as many of their bags as he could, Marie copying him and grabbing her valise and one of the smaller ones. Jackson took a moment to pick up the remaining two, then they turned and ran. Between the bench blocking Lucas's direct path and the crowd filing off the ferry that had surged forward at the perfect moment, the trio was given a decent head start. Lucas was caught in a wave of people and suitcases, fighting to make his way through them. They slipped into the crowd headed toward the ferry as they ran from Lucas, away from New York, away from everything they were trying to leave behind.

"Marie! I'll find you! This boat only goes to one place! I'll find you on that horrid little island and drag you back!" Lucas was shouting from the dock, waving his fist in the air, face burning as red as the cherries Jackson made into candy. They'd made it onto the deck of the boat, just enough out of the way of the crowd, and the gangplank was rising. Lucas would have to risk falling into the water to get them, and his line was drawn at ruining his expensive suit. Marie knew this, and laughed at the sight of him burning with anger over her escape, turning to Jackson. She tugged him by the lapels of his jacket, pulling him down the few inches that separated their heights, and kissed him solidly on the mouth. His laugh was against her lips, his arm wrapping around her waist to tug her close. Charles whooped, laughing and waving toward Lucas.

"Just try it, popinjay!" He cackled with glee, then turned to steal Marie from Jackson and lift her up, spinning her around, hiding their faces behind his hat to pretend he was kissing her as well. Marie laughed, tears gathering in her eyes from mirth, and held Charles's face to keep up the charade.

They were free, Lucas was trapped behind his need to keep his fancy suit pristine, and if what Charles had heard about Faodail was right, they'd be safe.

They would be safe.

Not too long after the trio had settled, someone cleared their throat within earshot, and Marie looked up to find a man holding his hat between his hands, a woman standing next to him and holding his arm while her other hand rested on her obviously pregnant belly.

"Oh, can I help you sir?" She asked, Jackson and Charles lifting their gazes as well. The man grinned.

"You already have, miss. That ten dollars you gave me the other day was the last bit of money we needed for our ferry tickets." His grin got wider, as did Marie's eyes. The construction worker who'd guarded her on the train!

"Oh it's you! I'm so glad to see you again."

"And I you, so I could properly thank you for helping us to our new lives." His partner nodded, smiling just as wide as he had.

"I'm so happy, and we're all headed there together now." Marie laughed, and reached her hand up to shake the worker's.

"It seems we are," he said, squeezing her fingers gently. "Seems we are."

Katiyana

Friday, October 2, 2020

My phone buzzing woke me up before my alarm did.
It was both Vinny:

RedSam

> can we have more dreams like that?

And the group chat:

QueenofGambits

> OKAY, THAT WAS MARIE AND JACKSON AND CHARLES, I'M GOING TO PULL A DAN.

Beefaroni

> Yeah I would like to pull a dan as well, that was very blatant, wasn't it???

RedSam

> hahah, it was!

BlondeBrainiac

Sigh, I'm feeling so left out right now...

QueenofGambits

Your turn next year fleur!!!!

BlondeBrainiac

You dorks have already told me everything so I hope you're not breaking rules.

I grinned, putting my phone back down, and closed my eyes until my alarm actually went off. The buzzing continued, and I smiled sleepily at the thought of the group chat going wild in the early morning hours. When I was properly awake, I allowed myself to unlock my phone and respond to Vinny first.

LilTriquetra

That would be great. I hope we get to see some of their life on the island too.

At the school gates, Vincent caught me off guard by being cutely dramatic and telling me he missed our music sharing on the train rides, complete with a deep wistful sigh I felt in my soul. The dream must have put him in the same great mood I was in. He was also probably allowing himself to take the risk since Dan was already off to Corp with Fleur, unable to tease him about it. I laughed and promised I'd tell Alex off for keeping me safe. That had gotten a grin, and it lightened my heart to see.

At lunch, Alena hurriedly detailed the dream she'd had that ended right when all of ours had, telling us that the construction worker she'd dreamed of before and the lady who she was dreaming through had packed up their belongings, said goodbye to a neighbor, and been on the same trains as the trio. She was struggling to remember the exact conversation with the neighbor when Jamari piped up, flushed but grinning.

"She was wishing them well in their new lives." Jamari's voice was the softest I had ever heard from her lips, and I blinked in surprise as my theory clicked into place. The construction worker was definitely, absolutely Jamari's past life. Which meant—

"Oh my god, Jamari, we were married in the twenties!" Alena was blushing too, her hands over her mouth, barely hiding a grin. Jamari nodded, poking shyly at her food. Vinny and I were both smiling from the other side of the table. "Jamari!" Alena laughed, flinging her arms around her almost-maybe-girlfriend's shoulders. Jamari's head tilted to rest against Alena's shoulder, her eyes closing contentedly.

"I've been waiting for you to find out for so long now, but I was banned from speaking about it." She was chuckling gently, and Alena laughed.

"Well don't tell me anything more, I want to find out myself!"

Jamari laughed and nodded her agreement, and just like that, another little puzzle piece fell into place.

After lunch, in art class, I'd finished my project and was breaking the rules by texting under the desk.

Bruadarach

Sorry i forgot to respond to the book, I'm so mad dorell and lore didn't let me have it so I could give it to you instead.

LilTriquetra

Bruadarach

LilTriquetra

Bruadarach

I felt a tap on my shoulder, and looked up to find Mx. Darling peering over my shoulder with a patient smile. "I don't care if you are texting the Bruadarach of Faodail, phones are not allowed in this class. If you're done with your project, I have plenty of things I need help with if you need something to fill your time."

I heard snickers around me and made a show of putting my phone in my bag and standing to follow the teacher, mumbling an apology. For the next half hour, I was in the supply closet separating colored pencils by color into matching bins.

By the time school was out, I was acting like a stereotypical teenager fiending for phone time. Due to the mishap in art, I'd just left my phone in my bag all day, not wanting to risk the wrath of any more teachers even in the hallway. My friends were sure to tease me later about being such a good student. So I texted Sinéad again as I headed toward the front gate.

LilTriquetra

A direct quote from my art teacher three hours ago "I don't care if you are texting the bruadarach of faodail, phones are not allowed in this class." And then I was forced to sort colored pencils for half an hour.

Bruadarach

Lmao that's what you get for texting in class, teenager

LilTriquetra

Oh I'm so sorry I forgot you didn't have cell phones when you were my age, and never felt the temptation, you geezer

Bruadarach

I HAD A PHONE JUST NOT A SMART PHONE I'll have you know I got in trouble multiple times and had my phone taken away you little stink

LilTriquetra

Oh I've been downgraded from being a little shit

Bruadarach

She started typing right away, but I pocketed my phone with a giggle and found my friends, and Alex waiting for me in his car already. I let out a forlorn sigh as I realized how much I missed riding the train with my friends, missed the routine of it. *It's only until Mom comes home,* I thought to myself, but half-jogged to my friends before acknowledging Alex at all. He'd understand.

Dan was standing against the wall, not chatting with the others, until Vincent nudged him. "What's going through your mind, sunshine?"

"I think Charles is me."

Vincent and I looked at each other briefly and burst out laughing. Dan looked up in alarm, his face clearly distressed, as Fleur and Alena joined in on the giggling, and Jamari held her Switch up to her mouth to hide a clearly amused grin.

"What? What, am I wrong? I just thought—" He was silenced by me reaching up to hold his face just the same as Marie had held Charles's on the boat.

"Dan, it's just hilarious it's taken you so long to figure this out." I grinned, leaning forward to kiss his cheek. Dan's blush was well worth my own.

I leaned back and released him, smirking at the shell-shocked Dan. Alena reached over and patted his back, chuckling.

"Dannyboy, of course he's you. No one else could have kept these two nerds out of danger like you could." Alena was right and we nodded in agreement, while Dan sucked in a breath and stood up straight to try and regain what he thought was lost dignity.

"Well of course, they clearly needed me so badly in every life that I had to be brought back in this one too." He pretended to be engrossed in his phone, and Vinny snickered, reaching over to flick his phone.

"Soulmates can be platonic, Dan."

Dan looked up at him and smiled, then took his hand. "Who said anything about our relationship was platonic, Vinny baby?" Vincent managed to snatch his hand away before Dan kissed it, leaving Dan cackling and no longer embarrassed since he'd passed the torch to Vinny.

"Okay this has gotten too romantic for my aro ass, I'm leaving." Fleur laughed and turned toward the train station alone, but it wasn't long before the rest of us caught up, me taking one of Fleur's arms, Alena her other, both of us singing the "Elephant Love Medley" from *Moulin Rouge*.

"Do you want to go to the event at Ladine's tomorrow?" Jamari asked as we settled at the station, holding out a little flier. I took it, looking it over. The information on it described what sounded like a lecture and demonstration on candle making and cleansing, and I nodded right away.

"Oh absolutely, that sounds fantastic. Are we all going?" I looked around at my friends, Fleur and Alena nodding, Vincent voicing his agreement, and Dan needing a nudge before answering.

"I managed to get a date, like Fleur said yesterday, so not me." He stuck his tongue out at Fleur who smugly clasped her hands behind her back. I giggled.

"Sounds great then. I'll see if Alex will drop me off at the station tomorrow so we can take the train like we did to the library." I hugged my friends tightly, squeezing Vinny's hand as it dropped into mine, then jogged over to Alex's car.

"You took your time." He grinned, starting the engine as I buckled myself in. I wrinkled my nose at him.

"Gosh, sorry I have friends that I like so much." I put more fake sass into my voice than was needed, but it made Alex laugh, so it was fine.

Katiyana

Saturday, October 3, 2020

THE DAY HAD DRAGGED on endlessly until it was finally time to head to the station. Alex walked with me, eyeing my family's apartment door warily as we passed it. My friends were already there, and the sight of them filled my heart despite seeing them less than twenty-four hours ago. After safely securing me in the hands of my self-appointed bodyguards, Alex waved and set off, not in the direction of Val's apartment, but somewhere surely just as mysterious as he was.

"Do you know who the presenter is, Katiyana?" Alena was squinting at the flier, and I peered over her shoulder to see the name I hadn't registered yesterday.

"Oh, Conner James, CJ! Yeah, he and Sinéad are friends. They went to school together. He also worked with the old Cabinet head, Milo, the one with the statue in the park?"

"Ohh, maybe I heard about him in passing then. I was staring at this trying to figure out why the name rang a bell." She tucked the flier back in her pocket, and Vincent came to my other side as she did. I grinned at him, slipping my arm through his.

"Hi there," he said, shifting his arm to hold mine, smiling back. "I have a present for you."

"Oh?" I brightened. "I love presents, especially surprise ones."

"You can't have it until after the candles." His grin was teasing, and I narrowed my eyes, only receiving laughter in return.

The demonstration was incredibly informative. I had previously had no idea how much effort actually went into making candles by hand. I ended up taking notes on my phone, even though I had no idea when I would ever end up making my own candles. But it felt important to save, and so I did. CJ's assistant for the demonstration ended up being his fiancée Connar, who I had met a couple of times since he was the IT manager for basically the whole island. I was always amused they had the same name with one letter difference. Sinéad had also attended, but sat in the back, so I didn't see her until she was talking with CJ and Connar after almost everyone else had left.

So of course, I went over and slugged her in the arm.

"Ow, the hell?" She scowled at me and held her bicep while I held my hands behind my back with a grin.

"That's for getting me in trouble in class." I giggled, and Connar laughed. One of those near-booming, head-thrown-back laughs that immediately endeared me to him.

"What did she do?" CJ asked, grinning as well. "She's gotten me in trouble for skipping class, but not during class."

"She was the one texting ME while she was in class." Sinéad slung her arm over my shoulders to pull me close, scrubbing her knuckles against the top of my head lightly. I squirmed out of her grip and stuck my tongue out, smoothing my hair down.

"Ah, cell phones. A teacher's bane," Connar mused, hopping off the table he'd been sitting on and moving to pack up the remaining candle-making gear. Sinéad leaned over to me, stage whispering.

"He would know, he never put his away while we were in school."

CJ chuckled and nodded in agreement, and I took my chance at making them all feel old, smothering my grin with a confused look.

"You guys had phones? Did you have to fight over who got the wall plug all the time? You had to plug them into that special socket to make them work, right?" My grin cracked, just a little, as Sinéad turned to stare at me with her jaw dropped. The joke seemed to have gone over CJ's head, unfortunately, and he started explaining.

"Actually, we had cell phones, a lot smaller than your smartphones, and it cost a lot of extra money to do anything but text and call—"

"CJ, she's yanking our chains." Sinéad sighed, flicking my forehead. I cackled.

"Oh." CJ turned and squinted at me. "You're just like your cousin. I can't believe there's two of you."

Vincent had come up beside me as I teased my cousin and her friends, and I absentmindedly slid my arm through his, only realizing I had done it when his hand settled over mine. I looked down with a gentle blush, then up at Vinny who just smiled and silently told me he didn't mind.

"Do you want your surprise now?" He asked, his grin getting bigger. I matched it.

"Yes! Absolutely I do."

He led me to the corner table where we'd tossed our coats and bags upon arrival, retrieved his backpack, then ushered me into a chair. I obliged.

"Alright, Dan and I talked about this yesterday after we separated at the train station, and he reminded me that scent is the biggest memory trigger, so I just wanted to see...well, I'll just show you."

I covered my eyes as he instructed, and waited. The soft thunk of him setting whatever it was down made me want to peek so badly, but I refrained until he said I could look.

The small box before me was terribly familiar but I couldn't place it to save my life. That was, until I opened it and caught the scent wafting from the little blue and gold bottle sitting primly in the bottom half of the box.

"Oh my gosh, oh my goodness," I whispered, reaching out to wrap my fingers around the bottle and pull it closer. My fingers found the familiar grooves along the edges, the exact feeling of them tingling in my fingers and distant memory, Marie's hands ghosting alongside mine. I could feel Vincent beaming beside me, clearly pleased to have found something from our past on his own. "Oh...this...this is mine—Marie's. Both of ours. Marie brought this over on the boat, I can remember it now." I grinned, uncapping the bottle and holding it to my nose.

"Gosh, it still smells so good! Usually perfumes this old have turned and smell like alcohol mostly."

Vincent put his chin in his hand and smiled across the table at me, very much enjoying my reaction. "You'll never guess where I found it.

"Where?" I spritzed a bit of the perfume on my wrist, rubbing it against my other, but before Vinny could answer, the door of Ladine's slammed open.

We both jumped. I barely managed to keep hold of the bottle, and I felt all the color and warmth drain from my face as I saw who was standing in the doorway. I don't know how, but Sinéad was immediately at my side and Valerie was approaching the door, Alex close behind.

"You're not welcome here. You need to leave," Val said, standing inches from Nick and crossing her arms. He remained in the doorway, glaring past her to where I was sitting, hands clenching and unclenching in and out of fists. "Did you hear me, Nick? You're no longer welcome in this establishment."

"Out of my way, demon bride," Nick growled, and Alex stepped forward to put an arm in front of Val. Nick looked up at him, raising his lip in a snarl. "And the demon himself. Move."

"The only person moving, Nicolae, will be you. Back onto the sidewalk, and off my property." Alexis had walked up behind Alex. Nick narrowed his eyes at her, as she'd effectively blocked his last path into Ladine's. Vincent stood and moved to my other side, laying a protective hand on my shoulder.

"Leon, come here now." I jerked my head up as I heard Sinéad whisper and saw her holding the large watch she always wore near her mouth. I didn't have time to ponder that it might not have been a watch at all.

"Let me take back what's rightfully mine, and I'll leave and never return." Nick's voice had dropped at least three octaves, and I felt Vincent's hand squeeze my shoulder as we both had the flashbacks of the most recent dream. "Marie has belonged to me and no one else for centuries. She was meant to be a Mortmore, not a MacAskill. Let her go so I can right this wrong and bring her back to the side she was supposed to be born into." I withdrew from his words, feeling Sinéad cringe with me, and she reached down to take my hand.

"Katiyana is a part of this island in ways a Mortmore could never be. In ways a Mortmore *should* never be." Alexis had narrowed her eyes now, hand gripping whatever it was in her pocket even harder. "And unless you're about to shock us all with some previously-unknown knowledge about Lucas's lineage, you should know your ramblings make absolutely no sense. Neither Marie nor Lucas were part of the bloodlines while they were alive."

Nick laughed, putting a hand to his forehead, eyes wide, shaking his head. "You're so stupid, all of you, so stupid and wrapped up in your little bubble—refusing to see any way but your own, not willing to acknowledge the fact there are others out there with power equal to, or greater than, your own—that they've completely slipped me under your radar! This is fantastic!" He laughed harder, maniacally, not even stopping when Alex moved forward and took him by the wrists, forcing him backward, toward the door, outside of Ladine's wards.

"Under our radar? Care to explain?" Valerie asked, and while I was just as curious, I was more than happy to remain in the corner and let the adults do the talking.

Alex had managed to push Nick mostly out of the store when Leon showed up, having used the back entrance. He stood at the banister that separated the café from the store, and therefore me from Nick. Sinéad visibly relaxed once her partner was between me and my brother. Nick fought his way back to the doorway, clawing at the sides of it.

"Slipped right under your pretentious, stuck up little noses. You were so busy thinking you were the best around, that no one could come close to your skill, that you failed to recognize when someone did." Nick was grinning now, his eyes wild as he stared up at Alexis. "Oh, High Priestess, Coven Mother, you were so certain that no one could do as you did and bind souls together, bind them to a chunk of land in the ocean. You were so sure you were the only one." His voice was taunting and he laughed again, struggling now against Alex's grip. But Alex didn't let go. Alexis revealed an athame that looked nearly as old as the shop itself, held surely in a hand that didn't raise it as a threat, but was clearly prepared to use it if she had to.

"Explain yourself," she demanded flatly, her voice suddenly filling the room. Alexis had always been intimidating, but I had never seen her downright scary. Nick chuckled, unphased.

"See how she takes on the countenance of Hecate just to make herself feel large? Just to make herself appear threatening?" He leaned toward the blade and my heart picked up speed. "Come on then, priestess. Take me in the name of your goddess, erase me as a problem instead of facing your own failures."

"Nicolae…what's Kabuto's ninja registration number?" Sinéad asked, and I looked up at her in absolute confusion. Why was she talking about a *Naruto* character, about anime, at a time li—

"Who the fuck is Kabuto?" Nick answered, and my rapidly beating heart dropped through my stomach and onto the floor. My eyes widened. That wasn't my brother anymore. He would know that answer immediately.

"Oh gods," I whispered, and Sinéad gripped my hand harder. Nick's face twisted into a grin. Alex had given up on pushing him out of the store and instead was trying to make him kneel on the floor, keeping hold of one arm and the back of Nick's neck.

"Oho, the little Bruadarach has figured it out. I'm not your cousin, am I, runaway?" Nick was taunting Sinéad now, and she leveled a glare at him. He snickered. "The girl with half a soul and a brain to match has figured it out, and the coven mother still can't. Do you want to know how they outsmarted you? How they—" He struggled to turn in Alex's grip, managing to get his feet under him, but remaining in a crouch. I saw Alex tighten his grip, Leo take a step forward. "—managed to do in one try what it took you three to figure out?"

"Explain. Yourself." Alexis ground her teeth against each other, and she kept the athame level at Nick's chest as he stood, Alex still fighting to keep him held. Nick chuckled at her once more, leaning his head on his shoulder to look at her teasingly.

"The Mortmores twisted fate. They pushed me into your little circle and allowed me to infiltrate. Of course, I couldn't take over until she remembered me, and the first few tries were a bust. But oh, this time, this time I got so much closer. I managed to be in the same apartment! I got to hold her as she grew up, guide her when she was about to be led astray." He sighed wistfully. "If only I had managed to get rid of the rest of you sooner."

The room was silent, filled to the brim with shock as we all processed what exactly Nick—or at least Nick's voice—was saying. Somehow, Lucas had gotten in contact with the Mortmores. All the way back in 1926, he had managed to worm his way in and gain their help in twisting the cycles of the island to let him be reborn here, on Faodail, as many times as it took to get to me, to get Marie back. If I hadn't been secured by Vincent's hand on my shoulder, I would have fallen out of my chair. As it was, my head was spinning, and there was so little air in my lungs.

"You sick bastard." Vincent's voice broke the quiet, and Nick turned to grin evilly at him. "You couldn't bear the idea of a single woman telling you no, so you literally manipulated both of your destinies to try and drag her back to you, when she clearly didn't want any part of you?" Vincent shook his head, letting go of my shoulder to move, to stand beside Leo. Sinéad caught my weight. "I can't believe you're so deluded. You really think just because you want something it belongs to you? You're the goddamned poster child for a spoiled rich kid, Lucas."

It would have been an absolute understatement of the century to say the rest of us were shocked. Vincent, who we had come to know as a gentle, soft-spoken, kindhearted person, had just ripped into a dangerous and unhinged soul, armed only with his voice.

And all Lucas could do was laugh. He threw Nick's head back, mouth wide open, a horrible pantomime of Connar's earlier jubilation.

"Jackson, Jackson, Jackson." He chuckled. "She does belong to me. She was betrothed to me at birth. It's not a matter of just wanting something. It's being denied something you were promised your entire life, and having it taken away by a Slavic bastard who thinks he can come in and sweep another man's woman off her feet and spirit her away."

"You know damn good and well Marie made her own choice to leave," Vincent spat back, making his way to Alexis's side. Alexis adjusted the athame in her hand, lowering her arm. Vincent's fists were shaking as he clenched them, his knees trembling, but he held his ground. "Don't you dare pretend any of it was Jackson's idea."

"Oh sure. You absolutely didn't taunt her with kisses, sweet words no man should ever whisper to another man's future wife. You didn't do any of those things, did you?" Nick's—Lucas's—laughter was fading, replaced by the cold steely anger Lucas had carried into the bakery the morning he bruised Jackson.

"We've all heard enough. You're leaving." Alex yanked Nick back, tugging him toward the doorway, but the movement afforded Nick just enough slack to slip free and lunge at Vincent, his hands finding Vinny's neck and squeezing. A cry ripped from my throat as I leapt out of my chair, flying down the two steps and to Vinny's side, grabbing Nick's shirt to try and drag him away.

I was pulled out of the way as Leo and Alex dove toward the pair, trying to rip Nick off him without hurting Vinny further, struggling to unwrap Nick's fingers from his throat.

Then Nick cried out, and fell to his side, hands gripping his stomach as red seeped through his fingers. Vincent scrambled away, one hand flying to his throat and the other...

"Vincent—" I whispered, staring at the ceremonial knife in his hand. He dropped it, letting it slide across the floor back toward Alexis, who looked down at it then back up to him.

"He must have snatched it out of my hand when Nick lunged—" She began, but was cut off by another cry of pain from Nick, and we turned to see Sinéad wrapping a pair of handcuffs around his wrists.

"Call an ambulance," the Bruadarach commanded, and Valerie had her phone in her hand in an instant.

Even with Nick/Lucas subdued, the tension didn't drain out of the room. I moved to Vincent's side, and knelt down near him. He stared up at me, pleadingly, keeping the hand covered in my brother's blood as far out of my sight as possible.

"I'm sorry, I'm sorry, I didn't want him to attack you, I'm so sorry." He coughed, holding his clean hand to his face.

"He was going to kill you. You protected yourself." I meant it, but the tremble in my voice betrayed me. I looked toward Nick, lying on his back on the floor and groaning, shouting out expletives, both at anyone who came near him and at Vincent, who he kept calling Jackson. This situation was unbelievable. My brother...could I even call him that anymore? He had tried to kill my friend, he would have tried to do unthinkable things to me. All because his spirit, his soul, couldn't get over a rejection from a century ago. And now my friend had literally stabbed him in self-defense.

I collapsed onto the floor, my hands falling into my lap, barely managing to take hold of my head as it slumped. Leo rushed over, making me lift my head so he could look me over, checking my eyes and pulse, before urging me to lean against the wall next to Vincent.

"What just happened," I whispered, to no one in particular, not expecting an answer. Leo squeezed my hand.

"We're figuring it out, Yana." With that, he turned and left us, moving to Sinéad's side as they discussed what type of security to put Nick under until he was able to be questioned.

I felt Vincent's hand tap lightly against mine, and turned to find him looking at me, his eyes full of unshed tears, his voice raspy, a terrible memory of Jackson's. "I'm so sorry."

I took his hand slowly, my own shaking, and squeezed. A large breath in, a larger one out, repeat until I could find words.

"Amazingly, I'm glad you did it." As awful as it felt to say about my own flesh and blood, it was true. Nick needed to be stopped. There was no telling what he would have done if he had been allowed to get his hands on me. Vincent squeezed my hand back as I shuddered. The almost-kiss in my bedroom a few days ago had been disgusting enough.

"...we're going to need so much therapy after this," Vincent whispered, and I broke. But not into sobs. Wheezing, desperate laughter, the kind easily mistaken for crying, complete with tears. As Vinny turned to wrap his arms around me—his bloody hand still not touching me—they dissolved into actual tears, and we cried together. What else was there to do? Everything had been horrifying, everything that we knew had been tipped on its head. Neither of us had gotten hurt, but now there was too much between us for us to just be normal teenagers ever again. Vincent was spot the hell on, we were going to need so much therapy after this.

Later, neither of us knew how much, we pulled apart at a tap on Vinny's shoulder, breaking out of our exhausted half sleep to see Valerie holding out a damp washcloth, looking at us with her brows knit in concern. Vincent pulled his arms free and set about cleaning up his hand as best he could, a bit easier now since the blood had dried. Val reached down to smooth my hair back, and I closed my eyes at the touch.

"They took him to the hospital. Sinéad has guards posted around his room, and when he's healed, he's undergoing an investigation and mental health assessment. I think the coven is going to be allowed to question him as well, since he made some sort of deal with the Mortmores. Sinéad's on the phone with your mom now." Valerie's explanation had been to the point and perfectly clarifying, and I couldn't thank her enough for not sugar-coating or embellishing anything. I just nodded, having no words to explain the thunderstorm of emotions currently plaguing me. She took the washcloth back from Vincent when he finished with it, leaned down to kiss my head, and went to speak with Sinéad and Alexis. I couldn't hear what they were saying, and I didn't try. They'd explain everything later. I was fine being ignorant for right now.

"I'm so glad none of our friends had to witness that." Vincent's voice was cracked, small, and I turned to look at him. He was staring at his shaking hand, a bit of blood still in the corner of his fingernail. I reached out to take it.

"Jamari and Alena would have cheered. Fleur would have started praying. Dan probably would have fainted." I smiled weakly, and Vincent smirked back.

"Dan would have fallen right to the ground, you're right," he whispered, then laughed, a soft, two-note noise that ended in a sigh. He closed his eyes. "I hope you can forgive me."

"For protecting me from my clearly psychological-ly-damaged brother? I might be able to let this one slide." I nudged his shoulder with mine, shifting to lean against the wall with him again, not letting go of his hand. His head dropped to my shoulder, so I rested mine on top of his. I was joking as a defense mechanism, but it was absolutely true.

We must have exhaustedly dozed off again, because the next time I opened my eyes, Leo was lifting me off the ground, and when I glanced over, Alex was picking up Vinny. Both of them lifted us as if we were five years old and weighed nothing.

"Wh-whats going on?" I stammered, holding onto Leo's shoulder.

"You're both staying at the Highlands tonight, Bru-adarach's orders," Leo informed me, looking down with a gentle smile. I nodded, knowing Sinéad would want to keep us close so she could keep an eye on us. I wouldn't have been surprised if Gautier and the rest of the security force camped out on her lawn for the night.

Vincent

Saturday, October 3, 2020

Katiyana told me later that Alexsander had carried me to the car, but I was asleep the entire time. I warred with my dignity and pride before finally succumbing to the fact that being briefly choked by someone and subsequently stabbing them had exhausted and drained me enough to not notice my body was being moved.

I woke to the sound of gravel under tires and blinked my eyes open to rest them on a much different sight than Ladine's. It was a three-story Queen Anne-style manor, and we'd just pulled through the main gate.

"Welcome to the Highlands." Leo's voice sounded from the front seat, and I looked to see he'd been the one driving, Sinéad in the passenger seat furiously texting someone.

"Brian got the guest rooms set up. There's two right next to each other so you two can be close." She turned in her seat to speak to Katiyana and myself, frowning in sympathy and worry. "I asked Val to get your stuff from her apartment, Yana, but I don't have Dan's parents' contact info for yours, Vinny."

"I texted Dan," Katiyana said, her voice muffled by the hand holding her chin. Her eyes were drooping, and she looked only a little less tired than I felt. I reached out to hold her free hand for the remainder of the short ride. She let me without protest and squeezed.

Minutes later, we had shuffled into the manor and were shown upstairs by a concerned but quiet man who I presumed to be Brian, and that presumption was confirmed as Katiyana hugged him and thanked him.

Valerie and Justine showed up simultaneously with our things. Justine worried over me and held me close, and it took a lot of strength to not just collapse into tears in her arms. She was more of a mother to me than my own had ever been, and I told her as much before she left. The sentiment earned me another tight hug and a kiss on the head, and I squeezed her just as hard back.

We had silently settled into our own separate rooms, parted by only a wall as we realized the beds were on either side of it. I was halfway to sleep before my phone went off.

LilTriquetra

> How mad do you think Sinéad would be if I punched a hole in her wall

RedSam

> furious. banished from faodail.

LilTriquetra

> Ugh

She went offline and I heard movement, registering it as her rolling over to fall asleep. Then my door creaked open and shut, and I sat up in bed.

"Scoot over," Katiyana instructed, nudging my hip with hers. My face immediately flushed hot, and I thanked the gods I didn't sleep in just underwear like Dan. I obeyed her request and scooted closer to the wall, making room for her to lay down at my side.

"Sorry, this is probably weird, but the idea of sleeping by myself tonight sounds absolutely, horrifically awful." She had brought the pillow from her bed and flopped it down next to mine, and I settled on my side to face her.

"You're alright. I just hope Sinéad doesn't turn into a mom on us when she sees this in the morning." I grinned, and Yana rolled her eyes.

"She can kiss my butt. We've been through hell tonight and I think we deserve a little of our own comfort."

"You're right."

We exhaled deeply in unison, and Katiyana rolled halfway to put her glasses on the nightstand. When she rolled back over to face me, I was awarded the sight of her silver eyes with nothing in front of them and felt my heart skip.

"Should warn me before you do that," I breathed, and Katiyana smiled so softly, reaching up to pat my cheek.

"Sorry, I'll remember next time."

We tucked in together, and Yana's hand found mine under the covers. Some distant part of me was freaking out that we were lying next to each other in the same bed and all the societal expectations that went along with that, but the larger, more weary and logical part was quickly smothering it. All Katiyana was seeking from me was the comfort that came from someone else experiencing the same traumatic event. As she closed her eyes, I let myself look at her for just a little bit longer before closing my own.

Sleep found us not long after, and for the first time in a while, we didn't dream.

Katiyana

Sunday, October 4, 2020

I WOKE UP FACING the wall, hugging the pillow Vincent had been using. When I realized I was in the bed alone, I sat up and squinted around the room for a second before putting on my glasses. He wasn't in the room, and part of me was sad to not find him next to me. But then I remembered whose house I was in and realized it would probably be better to not invoke Sinéad's wrath, and her subsequent telling of my parents.

Vincent stepped out of the bathroom as I headed toward it, thankfully dressed and with fairly dry hair so we could avoid having a teen-romance-movie moment. He grinned upon seeing me, though, and that was enough to make me melt a little. The only thing that ruined the moment was the bruise on his throat, and my smile faltered a bit. He noticed and reached up to rub it.

"I didn't want to wake you. You were completely passed out," he said in his still slightly raspy voice, stepping aside so I could make my way into the bathroom.

"I wouldn't have minded." I shrugged, and he just smiled at me before walking back to the guest room with his bundle of things.

After I'd cleaned myself up, I found him in the room scrolling through our shared info folder and chewing on his thumb in thought.

"Sinéad has a breakfast food stash if you want to raid it."

He looked up from his phone, blinking back into reality, and then nodded. We headed downstairs together, and I noted Vinny marveling at the Bruadarach's manor. The house was well over a century old, and every Bruadarach since the one who'd built it had lived here. I'd been in and out of it throughout my life, minus the years Sinéad was gone, and through Vinny's eyes, I realized I'd become numb to the old money opulence of the place. Suddenly I felt sheepish, parading about the house like it was my own, like all the antiques and priceless curios belonged to me. Luckily, my struggle to figure out how to remedy this was broken.

"Do you know if that sword in the stairwell is real?" Vinny was looking over his shoulder toward it, and I glanced up to see which one he meant.

"Oh, yeah I think it is? Sinéad would know better than me. She and Dorell curated and cataloged this whole collection."

By the time we'd made it to the kitchen, I could nearly hear the gears in Vincent's head whirring as he looked around at all of Sinéad's curios. We were both so distracted neither of us noticed the woman sitting at the island, until the tablet in front of her pinged.

"Good morning" she said, not looking up from her tablet. I stared at her for a moment, trying to see if I recognized her, but I didn't.

"Good morning. Are you one of Sinéad's employees?" Vincent asked, once more saving the awkward situation with ease.

"I am." The woman looked up, nodded, then offered a polite smile.

"Oh, we haven't met. And I know just about everyone," I blurted out, and she just nodded.

"That's the point." She grinned, slyly this time, and looked toward the doorway a few seconds before Sinéad walked in.

"Isolde, are you frightening my cousin?" Sinéad was looking through a clipboard full of paperwork, and nudged Isolde with her elbow as she passed. It was genuinely strange to see Sinéad act so familiar with someone I didn't know, and I was rethinking my knowledge of the island and how much I was actually privy to. It was turning out to be less and less. I was trying not to be uncomfortable with it.

"I'm not doing anything beyond introducing myself." Isolde was amused; clearly they'd had a similar conversation before.

"Oh, just tell them why you're here."

"Alright." Isolde shifted some papers on the counter toward us, and I leaned over to look. They were photos from a security camera of some sort that clearly showed Nicolae knocking on the door of the northernmost lighthouse, and someone opening it for him.

"Is that...is...is he *actually* working with the Mortmores? I thought they'd all left!" I looked back up at Sinéad and Isolde, brows furrowed in shock.

"They are very good at hiding," Isolde said, flipping the page to a list of dates and times. "We marked every time your brother went to the lighthouse."

Vincent had been silent since his first greeting, but spoke up again, his words holding an accusatory tone. "Hold on...wait. You had. A camera. On this place the whole time, and you never thought to look at it until he attacked us? Until I had to stab him to keep him from getting at Yana? What?"

Sinéad had noticed his rising annoyance and held up a hand. "I don't say this to excuse our actions, only to explain. The Mortmores have been silent and dormant for as long as I have been back on the island. We fell into a false sense of security, and it was wrong of us. We kept the camera on them—it's hidden of course—but we didn't think to routinely check it until recently, when Katiyana found Nick doing the rituals in the apartment. The lighthouse was built by the Mortmore family, and it honestly hadn't even crossed my mind that they'd try to use it as a hideout. We have been creating this list since then, but Nick made his move before we had the full picture. You have every right to be upset at our lack of foresight, and lack of action. I completely understand if it takes both of you a while to trust the authorities on this island again." Her diplomacy was annoyingly effective.

Vincent's fist uncurled as Sinéad spoke, but his brows didn't unknit. "Right."

I slid my fingers into his and squeezed, and he dropped his gaze. I was more shocked than angry. I had always thought the Mortmores were just not on the island at all, that their manor had been abandoned, and that didn't even change when Nick had started his bullshit.

Vinny shook his head in disbelief. "We got played. We really got played."

"Yeah, we did." Sinéad sighed. "Thankfully, on a much smaller scale than before I left."

"The blame falls partially on me. I should have been the one watching the cameras. I apologize for this." Isolde spoke softly.

I sucked in a huge breath. This was almost too much to process before breakfast. Vincent sighed, as if the breath had passed from me to him. He pushed his hair back, then let it flop.

"Okay, so are we passing this instance around as one of those 'it's no one's fault' things, or what? Because excuse my language, but that's kind of bullshit." His attempts to speak were taking their toll, and his voice cracked on the last word and he coughed. He was definitely still agitated but trying to remain polite. I admired him for it. Sinéad shook her head.

"No, definitely not. I failed you both by allowing the Cabinet to sink into the false sense of security. Isolde should have checked the camera more often, and even Leo and Dominick slacked on their patrols. The entire security force is being rearranged due to this." She laughed without humor. "Even Alexis and Val weren't keeping as close of an eye on the ley lines as they usually do. We all failed you, and in a larger sense, all of Faodail. If the Mortmores had been allowed to spread further than just Nick, if they'd added to their numbers, we could have been in the same situation as we were when I left."

"And that was definitely not a pleasant time." Isolde's voice was soft again.

Vincent had slowly been softening as they spoke, looking down at the kitchen island. I squeezed his hand again, then looked at my cousin who was pulling mugs from the cabinet to prepare tea.

"Okay. So...you have a plan to not let this happen again, right?" I asked quietly, looking between Sinéad and Isolde. Isolde looked to Sinéad.

"Yeah. It's not perfect yet, but we shifted observation of the camera to higher priority, assigned more walking patrols with a wider range of people so it's less suspicious than just Leo and Dom constantly casing the joint, and Nick is remaining in the hospital until we can have a full mental health examination performed. Once your parents get back, we're going to decide what to do with him." Sinéad spoke as she mixed a blend of loose dried herbs, setting the kettle to boil.

"Well, that's better than just sticking with the way it was," I looked to my left as Vinny muttered, shaking his head. He looked up finally.

"We can't just throw them off the island? Banish them? Wouldn't it be easier to not have any Mortmores here at all?"

Sinéad laughed. "Stars, you sound like me when I was your age. I wish it was that easy. Unfortunately, the lighthouse is public property, not government property, and my jurisdiction over it is minimal. I can't kick anyone out of there, especially not the family that built it."

"I thought Faodail was a sovereign nation?" Vincent asked.

"It is, but we still have laws to follow. Even if the judge and jury are likely to take my side, banishing a specific group of people is still unlawful and a sign of a corrupt government, which we strictly try to avoid here." Sinéad was clearly perturbed, her lips pressed tight once all the words were out of them.

I sighed, nodding. "I get it, just sucks."

"Yeah, quite a bit." Vinny released my hand and moved to sit beside Isolde, tugging the papers toward himself to look them over.

"I'm sorry, I really am. I asked Milo the same thing when..." Sinéad paused and closed her eyes. "When Aunt Mariana got murdered."

I shuddered at the memory, as fuzzy as it was. I had been little when it happened and didn't realize what was going on beyond everyone was upset and terrified, Aunt Mariana was dead, and the Mortmores had taken over everything. It was a dark time.

We fell into contemplative silence, Sinéad making the tea, Vinny shuffling papers, Isolde and me watching the steam in our mugs once they were set in front of us. Sinéad's phone buzzed.

"Oh, Alexis wants us all back at the café later today." Sinéad looked between Vinny and me after reading the message. "Sounds like you two left all your school things there, and a perfume bottle?"

"Oh yeah. I hope it didn't get broken." I'd forgotten all about it, about everything. The memory of homework due on Monday floated forward.

So we had tea, and Sinéad relayed to Vincent what she'd learned about the situation with his mother, and what decisions were being made. A lot of it I was hearing for the first time, and come to find out, she was being prosecuted for child abuse. Vinny sat silently as Sinéad spoke, holding his mug tensely in his hands.

"Does that mean I'll have to see her in court or something?"

Sinéad shook her head, setting down her mug. "No, no you do not. The Webers have asked if you can give your testimony privately, that's been approved, and we're working on instating them as your legal guardians. I hate to be the one to tell you, but your friend Dan is very good at secretly gathering evidence." Her voice held a small note of humor, trying her best to lighten the situation. Vincent just nodded like he'd known all along. He probably had. Dan's parents had definitely kept him up to date on everything that was happening, since it involved him. And if I knew Vinny like I thought I did, he'd purposely kept the rest of the Squad out of it.

"Is she...still. Around?" He said the sentence so hesitantly it felt like three separate ones, and Vincent's grip on his mug tightened. I wanted to reach out to touch his shoulder, but feared I'd scare the life out of him if I did.

"She's been in custody, awaiting a full mental examination. She's..." Sinéad paused, chewing on her lip. "I can't think of how to put it delicately, but she's not doing well."

Vincent just nodded, finally lifting his mug to his mouth to drink. And with that, the conversation was over. The situation with his mom was handled, as much as it could be before the court date.

Later, Sinéad walked Vincent around the collection of heirlooms as I followed idly, while Isolde disappeared somewhere downstairs. And then we headed off to Ladine's.

Opening the door to the café, I gasped and darted in, letting go of the door and hoping whoever had to catch it would forgive me.

"Mom!!!!" I shouted, running to where she and my aunts were standing, the unbroken trio. She held her arms out and wrapped me up in them, squeezing me tighter than it seemed she ever had.

"Oh Yana, I'm so sorry, you never should have had to go through this. We should have seen the signs so much earlier." Her face was muffled by the top of my head but I could feel the sincerity and regret pouring off her, so I just squeezed her tighter.

"I'm not mad at you." I spoke into her collarbone, feeling my aunts join the hug and surround us.

"No honey, we're mad at ourselves for not preventing this," Aunt Pearl explained, stroking my hair back. I lifted my head to look at her. "We should have seen this coming, we knew it was odd when Etta had a boy instead of a girl like we had foreseen."

"We should have known something had gotten muddled with." Aunt Jennie spoke from the other side, and I turned my head to look at her, as well. She had a much more sour expression than her sisters.

I stayed in my mom's arms, listening to her and my aunts discuss what to do now, until someone tapped my shoulder and I turned to see Alexis holding out my school bag and the box for the perfume bottle.

"I believe these are yours, my dear." She smiled tenderly. I nodded and took them, peeking in the box to see if the bottle was still there.

"Thank you for keeping them safe."

"Nothing in this shop is ever lost or damaged. It does wonders for inventory day." She waved her hand toward a sigil above the door, winking at me and then walking off to find Vincent and give him his backpack.

"I'm so glad Alexis and Valerie were here for you. I'll have to thank them somehow." Mom sighed, holding my face and tapping my cheekbones with her thumbs. It was something she did whenever I got hurt or upset, and it always helped somehow.

"I'm glad, too, I don't know where I'd be without the coven." I smiled and looked over as Vincent appeared in the corner of my vision. "Vinny! This is my mom!" I turned to him, slipping my arm through his, holding my other hand out to Mom. I noted he tucked his chin down, doing his best to hide the bruise on his throat.

"Nice to meet you and thank you for protecting my daughter." Mom gave him a wide grin, and my aunts did the same on either side of her. Vincent blushed, his free hand reaching up to grab his pendant.

"I did what anyone who was there would have done," he mumbled, squeezing my arm close to his side with his own.

"You still did it," Aunt Jennie said, reaching forward to gently stroke his hair away from his forehead. Surprisingly, he didn't flinch from the touch. Jennie had that way with people. She was a massage therapist and reiki master, so her hands were literally made for healing. "You protected an innocent, and that marks you for good."

"Marks me?" Vinny asked, lifting his gaze to meet hers and his hand to his throat. "How do you mean?"

All three of the sisters chuckled conspiratorially and shared a secret glance. Vinny and I looked at each other in confusion.

"You'll find out. Listen for Alexis's call." Aunt Pearl teased us with her tone and a wink, and after Mom kissed my forehead, she and her sisters set off downstairs.

"Well that wasn't cryptic in the slightest." Vincent sighed, and I giggled softly.

"If you're planning on being around the members of this coven more often, you'll have to get used to it." I nudged his side, and he groaned loudly, dramatically.

"Val told me she wanted to talk to us." Vin tugged my arm, leading me toward the café tables where Valerie was waiting with one of the coven record books. We settled down across from her and she smiled slyly.

"There you are, took you long enough." She spun the book, already open, toward us and tapped on a page. "Look here."

Vincent leaned over, ever the scholar, and I peered at his side. "Valerie Evans, born this day...nineteen...thirty-four? Wait. What—Valerie how..." Vincent looked up at her, bewildered, and I looked more closely at the page.

"Born to Jackson and Marie Evans, hereby protected by the Faodail Coven forevermore." My words tripped over themselves a little as I read, then I stared up at Valerie too. She was smirking at us, mischievous and amused and all sorts of pleased. "I'm sorry you're. How old, first of all, and second of all—"

"You're ours." Vincent's voice was quiet while mine gained volume.

"I've been making sure to keep an eye on you both throughout the years." Val settled her head in her hand, still grinning, and spun the book back around. She traced the ink markings of her birth with gentle fingers, her gremlin-level grin fading into a soft smile.

"So how old are you, really?" I asked, raising my eyebrow at her. She laughed.

"Now, *Mom,* you should know better than to ask a lady that." Valerie winked and scooped up the book, walking away to where Alex was waiting for her. I looked at Vincent, and he looked back.

"Why is it somehow more shocking to find out our daughter is still alive rather than the fact we had a daughter in the thirties? Also, why does she still *look* thirty?" He asked, and I shrugged, tossing my hands out to the sides and standing up.

"Nothing on Faodail makes any sort of sense anymore." I shook my head, but secretly it was...nice. A whole new worldview had opened up for me to explore.

Vincent chuckled as he stood and moved around the chairs to catch up with me, taking my arm and resting his hand on mine.

"We'll sort it out together."

"I'll hold you to that."

The Squad

Saturday, October 31, 2020

It had been about a month since Nick had tried to attack Vincent. He was still in the hospital, but his parents had gone to visit him and said he was acting much more like himself rather than Lucas. For Katiyana, it was somehow a surprise that her dad took the paranormal/supernatural stuff so well, but he reminded her that he'd married a MacAskill woman, and the unexpected was to be expected.

RedSam

what time are we supposed to be there? i don't know how long play practice is gonna go tonight, so I might have to dip out early.

BlondeBrainiac

Seven. Why am I the only one who remembers? (stop texting at practice)

GamezNStuff

Because you're the mom and I'm already there

BlondeBrainiac

Ugh, I'm not even invited to this and yet…

Beefaroni

You signed up to be mom, blondie.

LilTriquetra

You literally did, Fleur

QueenofGambits

I'd say sorry but I don't feel bad for you also you have new mando to watch why are you even sad??

BlondeBrainiac

I hate you all and I'm sacrificing you to the wild hunt tonight. But you're right I'll drown my sorrows in star wars.

LilTriquetra

I wonder if alexis would stop you or help you

GamezNStuff

She'd definitely hesitate and think about it

RedSam

lol

Beefaroni

STOP TEXTING AT PRACTICE! if we're not allowed to put vinny in the necromancy circle I don't think we're allowed to sacrifice people to the wild hunt

The hell is a wild hunt btw

LilTriquetra

Show up at ladine's at 7 and find out.

GamezNStuff

Is that the new f*ck around and find out?? "Show up at ladine's and find out"??

QueenofGambits

It is now

And so, they gathered at Ladine's at seven, on Samhain. It was a little odd to be called there when the official Sabbat festival had already taken place during the day, but who were they to refuse a request from the coven mother herself.

Etta met them at the door, dressed in what were obviously ritual robes to most of them, but probably looked ominous and possibly cult-ish to the others. "Hello my darlings, come downstairs." She was beaming with enthused delight, and the teenagers glanced at each other curiously before following.

What awaited them was the ritual room set up for a full ceremonial ritual, icons of the coven's deities spaced equally around the circle, a fire burning steadily in the center cauldron, and the entire coven standing with their chosen deities. The collection was a mix of Greek, Celtic, and Egyptian pantheons. In the middle of the circle, a line of four statues stood.

Katiyana felt a pull on her sternum, an invisible rope tugging her toward Brigit. She reached for Vincent's hand as he reached for hers. His eyes were fixed on a statue that Katiyana recognized as Calliope, one of the muses. A glance to the side showed Dan squinting in Zeus's direction, and Alena looking toward Hephaestus.

"What's going on?" Alena was the one to speak, ever the outspoken, and stepped to the edge of the circle. "Are we actually getting sacrificed to the Wild Hunt?"

The gathered coven members laughed, Dorell's ringing out much deeper than the others. "Of course not," he exclaimed, his eyes twinkling with excitement. He turned to Alexis, who nodded, then motioned to Etta.

"It is tradition that a Faodail witch starts their training on their sixteenth Samhain. We were hoping all of you would be born in the same year this time, but we had a couple rebels." She meant the sisters, Jamari and Fleur, one older and one younger than the rest of their Squad. Etta slid her hands into her sleeves, stepping away from her station and toward the cauldron. The light made her look mystical, every inch the witch Katiyana had been raised by. A thread of energy hummed between them, extending to everyone in the room. Based on the soft intakes of air, Vinny's hand squeezing Katiyana's harder, Alena reaching for Dan's, and Dan standing straighter, the newcomers definitely felt it too. Something bigger than them—something absolutely magickal—was about to start.

"So, let's begin."

Pronunciation Guide and Glossary

Places

FAODAIL - *FAY-UH-DALE*- A small island off the coast of Massachusetts, discovered by Angus MacAskill in 1739. He founded the first settlement on the island not long after, and the population has grown since.

Ceangal - *Kan-gull*- The largest populated area on Faodail. Ceangal is nearly in the center of the island. The majority of Faodail's stores and restaurants are here, along with the local theatre and shopping mall.

Meadhan - *Med-han*- The fertile fields of Faodail. This small town is home to all the ranches and farms on the island, and where a large majority of our food supply comes from. Also here is Corp school.

Dubhan - *Dove-an*- The entry point to Faodail, where our ferry connects with the United States mainland. This small fishing village is the least populated area on the island, but without it, we would have no contact with the outside world.

Cridhe - *Cree-ah*- One of the three schools that make up Faodail Academy. Cridhe offers courses that are focused on fine and performing arts, linguistics, history, and other similar subjects.

Inntinn - *Inn-chin*- One of three schools that make up Faodail Academy. Inntinn offers courses that are focused on engineering, external sciences such as physics and astronomy, along with computer science and other similar subjects.

Corp - *Core*- One of three schools that make up Faodail Academy. Corp offers courses that are focused on agriculture, internal medicine, holistic health and other similar subjects.

Ladine's Gem – *Lay-deen's Gym* – Metaphysical shop in Ceangal, also serves as headquarters for the Faodail coven.

People

Bruadarach- *Brew-daar-ark* - The leader of Faodail, somewhere in between a Queen/King and president. It's not an elected position but the Bruadarach can be voted out by the citizens if they are disapproved of.

Katiyana Randa – *Kah-tee-yawn-uh Ran-duh* (Lil'Triquetra)

Alena Chen– *Ah-leen-uh Chin* (QueenofGambits)

Jamari Miller – *Jam-ar-ee Miller* (GameznStuff)

Fleur Miller – *Fl-urr Miller* (BlondeBrainiac)

Vincent D'Avranches – *Vin-sent Dee-Ave-ran-chez* (RedSam)

Dan Weber– *Dan Web-bur (Beefaroni)*

Sinéad MacAskill – *Shen-aid Mac-ask-ull* (Bruadarach)

Nicolae Randa – *Nick-o-lie Ran-duh*

9 798991 106917